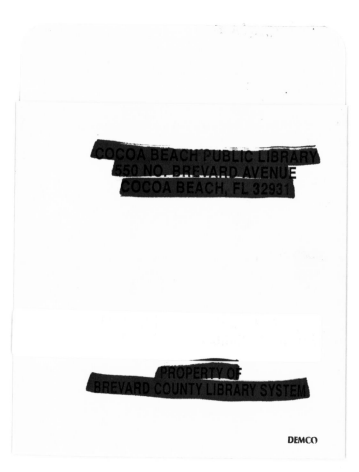

Widowmaker

OTHER MIKE BOWDITCH NOVELS BY PAUL DOIRON

The Precipice

The Bone Orchard

Massacre Pond

Bad Little Falls

Trespasser

The Poacher's Son

Widowmaker

Paul Doiron

MINOTAUR BOOKS
NEW YORK

WIDOWMAKER. Copyright © 2016 by Paul Doiron. All rights reserved. Printed in the United States of America. For information, address St. Martin's Press, 175 Fifth Avenue, New York, N.Y. 10010.

www.minotaurbooks.com

Library of Congress Cataloging-in-Publication Data

Names: Doiron, Paul, author.
Title: Widowmaker : a novel / Paul Doiron.
Description: First edition. | New York : Minotaur Books, 2016. | Series: Mike Bowditch mysteries ; 7
Identifiers: LCCN 2016001456 | ISBN 9781250063700 (hardcover) | ISBN 9781466868670 (ebook)
Subjects: LCSH: Game wardens—Fiction. | Wilderness areas—Maine—Fiction. | Missing persons—Investigation—Fiction. | BISAC: FICTION / Mystery & Detective / General. | GSAFD: Suspense fiction. | Mystery fiction.
Classification: LCC PS3604.o37 W53 2016 | DDC 813/ .6—dc23
LC record available at http://lccn.loc.gov/2016001456

Our books may be purchased in bulk for promotional, educational, or business use. Please contact your local bookseller or the Macmillan Corporate and Premium Sales Department at 1-800-221-7945, extension 5442, or by e-mail at MacmillanSpecial Markets@macmillan.com.

First Edition: June 2016

10 9 8 7 6 5 4 3 2 1

For my sisters

History doesn't repeat itself, but it rhymes.

—*Erroneously attributed to Mark Twain*

Widowmaker

I

On my first day as a cadet at the Maine Criminal Justice Academy, the instructors showed my class the most disturbing video I had ever seen. It was a montage of real-life footage—most of it taken during routine traffic stops—of police officers who had been ambushed in the line of duty. We saw cops being run over, cops being wrestled to the ground by multiple assailants, cops having their service weapons stripped from their hands and used to kill them.

"You only need to get careless once," our instructor told us. As if we needed to be told.

Five years had passed since I'd seen that video; I was no longer a twenty-three-year-old cadet, no longer a rookie, and yet those horrible images still made regular appearances in my nightmares. Every time I went on patrol, without exception, I would hear my instructor's warning in my head, and I would wonder if this was the day that some seemingly harmless stranger would smile at me through a window and then shoot me in the face.

I might have called myself paranoid if I hadn't watched those cops being murdered.

I had just taken off my gun belt and put a pot of venison stew on the stove to reheat when I glanced out the window and saw the Jeep parked across the road. It was late afternoon in mid-January and already getting dark, but I saw a flicker inside the vehicle that told me someone was lighting a cigarette.

I was all alone in the house.

Earlier that week, I had said good-bye to my girlfriend, Stacey, a wildlife biologist who was headed north to study why moose were dying off in record numbers across the state and what could be done to save them.

My nearest neighbors lived a quarter mile away through the woods in either direction.

So what reason would someone have for stopping here?

The state of Maine doesn't give out the home addresses of its game wardens, but the location of my rented house was common knowledge around Sebago Lake, especially among the resident poachers, petty criminals, and pill fiends. Hard as it was for me to believe, I had been stationed in the greater Portland area for nearly a year and a half now, more than enough time to make enemies, and I already had a long list of them from my years on the Midcoast and Down East. I could think of plenty of people I wouldn't have wanted to show up, unannounced and uninvited, on my doorstep.

I strapped on my gun belt again.

Without stopping to grab a parka or hat, I made my way through the kitchen to the back door and out into the frozen yard. The motion-sensitive lights snapped on, revealing my government-issue boat, canoe, and Jet Ski: all the tools of my summer trade stowed beneath cold-stiffened tarps. The people who were renting me the house had also left behind a jungle gym, for which Stacey and I had no use.

I circled through the leafless woods that surrounded the property, my feet punching postholes through the surface crust, and came out onto the road, downwind of the Jeep. There was a bite in the air that made me think more snow was on the way, even though none had been forecast. Even from fifty feet away, I could smell the cigarette.

The Jeep was a lipstick-red Grand Cherokee, neither old nor new, with a Maine plate and a ski rack on top. The shadows made it hard to see through the windows, but I thought there might be just a single person inside. I removed my flashlight from its holster and did my best to stay out of the rearview mirror as I came up behind the parked vehicle.

I rapped hard on the glass and shined the beam of my SureFire straight into the driver's face.

"Christ!" she said, jumping in her seat.

She was a middle-aged woman with wavy blond hair and blue eyes that were probably beautiful when they weren't stung with smoke and rimmed red from crying. She was wearing a white puff vest over a denim shirt that matched her eyes. My first thought was that she was stunning; my second was that I had never seen her before in my life.

In my hardest voice, I said, "Game warden. Can you roll down the window, please."

She had to turn the key in the ignition to get the glass down, and for an instant, I thought she might peel out of there. Instead, she released a cloud of smoke through the cracked window. I wondered why she even bothered wearing perfume if she was going to cure her skin with tobacco fumes.

She turned off the engine. "Is there—is there a problem?"

I moved the light from her face, flashing it around the interior of the Jeep. She had been using a Diet Coke can as an ashtray. Her purse was on the seat beside her. I saw a ski jacket thrown carelessly in the backseat. But no open containers of alcohol, no rifles mounted in a rack, nothing suspicious or illegal.

"Do you mind showing me your license and registration?" My breath steamed, as if I, too, had been smoking.

"What did I do? Did I do something wrong?" She had a jittery way of speaking, as if there was too much caffeine and nicotine in her bloodstream.

The law actually didn't require her to show me any identification, but I wasn't going to tell her that. I wanted to know who this strange woman was parked outside my house.

After a moment of hesitation, she reached for her pocketbook and pulled out a wallet. She looked even more attractive in the picture on her driver's license than she did in the flesh. Her name was Amber M. Langstrom, she was forty-eight years old, and she lived in Bigelow, which was a ski town up north, not far from where I had spent the first nine years of my life, back before my parents divorced.

"I saw you parked out here," I said, turning the light back on her, "and I wanted to see if you were all right."

"I just pulled over to make a call," she said.

"It's a dangerous place for that. This is kind of a narrow road—especially with these snowbanks—and a car coming around the bend wouldn't have much time to avoid hitting you."

She shut one eye. "Can you turn off that light, please? I can't quite—"

I pointed the beam at the ground. "Is that better?"

"Yes. Thank you." She blinked a few times to clear the spots away and then brought her face close to the window. She seemed to be squinting to read the name tag on my uniform.

"It says Bowditch," I told her.

Her lips parted and she gave the faintest nod. Then she laughed for no reason I could understand.

"Are you sure everything is all right?" I asked.

"Well, actually—"

"Yes?"

"The real reason I stopped is I'm lost and—this is so embarrassing—I've been driving around looking for a place to pee. There are no gas stations or McDonald's anywhere." She leaned her forearms against the wheel and smiled wide enough for me to see she was missing a molar. "I don't suppose—I don't suppose you live in that house?"

I felt my hand twitch in the direction of the .357 on my hip.

"If it's not too much trouble, I just wondered—could I use your bathroom?" she asked, with an extra tremble in her voice. "This is so embarrassing, but I drank too much soda, and I really, really, really have to pee."

"Can you excuse me a minute?" I said.

I retreated back to her rear bumper and took out my cell phone. I hit the auto dial for the state police dispatcher and recited the plate number and driver's license information.

The answer came back: "No outstanding warrants. No convictions. Record's clean."

"Thanks."

"Is everything all right there, Mike?" the dispatcher asked.

"I'll let you know."

I could see Amber watching me in her side mirror as I approached her open window.

I brought the flashlight beam back to her face. "What are you really doing here, Ms. Langstrom?"

"Your first name is Mike, right? Mike Bowditch?" She smiled

quickly, then bit down on her lower lip. The expression was supposed to be friendly, flirtatious. She had a small tattoo of a butterfly, the size of a gem, at the base of her throat.

A breeze lifted the hairs on my scalp. I kept my right hand by my hip.

She smiled harder. "I have a confession to make. I've been sitting here trying to get up the courage to knock on your door, and then you just—you just came out of nowhere like a ghost or something. The thing is, I needed to see you, and the Warden Service wouldn't tell me where you lived. I asked Gary Pulsifer, and he said it was somewhere near Sebago, but he wouldn't give me your home address. I had to ask around at some of the bars near the lake."

Pulsifer was the longtime district warden for the Rangeley Lakes region. He and I had a complicated acquaintance that was sometimes cordial, other times close to adversarial. Gary was known in the service for having a uniquely perverse sense of humor. But I had a hard time believing he would have sicced a stalker on me, even one as attractive as Amber Langstrom.

"Why have you been looking for me?" I asked.

"Can we go inside?" she said. "It's freezing out here, and it's kind of—well, it's kind of a long story. And I wasn't lying about having to pee."

I gazed into her eyes, but I didn't know what I should be looking for. If she was truly dangerous—truly a threat to my life—what would be the tip-off?

"Not until you tell me what you're doing here," I said.

"It's about your father."

The breeze lifted the hairs on my scalp again. "My father?"

"It's about Jack."

I wasn't sure what I had been expecting her to say, but it wasn't that.

"My father is dead."

"I know," Amber said, and her voice trembled again. "That's why I'm here."

2

Five years earlier, my father had been the most notorious criminal in Maine: a legendary poacher turned cop killer and fugitive. Needless to say, he was more than that to me; everything I was, for better or worse, I owed to him. I had lived my entire life in the shadow of his reputation, and that shadow had only grown longer and colder in the aftermath of his death. Over the past half decade, I had struggled to separate myself from the man and his crimes, successfully for the most part. In my mind, at least, I had buried Jack Bowditch once and for all.

Which was why the mention of his name now was like the sudden emergence of a repressed memory.

"Come inside," I told Amber Langstrom.

She gathered up her ski jacket and purse and climbed down out of the Jeep. She was shorter than she had looked behind the wheel and thin in the way many smokers are unnaturally thin. I watched her dance around a patch of black ice and thought that in bars, out of the light, she must have been frequently mistaken for a woman in her twenties.

She stomped her boots on the woven mat inside the door to loosen the snow from the treads.

"Bathroom's down the hall on the right," I said.

"Thank you!"

I heard the lock click on the door and began to wonder why—despite all my training and better instincts—I had just let a stranger into my house. It had to be more than her having mentioned my dead father.

I have always had a foolhardy streak. I used to mistake it for

7

bravery until it nearly got me killed for the umpteenth time. Then I saw it for what it was: a chronic addiction to adrenaline. My body craved danger the way a junkie does his next hit of heroin. I wondered how many of the dead cops in that video had suffered from the same weakness.

My girlfriend had only been gone a few days, and already the house was a mess: boot prints on the carpet, coats fallen from the rack in the hall, dirty plates on every tabletop. Stacey and I didn't live together—we hadn't yet taken that step in our relationship—but her irregular visits gave me the incentive to keep the place somewhat clean. I might have forgotten and left up my Christmas decorations all winter if she hadn't pointed out the brittle fir boughs over the mantelpiece.

"How can a man who is so curious that he notices everything not notice his house is a tinderbox?" Stacey had said, her long brown hair shaking as she laughed.

When Amber came out of the bathroom, I made sure to be standing to the side of the door with my hand resting on the butt of my SIG Sauer.

She gave me a nervous smile. "Oh, there you are."

I hadn't yet had a chance to stoke the fire in the woodstove; the house felt unnaturally cold. I motioned to the living room. "Have a seat."

Under the brightness of the overhead bulb, Amber had become middle-aged again. There were faint creases around her mouth and bags beneath her eyes. She was overdue for a visit to the hair salon. Her gray roots had begun to show. She sat with her knees pressed together, her jacket folded over her thighs, clutching her purse.

I remained standing with my back to the wall.

"You look so much like your dad," she said, gazing up at me. "It's a little spooky." She smiled briefly again and glanced around the room, taking in the cold woodstove, the fish mounts on the wall, the overloaded bookcases. "You have a lovely house. Do you live here alone?"

I made a vague throat-clearing noise and shifted my weight from one foot to the other.

She seemed to get the point. "So, I guess I should explain what I'm doing here."

"I would appreciate it."

She inhaled through her nose and exhaled through her mouth, as if performing a yoga exercise. "I knew your father. He used to come into the bar where I work. Well, he used to come in until he got banned for breaking a guy's arm. It was a different bar back then, the Red Stallion in Carrabassett. It's been closed a long time. I'm over at the Sluiceway now up Widowmaker."

It was a ski resort near Rangeley. My father had worked there briefly, long ago, driving one of the snowcats.

"Anyway," she continued, "I heard about what happened with Jack. I mean, who didn't hear about it? All that horrible stuff up at Rum Pond. It was just—just unbelievable."

"My father was a bad man," I said simply.

"No, he wasn't!" Without fully rising, she started to lift herself from the sofa, eyes widening with disbelief, then sat back down again. "Jack had a good heart. He was just so troubled." Her blood-shot eyes filled with tears again. "You don't really believe that he was bad. Why did you try to help him if you thought he was some sort of monster?"

I had puzzled over that same question for years, but I had no intention of baring my own troubled psyche to this unhinged woman.

Her smoky perfume hung heavily in the air.

"Ms. Langstrom . . ."

"Amber."

"I don't mean to be rude," I said. "But you really need to tell me what you're doing here."

"Of course. I'm sorry." She opened her purse and removed a photograph, which she held out for me to take. "This is my son, Adam."

It was a picture of a rugged-looking young man, probably no older than eighteen. He had the wavy brown hair of a Kennedy and piercing blue eyes set off by a skier's tan. The photo had been taken outside against a white mountain backdrop so beautiful, it looked fake.

"He's a handsome kid," I said, not knowing what else to say. I tried to return the picture, but she refused to take it.

"He doesn't look like this anymore," she said sadly. "He's been through so much. Anyway, the reason I'm here—" She took another yoga breath. "I'm hoping you can find him for me."

"I don't understand."

"Adam is missing."

"Have you spoken to the police?"

"You don't understand," she said. "The situation is—it's not that simple."

I had a feeling that I would regret my next sentence. "Then explain it to me."

"Three years ago, Adam was a senior at the Alpine Sports Academy outside Rangeley. Do you know it?"

"It's a high school for skiers," I said, hoping to hurry her along, "like Carrabassett Valley Academy."

"I wish he'd gone to CVA!" Her eyes welled up again and she dabbed at them with a wad of tissue from her purse. "But ASA offered him a scholarship. The school pays for a few local kids to go there—kids with athletic potential—everyone else is rich. And he did so well, too. I mean, his grades were never the best, but he was the best racer in his class. He had a shot at making the U.S. Ski Team and maybe even going to the Olympics."

I was still struggling to understand what any of this had to do with me. "So what happened to him?"

"Senior year, he met a girl from Vail. Her name was Alexa Davidson. She was a freshman."

From the way she spit out that last word, I suspected I knew what was coming next. "How old was she?"

"She was fourteen, although she looked and acted a lot older than that."

"And how old was Adam?"

"He was seventeen for most of the semester."

I set the photo on the table between us, facedown. "And then he turned eighteen. And someone found out he and Alexa were having sex?"

"The parents demanded that the school investigate. It would have been bad enough if they'd just expelled him, and taken away his dreams of skiing professionally, but the fucking headmaster decided to bring in the police."

"And they arrested Adam for statutory rape," I said.

"They totally set him up to make it look worse than it was." Her hair fell around her face. She pushed the strands away violently. "I had to sell my condo to pay for the lawyer—thirty thousand dollars—and all he did was lose the case. Adam still ended up going to jail. They were both just kids!"

Not in the eyes of the law. "How long was he in jail?"

"Two years."

"Where?"

"Bucks Harbor."

It was a prison in easternmost Maine, not far from one of my old districts. It was a minimum-security facility—low- to medium-risk prisoners. Informally, it was known to be a warehouse for convicted sex offenders, although the Department of Corrections would deny up and down that it was a dumping ground for the lowest of the low.

I noticed she hadn't mentioned Adam's father. There was no ring on her finger, either.

"How long has he been out?" I asked.

"Three months," she said with a sneer. "He's on supervised release, which means he has to register as a sex offender for the next ten years. He has to meet with a probation officer in Farmington every week and pay to go to counseling with a bunch of child rapists until he's 'cured' or something."

At least he hadn't been fitted with an electronic monitoring device, I thought.

She removed a pack of Capris from her vest and then seemed to realize she shouldn't light up in my house without asking permission. She stuffed the cigarettes in her pocket. When she looked up again, her eyes were full of fury.

"Do you know what the worst thing is, though?" she said. "They put his picture on the Internet! There's a Web site where you can look up who the sex offenders are in your town. So people see there's this new 'predator' named Adam Langstrom living nearby, and they freak out about their kids, even though he is completely normal and would never, ever hurt a child. My landlord wouldn't allow him to stay with me because the fucking neighbors saw his picture on the Internet. Adam had to go live at this logging camp in the middle of nowhere."

"A logging camp?"

"It's kind of like a halfway house, too. The probation officer sends people there who don't have anywhere else to go. All I know is that Adam hates the place. He said the man who runs it is a lying sack of shit who doesn't care about the safety of his workers. A man died there a month ago when a tree fell on him!"

I could guess the rest. "How long has Adam been missing?"

"Two weeks," she said. "He was supposed to check in with his parole officer, but he never did. She got a judge to put out a warrant for him."

In Maine, game wardens are trained alongside state troopers and have all the same arrest powers, but searching for fugitive sex offenders didn't normally fall within our purview—not unless they ran off into the woods. "And you haven't heard from him?"

Her voice had a sharp new edge. "If I had, I wouldn't be here, because at least then I'd know he was safe somewhere. His fucking PO thinks he ran off, but she's not going to go chasing him. She says he'll show up eventually, and then the cops will just arrest him again. Only this time, he'll be going to prison for ten years!"

"Your son is an adult, and he is going to have to live with the consequences of his actions."

"You don't understand. I'm afraid something happened to him!"

An image came into my mind of a friend, a veteran of the war in Iraq, who hadn't been able to escape his own demons after he returned home from the VA hospital.

"Was Adam suicidal?" I asked carefully.

"I don't know. I never used to think his father was."

Her answer raised so many questions, I had to resist diverting the conversation down a new path. "What about the people at the halfway house?" I asked. "Maybe Adam said something to them before he vanished."

"The asshole who runs the place wouldn't talk to me. He said he has a rule against violating his workers' privacy. But I'm Adam's mother!"

"I'm not a private detective, Amber."

She seemed stunned by my refusal. "What about Jack? You helped him. Everyone says you tried to prove his innocence."

"That was different. I'm sorry, but I just can't help you."

If I had known her at all, or been in any mood to explain, I might have confessed how embarrassed I was, humiliated even, by my past self. As a first-year warden, I had been reckless and headstrong. My insubordinate actions had nearly gotten me fired. I had no business getting a second chance in the Warden Service, but sometimes life rewards the undeserving. These days, I took every opportunity to distance myself from that Mike Bowditch. I treated him as a disreputable stranger—not even a blood relative—just someone who happened to share my name.

"You don't understand," she said yet again.

"I hope your son is all right and that he comes home soon."

She inhaled, then let out a long breath, as if preparing to jump off a cliff into deep water. Her eyes filled again wth tears. "Adam is your brother!"

I thought I had misheard her. "What did you say?"

She leaned across the table. "Jack and I had an affair—I was married to A.J. at the time—and I got pregnant."

I felt as if I had been punched in the sternum. "That's impossible."

"He is!"

How old was Adam? Twenty-one? I did the math. Twenty-one years ago, I had been seven, going on eight, and my parents had still been married. Soon after, I would come down with pneumonia when my father dragged me through the woods checking his trapline; my devoutly Catholic mother would get an abortion but pass it off as a miscarriage; she would pack her station wagon with little more than a few changes of clothing, and we would take off in the night while my father was out drinking, without even leaving a note, never to return. Twenty-one years ago my world hadn't yet fallen irretrievably apart.

Amber's face became fuzzier and fuzzier as she spoke: "I'd thought about telling you when Jack died—and then again after I heard your mom had passed away. I thought you should know you weren't alone in the word, that you had a little brother. But then Adam went to jail and everything spun out of control."

I found myself taking the photograph from her hand and sitting down hard in the armchair opposite her. I stared at Adam Langstrom's face, searching for a resemblance I hadn't noticed at first glance. He had the same brown hair and sky-blue eyes as my dad and me. Maybe the jawline looked faintly familiar. But the similarities were all superficial.

"How do you know?" The words came out as a croak. "How do you know that my dad is the father?"

"I know."

It felt as if every muscle in my body had gone taut. "Why should I believe you? You just dropped this on me after I refused to help find your son."

"What do you want from me?"

"A letter from him. A picture of you together. Anything."

"Your dad didn't write letters," she said, as if I should have known better than to ask. "And A.J. burned the only picture of Jack and me together when he found it."

I rose stiffly to my feet. "I'm sorry, but you need to leave."

"Wait!" she said. "I have these."

She reached into her jacket pocket again and pulled out a pair of dog tags on a chain. She passed them to me across the table. I read the words stamped into the stainless steel:

```
BOWDITCH
JOHN, M.
004-00-8120
O NEG
NO PREF.
```

My father had done two tours of duty in Vietnam with the Seventy-fifth Ranger Regiment and had returned home a hero. But the war had left him badly scarred, both physically and mentally. What he'd experienced in the jungles of Southeast Asia—killing men, nearly being killed by them—had managed to turn him into the worst version of himself, or so people told me who had known him before he left Maine.

He had continued to wear his dog tags long after he'd left the army. In every memory I had of him with his shirt off, they hung around his neck. They seemed to have some talismanic power, as if he credited them with having saved his life, while so many of his friends had died. I had been surprised to hear those tags hadn't been found on his body at Rum Pond. I had always wondered what had become of them.

"Jack gave those to me the night he first held Adam in his arms," Amber said. "He wanted me to give them to him when he was older."

Another invisible blow struck my chest. "You mean my dad *knew*?"

"He offered to take care of us, but I was still with A.J. and trying to make things work. Besides, as young as I was, I knew that Jack wasn't going to make a good husband—or a good father."

I was having a hard time getting my wind back. "You need to leave."

"What about Adam?"

"What about him?"

"You won't help me find him?"

"No."

"Not after what I just told you?"

"Especially not now," said a rough voice issuing from my mouth.

She remained seated, looking up at me. I could see her in the act of thinking. In the quiet, I heard the furnace start up in the basement.

Then Amber twitched her nose. "Is something burning?"

I had left the venison stew simmering, and it had begun to scorch the pot.

I hurried out to the kitchen. I used a dishrag to lift the handle and drop the bubbling contents into the sink. A haze hung in the air, its odor as foul as a failed animal sacrifice.

When I returned to the living room, I found Amber standing with her purse over her shoulder. I had thought I might have to throw her out, as emotional as she'd been. But she seemed strangely composed now.

I held the door open for her. Sure enough, it had begun to snow while we were inside.

"Don't you want to know how to reach me?" she said.

"I can always ask Gary Pulsifer."

Her expression softened. "It's better that you know about your brother, Mike."

I barely stopped myself from saying "It doesn't feel better."

I followed her out into the driveway and waited while the Jeep started up and the headlights came on. After she had driven off, the silence of the woods closed in around me. The sensation was of being imprisoned inside a snow globe.

I went back into the house to deal with the burned mess in the kitchen. It wasn't until later that I found Adam's picture where she had hidden it, under a dirty plate on the coffee table. She had scribbled her phone number on the back of the photograph. She had left the dog tags, too.

3

I read a lot as a kid. My mother used to come home from the library with free books she'd found in the donation boxes by the door. I remember one battered paperback in particular. It was an encyclopedia of different kinds of ghosts: phantoms, wraiths, apparitions, et cetera. A field guide to the undead. There was a chapter on poltergeists that has stayed with me. We tend to think of them merely as noisy, mischievous specters, but what this book explained was that, unlike other ghosts that tend to haunt places, poltergeists haunt specific people. No matter where you go, those loud, disruptive spirits will always follow you.

My father was my personal poltergeist.

I tossed the dog tags in my hand, listened to them jingle, turned them in my fingers, felt the stamped letters like braille I was unable to read. I had never known that we shared the same blood type. As if I needed another reminder of how much we had in common. I clenched my fist so hard around the tags that they left a rounded rectangle imprinted in the skin of my palm.

I knew that my father had always been a womanizer. He had been a handsome, red-blooded mountain man, possessed of an unshakable self-confidence and an animal magnetism I had seen on display in too many barrooms. But he had also loved my late mother in his own oddly ardent way, and the idea that he had fathered a child with another woman while he was still married to her—I didn't want to believe it.

And yet my dad had made a fool of me before. Why shouldn't he do it again from beyond the grave?

I tucked the tags into the chest pocket of my uniform and picked up the photograph Amber had left behind in a last-ditch effort to manipulate me into doing her bidding.

Adam Langstrom's eyes were so blue, many people would have thought they had been retouched, but I saw the same color every morning in the mirror. If she had been lying to me, either she was a terrific actress or she had also been lying to herself.

I felt a sense of panic growing inside my gut that I had never experienced before. For the past five years, I had thought I was the last in a cursed bloodline. But now . . .

Not knowing what else to do, I reached out for Stacey.

I dialed the number of the Department of Inland Fisheries and Wildlife's office in Ashland, a remote logging town north of the forty-sixth parallel in a part of Maine that had more moose than people. That was why Stacey and several of her colleagues were holed up there for the winter. They were investigating how an epidemic of blood-sucking winter ticks was devastating Maine's moose population. Thousands of the big animals from Minnesota to Nova Scotia had already died, and there seemed to be nothing biologists could do to stop the plague. The direness of the situation had only hardened Stacey's resolve. Like her father—my friend and mentor Charley Stevens—she seemed to fight the hardest for causes other people had given up for lost.

"Stacey's not back yet," said the man who answered the phone. "They're still out in the field."

"Isn't it dark?"

"Let me check. Yep, it's dark all right."

"Isn't it snowing?"

"It snows every day this time of year."

"What you're telling me is not to worry," I said.

"I'll have her call you when she gets back."

I tried to keep busy while I waited. I took off my gun belt again and changed out of my uniform into a flannel shirt and jeans. I even washed the dishes. But worrying about Stacey and not being able to tell her my news only added to my agitation.

I had a fifth of Jim Beam in my cupboard that I hadn't yet opened. My father had been an alcoholic, and I'd had more than my share of moments when things were going badly and I had felt the pull of the bottle. But if ever I needed a drink, it was now. I filled a glass with bourbon and sat down in front of my laptop to read the sad tale of Adam Langstrom.

And sad it was.

I started by accessing the state law-enforcement database to see if there really was a warrant out for his arrest. The page that came up showed a picture of Langstrom taken by the Department of Corrections and listed him as a fugitive, wanted for violating his probation. He looked older and more hardened than he did in the photo his mother had left behind. He had put on muscle, and his hair was dull and in need of cutting, but what was most noteworthy was his right ear. It was missing the lobe, as if something—or someone—had chomped it off.

It listed his age: twenty-one, as Amber had stated.

It listed his height as six feet two inches—my height.

It listed his weight as two hundred pounds—ten pounds heavier than me. Adam Langstrom was a big kid.

I then pulled up the public sex offender registry and typed in his name. The same photo came up, along with his "town of domicile," which was Kennebago Settlement, east of Rangeley on Route 16. It listed his place of employment, too: Don Foss Logging, also located in Kennebago. The site identified him as a ten-year registrant and said he had been convicted of one count of unlawful sexual contact and one count of unlawful sexual touching. No additional details were given about his crimes.

I had to continue my search elsewhere.

The Maine newspapers had barely covered his arrest and trial, in deference to the sensitivities of the Alpine Sports Academy, no doubt. It wouldn't have been in ASA's interest to trumpet the news that one of its scholarship students had raped the daughter of some captain of industry. The school tended to enroll kids who had spent their formative years on the ski slopes of Vail, Park City, and Jackson Hole. It had produced a handful of Olympians, but its greatest achievement was building its endowment, which some sources said rivaled that of some Little Ivies, including my own alma mater, Colby College.

There was no mention in any of the articles of a prior romantic relationship between Langstrom and the unnamed girl. To read the stories, you would have thought the case came down to a single assault. Langstrom had claimed the sex was consensual, but under examination, the girl had said she had been coerced.

Even though the papers hadn't identified her by name, I remembered that Amber had called her Alexa Davidson. From there, it was easy enough to search the academy's archived press releases and discover that a Seattle couple named Ari and Elizabeth Davidson had given a million-dollar gift to the school five years earlier. Now I could see why the headmaster had been so eager to turn the investigation over to the Franklin County Sheriff's Department.

The only other photograph of Adam Langstrom predated the picture on the registry. It had been taken at his sentencing. He was dressed in an ill-fitting suit, and his tie was askew, as if it were a noose he had managed to loosen. I couldn't see his right ear to see if it was missing its lobe. What struck me most about the picture was the expression on his face. So often defendants in court appear ashamed and already defeated; either that or emotionless and temporarily brain-dead. But Langstrom was glaring straight into the lens, as if he wanted to vault across the room and strangle the photographer with his own camera strap.

Langstrom's anger was as familiar as the color of his eyes. I had seen it too many times in my father's face and, sometimes, in my own bathroom mirror.

The cell phone buzzed on the desk. I took another sip of bourbon before I answered.

"Stacey?" I said.

"Graham told me you'd called." Her voice sounded nasal, her sinuses clogged, as if she was suffering from a bad cold. "What's going on, Mike? I'm too frostbitten for phone sex, if that's what you want."

"I was worried about you."

"What? Why?"

"You were late getting back to the office. And I saw from the weather radar that it's snowing even harder up there than it is down here."

She paused. "Your voice sounds funny."

I couldn't lie to her. "I've had a couple of shots."

"What happened?"

"I had a visitor earlier. This woman named Amber Langstrom tracked me down at the house. She says she knew my dad." My voice sounded like someone else's in my ears. "She says I have a brother, Stacey."

I pressed the phone against my ear. I heard nothing for a long time.

She spoke slowly. "You have a brother?"

"She says his name is Adam. And he just got out of prison for statutory rape, and now he's missing."

"You need to back up," Stacey said "Start from the beginning."

I remembered how Amber had taken yoga breaths. I closed my eyes, breathed in and then out, and began my tale. I am sure I rambled. Bourbon on an empty stomach hadn't been the best idea. But Stacey was good at keeping me on point.

When I had finished, she said, "Can you e-mail me his picture? I want to see if he looks like you."

"It might be fuzzy, since it'll be a picture of a picture."

"That's all right. Do you believe this Amber woman is telling the truth?"

"Maybe. I don't know. It's possible. My dad slept with plenty of women. And Amber seems like his type."

"What type is that?"

"Ready, willing, and able."

Not to mention hot as hell, I thought. But that detail didn't seem like one I should share with my girlfriend.

"Then you've got to help her find this Adam guy," Stacey said. "Aren't you curious to meet him?"

"No."

"Liar."

"My life was perfectly fine before I knew he existed."

"Perfectly fine? Who are you kidding?" she said with a laugh. She really did sound stuffed up. "You might have a half brother, Mike. You'll never forgive yourself if something ends up happening and you never get to meet him."

I pushed the bottle away. "I've been down that road before, Stace. It didn't end well."

"You're not the same person you were when all that shit happened at Rum Pond."

"Exactly. I'm not that person anymore."

"At least make some calls for the poor woman."

"Who would I call?"

"Start with Gary Pulsifer," she said. "Find out how he knows this Amber Langstrom. Then ask him what the hell he was thinking, sending her to look for you."

Those were good questions. But I wanted to talk about something else, anything else.

I tried to picture Stacey on the other end of the line. In my imagination, her dark hair was wind-tousled and her lips and cheeks were rosy from the cold. Like her mother, she had uncanny green eyes that were both beautiful and unsettling, as if she were descended from some supernatural race of beings gifted with the powers of telepathy and clairvoyance. I smiled at the face I saw in my mind's eye.

"So how are things going up there in Moose Vegas?" I asked.

"Winter just started. The moose still have full coats and haven't been sucked dry yet by the ticks. Ask me again in April."

"I'm not going to have to wait that long to see you, am I?"

"That depends on the moose."

"You sound like you have a cold."

"It's just the sniffles."

"So are you still too frozen for phone sex?"

She laughed that rowdy laugh of hers. "I'm thawing," she said. "But I'd better lock my door if you're going to start talking dirty."

4

That night, in my dreams, I found myself back in the mountains and hardscrabble farmland of my childhood. I was a boy again, standing outside my father's trapping shed, and there were patches of snow on the ground. I was watching him expertly cut the fur off the otters and muskrats he had caught in leg-hold traps, then throw the skinned carcasses into a fire he had lit in an oil drum. My father's hands were bloody, but when he looked up at me, he was smiling and his face was kind. He waved me over to come help him—something he had never done in life—offering me the bloody knife to take. But as is often true in dreams, I found myself unable to move, and he began to get red in the face. He started cursing and brandishing the knife as he came toward me, and that was when I woke up.

I felt no more rested than when I'd gone to sleep. There was a dull pain behind my eyes from the bourbon the night before. I swallowed some ibuprofen and stood under the shower for fifteen minutes, letting the hot water scald my back.

When I picked up my uniform shirt from the floor, my dad's dog tags fell out of the pocket. For some reason, I was seized by a sudden impulse to put them around my neck. Then the urge passed, and I was left wondering why I would have wanted to carry around a reminder of a man who had nearly ruined my life. I gripped the tags tightly in my hand and glanced around the bedroom for a place to hang them.

As I made my way down the stairs to the darkened kitchen, I made a conscious decision to focus on my work that day. I wasn't going to think about Amber or her misbegotten son.

Standing at the counter, watching the black windows fade to blue,

I ate half a box of Cheerios, then filled my travel mug with coffee for the road ahead. I was supposed to cover two districts that day: my own and the adjacent district to the northwest. The warden who normally patrolled that section, Tommy Volk, was in the middle of a knock-down, drag-out divorce and was taking a personal day to spend in court, battling with his soon-to-be second ex-wife. The joke around the division was that Volk already had a third ex-wife lined up.

Strange as it sounds, the love lives of game wardens were often the stuff of soap operas.

When I reported in with the dispatcher, he said, "I got a call from a lady who claims to have seen a timber wolf in her backyard."

"There are no timber wolves in Maine."

"Tell her that. She was pretty agitated. Said it was killing deer. She's called twice now, in fact. I think she's going to keep calling us every hour if you don't go over there this morning."

The woman's name was Gail Evans, and she lived over on Pondicherry Pond, near Bridgton, which was part of Volk's district and not a place I knew particularly well. Ms. Evans had probably seen an eastern coyote: an animal with which I had some unhappy history. It felt like a portent of a miserable day to come.

Outside, I found three inches of weightless snow on my truck and a scrim of frost on the windows that required five hard minutes of scraping to clear. The air was crisp enough to stiffen the hairs in my nostrils. I decided to replace my brimmed duty cap with a knit snowmobiling hat. I didn't want to lose any earlobes.

The road around the west shore of Sebago revealed an expanding sheet of ice that still hadn't yet hardened all the way across. Indigo waves continued to churn a mile out in the center. Some winters, Maine's deepest lake never froze entirely. The open water made me think of the World War II bomber who had crashed out there during a training mission. The fuselage had never been recovered. The plane was still down there in the murk and the mud, a rusting tomb for its skeleton pilots.

Lord God, I was in a morbid mood.

Most of the morning traffic was moving in the opposite direction, heading into the distant city of Portland. Southernmost Maine was the only part of the state that was growing, gaining in population. Everywhere else, it seemed, the old mill towns and fishing ports were losing their young people. The last time I had visited the mountains of my childhood, I had counted abandoned houses and trailers until the number got too depressing.

Which, inevitably, made me think about my father again.

And Adam Langstrom, my alleged brother.

It wasn't even seven o'clock yet, and I had already broken my promise to myself.

Gail Evans was waiting for me in the middle of the road, and I could tell from her expression that she had been waiting a long time. She stood beside a sign that read THREADS: FIBER ARTS STUDIO, WEAVING AND SPINNING LESSONS.

I guessed her to be in her late fifties or early sixties. She had sun-damaged skin, bright eyes the color of Navajo turquoise, and silver curls that escaped from under a fibrous, fuzzy cap that reminded me of a purple Furby. She was dressed in blue jeans, a rainbow-hued sweater, and heavy Birkenstock sandals ill-suited to the time of year. She held a snow shovel at port arms across her torso.

"What took you so long?" She spoke as if she suffered from lock-jaw.

I treated the question as rhetorical. "You reported seeing a 'wolf'?"

She waved the shovel at me. "Two hours ago! It chased a little deer right through my yard."

Contrary to popular belief, there is no population of wolves living in Maine. Occasionally, one might materialize in some northern corner of the state: a lonely wanderer from some distant region of Quebec. My father claimed to have seen a wolf once while he was hunting. There might also be some outcasts that had been let loose by crazies hoping to repopulate the Maine woods with species from the Pleistocene. But the official line from state biologists was that wolves had been eradicated from the northeastern United States in the nineteenth century, and there were no plans whatsoever to bring them back.

In all likelihood what this woman had seen was a coyote: a once-nonnative species that had migrated east to fill the ecological niche vacated by their larger cousins. As the small western coyote drifted into Maine, it evolved into a formidable predator capable of taking down everything from an adult deer to a newborn moose. I'd seen dead coyotes, shot by night hunters (because the best time to hunt them is after dark), that measured five feet in length and weighed in at nearly seventy pounds. Damned big dogs.

"Can you show me where, exactly, you saw this 'wolf'?" I asked.

The muscles in her neck stiffened. "Why do you keep saying it that way—'wolf'? You don't believe me, do you? Well, I can show you the paw prints."

I followed her down her driveway to a cottage that looked like something out of a storybook. The house was purple, with a green-shingled roof, bright orange doors, and numerous stained-glass windows. In the yard were all manner of sculptures—from enormous wrought-iron human figurines to granite birdbaths, now frozen, to immense metallic balls like gold meteorites that had dropped from the sky to become half-buried in the snow.

"See, there!"

She used her shovel to point at a heavily trampled plot of snow beside a flat-tray bird feeder. There were hoofprints of all sizes everywhere in the yard.

I scratched my nose. "You seem to get a lot of deer here."

"I put out corn and apples for them. Cortlands."

"That's a bad idea, Ms. Evans."

"Feeding deer in general or giving them Cortlands in particular? Whatever for?"

I started an often-recited speech: "I know you mean well, but feeding deer actually reduces their ability to survive during the winter. It makes deer more vulnerable to predators by drawing them out of their protective cover, and it lures them close to roads, where they get hit by cars. And when they congregate in herds, they pass on illnesses—like chronic wasting disease—to one another."

Her expression told me she didn't believe a word I was saying. "So I'm supposed to watch them starve?"

"You could invite hunters onto your land instead of posting it."

"Right!"

"Well, you shouldn't feed them, in any case."

Gail Evans remained unmoved. "That's ridiculous."

I had no doubt she would keep putting out feed corn and fruit baskets for the deer no matter what I said. "You're going to continue having problems with predators, in that case."

I circled the trampled area, which was littered with cracked kernels of corn and apple scraps the deer hadn't yet eaten. Sure enough, I saw the prints of a very large canine—five pads with visible claw marks. Felines, like bobcats and lynx, typically don't show their claws. By the size, I would have said they belonged to a domestic dog.

I rose to my feet and brushed my gloved hands together to remove the snow. "Can you tell me what you saw, exactly?"

She had a rare gift for speaking complete sentences through clenched teeth. "I was in my studio, and I heard howling, and then I saw the deer come through and, a moment later, this fast black shape. And I said, 'Oh, my Lord, that's a wolf!' It scared the hell out of me. No one ever told me there were wolves here."

"That's because there aren't any," I said. "Are you sure it wasn't more of a bark than a howl?"

"What—like a terrier?"

I tried to frame my words carefully. "Ms. Evans, I'm sure it seemed to you like a wolf."

Gail Evans flashed her jewel-like eyes at me. "Here we go."

"In all likelihood, what you saw was someone's dog," I said. "It doesn't take much to awaken their predator genes. You'd be surprised by some of the breeds I've seen—Shetland sheepdogs, boxers, even poodles—chasing deer."

"This was no poodle."

I tried another tack. "It could have been a coyote. There are a lot of them in this area, and they hunt deer. But the prints would be smaller."

She pushed her fuzzy hat back from her forehead as if it was itching her. "Didn't coyotes kill two hikers on the Appalachian Trail? If you're trying to reassure me, you're not doing a very good job! Besides, I saw dozens of coyotes when I lived in Santa Fe, and this was too big to be one. I'm telling you, it was a wolf."

I didn't want to rehash what had actually taken place on the AT;

I had spent too many hours trying to put a stake through the heart of rumors that refused to die. Nor did I want to get into a taxonomic debate about the subspecies of coyotes—western versus eastern—with this impossible woman.

There was a long silence while I tried to formulate a response that didn't sound even more condescending. Some crows far away in the treetops began making a ruckus.

Finally, Gail Evans lifted her chin as if trying to balance a Ping-Pong ball on it. "You're not even going to make a report of this, are you? Or if you do, you're going to write something about a crazy woman 'from away' who doesn't know the difference between a timber wolf and a poodle."

The complacent self-confidence of this woman was bringing out a side of me I disliked. As a rookie warden, I had sometimes been abrupt to the point of rudeness with difficult people, but I had worked hard at managing my anger during the past years. Nevertheless, I needed to get away from her before I said something I regretted.

"I think I'm going to follow these tracks a ways and see what I find. If you want to wait inside—"

"I'm going with you."

"This is something I need to do alone, ma'am."

She shook her head in frustration, causing her Furby cap to slide forward again. But she had recognized the seriousness in my tone. When I left her, she was attacking the snowbank around one of her buried statues with the blade of her shovel.

With the new coating of snow, running the track was easy. The prints led across the side yard and through a wall of white cedars that the deer had chewed to shreds. The track shifted course where the young deer had made long leaps trying to escape the death snapping at its heels. I found tufts of deer hair pinned to some bayberry thorns, telling me the chase had happened very recently. A strong wind would have blown those wisps of fur loose.

Stacey teased me about being a compulsive noticer, but I believed my attention to details was one of my better qualities. It certainly helped me in my work on days like these.

The temperature seemed to drop as the shadow of a cloud passed over me. I looked up and felt my heart skip. Directly over my head hung an enormous oak branch—roughly the size of a railroad tie—that had broken loose in a recent storm. The branch should have come crashing to the ground, but it had gotten snagged in the boughs of the surrounding pines. The weight was causing the boughs to sag, and it looked like the next strong gust might send it plummeting to earth. Maine loggers called these looming hazards "widowmakers," for obvious reasons. They had killed many men in the woods.

Widowmaker was the name of the ski resort where Amber worked. The universe seemed intent on nudging me in a direction I didn't want to go. I stepped out from under the death trap as the wind rustled the snow out of the boughs around me.

I kept following the deer trail.

A few hundred yards into the forest, I finally came across the corpse of the young deer. It was still warm. Flecks of spittle showed along its lips. The yearling had run until its heart had given out. The ribs rippled beneath my fingertips as I rubbed the animal's side.

The stomach was torn open, and a bloody pulp of half-chewed organs had spilled out onto the snow.

I pushed my cap up on my forehead and rubbed my fingers through my hair, trying to make sense of what I was looking at. From the size of the tracks, I had expected that it was a dog. But a dog chasing a deer is not unlike a dog chasing a car: If it ever catches its prey, it frequently has no idea what to do with it. The fun is all in the pursuit. Unless a dog is starving, it usually won't feed on the carcass.

So this must have been a coyote, but that made no sense, either. The prints were twice the size of any coyote prints I'd seen.

It had to be a dog—and a big one, too. Something had interrupted its meal. Maybe it had smelled me coming, or maybe it hadn't been that hungry to begin with.

Under Title Twelve of the Maine Criminal Code, the section primarily enforced by game wardens, I was authorized to shoot any dog I found killing deer, although I had trouble imagining myself actually doing so without hesitation. In my mind, the owner was the one who deserved a backside of bird shot. Fines for letting a dog run free to attack deer and moose rarely exceeded a few hundred dollars.

It seemed a pitifully small amount of money for such willful negligence.

Gail Evans bore some culpability here, too. By naïvely putting out food for deer, trying to help them survive, she had lured this young animal to its death. People never want to believe that their best intentions can lead to the worst outcomes.

I decided to leave the deer to the crows. Birds need to eat, too.

Then I followed my own trail back to the gingerbread house.

"Well?" asked Evans.

"It was a dog," I said loudly, leaving no room for rebuttal.

"I knew you were going to say that."

"I'll ask around and see if I can find out whose it is. We'll make sure it stops doing this." I handed her my business card with a number to call in case she spotted the renegade dog again. "You really should stop feeding those deer, too. It's hurting them more than it's helping them."

Gail Evans planted her feet and stared me in the eyes. "If it's not against the law, you can't stop me from doing it."

"Don't be surprised if the dog comes back, then."

She made a loud sniffing noise, as if her nose had begun to drip. "A dog! Right!"

"There are no timber wolves running around your neighborhood, I can assure you."

"I know what I saw," said Gail Evans. "It was a wolf, and nothing you say will convince me otherwise."

5

The prospect of canvassing the area for a deer-chasing dog didn't excite me. Knocking on doors is one of the fundamentals of police work; nothing yet has been invented to replace it. But that didn't mean I was eager to make the rounds.

I dug my hand into my pants pocket for my truck keys, but when I pulled them out, something else came with them. My father's dog tags. The willful chain had tangled itself around my finger.

I was certain that I'd hung them up back at the house. Hadn't I?

Obviously not, because here they were.

"At least make some calls for the poor woman," Stacey had told me. "Start with Gary Pulsifer. Ask him how he knows this Amber Langstrom. Then ask him what the hell he was thinking, sending her to look for you."

I drove to the Pondicherry Pond boat launch. I counted three ice-fishing shacks, all with trucks parked beside them. None of the vehicles was familiar to me, but I didn't patrol this district often enough to recognize all the local scofflaws by sight. The people in the shacks would see me driving toward them across the ice and have time and cover to dump any illegal fish they might have taken back through the holes they'd drilled. There was nothing I could do about them but check their licenses.

Besides, I was too preoccupied by the events of the night before. There was no point in denying it anymore.

I turned off the engine and keyed in Pulsifer's number. I was embarrassed to admit that I knew it by heart.

* * *

Gary Pulsifer was a district warden, like me, but he was also the designated representative to the Maine State Law Enforcement Association, the union that collectively bargains for our compensation and benefits and that defends us if we are ever the subjects of disciplinary proceedings from the Internal Affairs division.

In my five-plus years as a game warden, I had faced four such tribunals. As such, I was intimately acquainted with Article 11 of the union's bargaining agreement, the section titled "Complaints and Investigations." I knew my rights going into a disciplinary hearing. And Pulsifer had been at my side for every one of them.

The accused are given the option of taking a lie-detector test.

Nobody is foolish enough to take one.

Except me, of course. In the months following the manhunt for my father, when rumors were flying that I had conspired to help him elude capture, I had submitted to a polygraph exam. An assistant attorney general was hell-bent on proving that I had been Jack Bowditch's accomplice. I had seen no other choice but to surrender my fate to a machine widely known to be an imperfect determiner of guilt or innocence.

I'd spent five hours in that airless room, being asked question after question, *rat-a-tat-tat,* by a man who never displayed one recognizable human emotion. The examiner refused to make eye contact. He spent the entire time staring at his computer screen as if it were the true gateway to my soul.

"Is your first name Michael?"

"Is this the month of September?"

"Do you plan on telling me a single lie today?"

"Did you communicate with your father while he was a fugitive?"

"Did he admit to you that he killed Jonathan Shipman?"

"Did he admit to you that he killed Deputy William Brodeur?

"Did you love him?"

The examiner didn't ask me that last question, but I kept waiting for it to come.

When I came out of the interrogation room, I found that every muscle in my body was as sore as if I had just scaled a cliff without a rope.

"That was brutal," I told Pulsifer afterward.

"You think so, do you?" he'd replied, giving me that half-suppressed grin I would come to know so well.

Pulsifer was in his late forties and at a place in his career when many wardens consider applying for leadership positions, not just because they have families and can use the increased pay but also because pensions are based on the rank you have when you retire. Pulsifer didn't seem to care about money or rank. He lived simply with his wife and four children on a farm in Flagstaff, just down the road from where my family had once rented a ratty-ass trailer.

He had a narrow face and clever brown eyes that were set a little too close together over his nose. The effect was to make him appear somewhat foxlike. He wore his rusty brown hair on the long side, right at the limit of what was permissible in the warden handbook. Pulsifer seemed to inhabit that perilous borderland. He always seemed to be fighting back a smile, as if he were in on a joke the rest of us were missing.

"How do I know if I passed the test?" I'd asked him. "I'm worried I didn't."

"Well, how much were you lying?"

"I wasn't lying."

"Everyone lies," he'd said with a merciless grin. "It just depends how good you are at doing it."

That was my introduction to the untrusting, ever-mocking worldview of Gary Pulsifer.

He began our phone conversation the way he began all our phone conversations: "What fine mess did you get yourself into this time, Bowditch?"

"It's not what I did. It's what you did."

"Amber Langstrom found you, did she?"

"What the hell, Pulsifer?"

"I didn't tell her where you lived. I just pointed her in your general direction."

"Come on!"

"You're right," he said. "I shouldn't have done it, but I was curious to see what would happen, and I couldn't help myself. So what did she want to talk to you about?"

Pulsifer was aware that his last name sort of rhymed with that of a certain fallen angel. At times, it seemed, he liked to play up the resemblance.

"She didn't tell you?" I asked.

"She said it was personal. She didn't explain how you two knew each other, just that you went back a ways and she needed to get in touch."

"I never met her before last night."

He chuckled. "Well, it wouldn't be the first time Amber Birch lied."

"I thought her name was Langstrom."

"Birch was her maiden name. She was the hottest girl at Mount Abram High. She's still smoking. Don't you think?"

"Is that why you helped her find me—because you want to get in her pants?"

When he spoke again, his voice was different, harder. "I hope I haven't created a problem for you."

"Yeah, well, you have. What can you tell me about her? Is she crazy?"

"Crazy, no. Trouble, always. She works in the pub over at Widowmaker. Been there forever now, ever since the Red Stallion closed. She married A. J. Langstrom right out of high school. Who knows why. We used to joke they hooked up because A.J. had the biggest dick at Mount Abram. Everybody knew his only ambition in life was to take over his old man's gas station. But Amber had champagne wishes and caviar dreams, as my old man used to say."

He paused to take a sip of something.

"I think Amber realized she'd made a mistake pretty fast. I used to go over to the Sluiceway during my drinking days, and she had a reputation. I remember she didn't wear her wedding ring at work, said it would get scratched or something. I think she was hoping one of the rich skiers would sweep her up and take her off to Fiji. Then she got pregnant, and that was that."

I needed to be careful about what I said next.

One of the impediments to Pulsifer and me ever becoming friends was the history he had with my father. I might have called them archenemies if the rivalry hadn't been so one-sided. Gary had been a district warden during the heyday of my father's poaching career, and he had never managed to catch him in the act. My dad delighted in spreading stories about all the deer and moose he was taking out of season, knowing how much it would humiliate the local warden. The relationship between Gary Pulsifer and Jack Bowditch was not unlike the one between Wile E. Coyote and the Road Runner.

To his credit, Pulsifer never seemed to hold my dad's misdeeds against me, although he was far too subtle to reveal his true feelings. Still, I had no intention of asking him if my father might have been the one who knocked up Amber Langstrom.

"So what's the story with her son?" I asked.

"Her son?" He seemed genuinely taken aback. "Now I get it. She asked you to help find Adam, didn't she?"

"Yes."

"Christ! I should have made the connection," he said. "Amber came to see me first, asked if I could go looking for her kid. She flirted like hell, trying to get me to say yes. But I'm not going to risk what I've got for a piece of ass, not anymore. She was pissed when I turned her down. I can't believe I didn't make the connection."

Pulsifer was one of the smartest, savviest wardens I knew. The possibility that this hadn't occurred to him defied belief. "What can you tell me about Adam?"

"He fucked the wrong girl, first of all. I'm pretty sure it was consensual, but he should have realized that there's a different standard for eighteen-year-olds. Not that I feel sorry for him. Adam Langstrom was no angel. He beat up the Davidson girl's brother pretty bad when he tried to put an end to it. Did Amber tell you that part?"

"No."

"I think that's what set their father off, hearing his son had been busted up in a fight and then finding out why."

"Who's his PO?" I asked, meaning his probation officer.

"Shaylene Hawken in Farmington. Talk about a hacksaw! That woman could stare down a grizzly. I feel sorry for the guy in that respect."

"Amber said he was living at some sort of halfway house, but it shows up on his registry page as a logging outfit."

"It's a company owned by a guy named Don Foss," Pulsifer said. "He's got some sort of arrangement with the state where he takes in sex offenders who can't find a place to live. Gives them beds and jobs working on his crew. I can't decide whether he's a secular saint or a modern-day plantation boss."

It sounded like an unconventional operation, to say the least.

"Have you seen Adam since he got out?"

He took another sip of whatever he was drinking. "A couple times at the tagging station in Bigelow last month. I think he was hanging around just to torture himself. As a felon, he can't own a gun, and he can't hunt ever again. I'll tell you, before he went to prison, that kid was a wicked deer killer. Bagged two-hundred-pound bucks three years in a row, and we don't have as many of those up here as we used to."

As a convicted sex offender, Adam had to observe a crushingly long list of prohibitions: no owning guns, no drinking alcohol, no using a computer, no searching the Internet, no looking at pornography, no living where he wanted without approval, no unsanctioned travel out of state. While he was on probation, the slightest slipup—even just a speeding ticket—might be enough to send him back to jail. I tried to imagine how I would feel living with those restrictions, and I kept ending up at the same place.

"Do you think he might have killed himself?" I asked.

"You know, it won't surprise me if they find him hiding out with some skank and a gallon of Allen's coffee brandy in a motel in Machias, and it won't surprise me if they find him hanging from a redbud tree."

I had never heard of a redbud tree, but Pulsifer was full of obscure references to books and movies.

"I've got to go," I said. "I've got to get back to work."

The truth was, I had about a thousand more questions about Adam Langstrom, but I wasn't sure I wanted to know the answers.

"What are you up to today?" Pulsifer asked.

"A woman in Pondicherry swears she saw a wolf chase a deer through her backyard."

"Good luck with that!" The mischievous lilt returned to his voice. "So you're not going to tell me why Amber came knocking on your door? You said you didn't know her, so why did she pick you to be her knight in shining armor? You've got me intrigued."

"Good-bye, Pulsifer."

"I've missed seeing you at Loudermill hearings. You were always my favorite shit magnet, Bowditch."

"That isn't funny."

"It's a little funny," he said. "Seriously, I've been hearing good things about you lately. It made me wonder if there might be two Mike Bowditches. If you are ever up this way, give me a call and we'll grab a coffee."

After I'd hung up, I sat in my cold truck, watching frost form on my windshield. On the one hand, Pulsifer had confirmed my suspicion that Amber shouldn't be trusted. On the other hand, everything he'd told me about Adam's character—his cockiness, his fighting temper, his marksmanship with a deer rifle—made me think the missing man really might be my father's second son.

6

The driveway of the next house hadn't been plowed, and there were no lights in the windows or smoke coming from the chimney. I gave it a pass. The same with the one after. The homes along Pondicherry Pond seemed to be mostly seasonal cottages.

Toward the end of the camp road, I came upon an old guy in a green bathrobe, sweatpants, and pack boots. He was pushing a snowblower that was throwing an arc of glistening powder high into the air. When he spotted my warden truck at the end of his drive, he turned off the gas and leaned his weight against the handles in lieu of a walker. He studied me as I came around the front of the vehicle.

"Morning!" I said.

"Morning, Warden," he said in an accent that eschewed all *r*'s.

"Beautiful day, isn't it?"

"A mite chilly, I'd say." He had a roseate nose, a scruffy beard that was more like a really bad shave, and was probably bald under his fur-lined bomber hat. "What can I do for you?"

"You wouldn't have a dog, would you?"

"Used to."

"What about any of your neighbors along this road?"

"Some do. Some don't."

I could see how this conversation was going to unfold unless I took the initiative. "Any of them let their dogs run free? I got a call from a woman down the road saying a dog was chasing deer through her yard. It killed a little yearling in the woods back of her property. I'm trying to find the owner."

"Was it that lady with all that artsy crap in her dooryard?"

I nodded. "That's the one."

"Didn't know you wardens was moonlighting as dogcatchers," he said.

"Only when the dogs chase deer."

His bathrobe opened when he straightened up and revealed a faded T-shirt with a Green Beret logo on the front and the Latin words *De Oppresso Liber*.

"Think Carrie Michaud might have a new dog," he said. "Some kind of shepherd or husky mix, I think. Black as the Earl of Hell's waistcoat. Saw it riding in the truck with her the other day. Thought I heard it howling the other night, too."

"What do you mean, *howling*?"

"You know," he said, and let loose with a loud and shockingly accurate wolf call.

I was getting a churning feeling in my stomach that told me my strange day might yet take a stranger turn. "You sure it wasn't barking?"

He gave me a look as if the question was the most asinine thing he'd heard.

"Which house is Carrie Michaud's?" I asked.

"Blue one at the corner. Got lots of yard art out front. You can't miss it. Don't tell her it was me who told you, though. Carrie's a little thing, but she can get worked up pretty good."

"I won't."

Before I could thank him for his help, he restarted the blower. I watched him shuffle along behind the noisy machine, smelling the heady gasoline exhaust on the cold air and wondering what this old Green Beret's story was. You never know who you'll meet holed up in some backwoods shack. I suspected that it might take a long time to pry this man's tale out of him, and then I would be disappointed to learn he had bought the T-shirt for two bucks down at the Goodwill store.

Some breeds of dogs bark; others bay. I had heard dogs moan or wail when they were hurt or unhappy. They were capable of all sorts of unexpected vocalizations. But the old man had perfectly imitated a wolf's howl, and unless he was having fun with me, which was a distinct possibility, it meant that I might owe Gail Evans an apology.

I had no trouble finding Carrie Michaud's house. The front yard was littered with snow-covered appliances and rusting scrap metal. By "yard art," the old geezer hadn't meant sculptures like those outside Gail Evans's house. He had meant junk.

The house itself wasn't much better. Someone had once painted its cedar shingles bright blue, but the color had faded and had now turned a color I associated with the lips of people who'd frozen to death. The blinds were all drawn, as if whoever lived behind them was allergic to sunlight. A yellow plastic sign posted to a pine warned against trespassing. Another said BEWARE OF DOG.

In the driveway were parked two trucks: a Suzuki Equator and a Mitsubishi Raider, both painted black.

As I climbed out of my own truck, I removed my gloves and felt without looking for the canister of pepper spray on my belt. There were no dogs visible, but I did see prints in the snow, big ones like those I'd found in the woods behind Gail Evans's house, and, the pièce de résistance, an enormous pile of shit.

They hadn't bothered to shovel the walkway, but had worn a path from the drive that required me to place one foot in front of the other. I heard music pounding through the front door. Screeching guitars and machine-gun drums. I pushed the glowing doorbell and waited. I gave it a minute, then banged with my fist.

Eventually, the door was opened by a skinny guy who looked like he'd just walked off the set of a postapocalyptic horror movie. He had bleached hair, disk earrings that had stretched holes in the lobes wide enough to stick your finger through, and a bone-white complexion. He wore a sleeveless purple T-shirt, cargo pants, and leather boots with a surplus of nonfunctional buckles.

When Goth fashion had finally come to Maine—everything came to my rural state long after it was passé elsewhere—it had lost something in the translation.

"You wouldn't happen to own a dog, would you?" I said.

He turned and yelled over his shoulder into the darkened, thumping interior of the house. "Carrie!"

"What?" came a shrill voice.

"Do we own a dog?"

"What?"

"There's a game warden at the door."

The music stopped, as if a plug had been pulled. I heard staccato footsteps on a staircase.

"What's your name?" I asked the Goth.

"Spike."

"You don't know if you have a dog, Spike?"

"It ain't my house, man."

A moment later, a woman elbowed her male friend aside to face me. She stood no more than five feet tall and weighed, I was guessing, no more than ninety pounds. She had a pixie haircut (dyed black), a painful-looking sore on her lip, and bile-green eye shadow. Like her beau, she was outfitted for the end-time in a leather vest, with no shirt underneath, and black jeans rolled above her bare ankles. She also happened to have a new tattoo on her forearm. It was poorly drawn and still scabbed, but it was unmistakably the silhouette of a howling wolf.

"Didn't you see the sign!" she said in the overloud voice people use who are hard of hearing. Her eardrums must have still been stunned from all that metal. "No trespassing!"

"That doesn't apply to law enforcement," I said. "I also saw the 'Beware of Dog' sign. What kind of dog is it?"

"Why do you want to know?"

"A dog killed a deer down the road from here."

One side of her mouth—the side with the sore—twitched. "I don't have a dog no more. That sign is old. Who told you I have a dog?"

"You're Carrie Michaud, aren't you?"

"So what?" Everything about this hostile, manic, hollow-eyed person shouted *narcotics.*

"Look, Carrie, I know you own a dog. There are dog tracks and urine stains all over your yard. There's a big pile of dog shit next to that snowbank. You need to stop lying to me. Now, why don't you go get your dog?"

"So you can give me a ticket? Ha! No way!"

I was tired of playing coy about my suspicions. "It's a wolf dog, isn't it?"

Before I could say another word, she slammed the door in my face.

Wolf dogs are the hybrid offspring of wolves and domestic dogs, bred, mostly, for people who want the thrill of saying that they own the baddest animal on the block. They rank above pit bulls in that regard. They also happen to be illegal to possess in the state of Maine.

I backed slowly away from the front door and looked at the windows. Sure enough, one of the blinds was lifted, and I saw the Goth's tubercular face peering out.

I made sure to be loud. "Open the door, please."

Carrie Michaud appeared in the next window. "Fuck you!"

So much for negotiation.

I retreated back to my truck and turned the key in the ignition. Once hot air was finally blowing through the vents, and my face was feeling less like a death mask, I picked up my phone and dialed a friend.

"Kathy? It's Mike."

"Grasshopper! Long time, no speak."

Kathy Frost had been my field training officer and sergeant when I joined the Warden Service. For years she had headed all of the Warden Service's K-9 teams, until she was forced to take early retirement due to injuries she'd sustained from a gunshot. She still helped us out during search-and-rescue operations, directing the efforts of dog teams to cover the most ground in the fastest amount of time. No one I'd ever met knew more about dogs than Kathy.

"How's retirement?" I asked.

"I'm thinking of buying a metal detector. What does that tell you?"

"That bad?"

"Worse."

"Listen. What can you tell me about wolf dogs?"

"They're illegal to possess without a permit."

"I'm wondering how I can identify one."

"You can't," she said. "Not by sight. I mean, you can look for certain features—long legs, slanted eyes, small ears—but you still might be looking at an animal that's one part Siberian husky, one part Malinois. Breeders have gotten good at making fakes, since people will pay top dollar for an honest-to-Jesus timber wolf."

"What's top dollar?"

"Two grand for a high-content animal. Generally speaking, the more wolf DNA it has, the more expensive it is. Why do you want to know?"

"I've got a situation with some tweakers. I think they're keeping a wolf dog, and I am going to have to confiscate it. I was hoping there was a way I could tell if it was the real thing or not."

"The only way to know for certain is to do a lab test."

"I know it's been chasing deer," I said. "It killed a yearling this morning."

"That doesn't prove anything. But it gives you cause to take it to a shelter. They can test it for you."

"What happens if the results come back positive—that it's a high-content wolf dog?"

"Usually, the department would try to find someone to adopt it. But if yours killed a deer, it'll probably be put down."

"Anything else I should know?"

"Are you going to try wrangling the animal yourself?"

"I don't have a carrier or catch pole with me today, so I'll probably be calling an animal control agent."

"Be careful," Kathy said. "There's a reason why wolf dogs are illegal. Most of them are unpredictable and pretty near untrainable. They are superintelligent. I read somewhere that training a dog is like training a toddler. Training a wolf dog is like trying to train a thirty-five-year-old man."

"Thanks, I'll let you know how it goes. When are you going to get a new puppy, by the way?"

"I just haven't met the right dog yet."

Kathy had once owned a coonhound named Pluto, whose nose was the stuff of legend, but he had died the night she herself was shot, and she hadn't yet adopted another young dog to train. I had thought her grief for Pluto would abate over time, but as her period of mourning had stretched on and on, I began to worry about her.

"Let me know how it goes," she said.

"Ten-four."

I glanced back at the house, certain that they had been watching me the whole time, worried about what I might be doing. That was good: I wanted them to be spooked. For my plan to work, they needed to panic.

I put the transmission into gear and started forward. I drove a hundred yards, until I was well out of sight of Carrie Michaud's house. The snowplows had carved out a wide spot in the road where they could reverse direction. It was the perfect place to hide my truck. I wasn't sure how much time I had, but I didn't want to miss my chance. I reached into the backseat and rummaged around until I found the white poncho I used as wintertime camouflage. I pulled the hood over my head and got out.

Moving from shadow to shadow, I made my way back along the frozen road, expecting to see one of the pickup trucks come roaring in reverse out of the driveway at any moment. When I reached the tall snowbank at the end of Carrie's drive, I threw myself against it, then squirmed into position so I could peer over the top.

I didn't have long to wait. Within a matter of minutes, Spike emerged from the house, pulling a magnificent black animal behind him on a leash. Each dark hair in its coat seemed to shimmer as it padded along. Long legs, slanted eyes, small, sharp ears—I understood Kathy's caution about jumping to conclusions, but there was absolutely no doubt in my mind that this creature was, in any meaningful sense, a wolf.

And yet when Spike opened the passenger door of his truck, the animal leaped obediently inside, as eager as the family dog going for a ride.

"Good boy, Shadow," I heard the Goth say.

He had pulled on a black trench coat and fingerless gloves to make his getaway. He moved with surprising speed and purpose for a man with so few functioning brain cells. He hurried around the front of the truck, pushing the remote starter button on the key fob. I heard the engine turn over.

I tumbled down the snowbank and jumped into the driveway. "Hold it, Spike!"

The Goth stopped in his tracks, his arms dropped to his sides, and his mouth fell open. For about ten seconds, he gawked at me. Then he reached for the driver's door.

"Hold it right there!"

I sprinted forward as he climbed inside the running truck, and managed to catch the door handle before he could yank it shut. We played tug-of-war for a few seconds, and then he threw the truck into reverse. The pickup lurched away, forcing me to release my grip or be pulled along with it.

I would estimate that the backward-moving Raider hit the snowbank at thirty miles per hour—enough speed to fill the bed with snow and bury the rear wheels. Spike tried to drive forward, but he was stuck now. An acrid cloud of exhaust fumes and burning rubber gathered around the truck as he tried in vain to dislodge it.

I put my hand on the grip of my sidearm. I had reached the limits of my patience. The idiot might have dislocated my shoulder. "Step out of the vehicle!"

He stared openmouthed at me through the windshield as I got myself into position parallel to his door. Just as I was about to repeat my command for him to get out, he threw himself across the seat and pushed the passenger door open, shouting, "Go, Shadow! Go!"

The wolf dog gave a yelp when he hit the snow.

But instead of running off, the beautiful animal stopped. He stood there, looking back and forth between us with his luminous yellow eyes. He seemed to have no idea what was happening. I couldn't blame him. This whole comedy had me shaking my head. Wait until I told Kathy how it had gone down.

"Step out of the vehicle," I shouted again. "Step out of the vehicle now!"

It was then that a dark shape swooped into my peripheral vision. I was so focused on the ridiculous man behind the wheel that I missed Carrie Michaud running up behind me. I felt the knife between my shoulder blades before I saw it.

7

The sensation was like nothing I had experienced: somewhere between a sharp poke and a hard punch. At first, my mind couldn't connect the peculiar pain to a recognition of what had just happened.

Then, as I turned, I saw the blade glint in the winter sunlight. And the neurons fired.

She had just stabbed me in the back.

Carrie Michaud lunged at me again. I brought my left arm up to protect myself and received a slash across the forearm. This time I felt the pain fully, knowing what it was. I staggered away, trying to get my legs under me, but I stepped on a patch of ice and went down on one knee. I fumbled for my sidearm but couldn't find the grip.

She came at me again, this time from above. Her lips pulled back from her sharp little teeth.

All I could think to do was punch her. I jabbed with my left fist and hit her squarely between the eyes. Her head snapped back violently, the knife dropped from her hand, and down she went.

I spun around frantically for a few moments, trying to feel with one hand between my shoulder blades, certain it would come back wet with blood. But all I could feel was torn fabric.

The blade had sliced cleanly through my poncho and the parka underneath. My body armor had been designed to stop a bullet, not a knife. By all rights, the blade should have cut through my trapezoid muscle, severed an artery, and punctured a lung, if not my heart. Had I turned at just the right moment? I had no idea how I had been saved.

My other hand finally found the grip of my SIG and pulled it free of its holster.

Carrie Michaud lay crumpled on the ground. I had knocked her out cold, or maybe she had hit her head on the ice. Her body looked as delicate as that of a child. And yet this waif had come within inches of killing me.

Under the law, I would have been justified in shooting her dead. It didn't matter that she seemed to be unconscious. She had stabbed me, and that was all that mattered. I knew I could pull the trigger and end Carrie Michaud's miserable existence and the state of Maine would claim that I had been fully justified. The legislature had granted me an indulgence to commit homicide.

I lined up my gun sights at her narrow chest and slipped my finger inside the trigger guard. In shooting class, you are taught that is the point of no return. Out of the box, in single-action stage, the SIG Sauer P226 has a trigger-action pull rate of 4.5 pounds. The slightest squeeze and it would be done.

But I couldn't.

Instead, I swung the pistol around on her boyfriend. If anything, the Goth looked even more helpless and pathetic. He was still sitting wide-eyed and slack-jawed behind the wheel of the immobilized Raider. Smoke from the exhaust continued to melt snow and fill the yard with oily fumes.

"Don't you fucking move!" I shouted.

But his mind was afloat in some other drug-induced realm.

I flipped Carrie Michaud onto her stomach and twisted her arms behind her back. I felt a cruel urge to snap her wrists but resisted the impulse. I reached behind my belt and found my handcuffs. When I heard the clasps click, I took a breath.

The harrowing reality of the situation was slowly beginning to take hold. I had almost joined the ranks of the police dead, only there would have been no video to show the cadets at the Criminal Justice Academy. Just a cautionary tale to frighten the new recruits: *"Did you ever hear about Mike Bowditch? Poor guy got knifed because he tried to take away a drug addict's wolf."*

The knife had fallen into the snow. It was a Gerber tactical model: black, with a tanto point and a serrated edge. The blade was wet.

Blood was dripping from my arm. It spotted the smooth patch of ice at my feet. The cut wasn't deep, but it stung as if it had been rubbed with salt. I couldn't put pressure on the wound without re-holstering my weapon, which meant I had to deal with Spike first.

I used so much strength pulling him from the running truck that he sprawled on the ice at my feet.

"Don't hurt me," he whined.

"Shut up!"

I used my second set of cuffs to secure his wrists. The effort pumped more and more blood from my arm onto the snow. When I was convinced that both of them were restrained, I finally put my gun away and clutched at the wound. Only then did it occur to me to raise my eyes to the house. For all I knew, there was someone else inside the building; someone else out of their drug-crazed mind, only maybe this person was armed with a gun instead of a knife.

I retreated back to a position of cover behind an oak tree at the edge of the drive.

All the while, the wolf dog watched me with keen interest. He didn't run off, nor did he approach. He just studied me with his ee-rie eyes while I called for help.

"Can you describe your injuries?" the dispatcher asked.

"She struck me in the back first, but the knife barely punctured the skin. Don't ask me how. I've also got a cut across my left fore-arm. I'm losing blood, but I've got pressure on the wound, and it seems to be helping."

"You're sure your back is all right?"

"Pretty sure."

"Stay on the line until backup arrives. Nearest unit is five min-utes away. Ambulance is right behind."

"I'm not going anywhere."

"Keep talking to me."

"What should we talk about?"

"Is there anything else we should know about your situation?"

"You're going to need an animal control agent, too. Make sure he brings the biggest carrier he's got."

"Is there a vicious dog on the property?"

Even from a distance, I could see his luminous eyes. They looked possessed of an intelligence I had never seen before in a domestic dog. "Not exactly."

Above my head, the dead leaves of the oak made a sound like whispers whenever the breeze touched them.

The wolf dog kept watching me intently.

I lost count of the units that responded to my 10-74 call. That is what happens when a report goes out that an officer is down; every available cop—sometimes even those off-duty—rush to the scene.

The first to arrive was a Cumberland County Sheriff's deputy. He drove up with lights blazing and sirens wailing and emerged from his salt-splashed cruiser with his weapon already drawn. I think he was a little disappointed to find me alert and upright, albeit leaning against an oak tree, with only a bleeding forearm.

The deputy's name was Moody. He was about my age, black-haired, brown-eyed, with a smirky way of talking out of one side of his mouth. "You're sure you weren't stabbed in the back?"

"See for yourself."

He examined the holes in my clothing. "Man, all I can say is you got lucky. You owe your guardian angel a big tip."

He fetched a pressure bandage from his cruiser while we waited for EMTs to arrive. I pressed it tightly to the wound.

"This isn't my first visit to Casa Michaud," Moody said.

"When was the last time?"

"Halloween. Carrie had a party. One of the girls who showed up had too good a time, if you know what I mean."

"Overdose?"

"Heroin cut with fentanyl, according to the coroner."

I'd been trying to understand why she'd stabbed me over a wolf dog. You only had to look into her eyes to see that the wires had short-circuited a long time ago. Where there are drugs, there are almost always guns. If Carrie Michaud had come at me with a pistol instead of a knife, I would have been seriously screwed.

"I shouldn't have let her sneak up on me," I said.

He shrugged. "Looks can be deceiving."

Carrie Michaud had been unconscious for such a long time, I had begun to fear she might be dead, the way boxers sometimes die from single punches in boxing movies. But she chose that moment to wake up. She began flopping around, trying to get to her feet, shouting obscenities the whole time.

"You're not going to bleed to death while I go get her?" Moody asked.

"I think I'll survive."

Moody pulled Carrie Michaud, kicking and screaming, to the back of his car.

Meanwhile, Spike continued to lie compliantly on the cold ground, never making so much as an effort to move.

The ambulance arrived next. The EMTs made me sit in the back while they applied a serious bandage to my arm. I would need to go to the hospital and have a doctor look at the wound, they said. From the way the cotton was drinking up the blood, I would certainly need stitches. The doctor would also want to take a sample in case the blade had been contaminated with some pathogen.

More and more cruisers were arriving. The flashing lights—blue and red—gave the scene a disco vibe. All the attention made me uncomfortable. No one had ever thrown me a surprise party, but I imagined it would have felt slightly less embarrassing. Now that the adrenaline was wearing off, I could smell my own sour perspiration. I was going to have to file a detailed incident report about the assault, and the information I included would determine whether Carrie Michaud was charged with aggravated attempted murder.

I saw a state trooper escort Spike out to the road.

"Do I have to keep sitting here?" I asked one of the EMTs.

"It would be better if you did."

"I feel perfectly fine."

"But you lost some blood. If you stand up, you might faint."

"I'm willing to take the risk," I said with a smile that was not returned.

I climbed down out of the ambulance and went searching among the cruisers for the one with Spike in the backseat.

"Do you mind if I talk to him?" I asked the trooper standing outside the vehicle.

We'd met once before, but I didn't remember his name. He was one of the new recruits in the state police and still had the stalwart look of a rookie who had yet to see the disconnect between the job he'd applied for and the job he'd ended up doing every day. He shrugged and opened the door for me.

I leaned against the cold blue chassis, looking down at the absurd Goth. The front of his clothes were all wet from lying on the icy asphalt.

"Tell me about the wolf dog," I said.

He kept his bleached head bowed. "His name is Shadow."

That was certainly original. "Where did you get him?"

"We traded for him."

"Traded drugs?"

His head bobbed in what I took to be a confirmation. "Carrie's always wanted a wolf dog. She says wolves are her totem animals. A guy we kind of know said he could get one for us."

"What's this guy's name?"

He licked his chapped lower lip while he considered this. "Rafael."

"What's his last name?"

"I don't know, man. He hangs in the same clubs as we do down in Portland. You show me a picture, and I can point him out. We didn't know it was illegal to own a wolf dog."

"I never said it was."

He bowed his head again. "Shit."

"You've been letting him run loose?" I was surprised that the animal would have returned willingly to his new owners.

"He escaped last night. We drove around all morning looking for him, but then we saw him on Pondicherry Road. He just hopped right in with us. Carrie says she was gypped. She says he's a shepherd-husky mix or something and only looks like a wolf. She says she's going to get back at Rafael."

I closed the door on him. I could feel the cold air on my skin through the rip in my parka.

"How's your arm doing?" the young trooper asked.

"It'll heal. Do you remember that movie they showed at the Academy?"

"The one with all the cops being killed? I think about the video every time I look at my kid."

"I think about it every day, too," I said. "A lot of good it did me."

"You're alive, aren't you?"

I had imagined that all the commotion would have frightened off Shadow, so I was surprised to see him at the edge of the trees, close enough to the action to observe everything, close enough to cover to hide. No one else seemed to notice him there, but he could tell that I was watching him, and so he was watching me back with that intense gaze common to predators.

A group of armored officers was stacked up, preparing to enter the house. Protocol required that they go in as if there might be a gang of heavily armed criminals behind the door. But everyone seemed to recognize that this afternoon was not going to be as action-packed as they had thought when they responded to the "officer down" call.

I began searching for the animal control officer. Instead, I ran into one of the EMTs who had patched me up. He tried to persuade me to ride with them to the hospital in Bridgton, but I told him I would drive myself.

"That's probably not the best idea," he said.

"Really, I'm fine."

"Do you know how often we hear that from people who are anything but fine?"

I spotted a little pickup truck with the Cumberland County logo painted on the door and a woman standing beside it with a catch pole, looking vaguely lost. I thanked the EMT for his concern and went over to introduce myself to the animal control officer. She was a pear-shaped woman with kind eyes and tinted brown hair that was thinning at the top. When she introduced herself, I had to ask her to repeat her name.

She smiled, as if this request was a regular one. "Joanie Swette." She spelled it for me.

"I'm Mike Bowditch," I said. "I'm the one who found the wolf dog."

She turned her whole body to look, instead of just turning her head. "Where is he now? Has he run off on us?"

"He's still around. Did you bring a carrier?"

"It's in the back of my truck."

It was one of those plastic crates with holes punched in the side for air and a steel gate at one end. I manhandled it out of the back of her pickup and then used my good arm to carry it down the road toward the tree line beyond the house.

Joanie followed with her catch pole. It had a four-foot-long aluminum shaft with a spring-loaded noose that could be slipped over the head of an uncooperative animal and tightened without getting anywhere near the animal's jaws. It was the same model I had back home in my garage.

Shadow was exactly where I had last seen him. "There he is."

"He's magnificent! But I have no idea how we're going to get near him."

I had no idea, either. Secretly, I was hoping that he would just turn tail and run, thus relieving me of the responsibility of capturing him, at least for now.

"Hey, handsome," Swette called in that singsong voice certain people use with animals. "Aren't you handsome?"

Shadow remained motionless, his dark ears up, wisps of steam rising from his nostrils into the cold air.

She reached into her pocket and brought out a handful of kibble. "Do you want a treat?"

The wolf dog didn't so much as flick his tail.

"Shadow!" I shouted.

To our mutual surprise, the wolf dog took a step forward.

"I thought that was a name those two losers just gave him," I said. "Give me that kibble."

I extended my open hand as I called his name again, and the animal came closer. Halfway across the yard, he sat down in the snow and looked at us.

"Come here, boy!" Swette called.

I squatted down to his level. "Come here, Shadow!"

He came right over.

He was even larger up close than I had imagined. I remained absolutely still, with my arm out as he hopped over the snowbank. I had a momentary bout of anxiety as the enormous animal opened his mouth and began to gobble dog food from my palm. He could have taken off my hand at the wrist with a single bite of those jaws.

Swette stepped back to loop the snare around the wolf dog's head.

"Wait," I said. "Maybe we don't need that. Put some kibble inside the carrier."

She opened the gate and scattered pellets inside. The wolf dog looked at me, as if seeking my assurance.

"It's all right, boy," I said.

And he trotted right in.

Swette was quick closing the gate behind his tail. Through the holes in the side, I saw his muscles flinch beneath his coat of black fur, but he didn't snarl or bite. He simply acquiesced to being caged.

Swette backed off and rubbed her chin.

"What?" I asked.

"I've never seen a dog like this. He's a little too calm. It's weirding me out."

I knew what she meant. I could understand a trusting family dog—one that had never had cause to live by its wits—being lured inside a cage with dog food, but Shadow was obviously intelligent. As a rule, I do not believe in mythologizing animals, especially charismatic species like bears and wolves, but there was something about this one that unsettled me.

I helped Swette lift the carrier with Shadow inside into the back of her truck. He easily weighed more than a hundred pounds. And when he shifted from the front to the back, we both staggered to keep our balance.

"How old do you think he is?" I asked her before she closed the tailgate.

"He's not a puppy," she said, out of breath. "But he doesn't look old, either. The teeth will give Dr. Carbone some idea."

"Is there a chance that he's a hundred percent wolf?"

"You can't judge by looking at them," she said. "A lab test is the only way to be sure."

"Can you give me a call when you get the results back?"

"Absolutely." She peered through the grille of the carrier. "It's sad, though, isn't it?"

At first, I had no idea what she meant. Then I had this panicked realization that we were sending this healthy, intelligent, obedient creature to his inevitable death. Kathy was right that no one would adopt a wolf dog that had killed a deer. I had been so taken with him that I had lost sight of the endgame. If he tested positive as a wolf, as was bound to happen, he would be given a shot of barbiturates and put down.

One of my duties as a warden was to kill injured, sick, and nuisance animals. In the course of my career I had shot moose, bear, deer, raccoons, opossums, foxes, woodchucks, geese, ducks, and even, once, a rabid dog that the residents of a trailer park had managed to corner in a waterless swimming pool. None of them had affected me as deeply as this.

Maybe it was because I had almost been killed myself and the thought of mortality was hanging over me like a half-fallen tree.

Maybe I was punch-drunk from the loss of blood.

Or maybe it was my upbringing. I was raised Catholic. Guilt is my resting state.

8

At the hospital in Bridgton, I was treated by a nurse practitio-
ner. It look ten stitches to close the gash on my left forearm.
She checked my back and found a bull's-eye: a small puncture in the
skin surrounded by a contusion from the force of the blow. She applied a bandage to the wound and asked if I wanted the doctor to
write a scrip for pain medication. I told her I had what I needed in
a bottle back home.

"I'd advise against drinking any alcohol tonight," she said.

"I'll be good," I said.

"I don't want you to be good," the nurse said. "I want you to get
well."

The thought of what had almost happened—how close I'd come
to being killed for no good reason—had left me feeling ashamed and
angry at myself. I'd gotten careless, just like the dead cops in that
video. I felt a shameful urge to slink back to my house and hide
behind the curtains until springtime.

But there was no hiding from my visitors. A state police detective
I knew named Pomerleau arrived at the hospital to take a statement
from me; she was accompanied by both an assistant attorney general and an assistant district attorney for Cumberland County. The
state of Maine takes the attempted murder of a law-enforcement
officer seriously even when the attack only results in ten stitches.

Then there were my fellow wardens. Volk showed up in his civilian clothes: the same hundred-dollar suit he'd worn in divorce court
that morning.

Volk was a big guy, not muscular so much as heavy-boned and
beefy, who had followed a well-worn path to the Warden Service:

Marine Corps, jail guard, deputy sheriff, game warden. He still wore his hair shaved down to the scalp in the high-and-tight style he'd first gotten back on Parris Island. The severity of the cut made his ears seem unnaturally small, and I had noticed that they tended to turn red whenever he got angry, which was often.

"You punched her?" he asked in disbelief. "What happened? Did your gun jam?"

He seemed more disappointed that I had not shot Carrie Michaud dead than concerned for my well-being.

My redheaded sergeant, Cameron Ouelette, worried about the state of my mind.

"Do you want to talk with somebody, Mike?" he asked.

"What do you mean?"

"Should I call Deb or Kate?" he asked earnestly. The Warden Service had two top-notch female chaplains. Their job was to counsel officers who had witnessed traumatic events or who had suffered themselves from some assault on body and soul. "Or should I call a priest? You're Catholic, aren't you?"

"I don't need last rites, Cam. I've got a cut on my arm."

Ouelette had just returned from a training session in crisis incident stress debriefing, or CISD, and so I forgave his superabundance of caution.

The person I found most difficult to face was my newly promoted captain, John "Jock" DeFord. DeFord was a rising star in the Warden Service: a natural leader who was also a natural politician. It was a rare combination, I had found. Cameras loved his blond, all-American good looks. As Warden Service captain, his new duties included supervising the Wildlife Crimes Investigation Division (WCID)—our version of a detective unit—as well as all personnel matters. It was in the latter capacity that he had come to see me.

"The colonel wishes he could be here," he said first off.

"I didn't expect him to fly back from Patagonia for me."

Colonel Malcomb and his new wife were off on the fly-fishing trip of a lifetime in South America.

"Detective Pomerleau told me what happened," DeFord said, studying my bandaged arm. "How are you doing, Mike?"

"I'm fine."

"Those vests we wear aren't knifeproof. The Kevlar is designed to stop a bullet, not a blade." The captain was in his forties but looked a decade younger on account of being more physically fit than anyone has a right to be. "You're lucky you were a moving target."

"Yeah, I've definitely had a lot worse things happen to me."

"But each one hits you different."

"Really, I'm fine."

"I hope you weren't this cavalier talking to the AAG." His boyish face darkened. "That Michaud woman needs to go to jail for a long time, Mike. Her boyfriend, too. You should take a couple of sick days. I won't force you to do it, but before you start arguing with me, I want you to hear me out."

I leaned back on the hospital table. The paper under my butt rustled.

DeFord said, "If you're back at work tomorrow, Michaud's attorney might make it look like you exaggerated what happened. How many prosecutions have you seen screwed up because DAs went into trials overconfident in their witnesses, and then they got their asses handed to them by smart defense lawyers?"

"You want me to buy a neck brace to wear when I go grocery shopping?"

"This isn't a joke."

"I understand." I just hated to see myself as the sort of professional who could be sidelined by ten stitches. DeFord and I hadn't talked privately in a while. But I had the sense that he liked me—a lot more than most of my colleagues, at least. Which wasn't saying much. I was eager to change the subject from my injury. "So I heard Pete Brochu got promoted to the warden investigator job in Division D."

The position had been held for decades by a man named Wesley Pinkham. Stacey had encouraged me to apply for the post myself—warden investigator was my dream job—but I hadn't felt that I was ready. Kathy had told me that DeFord had floated my name, but Colonel Malcomb thought I needed to prove I had matured out of my youthful rule-breaking phase before I could be handed a WCID job. I had a hard time disagreeing with the colonel.

"Pete's a good man," said DeFord.

True, but Brochu had never impressed me with his intelligence, and I had heard he was considering taking a job in his brother's lucrative home-building business.

"I wish him well," I said.

"Me, too." DeFord and Pinkham had been longtime colleagues, and clearly thinking about his dead friend made him uncomfortable. "I'm going to find someone to drive you home. Maybe Volk—"

"No."

"You shouldn't get behind the wheel, Mike."

"All they gave me was Tylenol."

"Still."

"I'm driving myself, Captain. I screwed up today by getting careless. Don't make it worse by making me look bad to the rest of the division, too."

He nodded, shook his head, and smiled. "Whatever you do, Bowditch, just don't get in another accident."

When I got home, I stood in the darkened driveway, looking up at the stars. The night was moonless, and the stars and planets were as clear as the carefully drawn illustrations on a constellation map. I saw the faint wash of the Milky Way flowing across the sky from horizon to horizon. Orion, the hunter, was raising his club above the trees to the southeast. Across the heavens, Draco, the dragon, was uncoiling himself around the Little Dipper.

As a boy, I had yearned for my father to teach me about the stars and planets, but he never had. It was only after I had become an adult that I received instruction from Charley Stevens, who was scandalized when I'd informed him of my ignorance. Charley believed that a woodsman who didn't know the stars was no woodsman at all.

Staring at the sky, I began to feel dizzy again. It was as if I were looking *down* into the void instead of up into it. For an instant, I had the sense that gravity was about to let go of me and I might go spiraling out into the cold vacuum of space. I tipped my head forward and focused on my boots until the sensation passed.

I went inside, threw my parka across the sofa, and poured myself a bourbon.

I knew that I should call Stacey in Ashland. She would want to know what had happened; she deserved to know. We weren't engaged yet—maybe we never would be—but over the past year, she had become the closest person to me in the world, and I didn't want to imagine a future without her. But I was too embarrassed to call, and I convinced myself I didn't want to worry her when I was perfectly all right.

Instead, I sent her an e-mail:

Hey, Stace,

Crazy day today. Got into a scuffle with a tweaker when I tried to confiscate her illegal wolf dog. The poor thing's probably going to be put down—the wolf dog, not the tweaker. It's a story for another time. Anyway, I'm OK. Just tired and sore.

Love,
Mike

When I was a kid, my mother took me to Mass every week and made me go to confession once a month. I remembered a kindly priest telling me in the confessional that sins of omission were considered to be less grievous than sins of commission. It certainly didn't feel that way at the moment.

I returned to the living room and switched on the overhead light. Everything looked so cheerless and lonely. I reached for my parka on the couch, and my father's dog tags fell onto the floor. The poltergeist was having fun with me again.

I stuffed the bewitched tags into my pants pockets and sat down to finish my drink.

Adam Langstrom's photograph was faceup on the coffee table, where I had left it. I tried to resist looking at the picture, but the pull was too strong. I threw back the rest of the bourbon and waited for the heat of the alcohol to spread outward from my stomach to my heart.

I held the snapshot by the edges, pinched it between my thumbs and index fingers, as if afraid to leave prints.

Did I want this man to be my brother? Did it matter what I wanted?

Adam and I were far from being twins. His hair was wavier than mine. His nose was longer. His brow was heavier. But there was something there. The word I would use is that I *recognized* this person I had never met.

And I resented him, too, I realized.

To have thought for years that I was the last of a bloodline and then to learn suddenly that I had a younger brother—a brother who just happened to be a statutory rapist, a convicted felon, a pariah forbidden to live in polite society, another irredeemable fugitive in need of my help—what kind of cruel joke had God decided to play on me?

I had made so much progress in repairing my reputation and rebuilding my life since my dad blew a hole in it. After years of wavering, I had committed myself at last to my vocation as an officer of the law. I had earned the respect of my peers and superiors (most of them, at least). I had a woman who loved me and whom I loved. The last thing I needed now was to be sucked into a thankless quest to find a missing person whom no one seemed to be missing.

Except his mother, of course.

I had begun to feel the alcohol in my head: It manifested itself as a softening of my thoughts.

I turned Adam's photograph over and read aloud the telephone number that Amber had scrawled on the back. It almost felt as if I were speaking an incantation, uttering an irrevocable spell. Before I could change my mind, I reached for the phone.

Amber Langstrom picked up on the second ring.

"It's Mike Bowditch," I said.

"Oh, thank God."

"I've thought about it, and I'm willing to make some phone calls—"

"It would be better if you came up here." Her voice had its familiar rough smokiness.

"I'm willing to make some phone calls."

"Don Foss won't talk to you. I had to drive out to his gate because no one would give me his number, and even then he wouldn't let me inside."

"What makes you think he'll talk to me, then?"

"Wear your uniform when you go see him."

Her assertiveness shouldn't have caught me off guard. Pulsifer had told me she could be manipulative. I had seen evidence of it myself.

"I can't do that."

"Why not?"

"Because it's one thing for me to make some informal inquiries about a fugitive I saw listed in the WatchGuard database. It's another to do so in an official capacity, especially if Adam is my brother."

"He *is* your brother!"

"I could get myself into serious trouble."

"You still need to come up here." She was as hard to shake off as a terrier.

"Amber—"

"Come to Widowmaker first," she said. "You should talk to Adam's friend Josh. He was the last to see Adam before he disappeared, but he wouldn't tell me what happened. Josh works on the ski patrol. Stop at the Sluiceway when you get here. I'm working lunch." She spoke so quickly, I couldn't find a pause to break in. "I knew you would help me. You're going to like Adam when you find him. You have so much in common. Thank you so much! You're my hero, Mike."

And then she hung up.

Being told I had a lot in common with a statutory rapist did not lift my spirits.

My father had had a thing for attractive, calculating women. If I was going to be honest with myself, I had to admit that even my mother had fit the pattern. She was young when they married and naive at first. She had tolerated his absences and heavy drinking, put up with the rumors about other women, bandaged his bloodied knuckles—she had endured these indignations until she no longer could. The divorce had been her idea, and she had laid the groundwork carefully, planning exactly how she and I would make our escape, before she delivered the news to him.

When she was free of my dad, she had immediately set out to improve her station. She had gotten a temporary job as a receptionist in a law office in Portland, and wouldn't you know, six months later she was engaged to one of the partners.

I wouldn't be manipulated by Amber Langstrom into driving three hours. In the morning, I would call Adam's probation officer, and maybe follow up with the mysterious Don Foss, but that would be the extent of my efforts.

But as I finished my second drink, I found myself drawing a mental map about the specific roads I would drive to get to Widowmaker.

A fool for scheming women? Like father, like son.

After a while, I plugged the phone into the wall to recharge and went heavily up the stairs to bed.

9

The next morning, I was awakened by a throbbing in my arm. My head hurt, too, and the inside of my mouth was parched from breathing out alcohol fumes all night long. I should have listened to the nurse.

I had to put a bread bag over my bandaged arm in the shower so it wouldn't get wet. After I had toweled myself off, I stood with my back to the mirror, looking at the stab mark. Knives are supposed to slice right through Kevlar. How had that not happened?

The previous night hadn't been my first brush with death. I had come closer to being killed many times in the past. And yet I felt shaken in a way I never had before. Maybe it was because, for the first time I could remember, I felt as if I had something to lose. As a rookie, I'd been willing to risk my life, as if it had no value; I had naive ideas about the nobility of self-sacrifice, which were premised on my own dispensability. I hadn't considered the possibility of being mourned by people who loved me. People like Stacey and her parents. People like Kathy Frost. I hadn't felt afraid of death because I had mistaken selfishness for selflessness.

I found myself shivering, even though the bathroom itself was still warm from the steam. I returned to my bedroom, put on jeans and a commando sweater, and went downstairs to have breakfast.

I had slept late. The day looked like it was going to be cold, with one of those milky skies you get during the winter in Maine, when it might snow at any minute.

Stacey had sent me an e-mail message before dawn.

Hey, Mike,

Glad you're OK! I want to hear the details.

That sucks about the poor wolf dog. Can't you find someone to take it?

It's a helicopter day! We're going up in the Forest Service chopper to spot moose, since the forecast looks good. I wish they'd let me fly the thing. How hard can it be? Maybe I'll get my helo license next summer. When are you going to let me teach you how to fly, anyway?

> Love,
> S.

PS. Did you call Pulsifer? Have you decided what to do about your brother? He looks just like you.

I had plenty of reservations about my connection to Adam Langstrom, but clearly the photo I'd sent had convinced Stacey.

I replied:

Hey, Stace,

Your father says, "Friends don't teach friends to fly." I bet that goes double for girlfriends.

How's your cold? I hope it's better.

I spoke with Pulsifer and he apologized for sending that woman my way. I'm still deciding what I'm going to do about Adam Langstrom. I have mixed feelings.

So I have an unexpected day off today. If the weather is going to be good, maybe I'll get my skis out. Stay safe!

> Love,
> Mike

The longer I went without telling her about being stabbed, the worse it would be. But I couldn't reach her by phone if she was up in a helicopter; there was no cell signal for hundreds of miles in that part of the North Woods.

That problem would have to wait. In the meantime, I sat down with a cup of coffee to fulfill my promise to Amber. I found the number for Adam's probation officer. She seemed to work out of the Franklin County courthouse in Farmington.

"Shaylene Hawken," said a voice I might have mistaken for a man's.

"This is Mike Bowditch with the Maine Warden Service."

"What can I do for you, Warden?"

"Do you have a minute?"

"No."

"I can call back, then."

She seemed offended by my attempt at courtesy. "I won't have any more time later. Just tell me what you want."

"You have a client named Adam Langstrom. I saw on Watch-Guard that he violated his probation and that you got a judge to put out a warrant for him."

"That's right. Failure to appear."

"He's been missing for two weeks?"

"Let me guess," she said. "You found a dead body in the woods matching his description?"

It seemed significant that she had jumped to that conclusion. "You think Langstrom committed suicide?"

"It wouldn't surprise me if he had. He was always whining about how much his life sucked, and how unfair the system is, and how he wasn't like the other skinners."

"Skinners?"

"Sex offenders. Langstrom has been on a downward spiral for the past month. But I'm confused here, Warden. If you haven't seen him, why are you calling me?"

"I'm wondering if you have any leads on his whereabouts."

"No. Do you?"

"So you haven't been actively searching for him?"

She had a laugh that was more a series of sharp expulsions of air from her lungs. "Do you know how many clients I have? I don't have time to chase runaway ducklings, especially when most of them manage to deliver themselves into the hands of the police sooner rather than later. It's not like these guys are criminal master-minds. And you still haven't explained your interest in Lang-strom."

"He and I have some history, and I thought I might check a few of his haunts."

I had told myself I wouldn't lie, that no matter what, I would tell this woman the truth. So much for that pledge.

"Great," she said. "If you see him, arrest him."

You would have thought the fact that I wasn't coming clean with Shaylene Hawken would have made me feel less insulted. "I'm offering you my help."

"Really? Because I can count on one finger the number of times I've gotten a call like this. That includes this one."

"I understand you were the one who placed him with Don Foss."

For the first time in the conversation, she paused before she answered. "I place a lot of my clients with Foss, guys who have nowhere else to go and no other means of making money. He's the last chance some of these men will ever have to get their lives straight. What are you implying?"

"I'm just trying to get my facts straight."

I heard typing in the background. "You said you had history with Langstrom, but I don't see any hunting or fishing violations in his record."

"We never got past the warning stage," I said, throwing another lie on the bonfire.

"That's a shame. Maybe if he had been busted before, he wouldn't have raped the Davidson girl. Langstrom is like most of the statutory cases I see here. Even after spending a year and a half behind bars, he still doesn't think of himself as a criminal. I'm guessing that's the reason he took off. He still can't face the reality of his situation. I have to go now. I don't know what your real interest in this guy is, Warden. But I'd recommend finding another hobby if this is your idea of recreation."

Shaylene Hawken had seen right through me. But then, she listened to liars every day. Hopefully, she wouldn't check up on anything I'd said with the Warden Service.

At this stage, I had nothing to lose by calling Don Foss. I was surprised to find that there was no contact information for his company anywhere online. What kind of commercial enterprise has an unlisted phone number? I figured I could always call Shaylene back and ask her for Foss's number. Then I could be absolutely guaranteed she would be making a report to my superiors in Augusta.

Had Amber known this would happen? That curiosity would get the better of me once I'd started asking questions? At the very least, she must have understood that any conversation I had with stone-walling Shaylene Hawken was bound to leave me feeling angry and frustrated.

I glanced again out the window at the alabaster sky above the ragged treetops. I hadn't been back up to my father's old stomping grounds in ages, not since the manhunt. I could drive up to Widow-maker and be back home before the snow started to fall. As long as I understood where the lines were drawn and made certain not to cross them, I was at no risk of getting myself into trouble. No risk at all.

I kept my personal vehicle, an International Harvester Scout II, in the garage, out of the elements. I had always had an affinity for vintage four-wheel-drive vehicles. Maybe it was because I spent so much of my working life driving a state-of-the-art GMC Sierra that was loaded with more technology than I knew what to do with. My first antique had been a Jeep Willys that ran like a dream until rust ate it down to the bones. Then I had owned a cherry Ford Bronco, which I had watched being blown apart by shotgun rounds. Looking for a replacement, I had been torn between a Dodge Power Wagon and the International Harvester. I had gone with the hardtop Scout and had never had cause to regret my decision. The gas mileage was abysmal, but my trusted four-by-four took me everywhere I wanted to go.

In the winter, I packed the back with tire chains, a come-along, and a pull rope—as much to help motorists who might have slid off the road as to help myself. (I have always been an incorrigible Good Samaritan. My life would have been easier if I had been even remotely corrigible.) I kept a pair of snowshoes in there, too, as well as a wool blanket, a five-gallon jug of gasoline, and a first-aid kit.

As I backed out of the driveway, I reached into my glove compartment for a pair of sunglasses. I also carried one of my off-duty pieces in there: a Walther PPK/S that jammed on hollow-point bullets, no matter how well I cleaned the barrel. I kept it for softheaded, sentimental reasons. It was the first handgun I had ever owned.

I debated whether to call the shelter to check up on Shadow. Joanie Swette had mentioned doing a blood test. I supposed that it was probably more reliable in terms of determining genetics, especially when the stakes were so high for an animal. But they wouldn't have the results for a while.

The GPS on my phone said it would take more than two hours to get to Widowmaker.

The resort was located north of Rangeley, a lake town not far from the New Hampshire border. I decided to take the cross-country route, following the frozen Androscoggin River through Lewiston, Maine's second-largest city, and past the mill towns of Livermore Falls and Jay, where the air smelled like rotten eggs and every snow-bank seemed to have a crust of asphalt grit.

I had lived briefly along the Androscoggin as a small boy when my dad had a job at the old Atlantic Pulp and Paper mill, and I could still remember my mother's warnings. Below the dams, the plunging river was coffee-brown and frothy, but then it would slip beneath a sheet of seemingly solid ice for miles.

"You can't trust it," she'd said. "Not ever, Michael. Do you understand me?"

Her warnings had given me the idea that the river was an evil serpentine thing, a winding white dragon, slithering through the snow. The impression would be strongest at night, when I heard the ice forming and shifting. The grumbling sound made me think of sleepless monsters, and then in the morning I would see jagged new patterns in the surface, cracks and ridges that hadn't been there the night before. The term my mother used for those nocturnal noises was *river talk*, but to me it sounded much more like the growls of something that would swallow me whole if I didn't take care.

Then I would watch my father trudge out to the middle of the frozen river with a six-pack and his ice-fishing gear and sit there safely for hours pulling brown trout through holes, one after the other, while he got a buzz started for the coming night at the bars. When he returned with a bucket of trout, I knew for certain he must be the bravest man in the world. Who else could ride the back of that white dragon all day and return home alive?

* * *

The road to Rangeley took me through the college town of Farmington, where Shaylene Hawken had her office, and then northwest through the impoverished Sandy River Valley. Bleak little towns with names like Strong, Avon, and Madrid were strung like tarnished beads along the highway. Hunchbacked mountains blotted out the light for long stretches, and moose warning signs flashed amber at every curve in the road.

Surrounded on both sides by hills, the isolated shacks and trailers down in the river bottom must have seen the sun for only a few hours each day. I found myself imagining the domestic dramas that might be playing out inside those benighted homesteads—the drugs being injected, the alcohol being consumed, the blows and the screaming, the guns being placed speculatively against temples.

I pressed the gas harder to outrace my grim thoughts.

The crossing for the Appalachian Trail came into view. Few people attempted to hike this stretch of glacial terrain in the winter. There was a short ascent to Piazza Rock that got some foot traffic, but almost no one dared venture out onto the exposed ridges beyond. The foolish ones who did—the backcountry skiers and alpine snowshoers—often needed to be rescued by game wardens risking their own lives.

And then, suddenly, the mountains let me go, and I was back in the bright white world.

Down in the Sandy River Valley, almost all of the variety stores and motels had been closed for the winter—if not boarded up for good—but now I began seeing motor inns with glowing VACANCY signs, and restaurants with snowmobiles parked out front. SUVs with out-of-state plates and ski racks began to zip past. Finally, a great white bowl opened before me, and I saw the hard, shining expanse of Rangeley Lake. Bright-colored dots raced back and forth on the distant ice; the sledders were out en masse for Snodeo.

I'd never attended the winter carnival, but I understood it to be an extended weekend of snowmobile races, bonfires, and hard partying. While our fellow officers in the state police and the sheriff's department patrolled the roads, Maine game wardens were given the trails and frozen lakes to watch over. Most of what we dealt with on the sledding routes were speedsters and drunks. I assumed the wardens assigned to Rangeley for the carnival must have gotten cramped hands from writing tickets.

As I drove through the village itself, I had to stop several times to let pedestrians cross the road. They piled in and out of the clothing boutiques and sipped lattes behind the steamed windows of the restaurants along Main Street. After the poverty and desolation I'd witnessed in the Sandy River Valley, I found it disorienting to see so much money on display in what seemed, on the map, to be the middle of nowhere.

The GPS told me to make a right onto Route 16, locally nicknamed "Moose Alley" for the number of collisions that occurred along it. Just past the village, the road took another hard turn, and then I was leaving the town and the traffic behind again. The houses began to be spaced farther and farther apart, and the woods began to edge closer to the snowbanks, until the trees on either side became unbroken walls of green. I drove fifteen more minutes along Moose Alley before seeing the sign for Widowmaker.

IO

Widowmaker was situated on the steep southeast-facing slopes of East Kennebago Mountain. The last time I could remember the resort having been in the news was a decade earlier, when a chairlift had malfunctioned, sending dozens of skiers plummeting to the ground. A man from Connecticut, a father of two, had died. There had been a number of gruesome headlines in the tabloids playing on the Widowmaker name. After the accident and the subsequent multimillion-dollar civil suit, the mountain resort had struggled to stay open.

Then, last year, a big ski company from out west had bought the place for pennies on the dollar. Pulsifer had said the new owners were looking to renovate the outdated lodge buildings and lifts. I wondered if they were considering bigger changes as well. I didn't know the first thing about marketing, but it seemed like they might want to rebrand their new investment with a less macabre name.

The access road to the resort crossed the frozen Dead River on a bridge that looked like it should have been replaced a decade earlier. Almost immediately, I came upon a cluster of businesses that had been built since the days when my father had driven a snowcat on the mountain. There was a grocery store plastered with signs that seemed to make a big deal out of its liquor selection; something called Kennebago Estates, which I guessed to be condominiums, offering many discounted units for sale; and a family restaurant, the Landing, which had an overly large and empty parking lot, as if its owners had opened the place with unreal expectations of how busy they would be.

One of the few landmarks I recognized from my childhood was the campus of the Alpine Sports Academy. The dormitories and halls had been built in the style of Swiss lodges—a timber-frame design that now seemed dated—but they looked better maintained than the other buildings I'd seen so far. Somehow ASA had managed to thrive even while the adjacent resort had fallen into disrepair—a tribute to the fund-raising prowess of its head of school, or at least proof that having half a dozen alumni with Olympic medals was enough to make the pickiest of parents overlook a lot of the mountain's flaws.

Soon the ski slopes came into view. Dozens of white trails flowed in all sorts of crazy directions from the snowcapped summit; they followed the grooves between the dark forested ridges the way melt-water streams will find their own zigzagging paths downhill after a storm. There seemed to be a lot of empty seats on the chairlifts.

The big hotel in the middle of the village loomed into view: the hub of activity for everything going on at Widowmaker. I hadn't expected to find a parking spot this near the top at the height of the season, but, to my surprise, a Volvo wagon was pulling out as I pulled in.

It was colder here than it had been at home. The air had a sharpness to it that promised imminent snowfall. As I crossed the lot, I noticed that I was one of the only people not dressed for skiing. Just about everyone else was clomping around in ski jackets, pants, and boots, as heavy-footed as Frankenstein's monster. Unencumbered, I sprang lightly up the stairs that led to the center of the resort's little village.

A recently shoveled sidewalk led between two big buildings: the Widowmaker Hotel and a plazalike strip of stores and restaurants. I saw signs for a market, a Laundromat, a coffee shop, and a few restaurants. You had to pass through an alley to reach the base lodge. It was a big post-and-beam building with wide doors. I followed a family of skiers inside.

I paused to remove my sunglasses at the entrance. At first glance, the great room seemed like a cozy-enough space; it was lighted by elaborate chandeliers and warmed by an enormous river-stone fireplace. But a closer inspection revealed that the carpet had been scuffed down to the backing in spots, and on the ceiling there were water stains shaped like prehistoric continents. Drafts blew about the room, carrying clattering echoes from the cafeteria and voices from the changing areas, where people were putting on and taking off their boots and helmets.

A sign for the Sluiceway pointed me up the stairs to the second floor.

Inside an arch, a teenage hostess stood behind a podium. She had a skier's tan, which made her gray eyes look grayer, and she was wearing a tight sweater, which accentuated the muscles in her firm little arms. She showed me the braces on her teeth when she smiled.

"One for lunch?" She lifted a menu from the stand.

"Is Amber working today?"

"Amber? She should be here somewhere." She glanced around the room. Only the bar itself seemed to be illuminated by artificial lights. The rest of the place was awash with natural light from a wall of windows. The air smelled of french fries.

A shout went up from a table of guys in plaid snowboarding jackets. "No, she fucking didn't, dude! That's not what she fucking said!"

It wasn't even noon yet, but those shredders were already buzzed.

The hostess blushed. "If you want to sit at the bar, I'll send her over."

"Thanks."

She smiled brightly again, and I wondered how many drunken men mistook her innocent friendliness for flirtation. If I had been her brother, I wouldn't have wanted her working at a place where guys got wasted before noon. I took a seat at the bar, positioned so I could keep an eye on the rowdy snowboarders.

I had never skied Widowmaker during my Colby years. East Kennebago was the runt of the local ski mountains, with no interesting geological features—no horns or windswept snow plains—to amp up its sexiness. Because its trails had been built on the southeast-facing slopes, the sun had more time to melt whatever snow fell, turning powder into water, and water into ice. The ski term for the mountain's characteristic surface was *frozen granular,* but my classmates who had skied Widowmaker called it "death cookies" and warned me away.

I hadn't needed the excuse. The real reason I had avoided Widowmaker was that I hadn't wanted to run into my father unexpectedly. I knew that he frequented the roadhouses and saloons between Rangeley and Solon: a drinking territory that he roamed the way a predator will mark as its own a certain chain of mountains, or expanse of forest. The prospect of my wandering into a barroom and seeing my dad on a stool, unshaven, with a shot and a beer in front of him, had scared me off. It was easier to stick to Sugarloaf, where I knew he had already been banned for life, and where I didn't have to worry about being humiliated.

The bartender came over. She was an athletic-looking woman with short hair the color of squid ink. She was dressed in jeans and a black fleece sweater with a *W* on the breast. "Beer?"

"Coffee."

"I'm making a new pot, if you can hold tight for a few minutes." She pushed a basket of popcorn across the bar. I took a handful. It was almost inedibly salty.

Glancing at the wall of windows, I saw tiny flakes of snow beginning to fall—the innocent-seeming vanguard of the coming storm.

"Mike?"

I spun on the stool, directly into Amber Langstrom's embrace. She hugged me hard, as if we were old friends and not people who had just met two nights earlier. I felt a pain on the bruised part of my back. I didn't bring my own arms up, but waited for her to let go.

"I knew you'd come!" She looked better than she had at my house. The whites of her eyes were actually white, and her blond hair was done up in a tousled style that made her appear younger. She wore the same black fleece as the bartender, but her jeans were as formfitting as ski tights.

"I thought I should see the place," I said. "I haven't been here in a long time."

"If I didn't have to work, I'd show you around." She leaned in close and lowered her voice. Her eyes were gorgeous, as blue as the bottom of a swimming pool. "Gerald—he's my new boss—is such an asshole. He thinks he's hot shit because he used to manage an Olive Garden. I am so glad you're here!"

I had no idea how to respond, but it didn't matter, because she kept on going.

"First, you need to talk with Josh," she said. "I heard he's working up on the summit today, which is kind of a bummer. Did you bring your skis?"

"My skis? No."

"Then you can't ride the chairlift. Well, you can ride to the top, but they won't let you come down that way. Do you want me to ask Elderoy to drive you up in his snowcat?"

"Wait. Who's Elderoy?

"The lift-maintenance manager. He's been here forever."

"And who's Josh?"

"He's Adam's friend, the one I told you about. He works on the ski patrol. Josh Davidson."

"Davidson, as in Alexa's brother? The one Adam beat up? I thought they hated each other."

Her painted mouth tightened. "Where did you hear that?"

"Pulsifer told me Alexa's brother tried to put an end to the relationship. He said there was a fight, and the kid ended up in the clinic. That was how the parents found out about Adam's relationship with Alexa."

From her reaction, you would have thought I had insulted her. "Gary shouldn't be spreading lies."

"They didn't get in a fight?"

"Those two were always hitting each other for fun. You know how boys are. It had nothing to do with Alexa. If they hated each other, why did Josh stay in touch with Adam while he was in prison? He was the only one of his academy friends who wrote to him. The rest of them treated Adam like a leper."

A stern-faced man wearing the same black fleece as the other workers in the restaurant appeared behind her shoulder. "Amber, can I have a word with you?"

She rolled her eyes at me, mouthed a silent profanity, and then turned to her manager with a remarkably genuine-looking smile. "Of course, Gerald. I was just giving this gentleman some recommendations for lunch." She returned her attention to me, as if finishing a conversation. "You should definitely try the Sluice burger. It comes with bacon and onion rings on top. Now, what is it you wanted, Gerald?"

"A word."

"OK, but I have an order up for table four, so you need to be quick."

Amber moved purposefully toward the kitchen. The scowling manager stayed one step behind her through the swinging door.

I swiveled back around on the stool and found myself looking into the hazel eyes of the bartender as she poured my cup of coffee from a steaming carafe. "Amber's a piece of work, isn't she?" she said.

"Yeah."

"How well do you know her?"

I blew on the top of the mug. "Not very well."

"You might want to keep it that way. Just my recommendation."

She thought I had been flirting with Amber. I gathered that it must have been a regular occurrence at the Sluiceway.

11

As I waited for Amber to return, I tried to make sense of what she had told me about her son and Josh Davidson. Why would the brother of the girl Adam had raped remain friends with her rapist, especially if—as Pulsifer had suggested—a fight between the two boys had been the incident that started the investigation that led to Adam's conviction? And what was I to make of Josh Davidson being the last person to see Adam before he vanished?

Curiosity had gotten the better of me so many times in the past. And here I was back in its thrall again. I was such a sucker for unanswered questions.

Across the room, one of the loud snowboarders stood up suddenly and knocked over his mug. Beer spilled all over the table and onto the floor. His friends pushed back in their chairs to avoid being dripped on—a hard scraping sound that drew the attention of everyone present—and started laughing and shouting.

"Dude! No!"

"Ugh, it's on my pants!"

"You are *so* wasted!"

"You bumped the fucking table!"

"I didn't bump it! You bumped it!"

I glanced at the teenage hostess and saw her shrinking behind her podium, as if she hoped it would shield her from the mayhem. The manager, meanwhile, was still scolding Amber in the kitchen.

I slid off my stool.

I zigzagged my way through the tables until I was standing behind the boarder who'd spilled his beer. "Guys," I said. "You need to keep it down."

79

The snowboarder—a big brawny kid—turned around and exhaled a heavy dose of alcohol into my face. "Lighten up, dude."

"There are families here. You need to watch your language."

I figured he'd give me some guff but then relent. It was early in the day for barroom brawls. Instead, he said, "Why don't you step back?"

"Really?"

"Yeah." And he shoved me in the chest.

I caught one of his hands and twisted. A wrist lock is one of the first self-defense maneuvers I had learned at the Criminal Justice Academy. A simple turn of the radioulnar joints in the hand is enough to make an aggressor's knees buckle, and that was what happened with my drunk snowboarder.

"Ow! Jeez! Let go!"

"I think you guys need to leave."

"Fuck you!"

I gave his hand another twist. "What was that?"

I turned my attention to his friends, who were still seated at the table. They were either less drunk or less bellicose, because they all reached for their wallets. They began scattering bills on the wet table.

I let go of the shredder's hand.

He rose from his knees, shaking his wrist, his windburned face growing even redder with humiliation. "Ow! Jeez! What's your problem?"

I removed my wallet with my badge and flipped it open. "I hope you guys aren't driving anywhere."

"No, sir!" one of his more sober friends said.

"We're staying at my mom's condo," added another.

"I hope that's true."

One by one, they slunk out of the pub like so many kicked dogs.

I sat back down at the bar.

"Thanks," said the bartender. "Are you a cop?"

"A game warden."

"Is that like a forest ranger?"

"Not exactly."

I had lost count of the number of times people had asked me that question. Even some native Mainers didn't understand that wardens are essentially off-road police officers. They associated us with checking hunting and fishing licenses—an important part of our job—and not with all of the other laws we enforced.

The teenage hostess tapped me on the shoulder. "Those gentlemen would like to buy you a drink."

"Who?"

"Them." She pointed to an eccentric-looking trio of older men seated in the corner.

One of them was obviously ex-military. He had a straight spine, like someone who had stood at attention for a long time, and a physique that suggested he still pumped iron every morning. He was neatly shaved, and his gray hair had been trimmed almost down to the skull, probably cut that very morning.

The second man in the group was ruddy-faced, with a snow-white mane and a prominent gut. He was wearing a tweed jacket over a fisherman's sweater, wool pants, brogues, and a herringbone driver's cap. He looked liked he'd stepped off the label of a bottle of Scotch whisky.

The third man, dressed in canvas shirt and corduroys, had the gangling appearance of someone who might be very tall when he stood up. Everything about him—head, limbs, and hands—seemed to have been stretched. He had a yellowish complexion, gold-rimmed spectacles, and a blond mustache going white.

My first thought was, What are those characters doing drinking in a skiers' bar?

They all raised their glasses to me in a toast.

I whispered to the bartender, "Who are those guys?"

"The Night Watchmen."

"Huh?"

She leaned across the bar. "That's what they call themselves, but if you ask me, the only thing they watch at night is porn. They come in here for the free popcorn and to pretend they're not gawking at snow bunnies half their age. I made the mistake of debating drug legalization with them once. After five minutes, they were ready to send me to Siberia."

I gave the trio a subtle wave of recognition and said to the hostess, "Thank them for the offer, but tell them I'm not drinking."

I turned back to the bartender.

"You should come back tonight when things get really wild," she said.

"No thanks." I smiled and sipped my lukewarm coffee.

After a few minutes, Amber emerged from the kitchen with a tray balanced on her shoulder. Gerald, the manager, was still shadowing her. He stood watch over Amber as she passed out plates of hamburgers and nachos to a table of skiers. When he was finally satisfied, he left her alone and disappeared again through the swinging door.

Amber came over at once. "Meet me downstairs in the Black Diamond Room in five minutes."

She was gone before I could reply.

The bartender raised an eyebrow at me.

I shrugged and paid for my coffee.

I followed the signs downstairs, past a laundry room that smelled of detergent and dryer exhaust, and an old-time video arcade where a few kids were zapping aliens and steering furious hot rods. The Black Diamond Room seemed to be some sort of banquet hall. The lights were off and the room was vacant, but the spirits of past wedding receptions seemed near. I waited inside the door, in the dark, amid the round tables and stackable chairs, feeling ridiculous at being made an accessory to Amber's act of subterfuge.

Fifteen minutes later, a burly little man in a black snowmobile suit stuck his head into the room and flicked on the fluorescent lights.

"Are you my passenger?" he asked.

"I'm not sure."

He had the crow's-feet and weathered skin of someone who had never worked a desk job in his life. There was snow mounded on his fur-lined hat and snow melting in his grizzled brown muttonchops. He removed his deerskin mitten to shake my hand. "I'm Elderoy."

"Mike Bowditch."

"Bowditch? Jack's son? Well, isn't that something! I worked with your old man before he got the heave-ho. Wasn't he a ticket, though. Anyone ever tell you you're the spitting image?"

"Not today, but it's still early."

He flashed one of the wider smiles I'd seen. His teeth looked as strong as the rest of him. "Where's Amber?" he asked.

"Trying to get away from her manager, I think."

"Gerald may be the first het'rosexual man Amber hasn't been able to snake-charm."

On cue, as if summoned, she appeared, out of breath and flushed in the face. "Elderoy, I need you to take Mike up to the top for me. Josh is working the ski patrol, and Mike needs to talk with him. It's really important."

The old man scratched one of his impressive sideburns. "Let me get this straight. You expect me to stop the important work that I am doing and chauffeur this young man to the summit just because you asked?"

"It's really, really, really important."

"Goddamn it, Amber," he said, trying but failing to suppress another smile. "You know how to play me like a fiddle."

"You'll do it, then?"

He pursed his lips and tapped his furry cheek for her to kiss.

She obliged, leaving lipstick marks.

Elderoy turned to me, beaming. "I'll meet you over at the Shady Lane Lift. This pretty lady can tell you how to get there."

I couldn't remember having agreed to interrogate Josh Davidson. Those lines I thought I knew? They seemed to be getting wavier by the minute.

"Are you sure Josh Davidson is going to talk to me?" I asked Amber after Elderoy had left the room.

"He's worried about Adam. Josh is his only friend left in the world."

"You said that before."

"Did I? Adam used to be so popular, too. He was such a great skier, and all the girls thought he was so handsome." She winced, as if the admission had caused her physical pain. Then she gazed directly into my eyes. "You really do look like him, you know."

She seemed so convinced—and so convincing. I had made a life-long practice of building walls against my emotions. Now I felt something begin to crumble inside of me. Bricks coming loose.

The question was out before I could stop it. "Does Adam know?"

"Know what?"

"Who his real father is."

Her expression became soft as she studied my face. "Not yet. But I want him to know—especially now."

I cleared my throat, zipped up my coat, and made to leave.

She touched me lightly on the arm. "Mike? If you don't mind, there's a question I've been meaning to ask you, too."

"Go ahead."

"Where is your father buried? I want to go see his grave with Adam."

"I don't know."

She yanked her hand from my arm as if from a burning stove. "How can you not know?"

"I'm pretty sure the state had him cremated. I never bothered claiming the ashes."

"Did anyone?"

"I have no idea."

"Jeezum, that's kind of cold. Don't you think?"

I pressed my lips together hard to keep from saying something I couldn't take back.

"You need to find out where he is," she said. It was the first time she'd assumed a motherly tone. "You owe your father that much at least."

What I owed my father was not a subject I cared to discuss. Not with her. Not with anyone.

I was learning that Amber Langstrom had a prizefighter's gift for knocking me off balance. I needed to do a better job of keeping my guard up when I was around this woman.

The snow had begun to drift down steadily and silently. It seemed like such a tranquil scene. I made my way through the stream of skiers and snowboarders tromping back and forth through the village plaza.

I saw Elderoy waiting beside his idling snowcat on the far side of a chairlift.

When I was seven, my father had taken me up with him in his snowcat one moonless night. I didn't remember much about the experience except certain sensations: the stomach-churning fear of climbing up and down the icy slopes, the wolflike howl of the wind as it shook the windows of the groomer.

"Ever ridden in one of these contraptions before?" Elderoy asked.

The cold seemed to awaken the stitched wound on my arm. "My dad took me once."

"Not like this one, though!" Elderoy proudly told me that his snowcat was a new PistenBully with tank treads and a flexible plowing blade that could be adjusted to deal with different kinds of snow conditions. He circled the enormous chugging vehicle, showing off its premium features—adjustable tiller, high-performance suspension, heated seats, and a winch cat for grooming the steepest trails— as if trying to sell me one.

"Your old man used to drive our prehistoric Tuckers," he said with a grin. "I'll never forget the night he slid down Steep and Deep in his groomer and everyone thought he'd killed himself. Turns out he'd had a girl with him *and* a bottle of Allen's coffee brandy. Jack was a rogue all right. Of course, he always liked me, so I never saw his bad side, although I heard plenty of stories."

I wanted to say, "You're lucky."

"I don't suppose he ever mentioned me?" he asked.

"I think I would have remembered your name. You don't meet many Elderoys."

"There used to be two of us with the same first name—Elder Roy and Younger Roy. That was how they told us apart. But Younger Roy passed away some years ago. His snowmobile went through the ice over on Rangeley Lake during the Snodeo. Drunk, of course. Most everyone from the glory days is gone now, retired or passed away. I'm the last of the Mohicans."

When I opened the passenger door, heated air rushed out of the cockpit. Elderoy cranked up the reggae music playing over his speakers, took hold of the PistenBully's joystick, and aimed us away from the lodge.

"Ever ski Widowmaker, Mike?" Elderoy asked.

"Sugarloaf's more my speed."

"Not sure I would have pegged you for a Sugarloafer!" he said. "I suppose you've heard the saying, 'Sugarloaf is old money. Sunday River is new money. And Widowmaker is never had any money.' Too bad, since we've got some mighty fine trails here." He started reciting their names with the paternal pride of someone who had cared for them for ages. "We just passed Snow Bunny and Pow Wow. Wild Thing is the main run. Atta Boy and Gritty Girl are moguls. Over on the south side of the lodge, near the condos, are Free Ride, Big Dig, and Git R' Down. My favorites are the diamond ones up above—Steep and Deep, the Beast, and Take It from the Top. That's the summit trail." He thrust his arm in front of my face. "And over there's Hospital Air Park, where the boarders strut their stuff."

We started up the mountainside, grinding along an access road that curved away from the ski lifts and trails. A two-way radio murmured on the dashboard. I couldn't hear what was being said above the Caribbean steel drums.

"Can I ask you something?" I shouted.

"Shoot!"

"What can you tell me about Adam Langstrom?"

He turned down the volume and glanced at me out of the corner of his eye. "That depends, I guess."

"How well do you know him?"

"I've known Adam all his life."

"Did you know he was missing?"

"I did."

"Any idea where he might be?"

He stopped smiling for the first time since we'd met. "Not sure if that's any of your business."

"You're probably right," I said, "but his mother asked if I could help bring him home."

He ran his tongue over his chapped lips. "I hope you don't find him, in that case."

"Why not?"

"Because he should have taken off for Canada back before the trial, when he still had the chance."

"I'm not following you."

"Adam was never going to get a fair shake. He was screwed the minute the headmaster called in the cops."

I waited, hoping he would continue.

And he did: "In this world, it doesn't matter if you're guilty or not. What matters is if someone else *needs* you to be guilty. I've seen it happen before. I've seen decent men ruined."

"You're talking about the chairlift accident," I said slowly.

"That lift never should have been running; it needed so many repairs. Buddy of mine, Scott Dyer, nicest guy in the world, was the lift manager back then. He kept telling the VP of mountain operations that the lift should be shut down. Did the VP listen to him? No, because shutting down the lift would have meant lost money. Sure enough, the line snaps one day in a windstorm, and a skier dies, just like Scott was warning everyone was going to happen. Guess who gets thrown under the bus?"

On the sound system, the Wailers were wailing. The summit was lost in fog.

"The thing that burns me," said Elderoy, "is that I didn't have the guts to quit. Because I was afraid, I watched a good friend lose his job and get crucified in the press. Scott would have gotten sued, too—if the poor man hadn't shot himself. And here I am, ten years later. Only it's me who's in charge of the lifts now. And it's no secret who'll be blamed if there's another fatal accident."

The machine tilted as we started up a steep slope, and I found myself staring up at the white sky like an astronaut about to be blown into space. The coffee sloshed unpleasantly in my stomach.

"It doesn't sound like you're going to help me find Adam," I said.

"No, I am not," Elderoy replied. "I get that Amber wants to know where her boy is—because she's his mom and she's worried about him—but that kid has suffered more than enough, if you ask me. I hope he's a thousand miles away from here. I hope he's someplace where no one's ever heard of Widowmaker Mountain."

12

As we gained elevation, Elderoy paused a few times to push around some newly created snowdrifts that were blocking the road. It seemed that the groomers and snowmakers were engaged in an unending battle with the weather. Some days, my job felt that way, too.

Near the summit, looking out at the horizonless landscape, I began to get a sense of vertigo. The snow didn't seem to be falling so much as rising, borne aloft on intermittent squalls. We passed a boarded-up building with gaping holes in the walls where windows had been kicked in by vandals or broken by storms.

Elderoy turned off "Three Little Birds" in mid-chorus. The wind seemed to raise its voice outside the snowcat.

"That's where it happened," he said, gesturing toward the old wreck. "That's the Ghost Lift."

"Why haven't they torn it down?" I asked.

"No money to do it. Not until now, that is. The new owners have scheduled demolition of the towers and the lift building for this summer." He dropped his voice even lower. "Maybe then people will stop remembering. I never will."

I stared down the mountainside and saw, through the rippling curtains of windblown snow, a descending row of T-shaped towers. They were spaced evenly apart, like steel telephone poles that had been stripped of their wires. But in my imagination I could see the missing chairs, and I could picture what it must have been like on that fateful day when the cables snapped and everything came crashing down.

The road flattened out as we traversed a shelf seemingly cut from the mountain rock. Peering ahead, I saw the colorful helmets and jackets of skiers coming off a modern, functioning lift. Some of them shouted and raised their ski poles over their helmets when they recognized Elderoy. Someday they'd probably name a trail after the old mountain goat.

Beyond was a wooden shack perched on stilts above the hidden valley. It had a first-aid emblem painted on the side. The most remote outpost of the Widowmaker ski patrol.

Elderoy piloted the PistenBully up to the building. When he popped open the door of the groomer, the temperature dropped fifty degrees.

"Nippy!" he shouted above the wind.

And then he'd slammed the door and was struggling, bent over, toward the stairs up to the shack. It hadn't occurred to me that he might be joining me inside.

I had never worked a district where one of my primary duties was finding lost skiers and snowboarders, but I had participated in a couple of alpine searches, and I knew the drill. Generally speaking, the ski patrol handled whatever calls came in, but any time the situation began looking desperate—night was beginning to fall, or the snow was turning to sleet—the local wardens would get an emergency summons.

I tried to follow the compacted path the ski patrollers had made in the snow—just as Elderoy had done—but I took a wrong step and found myself thigh-deep in powder. With some effort, I managed to climb free of the drift. I fought the wind all the way up the stairs.

Elderoy was waiting. "We were just about to send out a Saint Bernard!"

"As long as it's carrying one of those little casks of brandy."

A gust of wind slammed the door shut for me. I found myself blinking through fogged glasses at three people. Elderoy, of course. The other two were a young man and a middle-aged woman, both dressed in red ski jackets and black synthetic pants.

"Hello?" the woman said.

I unhooked the sunglasses from behind my ears and made an exaggerated series of expressions, trying to loosen the numb muscles around my mouth. "Hello."

"This is Warden Bowditch." Elderoy had removed his fur-lined hat and held it in front of him like a vassal who has come to beseech his feudal lord. "This is Kat, and that's Josh. They didn't know we were coming."

Typical of Amber, I was beginning to realize.

Davidson had dark hair, a thin nose, full lips, and a complexion that told me he tanned easily. There was something delicate about him, not just the narrowness of his shoulders and hips but something else, too. I had trouble imagining him belaying an injured skier on a stretcher and transporting him down an icy incline. Most of the competitive skiers I had met had been sturdy specimens: weight-lifting athletes with oversized legs and muscular butts. Not so with Davidson.

"What can we do for you, Warden?" the woman asked. Given the rosiness of her cheeks and the whiteness of her teeth, she seemed to be one of the healthiest human beings I had ever met.

"I don't suppose you have any coffee," I said.

"We have cocoa."

"That'll work."

The ski patrollers must have assumed I needed a minute or two to warm up. The truth was, I didn't know how forthcoming Josh Davidson was going to be with me. And silence can be a useful tool when you're conducting an interrogation. I removed my gloves finger by finger and set them on the table.

Kat brought over a thermos and set it in front of me. "So what can we do for you?" she asked again, this time with less friendliness.

The main room included a kitchenette and table, a two-way radio, and a wall of stormproof windows overlooking the trails below. There were orange trail makers piled in the corners and stacks of sleds for transporting crash victims down to the bottom of the mountain.

I took a sip of the hot chocolate. "Is there anywhere Josh and I can talk in private?"

The young man blinked. "What? Why?"

"Josh is on duty here," Kat said. "We might get a call at any minute."

"It's about Adam Langstrom," I said.

The mention of the name caused Kat to scowl. "What's going on here, Josh?"

"Adam skipped out on his probation," he said. "Supposedly, I was the last to see him."

"There's a court order keeping him off the mountain. Why didn't you call security?"

"Because it happened two weeks ago. We just ran into each other in the parking lot of the Snow Bowl."

Kat looked puzzled. "Two weeks ago? This couldn't have waited until the end of Josh's shift?"

"I'm afraid not." I took another sip of cocoa. "Adam's probation officer has her hands full with other cases. I told her I was going to be in the area and that I would make some informal inquiries on her behalf. It would probably be better if Josh and I spoke privately."

"Well, the only other room is the toilet," Kat said.

"I have an idea," I said, rising to my feet. "Elderoy, do you mind if Josh and I talk in your snowcat?"

Elderoy had begun to look anxious. He stroked the rabbit-fur lining of his hat the way a nervous person might pet a cat. "That's a brand-new machine."

"I promise not to touch anything."

"In that case, you're going to freeze your asses off."

"I'll only touch the heater."

After a moment, Elderoy reached into his snowmobile suit. He pressed the keys into my open palm, as if afraid I might drop them.

Davidson smiled nervously around the room. "Is this really necessary? Can't we just grab a beer after my shift?"

"The sooner we talk, the sooner Elderoy and I can get going," I said.

"Just answer the warden's questions, Josh," said Kat.

"OK."

As I slid my fingers back into my gloves, I remembered what Elderoy had told me at the bottom of the mountain. Crashing a groomer was how my father had gotten fired from Widowmaker all those years ago. No wonder the old dude was nervous about handing me the keys to his new ride.

It couldn't have taken more than two minutes to cross the distance from the patrol shack to the PistenBully, but it was time enough to flash-freeze my face again.

Davidson climbed into the passenger seat beside me. I managed to start the engine but had trouble seeing the temperature controls. After a moment, Josh reached over and hit the button to blast the blower.

"I still don't understand why you had to come all the way up here," he said. "You could have just waited for my shift to end. You could have waited at the bottom."

The rime ice that had formed on the windshield—the condensation that had frozen while we were inside—was already beginning to melt.

"You want to know the truth?" I said.

"Yeah."

"I wanted to take a ride in a snowcat," I told him. "My dad used to work at Widowmaker when I was a kid. He drove one of the old Tuckers. I remember him taking me up the mountain in that hunk of junk. Scariest night of my life. This PistenBully is pretty sweet, though. It's still got that new groomer smell."

Davidson leaned away from me with a puzzled look, as if he was considering the possibility that I might not be a game warden after all, but some crazed impostor. The haphazard nature of our conversation was clearly unnerving him, just as I had intended.

"So you're from out west," I said. "Seattle, right?"

"Vail, too."

"How did you and your sister end up at the Alpine Sports Academy?"

"My dad went to school here. He raced in the 1988 Olympics in Calgary. Then he blew out his knee." He tried humoring me to hurry things along. "Elderoy said you're a game warden. You must know Gary Pulsifer."

"I know Gary all right."

"I worked some searches with him—seems like a class act."

It was not the description I would have chosen.

"So if you're a warden, and you're looking for Adam, does that mean you think he might be lost in the woods somewhere?"

"No."

Trying to follow my train of thought had made Davidson confused, which was just what I had hoped. "Did you bust him for poaching or something?"

"Was Adam a poacher?"

"Not that I know of." He couldn't stop himself from smiling. "But who knows? He liked causing trouble, seeing what he could get away with."

"Including with girls?"

"What are you getting at?"

"Like I said, I'm just making some inquiries because his probation officer has her hands full. You never know what information might be useful in finding someone."

He rubbed his chin and nodded, but he didn't seem entirely convinced. "What is it you want to know?"

"Tell me about the fight."

"The fight?"

"You confronted Adam when you found out he'd been having sex with Alexa. You two got into it."

Davidson touched the corner of his eye. "He broke my eye socket. My orbital bone."

"And that was how the school found out?"

He knocked his head back against the window of the cockpit so hard, I could hear it. "The nurse asked me what happened, and I was so pissed off, I said some things I shouldn't have. The next thing I knew, the headmaster was there, asking me all these questions, and a detective showed up, and I got freaked out."

"What did you tell them?"

"That I was mad at Adam because he was my friend, and he'd been banging my little sister."

I could imagine what had happened next. The detective would have gotten the parents' permission to confiscate Alexa's phone, and they would have found texts (almost certainly lewd) and photographs (even worse). Then, after they'd managed to convince Alexa to cooperate, the cops would have orchestrated a pretext call. It was a recorded conversation between the boy and the girl to get him to admit what he'd done. A simple "I'm sorry" was all it took to send people to prison for statutory rape.

"I would have been pissed if someone had raped my little sister," I said.

"Yeah, but it wasn't rape. I don't know what the right word for it is, but it wasn't rape. They'd been having sex for a month. Alexa wasn't even a virgin when they started going out."

Davidson had begun to perspire from the heat inside the cockpit.

"It's still against the law," I said. "You did the right thing by coming forward."

"But I didn't know what was going to happen to him!" He let out a groan, as if overcome with nausea. "If I'd just made up some story about how I'd broken that bone, Adam would have moved on to some new girl, and Alexa would have been sad for a while. But she's always had her skiing to focus on anyway. Just talk to my dad for two minutes, and he'll tell you who's the champion skier in the family. Alexa just made the U.S. Ski Team. And here I am working on the Widowmaker ski patrol, trying to figure out what to do with my life."

Davidson really did seem to be a sensitive, emotional kid. Not at all like other college athletes I had known. I had a hard time believing it had been his idea to attend ASA.

"Did you end up testifying at the trial?" I asked.

"They didn't need me," he said. "My dad got Alexa to do it. He convinced her, like he always does. Plus, the police had that phone recording, and some dick pics Adam had sent her. They didn't need me to testify. I never even went to the courthouse. I was too ashamed to look my friend in the eye."

"You still consider him your friend?"

He laughed bitterly. "I'm not sure the feeling's mutual."

"Adam's mom said you kept in touch with him in prison."

"I sent him some letters, apologizing for what happened. But I never heard from him until after he'd gotten out. That was a couple of weeks ago. He was living at some kind of logging camp over in Kennebago with a bunch of other— It sounded horrible. The guy who ran the place was a slave driver, Adam said. He asked if I could meet him at the Snow Bowl. That's the bowling alley in Bigelow."

"When was this, exactly?"

"Two weeks ago Thursday," he said, stroking his lips with his long fingers. "He was waiting for me in the lot. It kind of spooked me, because I didn't know how angry he was going to be."

"Were you scared of him?"

"Fuck yeah! He'd just gotten out of prison. I almost didn't recognize him. Someone had bitten off part of his ear! His hair was real long, and he was bigger than before he went inside. The guy was fucking jacked."

Prisoners in Maine no longer had access to barbells or pull-up bars, but some of them compensated by maxing out on body-weight exercises in their cells. A friend of mine named Billy Cronk, who was serving out a manslaughter sentence in the Maine State Prison, had told me that plenty of ex-cons were still coming out of the joint stronger than before they'd gone in. Meaner, too.

"So what happened that night?" I asked.

"He asked me for some money," Josh said. "I only had a twenty on me, but he asked if I could use the ATM inside the bowling alley. I took out the max—three hundred bucks—and I gave it to him. Then he drove off in a truck I didn't recognize."

"Do you remember what kind of truck it was?"

"An old Ford, maybe. Or a Chevy. I don't know trucks. I am pretty sure he was all alone, though." He let out another groan. "I was relieved after he'd gone."

"Did he threaten you?"

"No. But—"

"But what?"

"He wasn't very talkative. Not like the old Adam at all. I used to be his sidekick. I've always been someone's sidekick, I guess. But he was really cold and quiet. I asked if I could buy him a beer, and he said he wasn't allowed to go to bars or drink alcohol as a condition of his release. He said there was a long list of things he would never be able to do again. He said I should appreciate all the privileges I had in my life." He sat forward, sweating, with a strained look on his face. "There was one other thing, too."

"What?"

"He had a black eye. It made me wonder about the guy who'd given it to him."

I considered my next question carefully. "Did he say anything or do anything that made you think he might—"

"Kill himself? Yeah, I've wondered about it since that night. It was the reason I called his mom when I heard he'd run off. I was worried about him. But why would he have needed money if he was just going to shoot himself?"

That was an excellent question. "Have you told any of this to the police?"

He sat forward. "I'm telling you."

Earlier that morning, I had promised myself that I wouldn't cross any lines. But now I possessed information that Shaylene Hawken, at least, should know about. How the hell was I going to explain to Adam's PO how I had come by it?

Informal inquiry, my ass.

Elderoy cranked up the music even louder than before on the ride down. He seemed in no mood to talk. Not that I cared particularly—I needed time to think.

I hadn't expected to see Davidson suffering—literally suffering—from guilt. But his emotions had seemed heartfelt. It always boggled my mind that people could be so charitable to those who had hurt them.

That Adam had needed money was no surprise at all. What were the economic prospects of a convicted sex offender up here? Not bright, I was certain. Why not scrape together some cash and make a break for a better life?

My brother must have known he would be caught; must have realized that he was facing one of only two possible futures—prison or death.

My brother.

Did I keep repeating that word because I wanted to believe it or because I didn't want to believe it? All I knew was that Adam

Langstrom—whoever he was—had awakened a long-dormant sense of dread in me. Not since my father fired those shots into a police car had I felt such a fear of the truth.

My wounded arm jostled the center console as Elderoy took a couple of whacks with his plow at a drift that offended his sense of symmetry.

The week could have been worse, I realized. Carrie Michaud could have aimed for the jugular.

At the bottom of the mountain, Elderoy remained belted in and kept Bob Marley blasting and the engine running. He looked at me through his eyelashes and muttered something I couldn't hear over the noise.

"What?"

He scratched his muttonchops. Then he snapped off the music.

"You got me to drive you up there under false pretenses," he said.

"How do you figure that?"

"You're looking to arrest that Langstrom kid if you find him. Admit it."

Until that moment, I had never considered the question. If I did manage to locate my fugitive so-called brother—and was unable to convince him to surrender—what would I do?

I got out of the vehicle without answering my chauffeur and made my way through the thickening snow to the base lodge.

13

Amber was certain to press me for information. But there were details about my conversation with Josh Davidson that I preferred to keep to myself—at least until I could follow up elsewhere. Adam's black eye, for instance.

I scanned the Sluiceway from the doorway but didn't spot her circulating among the tables. The lunchtime tide had ebbed, but the three curious characters I had seen earlier—what had the bartender called them, the Night Watchmen?—were still hunched over their popcorn and beer. The British-looking fellow caught sight of me and said something to the others, who all looked my way again with the same mix of amusement and interest, as if I were the butt of some private joke among them.

The inky-haired bartender had her back to me and was watching the television screen above the luminous liquor bottles. The Weather Channel was showing a map with a deep trough of snow moving toward Maine. It looked like it had already touched the Clayton Lake area, where Stacey was flying her moose survey. I needed to come clean with her about what had really happened with Carrie Michaud. Every hour I delayed telling Stacey the truth just made it worse.

The cold had parched my throat. I let out a dry cough.

The bartender met my eyes in the mirror. "You're back."

"I am."

She braced her arms wide atop the bar. "You want another coffee, or are you ready for a beer?"

"Water. Is Amber still around?"

The grin melted away. "She got a phone call a few minutes ago and hurried out of here without telling Gerald. I think she's pretty much fired at this point."

The call must have involved Adam, I thought. I couldn't think what else would have lighted such a fire under her.

"Do you know who she spoke with or where she was going?" I asked.

"Amber and I aren't exactly friends." She picked up a clean dishrag and began playing with it as she studied me. "What's your name, anyway?"

"Mike."

She looked at me with a sort of pity in her eyes. "Do you really need me to tell you that Amber is bad news, Mike?"

"Bad in what way?"

"How many ways do you require?"

I turned my back to the bar, leaned on the rail, and checked my phone for messages. Nothing at all from Amber. Somehow her unexplained departure seemed fitting. She had sent me urgently up the mountain and then forgotten I existed. Pulsifer had warned me about her selfishness.

Maybe the time had come to end my fool's errand and return home before the snow made the road through the mountain pass even more treacherous.

Someone loomed beside me. "Sir?"

I looked up into the face of a man in a blue uniform. At first, I assumed he must be a police officer. He was wearing a gun belt with a holstered .45 and pouches for handcuffs, a flashlight—all the usual tools of my trade. He had a badge, too: Franklin County Sheriff's Department. But the cap on his head was emblazoned with the trademark Widowmaker logo. Was he a cop, a security guard, or what?

"Yes?" I said.

"Can I ask you a couple of questions real quick?" It was the same verbiage I had been taught to use whenever I began a conversation with a potential suspect that was serious and not likely to be quick.

"What about?"

The officer was a tall man in his early twenties with a nondescript face I might have had trouble describing to a sketch artist: dull brown eyes, mousy hair, lips on the thin side, a few moles on his pale neck. He wasn't overweight, exactly, or at least not obese, but he seemed to carry an extra layer of fat over his entire body the way seals do. It made him appear soft, but I had a sense that the muscles were solid under that coating of blubber.

"Were you in this bar an hour ago?" he asked.

"Yes, I was."

"We had a report of a man matching your description having an altercation with a kid."

"The 'kid' was old enough to drink. Who 'reported' this altercation?"

"That's not important. Can you come with me, please?"

What the hell was up with this half-assed inquisition?

"Where?" I asked.

"I have an office downstairs." The officer kept a blank expression that made it impossible to read his emotions. "I'm just trying to straighten some things out."

"Russo, leave the guy alone!" said the bartender.

"Lexi, you do your job, and I'll do mine." The words themselves had an edge, but he managed to keep his tone even.

"The guy's a fucking forest ranger. Show him your badge, Mike."

"Is that true?" the man named Russo asked.

"I'm a game warden."

"Are you on duty here today, Warden?"

"No, I'm not."

"And have you been drinking today?"

"No, I haven't."

"Can I see your badge real quick?" Russo had the patter down, that was for sure.

Whatever this guy was, he was no ignorant rookie following a script he'd just learned. He had shown up here for the deliberate purpose of hassling me, and I had no idea what it was about.

I reached slowly—very slowly—into my inside chest pocket.

Russo examined my badge and photo ID. His eyes remained as absent of human response as a doll's.

With all the noise from the dining room, I hadn't heard another person approach me from behind.

"That's all right, Russo," a man said. "We saw everything."

The officer stood at attention. "Mr. Cabot."

I turned and found myself face-to-face with the mustached member of the Night Watchmen.

The whites of Cabot's eyes were more of a lemon chiffon color. His breath smelled strongly of beer. "My friends and I witnessed the whole incident. Warden Bowditch acted appropriately. He defused the situation before it could get out of hand."

I had come to the conclusion that Russo must be some kind of deputized security guard. Perhaps Widowmaker had an arrangement with the sheriff that granted some of their people arrest powers. I had seen similar setups on certain offshore islands.

"That's good enough for me, Mr. Cabot," said Russo, as if he worked for the man.

The guard returned my badge to me. "Sorry for the inconvenience, Warden. Just trying to straighten some things out. You have a good day now."

Meanwhile, the man with the gold-rimmed glasses extended his hand. "Name's John Cabot. Like the explorer. I apologize for Russo. He's a zealous officer, and usually that's a good thing here. Widowmaker has always attracted a certain unsavory element."

The odor of alcohol coming off Cabot was overpowering, and yet he spoke more coherently than almost anyone else I'd met that day. Clearly he was a person of some power, too, the way the officer had practically bowed to him.

"Thanks for backing me up," I said.

"Those brats were out of line." He gestured to his corner table. "Are you sure you won't join us for a drink?"

I remained fixed in place. "How did you know my name, Mr. Cabot?"

"What's that?"

"You said, 'My friends and I saw the whole incident. Warden Bowditch acted appropriately. He defused the situation.'"

His sallow skin sagged around the mouth. "You have a remarkable memory, young man."

"So I've been told."

His teeth were as yellow as the rest of him. "I knew your father. He worked for my company years ago, although we never met at the time. I got to know him later at various watering holes. Jack was quite the character, needless to say. He made a sizable impression."

"You own Cabot Lumber?"

"I did before I retired. I'm still the president of the board, but my sons run the business."

It was one of the state of Maine's larger independent building suppliers and had several sawmills, lumberyards, and dozens of retail stores. My father had felled trees for the company before being fired for some offense or another.

I crossed my arms. "But how did you know who I was?"

"You underestimate your own notoriety, Warden. At least in this part of the state."

Looking over his shoulder, I saw the ruddy British-looking chap waving me enthusiastically toward the table.

I had come up to Widowmaker promising not to call undue attention to myself. Clearly, these Night Watchmen jokers had me at a disadvantage. The whole sequence of events since I'd returned to the restaurant—Amber's unexplained disappearance, the grilling I'd received from Russo, being "rescued" by Cabot—left me feeling uneasy.

"Please come join us at least for a coffee." Cabot extended his scarecrow arm toward the back table. It was a grand, welcoming gesture that made me think of the ticket taker at a haunted house.

What other choice did I have?

I followed him.

The ruddy man in tweed pulled out a chair for me as I approached. "Welcome! Welcome!" he said in a posh accent.

"This is Johnny Partridge, late of Fleet Street," said Cabot. "And this taciturn fellow is Chief Petty Officer Lane Torgerson, U.S. Navy, retired. Gentlemen, we were correct in our deductions. This is indeed Warden Mike Bowditch, the son of the notorious Jack Bowditch, whom we were discussing earlier."

Torgerson I didn't know. But he looked like someone who had seen combat in a handful of theaters—from Vietnam to Iraq—and who could still hold his own against you in a bar fight and might even help you pick up your teeth afterward.

Partridge, however, I recognized.

He was a British-born reporter who had worked at several Maine newspapers over the years. I had no idea what had brought him from London to our little backwater state, but he'd had a long and controversial career. Everyone who worked in state government knew him by reputation and few were willing to take his phone calls. I remembered one particularly cruel column he had written attacking two friends of mine after they had been involved in a tragic suicide-by-cop shooting. Partridge had called wardens Danielle Tate and Kathy Frost "frantic female fish cops."

He had written about me, as well, following my father's death. Or so my friends had told me. I had managed to avoid reading the column he had published questioning my worthiness to carry a badge and a gun.

"Have a seat, young man," said Partridge boisterously. "Join us for a drink."

Torgerson nodded respectfully.

"He says he's drinking coffee," said Cabot, pushed his sliding spectacles back up his nose again.

"You must have a beer at least!" said Partridge.

The thought of sharing a table with this vile man soured my stomach.

"I apologize, but I didn't realize how late it is," I said. "I need to get going."

All three of them stopped moving at once and went completely quiet long enough for an old-time photographer to have made a daguerreotype of them.

"We noticed you talking to Amber Langstrom earlier," Partridge said, showing off his British dental work. "How do you know her?"

"I don't."

"Didn't she hug you?" the Brit asked. "I'm sure she did."

"She mistook me for someone else," I said. "She thought I looked like someone she knew."

Cabot raised one of his bristling eyebrows. "Really? We were all sitting here envying you."

I forced a smile. "I really made myself the center of attention, it seems."

"You've got to excuse us for being nosy Parkers," Cabot said. "We're all retired—in Johnny's case, partially retired. We have too much time on our hands, which makes us dangerous, of course. And we pay particular attention to Amber for obvious reasons." If he had shaped the outlines of her breasts in the air, he couldn't have been any more lewd.

"It's a shame about the poor woman's son," said Partridge to me.

I didn't have Officer Russo's gift for maintaining a deadpan expression. "Her son?"

"Sex offender," said Cabot. "Convicted child rapist. The kid was a promising skier, too. And now he's run off."

"He's human garbage," said Torgerson. I'd been wondering if he possessed vocal cords.

"That seems like too strong a word," said Cabot.

Partridge followed a swallow of scotch with a sip of beer. "What would you prefer?"

"I'd say that young Adam has forsaken his personal savior."

"Foss?" growled Torgerson. He really did sound as if he'd spent a lifetime breathing in napalm fumes and desert sand.

Partridge laughed uproariously. "That's a new name for Don! Personal savior!"

Torgerson's cell phone buzzed in his shirt pocket. He rose quickly to his feet and turned from the table, making sure I, at least, couldn't hear what he was saying.

"Now tell us about you," said Cabot.

"You already know that I am a game warden." The conversation seemed to be careening in the wrong direction. "The bartender said you gentlemen are part of a club," I said, trying to change the focus.

Cabot fingered the beads of moisture on his beer glass absently. "We enjoy a pint together."

"She said you call yourselves the Night Watchmen," I said.

"In jest," said Partridge.

"I don't get the joke."

"We all own homes on the mountain," said John Cabot by way of explanation. "The irony in my case is that I don't even ski. But my wife and her children can't get enough of it. We have an interest in protecting our property values. That's all there really is to it."

"Protecting your property values from what?" I asked.

"Fugitive sex offenders!" said Partridge.

Cabot raised his pint glass. "Touché."

Torgerson leaned over the table. "I have to go."

He didn't wait for a reply from them. Nor did he leave any money for the bill. Maybe the Night Watchmen ran a monthly tab.

"Are you sure you won't sit down?" said Partridge. "I wrote about your father, you know. Horrible thing, and so embarrassing for you, as a warden. I am curious to hear what your life has been like over the past years."

For another column? "Thanks for the invitation, but I need to get on the road. Nice meeting you gentlemen."

Cabot and Partridge silently raised their glasses to me and didn't speak a word to each other while I made my way to the door.

Well, that was a first, I thought. Usually when you are being threatened, you have some clue as to why.

14

The sky was as white as the slopes now. It was a cold, dry, nearly weightless snow, beyond the ability of the snowcats to shape. Skiers zoomed along the trail beside the lodge—momentary flashes of color—and then were swallowed up again by the silent storm.

The powder came off my truck with the faintest push of my gloved hand. I didn't bother getting out the scraper. I started the engine and watched my breath, my life, unfurl into the cold before my eyes.

Had Officer Russo deliberately tried to bully me away from Widowmaker—or was he just another ham-fisted rent-a-cop? Did the Night Watchmen really suspect I had a secret relationship with the Langstroms that threatened them somehow—or were they just the drunken old busybodies they admitted themselves to be?

The phone buzzed in my pocket. When I saw that it was Stacey's number, I felt my pulse begin to ease. The calmness lasted all of two seconds.

"You asshole!" she said. "You lying son of a bitch! Did you think I wouldn't hear what really happened, Mike? You had a 'scuffle with a tweaker'? Is that warden code for being stabbed in the back?"

"I'm sorry, Stacey. I didn't want to worry you."

"You lied to me."

"I lied by omission."

"What the hell does that mean?" Her nose still sounded plugged up. "My dad told me you could have died. He said every cop in the county came to the scene because they thought you were bleeding out."

Of course I should have anticipated that her father would have heard the news of my stabbing. Charley Stevens had been the worst gossip in the Warden Service before he retired, and he was even worse now that he was uninhibited by department politics. The old pilot had sold me out to my girlfriend—not that I could blame him.

"It wasn't that bad," I said.

"That's not the point." She began to suffer a coughing fit. "You need to tell me what happened, Mike, or I swear to God, I'm going to come down there tonight and kick your lying ass."

"I let a woman named Carrie Michaud get the drop on me. She's this little ninety-pound drug addict, and I didn't take her seriously enough. She stabbed me in the back, but the blade didn't puncture my vest. She did manage to cut me in the arm before I subdued her. I only needed ten stitches."

"You *only* needed ten stitches? And what do you mean, you subdued her? You didn't shoot her?"

"I didn't need to. I knocked her out."

"If it had been me, I would have shot her!"

"Where are you?" The question slipped out before I realized how it might sound.

"Ashland. We got grounded by the snow. Where are you?"

"I'm not sure you want to know."

"I am so going to kick your ass."

"I'm at Widowmaker."

She coughed some more. "What?"

"DeFord said I should take some sick days, but since I felt all right, I thought I would drive up to ask around about Adam. I told you I was coming here in my e-mail this morning."

She fell silent for a moment before launching her second offensive. "Ever since that woman showed up at your house and told you about your brother, you've been on this downward spiral."

"I wouldn't say that," I argued, despite the black thoughts that had been plaguing me only minutes earlier.

"It's your dad, isn't it? You've let him back into your head again. Jesus, Mike, get a grip!"

"I can explain everything if you just calm down."

"Don't talk to me like that. You should have called me from the hospital. If you don't understand how much that breaks my heart, there's nothing more to say. I'm not interested in being with someone who'd rather be lonely than be loved."

Then the line went dead.

A moment later, the phone buzzed again.

This time it was a message. Just one word: *Asshole!*

Before I had become a warden, and during my first years on the job, my thoughts had been so clouded with guilt and anger that I couldn't see anything clearly. At the time, I had believed my mind was perfectly sound. It was only later—after I had participated in my fourth or fifth critical incident stress debriefing—that I had realized I couldn't necessarily trust my own mental process; a sick psyche is, by its very nature, incapable of understanding it is sick. I remembered a question I had asked a counselor after she had diagnosed me with post-traumatic stress syndrome: "How can you think through your problems when your problems are your thoughts?"

If Stacey was right, I might be suffering some sort of psychological relapse brought on by that knife in my back. I needed to take a step back and make an attempt to assess my present difficulties with some objectivity.

I was miles from home—and my distance from Stacey at the moment couldn't be measured in mathematical units.

My superiors at the Warden Service had forbidden me to return to work until my wounds healed, but they would hardly have been pleased to learn how I had spent my so-called sick day.

Not to mention that Amber had taken off without so much as a note about where she was going.

And then there was the matter of the snow. Another inch had accumulated on my windshield since I had returned to the Scout, with only more to come. I flipped the switch and watched the hard rubber blades clear half-moons in the powder.

The easiest problem to deal with was Amber.

I keyed in her number and, of course, got her voice mail. "It's Mike," I said, trying to keep the frustration I was feeling out of my voice. "I thought you were going to be waiting for me at the Sluiceway, so we could talk about Josh. What happened? If you've heard from Adam, I'd appreciate your calling me back, since I froze my ass off going up that frigging mountain."

As soon as I hit disconnect, I felt a pang. Amber might have been a self-involved schemer, but I had no business taking out my self-disgust on her. For all I knew, she had received horrible news.

With everything that had happened at the Sluiceway, and then my disastrous conversation with Stacey, I had nearly lost track of the important details I had learned from Josh Davidson: about Adam's needing money, about his having a black eye, about his driving a truck no one knew he even owned.

Amber had told me to seek out Don Foss, though she doubted he would speak to me. I had to admit that every mention of the man had left me more intrigued.

Pulsifer had called him "a secular saint or a modern-day plantation boss."

Shaylen Hawken had said he was "the last chance some of these men will ever have."

And to Cabot and the Night Watchmen, he had been Adam's "personal savior," in ironical quotation marks.

What else did I have to do tonight but go searching for this enigma of the North Woods?

On my way down the mountain and out of the resort, I passed an open maintenance hangar. A PistenBully was idling out front, and I saw someone who looked like Elderoy having a conversation with another man while two dogs played in the open lot. The men seemed to be watching the animals leap into the air and bite at the snow-flakes.

As I drew closer, I saw that it was indeed Elderoy. The other, younger man I didn't recognize, but he was dressed in a Widowmaker snowsuit and leaning on a shovel. The dogs were large hounds of some sort; they had appeared black from a distance, but the coloring of their coats, even coated with frost, seemed to have more nuance than I had first thought.

I honked my horn and waved.

Elderoy glanced at my Scout, and we made eye contact, but he didn't reciprocate my gesture. We hadn't parted on the best of terms, it was true. He must also have muttered something to the snow shoveler, because the man gave me a look of such intense interest, I lifted my foot from the gas pedal. Then something even more curious happened: The man whistled. I couldn't hear the sound from the moving vehicle, but I saw the reaction of the hounds. Both dogs ceased to play and faced their master with absolute attention. It made my untrustworthy brain wonder what Elderoy had told the stranger about me.

The road down the mountain had begun to get slick. Cars lined up behind me. Most of the traffic was heading south on Route 16, back into Rangeley. I turned north onto the stretch of highway everyone called Moose Alley.

The road deserved its name. The slow-flowing Dead River ran along one side, slithering through a lowland of swamp maples and gray birches: a landscape custom-made for moose. In all seasons, there was something good for them to eat within a few feet of the unfenced road. During warm-weather months, moose loved to hang out in the open, where the breeze could push away some of the biting flies that followed them, and they could submerge themselves in refreshing pools while dining on catkins and water lilies. When the cold weather came, the animals would switch to a diet of evergreen needles and pinecones. They also enjoyed licking up the mineral-rich salt from the asphalt itself.

On average each year, four hundred Maine drivers collide with a moose. Most humans survive the encounters (albeit with totaled vehicles and broken bones); far fewer moose do. I kept my eyes open and both hands on the steering wheel, ready for what might come crashing out of nowhere.

I hadn't imagined Don Foss Logging would be hard to find. There was pretty much only one road through Kennebago, and I was on it, driving slowly enough that I should have been able to spot a business sign, even half-hidden behind the falling snow. But somehow I managed to miss it.

When I came to the crossroads in Bigelow half an hour later, I knew I had gone too far. I supposed I could have called Pulsifer for directions. He was the district warden, after all. When we'd spoken on the phone the day before, he had invited me to drop in the next time I was in town. Wouldn't he be surprised to see me pull up outside his farm.

Instead, I decided to drive into the village. Bigelow was a haven for snowmobilers who raced up and down the trails to Quebec, ran shopping errands on their sleds the way people elsewhere did in their cars, and lined the streets with their parked snow machines.

I stopped at the first business that looked open, a general store with a North Woods vibe.

Most of the crowd inside consisted of sledders in snowmobile suits that made them look fat, even if they weren't, and caused them to rustle and clomp when they walked to the registers with their bottles of sodas and bags of chips. At the lunch counter sat a couple of French-Canadian truckers coming from or going to the border crossing twenty-seven miles to the north, where my late grandfather had once worked. Beside them sat a couple of well-appointed skiers, lost on the road from Widowmaker to Sugarloaf.

To me, this scene felt like coming home. My grandparents, whom I'd never met, had lived nearby in Chain of Ponds, and I had spent an itinerant childhood living with my mom and dad in these same sorts of backwoods hamlets. The suburbs around Portland, where my mom and I later took up residence, and where I went to high school, and now worked, would always feel to me like a place of exile.

"Can you give me some directions?" I asked the very pregnant woman clearing plates behind the lunch counter.

"That depends." She had an acne-spotted face but a pleasant way about her. "Where're you headed?"

"I'm looking for a logging company."

"Cabot's? They're over in Rangeley."

"No. Foss's."

You might have thought I'd asked her to guide me to the nearest whorehouse. "Why are you asking me?"

"I thought if you worked here, you might know."

"I never go out that way."

"Which way?"

"Are you going to order something or not? I'm too busy to make chitchat."

She spun away from the counter before I could place an actual order (the truth was, I was famished). I did a quick scan of the store, searching for someone else who could give directions to the local sex-offender sanctuary. Few faces looked promising. If the people who owned Widowmaker condos didn't appreciate having convicted rapists, pedophiles, and pornographers living among them, why should I have expected their poorer neighbors to be more welcoming?

Rather than taking a seat between the truckers and the skiers, I grabbed a bottle of Moxie from the cooler, a couple of slices of pizza from the heated cabinet near the register, and a pint of Jim Beam for later. Stacey had been nagging me to cut down on the gas-station breakfast sandwiches and fried chicken that made up so many of my meals while at work.

The door blew open again and a person hurried in from the cold.

I mistook him for a boy at first, he was so short. He was dressed in an oversized lumberman's coat, jeans, and pack boots. His shoulders were heaped with snow, and there was a layer of frost on a brown fur hat that looked like nothing so much as a sleeping mammal.

The small person hadn't taken three steps inside before the clerk behind the register—a bearded dude who had the lordly bearing of the store owner—shouted, "Out, Mink!"

The voice that issued from his small body was shockingly deep: "But it's snowing!"

"You know you're not allowed in here."

"I need a ride home."

"So hitchhike."

"But no one's on the road. It's a freaking storm out there."

"I'm not kidding around, Mink."

The little man let out an audible huff. It reminded me of a sound an exasperated teenager might make. Before he ventured outside again, he paused at the door to deliver one last appeal. "If I freeze to death, it'll be on your conscience."

"Out!"

"I'll probably get hit by a freaking snowplow."

As the door slammed shut, the owner rolled his eyes at the ceiling. "That guy."

When it came my turn to pay, I asked, "What's his story?"

"Buddy, you don't even want to know," he replied with amusement.

"Tell me," I said. "What did he do?'

My interest must have made the owner suspicious, because his tone hardened. "Forget about him. He's harmless."

One of the things I have learned about Maine villages is that every one has its mascot (if not its idiot). He or she might be a a developmentally disabled boy who likes to greet you at the gas pump, or a brain-damaged logger who got hit by a falling tree. Some of these people are objects of great local affection and are treated with protectiveness. Others are regarded more as nuisances who might try your patience from time to time but who are ultimately, grudgingly accepted as members of the community.

Mink, whoever he was, seemed to fall into the latter category. Nothing about his speech suggested he was mentally or physically impaired in any way. But I had seen enough scenes like the one with the store owner to recognize the status the little man occupied among the good people of Bigelow.

The visibility was getting worse by the minute. It wasn't the storm of the century; we were just being dumped on. Welcome to winter in the Maine mountains, I thought. At least the skiers and sledders would be celebrating.

I intercepted Mink a hundred yards down the road. He had his collar up against the wind and his bare hands dug into his pockets and was trudging determined in the direction of the crossroads. I rolled the window down as I pulled up beside him.

"Need a lift?"

He scrambled into the Scout so fast, I barely had a chance to clear the junk from the passenger seat.

"It's colder than the North Pole out there." There was not the faintest trace of a Maine accent in his speech.

"Where are you headed?"

"Kennebago Settlement."

"That's a long walk! Especially in this weather."

"Usually, it's not such a slog, you know. My mom has a place in Bigelow. I like to check in on the old bird every couple of days. She makes me dinner."

Seen up close, his features appeared more unusual than when I'd briefly glimpsed them inside the store. Beneath his fur hat—which might well have been mink—he had jet-black hair that looked dyed, a nose that had been broken more than once, and a nasty scar on his chin. His fragrance was also distinctive. He smelled like he'd just emerged from a vat of cologne.

"My name's Mike," I said.

"Mink."

"I don't meet many people with that name."

"I like to stand out."

I knew the answer to my next question. "Did you grow up around here?"

"Nah, man. I'm from Jersey. What kind of antique vehicle is this? It rides rougher than Farmer Brown's tractor."

"It's an International Harvester Scout Two." I resisted telling him how much I had paid for the custom-restored four-by-four. "Can I ask you something?"

"Why stop now?" he said with a laugh.

"I'm looking for a business around here, but I can't seem to find it. Can you give me directions?"

"That depends. Where do you want to go?"

"Don Foss Logging," I said. "Ever heard of it?"

He unsnapped his seat belt. "Stop the vehicle!"

I hit the brakes so hard, we began to slide. I wasn't sure what I should focus on: keeping the Scout from crashing into a telephone pole or protecting myself from the suddenly frantic man to my right.

I steered in the direction of the skid. "Hey, man. It's all right. Don't get upset."

"I want to get out."

"I'm going to let you out—as soon as we stop sliding."

After a few tense seconds, the Scout came to rest with the passenger side pressed against a snowbank. Mink jerked the handle up and down and threw his shoulder against the door. I heard metal scrape against ice as he tried to pry it open, and groaned internally at the thought of my damaged paint.

"Stop! Let me pull forward so you can get out."

He whipped his furry head around. Bright tears sparkled in his eyes. His voice had risen to a higher pitch. "It's not funny, you know? Playing jokes on people."

"I'm not playing a joke on you."

His mouth curled in disgust, and he slunk against the door. "I'm not going to blow you, if that's what you're after. I don't go that way."

"What?"

His nostrils flared with disgust. "I'm not a freaking pervert. I am not like those creeps who live at Foss's."

"Mink?"

"I'm a law-abiding citizen!"

"Mink?"

He wiped the tears from his cheeks and squared his luxuriant hat on his head. "What?"

"This is all a misunderstanding," I said. "I just heard you needed a ride. I thought you might be able to give me directions. I don't know anything about you, and I don't care. I just need directions to Foss's."

The windshield wipers beat steadily back and forth.

"Why do you want to go to that shithole?" he asked, suddenly curious.

"It doesn't matter," I said.

"Does to me."

"I'm a game warden." I opened my wallet and showed him my badge. "There's someone I need to talk to at Foss's."

He sat up in his seat, but he could still barely see above the dash. "Is it that piece of trash Butera? Because he doesn't live there any-more."

"So you know where it is?"

"I know where it is."

"Can you show me on the map?" I reached for the dog-eared De-Lorme atlas under my seat. I opened to the page showing this cor-ner of Franklin County.

Mink squinted at the coffee-stained page as if he desperately needed reading glasses. "It would be better if I guided you in per-son. You won't find it on your own."

Clearly he hoped to ride along now that he realized I was a law-enforcement officer. He wanted to know who I was looking for, because the Rangeley Lakes region was essentially one big small town, and he was one of its snoops.

"I can't take you along with me," I said.

He removed his fur hat and shook off some of the melted snow from the pelt. Then he ran his hand through his dyed hair, causing it to stand up. He had the face of a boxer, if there was a division below flyweight. "Why? Will it be dangerous?"

Now who is the one asking invasive questions? I thought.

"I just can't do it," I said firmly.

He moved his tongue around his mouth so that one cheek bulged, then the other. "All right. You can drop me at my house first. The road to Foss's is just past that. I'll point you where you need to go."

He snapped his seat belt back into the latch and made himself comfortable for the ride.

15

Mink hummed to himself as we drove back down Moose Alley. I didn't recognize the tune, but he carried it well.

"Do you know Charley Stevens?" he asked out of nowhere.

"He's a friend of mine."

"I figured, since you are both wardens."

"He's retired now."

"That makes sense. Charley and his wife, Ora, used to have a place on Flagstaff Pond before Wendigo bought up all that land. Good people."

It shouldn't have been so surprising. Flagstaff Pond was just down the road from Bigelow, and Charley had been a familiar and friendly presence in the woods around here for decades. I had plenty of misgivings about this character Mink, but if he liked and respected the Stevenses, he couldn't be too bad.

"Do you know their daughter Stacey?" I asked.

"Which one is she? The blonde or the brunette?"

"The brunette."

"Yeah, I remember her. She's got great eyebrows."

Those were not the features I personally would have identified as her best, but I supposed her eyebrows might have warranted the compliment.

Now that we had gotten over our initial misunderstanding, Mink seemed eager to chat again. "What did you say your last name was again?"

"Bowditch."

"Oh yeah, I know who you are now. Your dad was a scary guy. He used to come into the Bear's Den when I was washing dishes, and the whole place would go quiet. Even from inside the kitchen, I could hear the dining room go dead."

It had been a long time since I had felt so defined by my father's reputation. But what had I expected, returning to his old hunting grounds? Jack Bowditch had been infamous, never more than in his last days.

"How did you end up in Kennebago?" I asked. "You said you were from Jersey?"

"South Orange. My dad had a hunting camp in Kennebago. He sent me up here to stay for a while. Wanted to make a man out of me. That was a long time ago. He's dead now. Heart attack. My mom moved up a few years ago. She hates it here, the old bird. Says there's no culture. Personally, I think she's lonely because she's too high-and-mighty to make friends."

"Do you still work at the Bear's Den?"

He let out a laugh. "That dump? No way. Don't ever eat there. You'll get intestinal parasites."

I had a bad habit of always asking one question too many. "Does the name Adam Langstrom mean anything to you?"

"The kid who raped the girl at ASA?" He swung his head around, dark eyes opening wide. "Is he the creep you're looking for at Foss's? I'd heard he was living with that freaking crackpot since he got out."

We drove on for another five minutes without seeing a single vehicle. At no time did my speedometer top thirty miles per hour.

"Do they call you Mink because of the hat?" I asked.

"Nah. My real name is Minkowski. Nathan Minkowski." He leaned against the dash suddenly. "Take a left here."

I turned down a wooded camp road, unnamed and unmarked except for two signs at the corner. One was a HOME FOR SALE notice with an arrow pointing into the forest. The other said DEAD END. My tires made a crunching noise as we left the highway and crept into the woods.

"You actually live up here?" I said.

"Yeah."

Fortunately, the plow had recently come through. It had scattered a gritty carpet of sand across the woods road to make the going easier.

"Who plows this road for you?" I asked.

"There's a guy who does it," my passenger said.

Sparsely populated townships like Kennebago, which were part of Maine's Unorganized Territories, did not have public works departments. The handful of people who lived within its boundaries relied on the state to provide municipal services. Most of the North Woods consisted of remote plantations and townships whose residents were effectively serfs under the rule of distant czars.

A hundred yards in, we passed a homestead made up of a single farmhouse and assorted sheds and barns. It had seen better days— half a century earlier. There was a sign out front announcing that this was the property for sale and that the price had been reduced. But no one seemed to be at home.

"Who's your neighbor?" I asked, slowing down.

"Just some mook."

Densely branched evergreens closed in around us. Snow pillowed the dark boughs and clung tightly to the electric line that stretched from pole to pole overhead: the only indication that anyone else might actually be living farther up in these woods. Little by little, we made our way up a hill, heading east. So far, we had passed only that single house.

I noticed that some of the higher branches had been broken by big trucks coming through. That should have been the tip-off.

We came around a corner and saw the gate with the sign. I read the notice in the glow of my headlights.

```
PRIVATE PROPERTY
ACCESS BY PERMISSION ONLY
24 HR VIDEO SURVEILLENCE
```

The sign included a number to call if you wanted someone to come let you onto the property.

"This isn't your house," I said. "This is Foss's place."

"Yeah, I shouldn't have fibbed."

I found myself wishing International Harvester had put ejector seats in their Scout IIs.

The plow had helpfully cleared a turnaround at the gate. I imagined the U-turn was well used by the locals who came here to gawk at the sex-offender colony. I began to reverse direction.

"What are you doing?" Mink asked in alarm.

"Leaving."

"You don't want to call that number?"

"I'm going to call it," I said. "But first I'm going to drop you at home—or at the side of the road. I haven't decided which."

"But we're already here!"

I had been planning on driving home after I had finished with Foss, but it was already getting late. With the snow piling up, the trip was bound to be a nightmare. My head ached, and my stitches ached, and the bruise on my back where Carrie Michaud had tried to impale me ached.

And Mink was right: I was already here.

I snatched my phone from the console and dialed the number visitors were instructed to call.

A recorded voice answered: "Please state your name and the purpose of your visit. If your business with us is legitimate, someone will be at the gate shortly to grant you admittance."

"This is Mike Bowditch with the Maine Warden Service," I said. "I would like to speak with Mr. Foss, please."

I turned off the engine to wait.

"At least I got you here," Mink said, picking his teeth with a fingernail. "You've got to admit you never would've found it without me."

At first, the snow melted the instant it touched the windshield, but as the warmth ebbed from the truck, a sheer white sheet began to form over the glass.

I kept the phone in my hand, ready for a callback. But none came.

After a while, I turned on the engine again and let the wipers clear away some of the snow. I wanted to be able to see the gate.

"About freaking time," said my passenger. "My nuggets were starting to go numb."

I turned off the engine again.

"Oh, come on!" Mink said.

Fifteen minutes passed before we finally saw headlights arcing through the trees. Then an enormous Ford Super Duty came rumbling down the hill to the gate. The driver left the engine running and the headlights blazing as he climbed down out of his oversized vehicle. The glare made it hard to see him clearly, but he appeared to be very large and was wearing a brimmed hat. He also happened to be carrying a shotgun.

I began to reach for the door handle. Mink followed suit. I closed my hand around his collarbone.

"You're staying here," I told him, tightening my grip. "I'm done kidding around."

He gave me the familiar exasperated sigh, but he didn't resist.

I stepped out into the falling snow. As the afternoon had waned, the sky had gone from a dull white to a sort of a lavender gray. I walked slowly toward the gate with my arms at my sides.

"Mr. Foss?" I called.

"What can I do for you?" He had a deep and resonant voice.

"My name's Mike Bowditch. I'm a Maine game warden."

"That's what you said in your message. What can I do for you?"

Don Foss was a big man in every way. He was tall, broad-shouldered, with a big chest that merged seamlessly into a bigger belly. His head was the size and shape of a basketball. He probably could have throttled a horse with his hands. The only thing small about him was his wispy little mustache.

"I'd like to ask you a few questions about Adam Langstrom, if you don't mind," I said.

"He's not here."

"Yes, I know. His probation officer told me."

"You spoke with Ms. Hawken, then?"

"She told me that Adam has been working for you since being released from prison," I said. "I wonder if I can come in and you can answer some questions for me."

"Such as?" The pump shotgun looked like a toy in his enormous hands.

"I'd like to know more about the nature of your facility."

He let out a booming laugh. "I don't offer tours of my property to strangers. I run a business, not a zoo. You identified yourself as a warden. In what capacity are you acting, exactly?"

"I'm not here as a law-enforcement officer," I said. "Amber Langstrom is worried about her son and wants him to come back. She asked me to help find him, and I agreed to do so as a personal favor."

I expected him to ask me for identification. The fact that he hadn't seemed a bad sign.

"Langstrom is not a child in need of protection." The man's voice rolled out of him like distant thunder. "He is a man responsible for his own actions."

"So you have no idea where he might have gone?"

"If I did, I would not tell you," he said. "It was a condition of his release that he submit to regular searches and blood tests. I have made his room and his personal effects available to his probation officer. I have also answered all of Ms. Hawken's appropriate questions. Beyond that, Langstrom has certain inalienable rights, which he did not forfeit upon his conviction. Unless I believe him to be a risk to himself or to others, I shall not violate those rights. "

The diesel engine of his truck chugged along, the only sound in the clearing.

"That's quite a speech," I said.

"I hope you are not mocking me, Warden."

"I've just never heard anyone talk that way about a sex offender before." I brushed snow off the bridge of my nose. "In my experience, even defense attorneys take hot showers after shaking their hands. And here you are, giving them jobs and welcoming them into your home. I'm curious to know why."

"Are you a religious man, Warden?"

"It depends on how scared I am."

"I am not a religious man," Foss said proudly. "But sometimes I find it useful to quote the Bible to those who profess to believe in it: 'Christ redeemed us from the curse of the law.' I don't believe in Jesus Christ, but I do believe in second chances."

"That makes two of us," I said. "I mean the part about believing in second chances. I'm here to stop Adam from throwing his away."

"How well do you know Langstrom?"

I thought back to the photograph I had seen of him taken at his trial: the familiar face filled with the familiar anger. "Well enough."

"Then you should give him the courtesy of assuming he knows his own mind and is responsible for his own actions." He lifted the barrel of his shotgun. "Who is that with you?"

I swung around and saw Mink standing behind me in the snow.

I had to hand it to the little guy. He was as stealthy as his namesake weasel.

"Get back in the truck, Mink," I said.

"I'm just getting some air."

I turned back to Foss. "He's just someone I'm giving a ride to. I picked him up hitchhiking."

"I know who Mink is." In the headlights shining behind him, his steaming breath made a wreath around his head. "I'm sure you understand that my men and myself are the subject of frequent threats."

"That's because they're a bunch of creeps," muttered Mink.

Foss seemed to ignore him. "This place is a sanctuary for men in need. I have given them my word that they will be safe here as long as they abide by my rules."

I gestured to the gate. "Your sign says that you have cameras monitoring this entrance twenty-four hours a day."

"That's correct."

"So you know when Adam left here on a Thursday night two weeks ago?"

For the first time, the big man seemed to falter in his confidence. "I do, but I am not going to tell you."

"He was last seen driving a pickup truck, but no vehicles are registered in his name. You wouldn't know whose that was?"

"As I have explained, I was Langstrom's employer, not his keeper. My men are free to come and go as they please so long as they abide by the orders of their probation and the agreement they signed with me."

"May I see that agreement?'

"You may not." Foss removed his fedora and whacked it against his thigh to remove the snow from the brim. "Please express my sympathies to Langstrom's mother. Tell her that I will welcome her son back if he chooses to return, but it is unlikely the state will give him that option now."

"Is that piece of trash Dudson still hiding in there?" Mink shouted.

Foss let out another of his thunderous laughs. I had the sense that he didn't take my passenger seriously. Nor did he extend his exagerratedly formal courtesy to him.

Mink surged forward. "You've got a funny sense of right and wrong, buddy!"

"Good night, Warden," Foss said, returning to his truck.

I couldn't really be mad at Mink for his outburst. Foss was obviously well practiced at resisting inquiries about his operation and about the ex-cons he sheltered. As I had feared, I had come all this way only to run into a steel gate.

16

The farmhouse at the base of the hill was still dark. The HOME FOR SALE sign in the snowbound yard had taken on added poignancy now that I understood the circumstances. No wonder the poor owner can't unload his house, I thought. Living down the road from a bunch of sex offenders was not unlike living beside a toxic-waste dump.

Mink and I had almost reached Moose Alley again when we saw headlights headed in our direction. The road here was narrow, especially given the snowbanks, with no place to pull aside to let another driver pass.

I stopped.

The driver of the oncoming vehicle stopped. He turned on his high beams.

With our headlights focused on each other, neither of us could see the other one.

Mink pressed his chest to the dash. "What's this mook's problem?"

For me to back up would have meant negotiating a hundred yards of turns—in reverse—into the woods. The driver of the other vehicle had only to scoot back fifty feet to the highway. But he didn't budge.

I drummed my fingers on the wheel. The height of the headlamps told me we were facing a truck, but I had no clue what kind. All I knew was that the driver was a jerk. The way the day had gone already, I shouldn't have been surprised to find myself engaged in a meaningless Mexican standoff.

"Honk your horn," said Mink.

"I'm not going to honk my horn." I unfastened my seat belt and made ready to get out to confront the unseen person behind the wheel. "Don't pull any shit this time, or you'll be walking home."

"We'll both be walking if this mook doesn't back up."

Half-blinded by the glare, I saw movement as the driver's door opened. The silhouette of a man appeared, clinging close to his vehicle. He moved toward us. I had a flashback to that damn video again, one cop after another being gunned down as they made what should have been a routine traffic stop.

I leaned across Mink's lap and got another big whiff of his cologne as I opened the glove compartment. The Walther pistol was hidden under a stack of auto-service receipts. I checked to make sure there was a round in the chamber.

"What do you need that for?" Mink asked.

"It's my Binky."

"Some Binky!"

The man stepped into the headlights finally, giving me the look I had been waiting for. He had brown hair that needed cutting and a stubble beard that needed shaving. He wore a ripped long underwear shirt beneath a black snowmobile suit unzipped nearly to his navel. His mouth was thin and drawn as taut as a garrote.

"Oh shit," said Mink.

"Why? Who is he? Do you know him?"

The driver advanced toward my door. I tucked the gun between my legs, keeping my right hand tightened around the textured grip, my finger close to the trigger. With my left hand, I rolled down my window.

The man leaned his body weight against my side mirror and stared at me.

"Hey, I know this vehicle." He seemed to have a speech impediment: a difficulty hearing or a problem fully manipulating his tongue. "This is a '76 Scout, right? Nice ride. I saw you up on the mountain this afternoon."

He was the young man Elderoy had been speaking with, I realized. The man with the hounds.

"Who's that with you?" he asked, peering past me. "Is that Mink?"

"Hey, Logan," said my passenger in a tone that went out of its way to cover up the fear he seemed to be feeling.

The driver, Logan, said to me, "Can you back up, so I can get by?"

Technically, it was a question, but it felt more like a demand. He seemed to have the drained complexion and sunken eyes of an insomniac, although it might have been a trick of the light.

"I could," I said. "But it would be easier if you did it. The highway's just right there behind your truck."

Without glancing back, he said, "Yeah, it is. You been up at Foss's just now?"

"That's right," I said.

I couldn't see hearing aids in his ears, but there was definitely something off about his voice that made him hard to understand.

"One of the perverts get loose or something?" he asked.

"Or something." I kept my handgun between my thighs. "I take it you live in the house for sale back there."

"You want to buy it? Make me an offer. I'm willing to let it go cheap."

"Your name's Logan?"

"That's right. Logan Dyer."

"You work over at Widowmaker with Elderoy?" I said.

The snow melted almost immediately when it touched his head. "He's my boss. I shovel snow. He said you're a game warden. Is this Twenty Questions we're playing?"

Suddenly, a loud, unearthly noise started up inside his truck—the baying of hounds.

"Yikes!" said Mink.

"I noticed your dogs at Widowmaker before," I said. "They're beautiful. What breed are they?"

"Plott hounds." He kept his eyes locked on mine, but I had a prickly feeling he had noticed I was hiding my gun hand. "You ever heard of those before?"

"No."

"They're from down south, bred for wild boars. I use them for bobcats and coyotes mainly. Sometimes bears." He swung his head around to his idling truck and baying hounds. "Shut the fuck up!"

The dogs went instantly quiet.

"You want to show me your hunting license, Logan?" I asked in a soft voice.

"I'll show you mine if you show me yours."

Carefully, I removed my badge from my parka pocket with my left hand and held it out, making sure not to lose the grip on my gun.

"I know who you are," he said. "You're the big hero. I saw you in the news. You were getting medals."

I had been honored by the Warden Service a couple of years earlier for apprehending the man who had ended Kathy Frost's career. I received the Meritorious Service Award for conduct above and beyond the call of duty at a danger to my own life, and, to the surprise of nearly everyone in the room, Warden of the Year honors. I had gone from zero to hero in the span of a single awards banquet.

"What's it like to get a medal?" he asked. "You got it on you now?"

I ignored the question and held out my left hand. "Now, how about showing me your license?"

Dyer looked me over without haste, as if he was taking his time making an important decision. Eventually, he produced a folded piece of paper. His hunting license said his name was Logan Dyer and that he was twenty-eight years old. I would have guessed thirty-eight, but hard living can age a man well past his actual years. He had purchased special permits to hunt every big-game species in Maine in every manner possible.

I was aware of how Mink seemed to be trying to make himself as small as possible in the seat beside me.

"Are we cool?" he asked, taking the paper back.

"There's just one more thing," I said. "You said you work at Widowmaker?"

His tongue seemed to flail around words. "You saw me working there, didn't you?"

"And you live in that house back there?"

"I already said I did."

I reached into my shirt pocket for the picture of Adam. "Does this guy look familiar at all?"

While Dyer examined the photograph, I watched his eyes, but there wasn't the faintest flicker of recognition.

"Who is he?" he asked. "What did he do?"

"Do you remember seeing him driving in or out of here? He might have been in a pickup."

He scratched his ear. "What kind of pickup?"

"I don't know."

"Sorry." He stretched out his arm, holding the picture clamped between two fingers. For an instant, I thought he might be planning to drop it as a joke. But he didn't. "Who is he?"

"No one important," I said. "How about moving your truck for me, Mr. Dyer?"

"Right. Sorry." Dyer waved at my passenger with just his fingers. "Toodle-loo, Mink. See you on the trails."

He stepped back away from my door slowly with his hands slightly raised, as if he feared to turn his back on me. I lost sight of him in the glare of his headlights again but heard the door slam. Then the truck went roaring backward.

"So I take it you know that guy?" I asked Mink.

"I know him."

"Not the friendliest person."

"No."

I barely tapped the gas until we had reached the intersection of Moose Alley. My headlights lit up the side of Dyer's vehicle. It was an old Toyota Tacoma, more rust and Bondo than steel. The windows were all fogged up, as if two teenagers were going at it inside. But I knew the condensation came from the panting dogs.

"Which way?" I asked Mink.

"Left."

I pressed the pedal and fishtailed all over the slick road before the tires caught. I watched the lights of Dyer's truck grow smaller and smaller in my rearview mirror. Only then did I realize that I still had my hand clenched around the Walther.

"Are you going to tell me how you know Dyer?" I asked Mink.

"He's just another asshat. Nothing special. He works over on the mountain, shoveling snow."

"Does he have difficulty hearing? He seemed to have a speech impediment."

"I heard he's missing part of his tongue."

"What?"

"Had some sort of seizure as a kid and bit part of it off. That's what I heard. Lots of people think he's stupid because of the way he talks. He's not stupid."

"Are you afraid of him?" I asked.

The question seemed to offend the small man. "If I was afraid of asshats like him, I'd never leave my freaking house."

From his flattened nose, I should have guessed that Mink had been in his share of scraps.

"Can I see the picture?" he asked suddenly.

"What picture?"

"The one you showed Dyer."

He brought the photograph very close to his myopic eyes. "This is that Adam guy, yeah? He kind of looks like you."

"Ever see him around Bigelow? Maybe at the Snow Bowl?"

"I think I'd remember him."

"Why?"

"Because he looks like trouble I'd want to avoid."

Based on the past couple of days, I couldn't argue with him on that point. What I was having trouble understanding was how Logan Dyer could work at Widowmaker and claim not to recognize Adam Langstrom: the most notorious student ever in the history of ASA.

Mink directed me another mile down the road and then told me to take a right into the woods. We passed a farm on one side and then a farm on the other side. The wind blew the snow from the white fields onto the road. It was banked in the shapes of waves, like a flash-frozen sea. We were in the flat bottomland of the Dead River, although we still hadn't crossed the river.

"You walk all the way into town from here?" I asked.

"It's good exercise."

"Don't you have a vehicle?"

"Cars are too much aggravation."

The sky had gotten completely dark, but the falling snowflakes reflected the beams of my headlights, and it felt as though we were traveling through a shimmering tunnel of ice. Finally, we reentered the forest again. We crossed a rickety bridge that should have broken beneath the weight of the state plow truck. The windows of a few more farmhouses glowed as we climbed yet another hill.

A line of snowmobiles crossed the road in the distance, their headlights flashing one after the other. I knew that one of the state's major sledding trails passed along the base of East Kennebago Mountain. We were nearing its northeastern slopes.

"Can you see the lights of the resort from here?" I asked.

"Wrong side of the mountain. This is my stop up here."

A steep, unplowed driveway branched off from the farm road through a Christmas-card forest. The driving might have been hazardous, but the scenery was undeniably beautiful. I brought the Scout to a halt and pulled the emergency brake while Mink straightened his fur hat.

"Welcome to East Bumfuck," he said. "Population: me."

"Are you going to be OK hiking in there?" I asked.

"Christ! You sound like my freaking mother."

He hopped out, slammed the door, and began trudging up into the dark woods without so much as a thank you. Mink was a piece of work, but the strange little man could clearly take of himself. The cloying smell of his cologne lingered inside the truck. I drove back out of the woods with the window down.

17

Even in good weather, the drive home would have taken me a solid three hours. But with roads like greased glass, and probably worse in the pass through the mountains, my estimated time of arrival would be well past midnight. Should I make the attempt or try to find a motel room between the mountain and Rangeley? I wondered.

My body voted for sleep.

Unfortunately for my body, my phone buzzed when I reached the bottom of the hill. I hadn't noticed the lack of a cell signal when I had been higher up the mountainside, near Mink's cabin. I grabbed the phone, hoping to see Stacey's number on the screen, but it was Pulsifer, of all people.

"Don't start with me," I said, foreseeing what he would say.

"I had to hear you were stabbed from DeFord? I thought we were amigos, Mike. What else have you been hiding from me?" His voice sounded ragged, as if he was outdoors, trying to speak above blowing wind.

"I am not kidding, Gary. I'm too tired for one of our usual conversations."

"Which are what, exactly?"

"Your giving me endless grief."

His response was to cackle. "If you don't want to hear my exciting news, then just say so."

I pulled the Scout over and put the transmission into park. "What is your exciting news?"

"I was out on my sled today," he said. "Snodeo is coming up this weekend, and I wanted to get a head start on the inevitable drunks."

No matter how hard I tried, I was unable to keep Pulsifer from spinning his yarns at his usual spider's pace.

"Please don't tease this out. I really am beat."

"Two hours ago, I got a call. It was a Rangeley cop I know. He was over in Dallas Plantation and wanted me to come look at something."

It was a township located between Kennebago and Rangeley, with no population to speak of. The summit of Widowmaker stared down at the unpeopled patch of forest at the foot of Saddleback Mountain.

"What was a Rangeley cop doing in Dallas Plantation?" I asked.

"He just happened to be closest to the scene."

"The scene of what?"

Pulsifer must have realized he was reaching the limit of my patience. "A couple of cross-country skiers from Saddleback found an abandoned truck this afternoon parked near the Navy Road. That's not unusual. People abandon a lot of old beaters in the woods. It just so happened that these skiers were the curious type. They decided to poke around. The windows were all smashed. Again, nothing unusual there. What was unusual was the blood all over the inside seats."

My heart tightened like a fist. "How much blood?"

"Enough for them to call the Rangeley PD. My buddy Steve drove out there to see for himself, and of course the truck had no plates. So he got on the horn with Dispatch and called in the VIN. Guess who the vehicle was registered to?"

I was afraid to say the name. "Adam Langstrom."

"Close! Amber Langstrom."

"Shit."

"It gets worse. Steve and Amber used to be friends—if you know what I mean. He called me up and asked me what he should do, and I said, 'Call the sheriff. Have them send a detective. But whatever you do, don't tell Amber.'"

"But it was too late. He already had."

Pulsifer reacted as if I had stepped on the punch line of one of his jokes. "How did you know that?"

"I'll explain in a minute. Where's the truck now?"

"In a clearing off the Navy Road, but it's about to be towed back to Farmington. Jim Clegg is here from the sheriff's department and he is going to have his forensics guy go through it from A to Z in the morning."

Amber had neglected to tell me that the truck her missing son was driving was registered in her name. Had he been using it with her permission, or had he taken it without asking? Either way, Amber's abrupt departure from work that afternoon suddenly made sense. What else had she neglected to tell me?

"I need specific directions."

"Mike, it's in Dallas Plantation."

"And I'm just down the road in Kennebago."

"What the fuck?" Now he was the one who sounded as if he'd been sucker punched.

"Just tell me how to get there, and I'll explain everything when I see you. And don't let them move the truck before I arrive."

I drove at an unsafe speed down Moose Alley, past the turnoff to Widowmaker, until I crossed the line into Dallas Plantation.

On my GPS, the Navy Road showed as a thin brown line that curved up from the Dead River valley into the high peaks between Saddleback and Sugarloaf. I looked for a sign telling me where to turn, but the road, like so many in this area, seemed to be unmarked. Even so, I had no trouble finding the turnoff. Multiple tire treads showed that there had recently been heavy traffic into and out of the snowy woods.

The location of the abandoned truck only added to the mystery.

To the extent that Dallas Plantation was known for anything, it was known for its semisecret navy base. On maps, the facility appeared under the acronym SERE. The letters stood for survival, evasion, resistance, and escape. SERE school was a camp where the military trained U.S. Navy and Marine Corps pilots in what to do if they were shot down behind enemy lines.

A cloud of folklore surrounded the mountain base. Some conspiracy theorists claimed that the military trained black-ops contractors on the grounds; they said the instructors waterboarded pilots to train them how to resist torture. Defenders of SERE said those accounts were slanders cooked up to discredit the navy.

All I knew was that the road I was traveling ended at a gate guarded by men with automatic weapons. And for some unknown reason, Adam Langstrom's bloody pickup had been left in the forest outside the perimeter.

I followed the main branch of the road a mile, past cutoffs to Redington Ridge and Saddleback Lake, until I could go no farther because there was a heavy military vehicle blocking the way. As I came to a stop, a man in a camouflage uniform and black gaiters and boots stepped forward to meet me.

"You're going to have to turn around," he said, coming around to my window. He wore a black watch cap and fingerless green gloves. "The road is closed."

I produced my wallet and badge. "I'm a game warden. Gary Pulsifer called me."

He motioned me forward. "Drive through, Warden."

Glancing through the trees ahead, I saw an eerie glow, as if the haze itself had been electrified. As I drew near, I saw that the strange illumination was coming from a construction light mounted to a trailer. Its bright halide lamps were all focused on a blue Ford pickup with a smashed window. I did a quick scan of the scene and spotted a second Humvee, a sheriff's police cruiser, and a flatbed tow truck.

Thankfully, I saw no sign of Amber.

Pulsifer was standing beside his bright yellow snowmobile, speaking with an older man in a brown uniform. When he saw my Scout drive up, he paused and shook his head in a theatrical show of vexation. His vulpine features seemed more pronounced in the weird light. His nose and chin seemed extra pointed.

"That was fast," he said.

"I told you I was in the neighborhood."

Pulsifer was wearing his black-and-gray snowmobile suit. He had set his helmet on the seat of his sled. "I have a few questions about that, but they can wait." He waved his hand at the older cop he had been speaking with. "Mike, do you know Jim Clegg? He's a detective with the sheriff's department. Jim, this is the infamous Mike Bowditch."

I pressed my teeth together behind my smile. *Infamous* was not how I wished to be known.

The detective had chalk white hair and a red roll of fat under his chin. We exchanged greetings and handshakes.

"What's the story?" I asked.

"You know most of it already," said Pulsifer. "The truck's registered in Amber's name."

"She bought it last month in Farmington at a private sale," said Clegg, who seemed to have a runny nose. "Paid two grand for it."

She had been overcharged. The truck was a battered Ford Ranger, manufactured well before the millennium and poorly maintained in the intervening years, to judge from the missing bumper, rust spots, and assorted dents and scratches.

"It was her get-out-of-jail gift for Adam," said Pulsifer.

"She told you that?" I asked.

"She told Steve. I mentioned that they were old acquaintances."

I was aware of people moving in the shadows outside of the glare of the construction light. "Where is she now?" I asked.

Clegg's double chin grew a little redder with frustration. "After I had a chance to interview her, I asked officer Haines to escort her home."

There was a warrant out for Amber Langstrom's son, and some lovesick cop had violated every rule in the book by inviting her to the scene of what might well have been the young man's murder.

"Tell me about the blood."

"Splatter on the dash and the seat," said the detective. "Consistent with a gunshot wound to the head, but not necessarily."

"But there's no body?" I said.

Pulsifer dug his hands into his pockets and rocked back and forth on his heels. "The navy brought down one of their dog teams to do a sweep around the lot. But they haven't found anything."

"What about the glass?" I asked.

"What about it?"

"Is there any glass on the ground, under the snow? If not, it means the windows were broken someplace else and then the truck was moved here."

"Get a load of Sherlock Junior!" Pulsifer almost sounded proud of me.

"Can I have a look?" I asked.

Clegg shrugged. "We've been waiting for you to arrive before covering the vehicle, so now would be the time."

"I explained to Jim that Amber had come to you for help," said Pulsifer. "I suggested you might have some useful information that was worth waiting for."

"I'd like to hear more about your involvement with Ms. Langstrom later," said Clegg.

"*Involvement* is the wrong word."

"I hope you're not going to tell me you're screwing her, too," said the detective.

"No!"

"So what is the story with you two?" said Pulsifer. He hadn't forgotten how elusive I had been with him.

The cold skin of my face stung as blood rushed into it. "It might take some time to explain."

"Can it wait for morning?" asked Clegg.

"I think so."

"Good, because I've been standing in the snow for two hours already, and I'd like to wrap up what we can here and go get some sleep."

Clegg meant that literally. The pickup would be covered tightly in plastic to protect it against the elements while it was hauled to the department's garage. Pulsifer had done me a real favor in postponing that process until I arrived.

I made my way into the cold circle of light around the Ranger. The right side of the dashboard and the passenger seat had a dull maroon tint. Some of the blood had been smeared toward the passenger door, as if something—a body—had been pushed out. The right window had been almost entirely shattered; all that remained was a jagged fringe of spiderwebbed glass around the edges.

I circled around to the other side of the truck. There was no visible broken glass.

Clegg appeared at my shoulder. "Satisfied?"

"I thought it was the driver's window that was broken."

"No, this one was just rolled down," he said. "It's the other one that was smashed."

I made my way around to the back of the truck. Snow had piled up in the bed, but it was thicker along the sides and near the cab, as if the pickup had been carrying something big recently. I glanced around the lot, gauging the heights of the snowbanks along the perimeter.

"I think there was a sled in the back of this truck," I said.

"A snowmobile?" said Pulsifer.

"Look at the shape."

In the winter, I would often go on patrol with a snowmobile in the back of my Sierra. When the banks got high enough, all you had to do was back up to one, throw open the tailgate, and drive your sled out. No need for a ramp.

Unfortunately, half a foot of snow had fallen that afternoon. Whatever snowmobile tracks might have been visible earlier had become soft, unreadable grooves.

I gazed around the clearing. "I expected to see Shaylene Hawken here."

"Are you kidding?" said Pulsifer. "If Langstrom's dead, it means less work for her."

Standing beside the construction light were two men, one in camouflage utilities, the other in civilian clothes. The man in civvies seemed totally focused on me. I was shocked to realize that I knew him.

"Is that Torgerson?"

"How do you know Lane?"

"I met him this afternoon at Widowmaker along with a couple of his drinking buddies. What the hell is he doing here?"

"So you met the Night Watchmen," said Pulsifer with a toothy grin. "Someone from the school must have called him. Torgerson used to be a SERE instructor. He moved back to Rangeley after he retired from the navy."

No wonder the old guy was such a badass; he'd worked at a survival school, teaching pilots how to resist abuse by abusing them.

Amber's truck had been abandoned at a trailhead just outside an off-limits navy base. The proximity to the SERE school might have been coincidental or it might have been significant. The same could be said about Torgerson's presence at the scene. The so-called Night Watchmen had a legitimate connection to the base. He and his friends had also voiced contempt for the local ex-cons whose names were on the sex offender registry.

"I'm going to go talk to him," I told Pulsifer. "I want to know what he's doing here."

"Do I actually have to tell you what a bad idea that is?"

Torgerson watched me approach with the same welcoming expression with which he might have greeted a door-to-door salesman.

"Chief Torgerson," I said. "I didn't think I'd be seeing you again so soon."

You might have thought he was totally deaf.

"This must have been the call you got at the Sluiceway," I said. "Someone from SERE wanted you to know Adam Langstrom's truck had been found."

The SEAL beside him said, "Do you know this guy Torgy?"

Torgerson's eyes bored into mine. "I know exactly who he is."

Without uttering another syllable, Torgerson turned his back on me. He dug his fists into the pockets of his peacoat as he tromped away through the snow toward a cluster of parked vehicles. The SEAL remained behind for a few seconds, his eyebrows knit together, his mouth twisted in confusion. After a while, he also left the halo of the construction lights for the darkness of the trees.

Torgerson was an expert at manipulation and intimidation. I had to hand it to him. He'd left me feeling as naked as if I'd just stepped out of the shower. And he'd done it without making a single explicit threat.

Pulsifer had been standing five paces behind me the whole time. His snowmobile helmet hung from his hand. "You and I need to talk about a few things."

"I know."

Car doors slammed around us. Engines roared to life. The tow truck driver went to work wrapping the bloody pickup for its trip to the forensics garage in Farmington.

Pulsifer bounced the helmet against his thigh. "You got a room somewhere for the night?"

"No."

"You can stay at my place, then."

The exposed skin of my face had taken on a cold, rubbery texture. "I don't want to impose."

"Lauren won't mind. I've told her so many stories about the shit you've pulled, she doesn't believe you're real. It'll be like I'm bringing home Bugs Bunny."

Typical Pulsifer: trying to cheer me up by comparing me to a cartoon character. The humor left me untouched.

Two days earlier, I had learned that I had a brother I had never met.

Two days later, I had come to the place where he might well have died.

The thought was having a hard time taking hold in my head.

"I have a stop to make first," I said. "There's someone I need to see."

18

At the intersection of the Navy Road and Route 16, I waited for the next plow to come along and followed it back toward Bigelow. I was exhausted but in no hurry, and I needed time to collect my thoughts.

Driving in a Maine blizzard is a matter of timing. Get ahead of a plow, and you'll find yourself blazing a path through unbroken snow, unable to see the edge of the road, oblivious to whatever ice might be hidden underneath. Get behind a plow, and you'll find the going easier, provided you're content to crawl along at twenty miles per hour and have your vehicle splashed with salt brine and sand.

It sure looked like someone had died in Adam's truck. You could have butchered a deer inside and spilled less blood. I saw two possibilities: Either a corpse had been taken away from the site for reasons unknown or it had been dumped somewhere before the vehicle was abandoned at the trailhead.

Up ahead, Widowmaker's sign glowed at the base of its access road. The light touched the snowflakes drifting past, making them look like a cloud of winter moths. The mountain itself was invisible in the hazy grayness. There wasn't even a glow in the sky from whatever trails might be open for night skiing.

A new question intruded into my thoughts: Why dump the truck at that particular trailhead?

Maine's western mountains were crisscrossed with logging roads and ATV trails; pockmarked with old gravel pits and remote clearcuts. Anyone looking to conceal a vehicle beneath a blanket of snow had thousands of potential hiding places to choose from. The decision to park the Ranger just outside the heavily guarded SERE school had to have been deliberate. Maybe someone had *wanted* Amber's blood-soaked truck to be discovered quickly. But why?

Once again, I passed the farm road that led across the frozen river and up the backside of East Kennebago Mountain to Mink's house. What a strange little man. I would have to ask Pulsifer what his story was.

Soon the plow turned west toward Eustis, and I turned east into Bigelow. I followed Pulsifer's directions south of town. Amber lived in an unnamed apartment complex built in the backwoods style you see in Maine. It was as if the builder had visited some suburban cul-de-sac in Massachusetts or Ohio and come back to the North Woods and tried to reproduce the architecture in the least appropriate setting imaginable. There seemed to be a dozen or so units, scattered over three identical buildings. I spotted Amber's Grand Cherokee—covered by only the thinnest scrim of snow, which told me she hadn't been home long—and pulled in behind it.

Light leaked around the edges of the curtains in the living room. I heard sorrowful music playing on a stereo inside. Amber hadn't bothered to shovel the walk leading to the front door when she'd gotten home. I kicked my way through the snow.

I didn't hear the bell chime over the music, but after a minute or so, the door opened a crack, and I got a faceful of marijuana smoke. Amber stared up at me with eyes like cherry tomatoes. She was still wearing her waitress outfit, but her hair looked as if she'd been caught in a sudden tempest.

"Can I come in?" I asked.

"Are you gonna bust me for the pot?"

"What pot?" I deadpanned.

But her mind had been dulled by whatever drugs she had taken.

"I'm not going to bust you," I said. "But you need to put it out."

She stood aside. I stomped as much snow as I could off my boot treads and stepped through the door. The apartment was neat enough. All the furniture matched, but it had seen better days. She seemed to have a taste for silk flowers, posters of exotic locales, and framed photographs of herself with male skiers, whom I guessed to be visiting Olympians. The only sign of neglect was the profusion of ash burns in the wall-to-wall carpet. No amount of cleaning would get those out.

I remained standing on the doormat while she flung herself down on a futon sofa. "Have a seat."

"Do you want me to take my boots off?"

She laughed through her nose.

"I've just come from where your truck was found," I said. "Why didn't you call me when you heard what happened?"

"I wasn't thinking straight." The marijuana had slowed her usually rapid-fire way of speaking down to half speed. "Can you fucking blame me?"

On the stereo, Reba McEntire was singing about a woman who got AIDS from a one-night stand.

"Can you turn down the music?" I asked.

She tossed the remote control at me. I pushed the off button.

"You don't have to keep standing there," she said. "I really don't give a shit about the rug."

Meltwater had formed around my boots. I tried to shake some of it off before I crossed the carpet to an armchair.

"I didn't know where you'd gone," I said. "All the bartender told me was that you'd gotten a phone call and run off."

She let her head loll in my direction. "Steve—he's a cop I know—he called me when he found Adam's truck. It's funny, you know? I rushed all the way out there, but when I got there, all I could do was wait. Wait to give a statement. 'Yeah, Officer, that's my truck.' Wait for the dogs to search the area. Wait for the CSI people to show up. Now I get to wait to hear if the blood they found matches my son's."

I had no idea if the police had Adam's DNA on file; it isn't always the case with prisoners, despite what many people think. The investigators would only be able to cross-reference the blood type in Adam's medical records. A true DNA test would likely take weeks, unless Clegg pushed to expedite. I had no idea where Adam Langstrom ranked on his to-do list.

"You weren't honest with me, Amber," I said. "You never told me you'd bought Adam a truck. Don't you think that was information I could have used to look for him?"

"I guess." She picked at a full ashtray on the table beside her until she found a roach with something left in it. She pinched the stub to her mouth and flicked the lighter.

"No more pot," I said.

"You're such a fucking Boy Scout, aren't you? Colby graduate. Game warden. The perfect son."

Hardly, I thought.

She sighed and lit a cigarette instead. "Or maybe you're just a tight-assed prick."

"Tell me about the truck."

"I knew he'd need a vehicle when he got out," she said, "so I paid cash for it over in Farmington. I drained my checking account to buy it. After he disappeared, I didn't want the cops to know he was driving it. I didn't want them to put out an APB—or wherever you call it—on the license plate. I was hoping you would find him or he would turn himself in and not have to go back to prison."

"I thought you'd want to hear what Josh Davidson told me," I said.

"What's the point?" she said. "It doesn't matter anymore."

"It might matter." I massaged my kneecaps. "Josh told me he loaned Adam some money the night he disappeared."

She leaned her head back and exhaled a cloud at the ceiling tiles. "So?"

"What did he need the money for?"

"I don't know."

"Think hard."

"I'm tired of thinking." Her eyes had a sheen that looked more like oil than water. "That's all I've been doing since I got home—thinking how Adam's life was cursed on account of me. It wasn't his fault I fell for Jack, or that A.J. could never look at him without picturing what I'd done. I was kind of relieved when A.J. finally ran off with that whore from New Hampshire. It seemed like a good omen. Then Adam got into ASA, and for a while it seemed like his luck—our luck—might have been turning around. He was winning ski races. Getting OK grades. Why'd he have to meet that cunt Alexa Davidson?"

Smoke had begun to slither toward me across the room. "I know you're grieving, but—"

"Adam was raped in prison," she said, lapsing back into monotone. "He told me about it one day when I went to visit. Just broke down into tears and called me 'Mommy' and whispered what they'd done to him. One of them bit off part of his ear! He'd been trying to act so tough before, like he could take care of himself. I'd been trying to tell myself not to worry, and then all my worries came true. He begged me not to say anything to the guards, said it would be even worse if I did. I remember coming out of the prison, and it was seventy degrees and bright sunshine, and I realized it was the worst day of my life. Until today."

Suddenly, she let out a curse as the cigarette burned her finger. Reflexively, she dropped the butt to the carpet, where it continued to smolder. She watched it, unmoving, uncaring, until the ember died.

"I would have done anything for my son," she said. "And I mean *anything*. I would've let every HIV-positive scumbag in that prison gangbang me if it meant they left Adam alone. I would have traded places with him in a second."

I wasn't sure what to say. "It must have been hard for you."

"Not as hard as when he got out," she said. "I thought it was going to be a second chance for him—for us. But Adam had already given up. 'You know what the worst thing is, Mom?' he said. 'The worse thing is they'll never stop punishing me. Any other crime—I could've run over a kid or stabbed someone in a bar—and eventually they'd say, "All right, you've paid your debt to society, go live your life." But they're never going to let me pay my debt,' he said. 'Every time I ask a girl out now, she's going to Google my name. "Once a sex offender, always a sex offender." And all I did was have sex with my girlfriend.'"

Amber reached for her lighter again and her pack of Capri cigarettes.

"Did you end up going out to Don Foss's place?" she asked, seemingly out of nowhere.

"I did."

"That self-righteous asshole. I don't trust him, and neither did

Adam. What kind of person takes in sex offenders like stray puppies, then works them for slave wages? There's something weird about that man. Holier-than-thou, my ass."

The tobacco fumes swirling around the room had begun to make me light-headed.

"Maybe Foss really does believe in redemption," I said.

"Adam hated living there. Said it made him feel even worse about himself, sleeping in the same bunkhouse with *actual* perverts. There was one guy who had done twenty years for raping a toddler. And another guy who used to be a wrestling coach. He'd molested dozens of boys. You know what Adam said to me? He said, 'Mom, someone should take a match to this place and burn it to the ground.'"

I remembered what Davdison had told me about Adam's having a black eye.

"Did Adam mention anyone in particular to you?" I asked. "Anyone he was afraid of at Foss's?"

"He said prison burned the fear out of him. It was true, I think. How can you be afraid if you don't care if you live or die?"

"Maybe *fear* is the wrong word, then. Did he have any enemies?"

When she laughed, she opened her mouth wide, revealing her missing molar. "My son didn't have anything *but* enemies!" She leaned her head back to study the smoke-stained ceiling. "What does it matter? It's too late anyway."

"We don't know that."

"It's too late," she repeated. "Adam is dead. I'm his mother, and we've got a special connection. As soon as I heard the news tonight about the truck, I felt the knife go through my heart. He's dead, and I'm done."

I wanted to shake her. "Amber, you asked me to help you find Adam, and that's what I'm still trying to do. I'm not giving up hope yet, and you shouldn't, either."

"What do you care?"

"I care because he's my brother." I rose to my feet and stood over her limp body. "If you're telling the truth."

She measured me with her eyes, all the way from head to toe. Then she stubbed out the cigarette and climbed awkwardly to her feet. "Do you want to see his room? Come on, I'll show it to you."

19

I had to sell my old condo to pay for Adam's lawyer," she said, leading me down a darkened hall. "That's how I ended up in this dump."

She opened a door at the end and turned on a light inside.

The room obviously belonged to a teenage boy with two absolute passions: deer hunting and ski racing. The bed was covered with a camouflage-patterned comforter, which matched the drapes. Three mounted deer heads stared down from the wall, their real eyes having been replaced with obsidian marbles. A dozen ski medals hung from the antlers. Ski posters covered every other inch of the walls.

"I thought he was going to stay here," she said, letting her arms fall slack. "I fixed it up just like his old one. Then the neighbors heard he was coming and complained to the landlord, and that was that."

"Do you mind if I look around?" I suspected she would be receiving a similar request from Detective Clegg very soon.

"Knock yourself out."

On the bureau I found two framed photographs. One showed a younger Adam and Amber with a man I assumed to be A. J. Langstrom. It must have been taken after one of the little boy's first ski victories, because he was holding a gold medal. A.J. was big and blond and blocky and looked nothing like Adam. Nor was he smiling.

The second, newer photo showed a dozen celebrating skiers posed atop a mountain in various stages of undress. Adam was in the forefront, shirtless, his abdominal muscles bulging, his strong arms raised triumphantly above his head, holding two bottles of beer. Two girls lay in the snow at his feet in their sports bras, arms curled around his ski boots, posing like harem slaves. Josh Davidson hung in the back. He had kept his shirt on and was staring at something beyond the camera's range, as if he had caught sight of a potential threat: an adult headed their way to break up the party.

"I'm surprised he kept this picture," I said, handing the photograph to Amber.

"Why?"

"Because it has Josh in it."

"Josh is in most of the photos Adam has from school. I told you they were best friends."

"What about Alexa?" I asked.

Her mouth twisted. "What about her?"

"Did Adam keep any pictures of her?"

"Of course not!" she said. "That bitch ruined our lives."

But I noticed that her eyes had darted toward a stack of magazines beside the bed.

I made my way along the wall of deer mounts, pretending to inspect them. Each had a more impressive rack than the next. Pulsifer had told me Adam was a natural-born deer slayer.

Just like my father.

Just like *our* father, I thought, correcting myself.

Maybe it was having seen the gore-drenched truck, but something had changed for me over the past twenty-four hours. My absolute certainty that Adam Langstrom couldn't be my half brother had steadily eroded until it had become a real possibility. Now it seemed closer to a likelihood. I was almost, but not fully, convinced. What else did I need to find before I could accept Amber's claim as the truth?

When I got to the stack of magazines, I knelt down and shuffled through them. Under the ski mags, I found a *Sports Illustrated* swimsuit issue that was four years old. Convicted sex offenders in Maine are prohibited from possessing pornography. Did bikini shots qualify? There was something sad and touching about the thought of Amber saving this magazine for her son's return.

I found the yearbook at the bottom of the pile. The cover was blue and silver, the colors of the Alpine Sports Academy. One page was dog-eared. I turned to it and came upon Adam Langstrom's senior portrait. He had never looked more handsome than he did in his blazer and tie, with his thick hair expertly cut and his eyes as blue as sea glass. Other pictures of him—racing downhill through the gates, laughing in a pool with friends—surrounded the posed photograph. The quote beneath his list of athletic accomplishments read: "Waking up is the second hardest thing in the morning."

My brother, the philosopher.

Amber had begun to cry. "That yearbook came out a week before he was arrested. His missed his final exams, so no diploma. I told him he should get his GED in jail, but he didn't see the point."

I paged through the yearbook until I found the section devoted to the underclassmen. Alexa Davidson was with the other freshmen. She resembled her brother—same wavy hair, big eyes, and an olive complexion. Her teeth were perfect. Her lips were very full; if she had been an adult, they would be described as sensuous. But you could see she was just a kid here.

"I still can't believe he threw everything away for that," Amber said with venom.

"She was pretty," I said, as if speaking of someone dead.

"His other girlfriends were prettier."

I found another picture in the yearbook of Alexa and her brother at a race. They were wearing helmets, dressed in skintight ski suits, and had their arms around each other's shoulders. She was beaming. He looked seasick. I flipped back to Josh's senior page and found his portrait. Unlike all the others, it had been taken in black and white, giving it a somber, old-fashioned look that might have been intended to be ironic. His quote: "Victory is an illusion of philosophers and fools." It was a strange sentiment coming from a student about to graduate from a school devoted to competitive athletics.

"Do you know where Josh lives?" I asked.

She sniffed and rubbed her eyes. "Why? You just talked to him."

"I might have more questions for him down the line."

"He has a house over in Rangeley, on the lake. Adam told me his dad bought it for him. That family is loaded."

Maybe I had been too quick to believe Josh Davidson. I had only his word about having met Adam outside the bowling alley that night.

The glass eyes of the deer kept catching my gaze the way the eyes of a portrait seem to follow you around a room.

"Whatever happened to Adam's guns?" I asked.

"His guns?"

"Gary Pulsifer told me Adam was a serious hunter. He shot all these bucks, didn't he? What happened to his rifles?"

She cleared her scratchy throat. "Adam's not allowed to own firearms. He's a felon."

"I know. I'm just wondering where they went. Did you sell them for him?"

"Yeah."

"What kind of rifles were they? How much did you get for them?"

Her hands flew up into the air. "Who cares? Why does it matter? You saw the inside of that truck."

"Amber, the detective is going to want to know if Adam had access to a firearm."

"That fucking Pulsifer," she said with a bitterness that shocked me. "I could tell you stories about Gary back in the day. You wouldn't believe some of the stories I could tell you."

She'd recognized how curious I was about the guns and was trying to divert my attention.

"Where are the guns, Amber?"

"I told you he doesn't—"

"I'm trying to help you both. Please let me help you."

Her shoulders sagged. "Adam's past help. I know he is."

"Maybe, but you're not."

Without a word, she turned and left the room. I switched off the light and followed her into her own bedroom. She had a fish tank that projected aqueous light on the ceiling and filled the space with the sound of bubbles. But I didn't see any actual living fish behind the glass.

She went down on her hands and knees beside the bed. She pulled out a long plastic box, the kind a person might use to store sweaters for the summer. Inside were two rifles: a scoped, bolt-action Ruger and a lever-action Winchester identical to the one I'd used to shoot my own first deer.

"Adam gave these to me," she said, sitting up again. "They're mine, and no one can prove otherwise."

I knelt down beside her and inspected the bin. The rifles had recently been cleaned. I could smell the bore solvent and lubricating oil. There were boxes of rifle cartridges in .30-06 and .30-30 calibers. Also a smaller box that had once contained 9mm rounds. But when I shook it, I could tell it was empty.

I held the box in my hand. "Where's the pistol?"

"What pistol?"

"The one that fires these rounds."

She drew her lips back from her teeth in an unsuccessful attempt to appear affronted. "A friend of mine left those in my Jeep. We went target shooting once behind the Sugarloaf snowmaking ponds."

"Why would you keep an empty box of ammo?"

She leaned past me and snapped the plastic lid back down on the bin.

My legs were stiff from driving all day as I rose to my feet. "Does Adam have a key to your apartment?"

"What? No. I told you he's not allowed to be here."

"But he has been here. He came here, and he cleaned his guns, and he took a pistol that was also stashed inside that bin. Don't deny it, Amber. I don't know why you keep lying to me. I don't know if you just can't help yourself or if you're keeping a secret you don't want anyone else to know."

She stretched out her legs on the floor and leaned against the bed for support. "I told you he has enemies."

"Who? You've got to give me a name, Amber."

"I told him not to take that gun," she said. "I told him he'd be sent back to jail if he was caught with it. But he wouldn't listen. He said he needed it for protection. He said he'd rather risk being arrested again than get shot in the back of the head. He wouldn't tell me who was after him."

"Do you know what kind of handgun it was—the make or model?"

"Why?"

"The police are going to need all the information they can get. If a gun turns up before—" I stopped myself from saying "before his body is found."

But she knew what I meant. "A Glock. I think that's what he called it. Or maybe that's from a movie. I don't know."

"Is there a box for it? Papers?"

"Not that I ever saw."

I extended my hand to her. "Get up."

She looked at my hand as if reluctant to touch it. Then, slowly, she stretched out her arm. I gripped her by the wrist and pulled gently until she was on her feet. She was wobbly but standing.

"I offered to help you find Adam if I could. But that was before they found the truck he was driving covered in blood." I put my hands on her shoulders and stared into her eyes. "Tomorrow, we're going to have a conversation with Detective Clegg. You're going to tell him everything you've told me about the threats and the gun. You're not going to hold anything back."

She had a way of pouting that reminded me of a little girl. "I thought you were on our side."

"I am on your side. That's why I'm telling you to come clean. I don't know what happened to Adam, but it looks bad whatever it was. I am not going to lie for you, Amber. And I'm not going to withhold information."

"But he's your brother!"

"It doesn't matter," I said. "I swore an oath to uphold the laws of the state of Maine. I'm not going to break my oath."

"You never had a problem breaking it when Jack was in trouble."

"I told you the night we met," I said, "I'm not that person anymore."

She shoved me in the chest. She wasn't particularly strong, but she caught me off balance. "Get out!"

"Amber—"

"Get the fuck out of my house!"

There was nothing left to say. She followed me to the living room. She yanked open the door, letting in a blast of cold air that passed through me as if I were a ghost.

"I thought you were different," she said. "But you're just like all the other assholes."

"You should get some sleep," I said.

"I thought you were a good person. I thought you were loyal. But you're just as much of a heartless bastard as Jack was. What kind of asshole son doesn't even claim his dead father's ashes?"

I had no answer.

20

Gary Pulsifer lived on a hardscrabble farm outside the little town of Flagstaff, in the shadow of the Bigelow Range.

Back in the 1940s, Flagstaff had been the epicenter of a political fight between the Central Maine Power Company, which had wanted to build a dam at Long Falls to generate electricity downstream in Moscow, and conservationists, who had opposed flooding most of the valley. The dam would have meant the demise of Flagstaff and the neighboring village of Dead River, the residents would have been displaced through eminent domain, and both communities would have vanished beneath the rising waters of Maine's newest lake.

But in the end, the opponents had managed to mobilize a public outcry, and the project was abandoned. In recent years, the developers had quietly returned. They had revoked the leases of dozens of camp owners on Flagstaff Pond, including my friends the Stevenses, and clear-cut massive tracts of timberland. They had pushed forward schemes to build wind farms atop the scenic mountains. Such is life in remote, unpeopled places. Every victory is inevitably short-lived.

I knew I had found Pulsifer's farm when I saw his patrol truck in the dooryard. The blowing snow had pushed a drift clear over the hood and halfway up the windshield. I parked beside his pickup in the lee of the wind.

Someone must have seen me coming. The front door opened and two curly-haired little dogs came bounding out at me through the snow, yipping and yapping.

"Don't mind them!" a woman called through the open door.

They were English cockers. Pulsifer had told me they were the best upland hunting dogs in the world—also the most headstrong and mischievous. It sounded like the perfect breed for him. I leaned down to pet the spaniels, but they sprang away with tails wagging, as if inviting me to give chase back into the house.

Lauren Pulsifer stood in the doorway, surrounded by a light that made her look like a movie angel. She had short blond hair, wide-set gray eyes, and a figure that suggested she had borne multiple children. I remembered Pulsifer saying that she used to be a teacher until the demands of the family and the farm had forced her to quit. She still did some substituting for extra cash, he'd said.

She stepped aside to let me into the mudroom. "Thank you for putting me up," I said.

Her eyes told me I should remove my boots.

"Gary's taking a shower." She hung my wet coat from a deer-foot rack on the wall. I hadn't met a game warden yet whose house wasn't a showcase of taxidermy. "Here, let me show you where you'll be sleeping."

The house had a pleasantly earthy smell, a combination of apples, wood smoke, dried flowers, and wet dogs. Children's finger paintings hung on the walls.

"How many kids do you have?" I asked out of politeness, already knowing the answer.

"Four. But Glen is away at college, and Jodi is staying at a friend's in Kingfield. You'll meet the others in the morning. We don't need an alarm clock in this house. Those kids are up before the rooster."

She showed me into a first-floor guest room with an ancient brass bed, an obviously homemade quilt, and a requisite deer-head mount to watch over me while I slept. She directed me to the nearest bathroom, then said to join her in the kitchen after I'd had a chance to clean myself up.

After she'd closed the door, I threw my duffel on the floor and sat down on the bed, feeling the weight of the day settle on my shoulders. Stacey had been right about Adam. Now that it seemed he had been murdered and that we would never meet, I found myself feeling a sadness that approached physical pain.

I missed Stacey so much and was so mad at myself for having lied to her. I checked my phone and found nothing—no voice mails, e-mails, or texts—from her. I considered calling but dreaded the prospect of her hanging up on me again.

Coward that I was, I sent her a text message instead.

> I can't begin to tell you how sorry I am. I am such an idiot. Please forgive me.

> I'm spending the night at Pulsifer's house in Flagstaff. Long story. I hope your cold is better. The room is cold here and the bed is small. I miss you, Stace.

> I love you,
> Mike

There was a knock at the door.

"Come in," I said.

Pulsifer poked his head in. His hair was still damp from the shower. "I've got coffee brewing."

The spaniels surged past his legs suddenly and leaped onto the bed beside me.

I scratched both under their ears. "So what are these guys' names?"

"Flotsam and Jetsam," he said. "Don't blame me. The kids named them. Come on, I want to hear about your day." He held up a finger, as if remembering something important, and stepped into the room. He closed the door and lowered his voice. "One word of warning: Lauren really hates Amber Langstrom. It goes back to when we were kids. Anyway, if she starts acting weird, I wanted you to know why."

I remembered the unopened pint of bourbon in my coat pocket. Should I offer it as a gift for putting me up? On my way to the kitchen I stuck the bottle in my back pocket.

Lauren was frying pork belly and onions to make baked beans. The smell was intoxicating. The Pulsifers had an enormous wood-fired cooking stove that radiated so much heat, she had been forced to crack one of the windows.

Pulsifer removed two mugs from a cabinet and set them on the table.

"I don't know if my stomach can take any more coffee," I said.

"Do you want me to make you some decaf?" asked Lauren.

"Decaf?" said Pulsifer with a shocked expression. "What in the world is decaf? It sounds like an abomination."

The dogs plopped down, one on each of my feet. I removed the pint of Beam from my back pocket and set it on the table. "I brought you this."

Lauren set down her wooden spoon and smiled at me with her teeth together. "We don't keep alcohol in the house."

I thought I remembered drinking beer with Pulsifer some years back after one of our qualification days at the Maine Criminal Justice Academy. Maybe he'd given up the sauce. I felt my cheeks flush with embarrassment.

"I'm sorry," I said, returning the pint bottle to my pocket.

"How about cider?" Gary said. "It's from our own orchard."

"That sounds great."

"Maybe I'll have some, too."

Pulsifer filled my mug with apple cider and sat down at the table. There was a wooden bowl filled with dusty-looking apples between us. He took one out and began to shine it against his pant leg. "Before you tell me what you've been up to all day," he said, "I have another question. How is she doing?"

Amber, he meant. "Pretty much what you'd expect. She's convinced Adam's dead."

"That makes two of us, then."

"I found out one interesting thing. She was hiding guns for him, including a Glock Nine, which he's been carrying around ever since he got home."

Lauren began pouring beans into a cast-iron pot. "Of course she hid guns for him."

"Honey," said Pulsifer.

"That woman is the most dishonest person I've ever met. Remember how she was in high school?"

"That woman just lost her son," said Pulsifer.

"Her son, the rapist. And why are you, of all people, defending her?"

So Gary and Amber had some history? Why was I surprised? The big question was, How long ago had they been involved—before or after his marriage?

Lauren's face flashed orange from the fire as she slid the pot of beans inside the wood stove. "If you ask me," she said, "both of them are finally getting what they deserve. God knows, it's taken long enough."

"Lauren!" Pulsifer seemed genuinely surprised by his wife's lack of compassion.

"I had Adam in my third-grade class," she said. "I always knew he was going to end up in jail. That kid is a bad seed."

I looked down at my hands.

"Lauren, that's enough," said her husband.

"She's always felt superior to me because she used to date you," she said. "Like I was pathetic for marrying one of her rejects."

Pulsifer stood up from his chair. The apple rolled hard off the table and both sleeping dogs sprang to their feet. "I said that's enough!"

They glared at each other for a long time—long enough for me to become aware of my heart beating faster—and then she went down on one knee and retrieved the fallen apple with her thumb. She examined the bruised spot, then she tossed the damaged fruit into the trash can.

"Mommy?" The voice was faint, coming from the top of the nearest stairs.

"Wonderful," Lauren said to her husband. "I should make you put her back to bed."

"Fine."

"No, you stay here with your warden friend."

After she'd left the kitchen, Pulsifer tilted back in his chair, holding on to the table with both hands to keep from toppling over. "I told you she was touchy."

"So you and Amber, huh?"

"You ever wish you had amnesia?"

"I used to."

The familiar foxlike smile of his made a reappearance. "I bet you did. You kept me pretty busy when you were a rookie. Every time you got called up on some new charge, I'd think, This is it. Bowditch has finally gone too far. He's done this time. And yet somehow you kept managing to dodge the bullets."

"I didn't dodge that knife," I said.

"Something saved you," he said. "Those vests aren't stabproof."

"So I have recently learned. I must have turned in time or something. The whole thing was a freak occurrence." I took a sip from the mug. "This cider is good."

"It's my own secret brew. You want a mix of sweet, bitter, and sharp apples for good cider." He seemed to cock an ear to the stairs. "Let me see that bottle of Beam."

I felt reluctant to hand it to him. Lauren definitely would not have approved.

Pulsifer unscrewed the top and splashed some bourbon in both of our mugs. "Here's to Amber."

The bourbon gave the cider a kick and an added sweetness. But I found that I had no real interest in getting drunk. And I was thinking I might have done something wrong in tempting Pulsifer.

"I appreciate your putting me up for the night," I said.

"I didn't want your ghost haunting me if you decided to sleep in your Scout."

"Do you mind if I ask a personal question? What made you sign up to be the union rep? It just seems like a shitload of aggravation."

"You want the truth?" He shook his head in mock sorrow. "I thought it would put me in good with everybody. Instead, the reverse happened. The thing about being the union rep is that you end up learning people's worst secrets. Drinking problems, domestic issues, gambling, drugs—you name it. Some guys are grateful to me for helping them out of a jam, but others resent me because of what I know about their personal failings."

"I'm grateful. You saved my ass more than once."

"The people you should be grateful to are Frost and Malcomb. How is Kathy doing anyway? I was sad to hear she'd retired. That woman was the original badass bitch."

"I think she's feeling a little lost," I said. "She hasn't figured out what comes next."

"Join the club."

"You thinking of retiring, Pulsifer? I thought you were serving a life sentence."

"Lauren wants me out. She's tired of my being gone all the time, leaving her with the kids and the animals. And the union stuff is burning me out. I'm tired of hearing everyone's sins. I never signed up to be the father confessor for the Warden Service. All right. You've stalled long enough. Why don't you tell me what happened today."

He poured himself a fresh cup of cider and added a bigger splash of bourbon. When he offered the same to me, I shook him off.

"You sure you want to hear all the gory details?" I said.

"No, but tell me anyway."

It took me half an hour to tell the story. Lauren didn't return to the kitchen, but sometimes I thought I heard a creaking at the top of the stairs, as if she might be standing at the banister listening.

I left out only one important detail, and that was about Adam's being my half brother. Pulsifer was an experienced investigator, and I could tell that he suspected I was deliberately concealing something. Hell, I would have been suspicious, listening to myself. How had Amber Langstrom managed to convince me to assist her in finding her fugitive son? After I had worked so hard to rehabilitate my career, why would I risk it for a total stranger? Something didn't add up. I could see it in his eyes.

"Amber certainly can be persuasive," he said.

The dogs were snoring at my feet. "I would call her persistent instead of persuasive."

"You wouldn't be the first man she bewitched."

But I refused to bite on any of the baited hooks he was throwing me. "She appealed to my sense of chivalry."

"So what's your theory?" he asked. I could hear the alcohol in his voice now.

"My theory?"

"What do you think happened to Langstrom? Don't tell me you don't have any ideas."

"I'd say that Adam was afraid of someone—someone specific. Amber said he had nothing but enemies, and I met a bunch of them today. Maybe it was someone who held a grudge against him from the rape."

"Davidson?"

I pictured the delicate doe-eyed skier. "I doubt it, but who knows?"

"It seems more likely another sex offender from Pariahville," Pulsifer said.

"What?"

"That's just my nickname for the place."

"It's possible. It didn't sound like Adam and Foss got along particularly well. But I keep thinking it was someone from outside. For instance, those guys who call themselves the Night Watchmen. At first, I thought they were just a bunch of old boozehounds. But there was something definitely creepy about them—how closely they were paying attention to me. It was as if they didn't want me asking around about Adam."

Pulsifer seemed to find the idea hilarious. "You think the popcorn posse is a group of vigilantes?"

"Torgerson seems like a tough old bastard. And the fact that he showed up at the scene—"

"Torgerson was there because he's a retired SEAL. A bloody truck is found outside the school. Of course someone is going to call him. Don't tell me you're one of those conspiracy theorists who think SERE is some sort of black-ops base."

The bourbon had brought out Pulsifer's mocking side, and I wasn't thrilled by its reemergence.

"I'm not a conspiracy theorist," I said. "What about the guy who lives down the road from Foss's?"

"Logan Dyer?"

"He's having trouble selling his house because no one wants to live near Pariahville. And I got a weird vibe off him when he looked at Mink."

"Mink!" The name made Pulsifer smile wide enough that I could see his canine teeth. "I should have realized you would've found a way to hook up with Nathan Minkowski in your travels."

"So what's his story?"

"No, no, no. We're not done with you and Adam. What were you saying about Logan Dyer?"

"Just that he seemed like bad news."

"I wouldn't bark up that tree if I were you. The poor guy has had a rough life. First his mom and sister died in a car crash. Then his dad causes a fatal chairlift accident."

I couldn't believe I was only now making the connection. "Logan is Scott Dyer's son?"

"How did you know Scott?"

"Elderoy told me about him. He said Scott Dyer warned the Widowmaker owners that the lift was unsafe. And then, after it happened, they used him as a scapegoat to shift the blame off their business."

"That's Elderoy's version," said Pulsifer. "Most of the people I know blamed Scott for negligence. The mountain had been doing fine before the crash. Then the accident happened and the whole economy went to crap."

I could easily imagine what life had been like for Logan Dyer; I also had a father who was widely considered a villain.

Pulsifer seemed to be reading my thoughts. "I never told you this, but I hated your old man. The way he used to rub my nose in shit around here. And then, after he shot Shipman and Brodeur, and everyone was hunting for him, I remember praying, 'Please, let me be the one who finds that son of a bitch.' And I didn't even believe in God back then."

My mouth had gone dry listening to him. I took a swig of cider but was repulsed by the taste of alcohol.

While Pulsifer had been talking, a film had formed on his eyes, as if we were drifting backward into the past. Now that the room had fallen silent (but for the crackling fire in the stove), he seemed to return to the present. He blinked several times to clear his vision.

"All I'm saying is that your father was a bad guy, too, and you turned out OK," he said.

"That seems to be a matter in dispute."

"Logan's not the brightest bulb," Pulsifer said defensively. "Look, the poor guy works as a snow shoveler. That's the lowest man on the totem pole over at Widowmaker. And sure, he's a little rough around the edges. He's the kind of person Lauren calls a 'sheep in wolf's clothing.'" He seemed suddenly disgusted with me. "I would think you, of all people, would understand his situation."

"Which is what?"

"You've both spent your lives trying to prove you're not like your fathers."

And with that he tossed another birch log into the stove and said good night. I remained seated at the table a while longer. Pulsifer had drunk nearly all of the bourbon. I poured the rest out and took the empty bottle back to my room so his wife wouldn't find it in the morning.

21

When I went into the bathroom to brush my teeth, I was surprised to find that the mirror over the sink had been shattered. Cracks spread out in a spiderweb pattern from one smashed spot. I didn't want to jump to conclusions, but it appeared someone might have driven a fist into the glass.

Accidents happen, I told myself. Especially in a house full of rowdy children.

I spit into the bowl and rinsed my mouth under the tap. The Pulsifers' well water tasted faintly of sulfur.

After having sat for an hour in the heat of the kitchen, the guest room felt frigid. I touched the radiator and found it cold. I crawled fully dressed under the covers. The quilt was too thin, the blanket inadequate. When I exhaled, I could see my breath dissipate on the drafts moving about the half-dark room.

I hadn't felt so alone in a long time. I reached for my phone on the nightstand, not expecting to find a note from Stacey. But when I tapped the screen, there was a text message:

> I'm sick as a dog. Sinuses packed with snot. My ears felt like they were going to explode on the chopper ride. But I'm going up again tomorrow, even if it kills me.
>
> I am having trouble forgiving you.
>
> S.

It was something at least: a reason not to give up hope. Tomorrow I would reach out to her again. I would make amends.

I had just fallen asleep when the door nosed open and the two spaniels, Flotsam and Jetsam, came bounding onto the bed. I got up to let them out, but they refused to budge. I crawled back under the covers.

It had been a long time since I had slept with dogs. My mother had been allergic, and so I had grown up with a series of cats, each more neurotic than the next. Nearly every warden I knew owned at least one dog, usually a hunting breed. Labrador retrievers were popular, as were Brittanies and English springer spaniels. Some of the wardens assigned to the K-9 search-and-rescue teams had German shepherds or Belgian Malinois.

Why didn't I own a dog? The reasoning I used, when anyone asked, was that I moved around too much. I lived alone, and my hours were erratic, and I couldn't put myself in a position to have to hurry home from a stakeout to feed a pet. But these same excuses applied to other single wardens, and most of them had canine companions. What was I waiting for?

When I closed my eyes again, I pictured that wolf dog, Shadow, caged in a pen at the animal shelter. His intelligent yellow eyes seemed fixed on me with the predatory intensity you associate with large carnivores. Had the test results come back, proving his wild bloodline? Was his fate now sealed? Joanie Swette had said that the shelter would make every effort to place him with a licensed caregiver, or even arrange transport to some distant sanctuary, and yet I had heard the lack of optimism in her voice.

I scratched the nerve bundle at the base of the cockers' spines and listened to the contented thumping of their tails.

No bed with a dog in it is ever cold or lonely.

The staccato pounding of children's feet on the stairs woke me. It was still dark. The skin of my face had tightened from being exposed to the cold air. And the dogs had disappeared from my side in the night.

I reached for my cell phone on the bedside table and saw that it was six o'clock. No new messages.

I shuffled into the bathroom and studied my fractured reflection in the mirror. I splashed some cold water on my eyes to remove the crust. I rubbed a wet hand towel under my arms and applied a fresh coat of antiperspirant. Then I brushed my teeth.

The kitchen was so raucous, I had trouble picking out individual voices as I made my way down the hall.

Lauren Pulsifer stood at the woodstove, pouring pancake batter on a greased griddle. Her hair was wet, but she was fully dressed and ready for the day, as were the two small children seated at the table. The room felt as hot as a sauna.

"Good morning! I hope the kids didn't wake you."

"This is when I get up anyway."

"Kids, this is Warden Bowditch. He works with Daddy. Mike, this is Jacob and this is Isabella."

The boy looked to be about seven. The girl might have been four. They both had their father's fox-colored hair. They grunted hellos and returned to their project of getting maple syrup all over their faces.

"Gary's out feeding the animals," she said. "Would you like some coffee?"

"Thank you."

She seemed in better spirits than she had the night before. I had expected her to be angry with me for smuggling booze into the house, where it was obviously not welcome.

The windows had begun to fill with an indigo light as the sun crept closer to the eastern horizon. Lauren put a plate of pancakes in front of me. "The syrup's from our sugar house. We try to grow what we eat here. It's a lot of work, but Gary says it helps him with his recovery."

Pulsifer had never told me he attended Alcoholics Anonymous. If he had, I definitely wouldn't have offered him bourbon. Even worse, I realized, Lauren's cheerful manner meant that she didn't know Gary had gotten drunk the night before. Somehow he had managed to hide it from her. I felt assailed by guilt—for tempting Pulsifer into breaking his pledge, and for my silent complicity in concealing his slip from his wife.

"Gary says you're dating one of the Stevens girls," she said.

"Stacey," I said.

Her eyes crinkled at the corners. "The pretty one."

It should have registered with me that Lauren would have known Charley and Ora Stevens and their daughters. For years, the Stevenses had owned a camp just across Flagstaff Pond. And Charley and Gary must have worked plenty of cases together before my old mentor retired from the Warden Service.

Lauren hovered with a dishrag behind her children, watchful of messes. "How are Charley and Ora doing?" she asked. "We miss them so much here. So many good people left the area when Wendigo canceled their leases. That company is as close as you can come to pure evil. Gary says they bulldozed every decent deer yard between Eustis and the Kennebec River. Their plan is to take all the good wood and then develop the waterfront properties for real estate. Maybe sell it to some billionaire to create his own North Woods Kingdom. Don't you hate it when your predictions come true?"

"Only the bad ones," I said.

She had an unconvincing laugh. "I guess it's been a long time since I was an optimist."

"What's an optimist?" the boy, Jacob, asked.

"It's someone who thinks good thoughts," Lauren said.

I ate quietly while Lauren did her mother thing, and we all waited for Gary. The kids seemed well behaved—loud as most kids, but well behaved. Eventually, she cleared them out of the kitchen with instructions to finish getting ready for school. Almost anyplace else, twenty inches of fresh snow would have meant canceled classes, but not in Maine, where natives consider anything less than four feet to be a dusting.

She removed my empty plate and poured coffee for the both of us. Then she sat down heavily across from me. It was as if she hadn't wanted her children to see how bone-tired she was.

"The older I get, the more I seem to hate change," she said. "Don't you find that's true? Even when it's good change, like with Gary. I have a hard time trusting things will be better in the future. I keep waiting for the sky to fall."

I thought of that empty bottle of bourbon in my duffel. "Stacey says I'm the same way."

She gave me another of her wrinkly smiles. "I remember her when she was a little girl. What a tomboy! And just as fearless as her dad."

"She still is," I said.

"They're such a wonderful family. Charley helped Gary out of so many scrapes. He could have let my husband self-destruct." She caught herself, as if she had suddenly remembered I was a relative stranger in her house. "You're easy to talk to, Mike. You have a comfortable way about you. And those blue eyes don't hurt, either. They must be your secret weapon with women."

"I wish that were true."

"I'm sure people must tell you that you have your father's eyes," she said. "I knew him, of course. Everyone around here did. And Gary was obsessed with him because he was so blatant about all the deer and moose he was poaching. He used to come home so, so angry. I know it was one reason he drank. Gary's sponsor says alcoholics drink because they have a spiritual disease. But I blame your father for a lot of the bad times we had. I am sorry, but that's just how I feel."

A door opened down the hall and a gust of cold air rushed into the kitchen before the door shut again and the finger paintings stopped flapping on the walls. Flotsam and Jetsam barreled into the room, their coats matted with snow, their nails clicking on the floorboards. I heard Pulsifer stomping his boots.

Lauren flushed, as if with embarrassment, and stood up from the table, as if she feared being caught with me in a compromising position. Living on an isolated farm in the woods, cooped up with four kids and a husband with a history of alcohol abuse, she probably had no one to talk to about her own problems. We both knew that she had confided far more than she had intended in me.

"Charley Stevens used to be the district warden here before he became a warden pilot," she began, as if in the middle of a conversation. "I remember when I was in elementary school he came to talk to my class and brought a three-legged raccoon with him on a leash. They probably wouldn't allow that now."

"I highly doubt it," I said.

"Highly doubt what?" Pulsifer was wearing his winter uniform: black parka and snowmobile pants.

"We were just talking about some of Charley Stevens's escapades," Lauren said.

"Those could fill a book." Pulsifer filled a glass of water from the sink and drank it down in one gulp, then did it all over again. "You used to be able to get away with a lot more in the old days." His voice sounded parched. "There was one state cop—I won't say who—who had three women he used to visit while their husbands were at work at the same mill. All three husbands worked different shifts, so there was always one open bed."

"That's not funny, Gary," Lauren said.

He hadn't yet made eye contact with me. "When I started, no one ever knew where I was or what I was doing. As long as I kept my picture out of the paper and wrote my quota of tickets, the colonel didn't care."

"It's a brand-new day," I said.

"And a cold one, too," said Lauren. "Thermometer read five below this morning, and the wind's out of the northwest. It must be one of those Alberta clippers the weathermen always go on about."

I hadn't yet decided what I was going to do. On my way south, I could stop at the Franklin County Sheriff's Department and see how the examination of Adam's truck was coming along. Maybe I'd run into Clegg there, and I could tell him about the handgun the missing felon had taken from his mother's apartment.

"I should probably get on the road," I told my hosts.

Pulsifer put an apple in his pocket for later. "I'll show you around the farm before you go."

"I just need to grab my duffel."

The dogs followed me into the chilly guest room and then decided it was too cold for them, leaving me alone to strip the bed. I piled the sheets, blanket, and quilt at the bottom of the bed and sat down on the bare mattress.

I suspected that Pulsifer's "tour of the farm" would be an excuse to talk about the previous evening. I dreaded the conversation on all sorts of levels. Would he be contrite, or would he make excuses? Did he blame me for leading him into temptation, or had he decided I was going to be his secret new drinking buddy?

I braced myself for the possibilities and started for the door.

Pulsifer was waiting for me in the mudroom with a displeased expression that confirmed my forebodings.

"What's going on?" I asked.

"I just got off the phone with Jim Clegg."

"Did they find any new evidence in the truck?"

"Too soon for that. Clegg and Shaylene Hawken are headed out to Pariahville this morning. In light of recent events, they want to have a chat with Foss and his flock of deviants. Clegg also reminded me that he still has a shitload of questions for you. I made the mistake of saying you were here. My head's a little fuzzy this morning."

"Should I follow you?"

"We'll take my truck. You and I need to talk."

22

In the mountains, in the winter, dawn comes late and dusk comes early. The sun hadn't yet made its way above the Bigelow Range, but the sky had turned the color of rose gold: a promise of light and warmth to come.

Pulsifer didn't speak as we brushed the snow off the hood and windows of his patrol truck with our gloved hands. When we were finished, I pried open the passenger door of my Scout. I unlocked the glove compartment, removed my Walther .380, and tucked the weapon inside the waistband of my jeans. An image of Carrie Michaud wielding a knife flashed through my mind. I dropped a couple of extra magazines in my pockets.

Pulsifer was behind the wheel with the engine running by the time I returned. He had turned up the police radio, as if to forestall our inevitable conversation. I had no intention of being the first to speak.

The plows had done expert work clearing the road into Bigelow, not that the locals were ever slowed down by a little snow. Just about everyone in the mountains seemed to own a four-wheel-drive vehicle. Those who didn't soon discovered how long the wait could be for AAA to come and pull you out of a ditch.

"I want to show you something," Pulsifer said suddenly.

I had expected he meant that he wanted to take me somewhere nearby.

Instead, he reached into his pocket and removed what looked like a foreign coin. He held it flat on his palm for me to look at. It seemed to be made out of bronze and was stamped with a triangle with the Roman numeral III at the center. There was a different word on each side of the triangle—Unity, Service, and Recovery—and around the perimeter there was a motto: To Thine Own Self Be True.

"Three years, four months, and twenty-seven days sober," he said. "Before last night."

"I'm sorry."

"Don't apologize. You're not to blame. It's all on me."

From the tone of his voice, it certainly sounded like he was blaming me.

"Gary, I had no idea."

"That's why they call it Alcoholics Anonymous. Oh, well." He pushed the window button on the door so that it went all the way down. Then he threw the coin out onto the icy road. "Just a piece of metal."

I wasn't sure what response would be appropriate under the circumstances.

Eventually, we emerged from beneath the shadow of Bigelow Mountain. We passed a snow-covered field edged by white birches and red pines, in the center of which stood the burned-out remains of a mobile home. I almost exclaimed aloud for Pulsifer to stop but managed to catch myself in time.

My vagabond family had lived in that trailer briefly when I was a child, before my father lost whatever job he'd had at the time. He'd come in half-drunk or mouthed off to the boss or slugged some coworker whose face he didn't like. Maybe all three. Suffice it to say, Jack Bowditch had never been the employee of the month at any place he'd ever worked. It was no wonder I had grown up in those early years eating day-old bread from the food pantry and venison burgers from deer my dad has secretly shot out of season.

I hadn't noticed the torched building on my drive in, but now I found myself overwhelmed by nostalgia. Most of my memories of my early childhood were bittersweet at best, chilling at worst. But what I was feeling now, I realized, was sadness and loss. Someone had burned down my old house.

Pulsifer didn't notice that I'd bolted upright in my seat. He was probably thinking about what he was going to tell his AA sponsor.

As we turned onto Moose Alley, he leaned over the wheel, peering at the road ahead. "What's going on up there?"

Four or five vehicles were parked in a line along one side of Route 16. A group of men and women were gathered together atop the snowbank. They were all bundled up against the cold and staring through binoculars at a dead tree.

"Birders," I said.

Pulsifer hit his blues and swung in behind the last car. He jumped out of the truck before I could ask him what he was doing.

"Folks, you can't park here!" I heard him say.

A man in a hat with earflaps said excitedly, "We're looking at a Great Gray Owl."

I squinted up at the snag and saw an enormous bird, as big as an eagle, perched on the twisted topmost branch. Its feathers were the same color as the bark of the leafless spruce. It was the first Great Gray I had ever seen. I reached for the binoculars on Pulsifer's dash to get a better look at the massive owl.

"I don't care what you're looking at," said Pulsifer. "You can't be blocking the road."

"You don't understand," the man in the hat said. "This is an extremely rare bird."

"We're not blocking the road," someone else said.

"People can still get by."

Pulsifer stood with his hands on his hips. "You need to move, folks. It's not open for discussion."

The birders mumbled at one another. Steam from their open mouths created a single cloud among them in the early-morning air. For their sake, I hoped they wouldn't put up a fight, but they must have agreed that discretion was the better part of valor when dealing with a pissed-off law-enforcement officer. One by one, the Priuses and Outbacks pulled away from the snowbank and started off toward Rangeley.

Pulsifer remained standing like a statue until the last one had driven off. I don't think he so much as glanced at the owl.

"Some people don't have a fucking clue," he said as he climbed back inside in the truck.

"Great Gray Owls are pretty rare sightings," I said. "They don't usually show up in Maine. I'm sure this one was reported on some bird Listserv. Birders are going to be coming from all over to see it."

"As if I don't have enough to do but play meter maid to a bunch of bird-watchers." He sneered in the direction of the dead tree. "I'm tempted to scare that bird off."

I was torn between keeping quiet and speaking my piece. Being me, I inevitably chose the latter. "It's not exactly rush hour out here. You didn't have to be such a hard-ass."

"Don't tell me how to do my job, Mike. I'm not the one with the folder full of reprimands."

I stared straight ahead. "Fine."

"I thought I was doing you a favor bringing you along. But if you don't appreciate it—"

I put on my sunglasses because I didn't want him to see the annoyance in my eyes.

When it became obvious that I wasn't going to continue the argument, he put the transmission back into drive and we lurched forward again. We went a full mile before he remembered to turn off his pursuit lights.

Now that the sun had risen above the mountaintops, the world had become too bright to look at. The new snow, piled high along the roadsides and clinging like cotton to every tree, didn't just reflect the light; it intensified it a hundredfold. Soon Pulsifer was also reaching for his shades.

We didn't speak again until we had turned off Route 16 onto the camp road that led up to Foss's gate. Tire marks in the snow indicated that the detective—I assumed it must be the detective—had arrived ahead of us.

Smoke from Logan Dyer's chimney was visible even before we saw his house. It drifted straight up above the treetops, a perfect tight spiral. As we approached his property, I could smell and taste the wood burning in the stove.

Dyer must have parked his truck inside the garage, but there was a Ford Explorer in the driveway. The SUV was the Interceptor model, issued exclusively to law enforcement and other first responders, but it was painted in the same black and silver tones as the Widowmaker company vehicles I had seen on the mountain. It was equipped with pursuit lights, too.

"Do you know who that is?" I asked.

"Widowmaker security."

"Russo?"

"Maybe," Pulsifer said. "The mountain has a half dozen guys who work security. A couple of them are deputized by the sheriff in case shit breaks out requiring a real police presence. Don't tell me you met Rob Russo, too?"

"What's he doing there?"

"I don't know. Having breakfast?"

"Ease up, Pulsifer."

"Maybe Clegg asked someone from Widowmaker to talk to Logan about what he's seen recently. The guy does have a bird's-eye view of the only road in and out of Pariahville."

The newly fallen snow gave the house and yard a cheerier aspect, although it couldn't help the flaking clapboards, and the dark, wet shingles showed how much heat was escaping through the underinsulated attic.

"Poor Logan," said Pulsifer. "He's never going to find a sucker willing to buy his house. I told you he's even unluckier than you."

As we passed by, Dyer's hounds began to bay inside: a loud and mournful noise that was nearly a kind of howl. The Plotts must have heard our vehicle with their supersensitive ears. If nothing else, they were effective watchdogs.

The road up the hill was slick, but the studs in Pulsifer's tires bit through the surface ice. When we got to the steel gate, we found it standing open. Two sets of tire tracks led in, but none led out.

"Have you ever been up in here before?" I asked.

"Not since before Foss started running his home for wayward creeps."

We were driving now through a majestic stand of old-growth pines. Very often the old lumber camps were surrounded by groves of massive trees like these. The loggers kept the big evergreens standing for scenery around their bunkhouses and kitchens, while they cut the surrounding forest down to the nub.

"How does Foss even make money?" I asked.

"The man cuts a shitload of wood."

"How? I couldn't even find a phone number for him."

"He doesn't need to advertise his services. The big developers know how to get ahold of him. Foss always comes in as the low bidder when a developer needs land cleared to build ski condos or whatever. It's one of the advantages to having ex-con employees who can't get a job anywhere. He can pay them pennies on the dollar and then turn right around and get his money back charging them room and board."

"It sounds like a sweet deal if you don't mind treating your workers like plantation slaves."

"Maybe in his mind he's helping them," Pulsifer said.

"What do you think?"

He raised an eyebrow to tell me how stupid my question was. "I think the guy's a genius."

Snow was dropping in clumps from the evergreens where the sun was shining, but it clung tightly to the trees that remained in shadow.

After a few minutes, we came to the first building. It was a generator station in a clearing, with a big solar panel on the roof and wires leading off through the tree limbs. I could feel the vibration of the machine in my fillings.

The next structure was a trailer, no different from those used at construction sites, with a satellite dish mounted on the roof. Two state vehicles, a Franklin County Sheriff's Department cruiser and a late-model Chevy sedan with state-government plates, were parked out front. I recognized the former as the car Clegg had been driving the night before. I figured the latter must belong to Adam's probation officer.

Pulsifer unfastened his seat belt. "Have you ever met Shaylene Hawken?"

"Not in person, but we had a pleasant chat on the phone the other day."

"Isn't she a charmer?"

As I stepped out of the vehicle, I heard a fast-paced chittering overhead and saw a mixed flock of birds swoop and settle into the cone-laden branches of a pine. They were Red and White-winged

Crossbills. Those bird-watchers Pulsifer had chased out of the road would have paid money to get such a good look at those elusive winter finches.

Pulsifer took no notice. He made his way to the door and rapped on it three times.

No answer.

When he glanced back at me, I pointed to the snowy ground outside the door. There were boot prints all over, as you would expect, but three distinct sets of fresh tracks led farther down the road. I set off in that direction while Gary hurried to catch up.

Pulsifer didn't strike me as a poor woodsman, exactly. He just seemed to be wearing blinders all the time. He was so focused on the job at hand that he failed to notice disturbances in the landscape around him. The more time I spent with him in the field, the more I understood how my poacher father had managed to outwit him for so many years.

23

U p ahead was a complex of buildings: garages, a dining hall, a bunkhouse, and assorted sheds. The usual construction equipment, too: skidders, crew vans, pickups, a bulldozer, and a flatbed truck for hauling logs. In short, Pariahville resembled just about any other logging operation you might find in the forest.

Pulsifer and I approached the dining hall. A single voice was issuing from inside the building. Loud, resonant, and commanding—it belonged unmistakably to Don Foss. Pulsifer didn't bother knocking.

When he opened the door, the room went quiet. Nine or ten men seated at picnic tables turned to see who had let in the sudden blast of arctic air. Beyond them, on a raised stage at the end of the hall, stood Don Foss, flanked on either side by Jim Clegg and Shaylene Hawken.

Foss was wearing an outfit that Paul Bunyan himself might have bought off the rack, and in the same size, too. The big man turned to Clegg. "What's going on here? Who are these men?"

"The wardens are here at my request," said the detective.

Clegg had on his brown-and-khaki uniform and was holding his drill sergeant's hat at crotch level, as if to protect his privates from the imaginations of the assembled sex offenders.

Shaylene Hawken appeared strong enough to wrestle a moose calf to the ground. She had a hard red face that looked as if she scrubbed her skin with steel wool, and gray-brown hair that she had probably cut herself. She was dressed in civilian clothes appropriate for tromping around the woods but was wearing a ballistic vest with a badge pinned to the fabric. A semiautomatic pistol rested in a holster on her hip.

"Should we expect additional visitors?" asked Foss.

The men at the tables had contorted themselves to look at us. Most of them had faces that were young and bearded; they were the same age, more or less, as Adam. The older ones among them look prematurely aged by bad habits and more recent exposure to the elements. Almost without exception, they looked dead-tired.

"Please continue, Don," said the detective.

Foss's natural tone of voice seemed to be a bellow. "Detective Clegg and Officer Hawken will be speaking with each of you privately in the bunkhouse. I have their assurance your conversations will be confidential unless—" He turned and looked down again at the detective at his side. "I fail to see how this concerns the Warden Service."

"The wardens are assisting our department in the search for Langstrom," Clegg said patiently.

I counted ten men in all seated at the tables. So there had been eleven in the camp when Adam was here.

One pudgy, pink-cheeked guy raised his hand. "Why are we being interrogated if Langstrom was the one who skipped?"

"These are interviews, not interrogations," said Detective Clegg. "We're asking for your help."

"What kind of help?"

"Information—what do you think?" said Shaylene Hawken. She swayed from side to side, her hands clasped behind her.

"So we don't have to talk?" asked another man.

"Fuck yeah, we do," said a third. "You think they won't violate your ass back to Bucks Harbor if you don't say nothing?"

Foss raised his huge hands in a placating gesture. "The officers have given me their word this isn't a pretext to violate anyone's probation."

"Sure, they say that now, but what happens when you ain't there?" asked the suspicious one.

"I will be in the room for each interview," said Foss.

I heard one man at the nearest table whisper to another, "He just wants to hear everything we say."

Foss continued: "I've told the officers I'm prepared to end the interviews if there is any coercion."

"Are they going to search our lockers, too?" asked the pink one.

"We'd prefer not to have to do that, Dudson," said Hawken.

I could tell that the implied threat rubbed Foss the wrong way. "As all of you know, the officers have the right to inspect your belongings at any time. But given that the focus of these interviews is the whereabouts of Adam Langstrom, I see no need for a sweep of the bunkhouse. Isn't that right, Detective Clegg?"

"All we're asking is that you answer our questions truthfully—no bullshit, no evasion—and we'll be on our way."

"Yeah, right," said one of the men at the tables

"This is bullshit."

"You know someone's going out of here in handcuffs," whispered the quiet man near me. "They're just looking to violate one of us so we don't take off like Langstrom."

Beside me, Pulsifer had remained quiet, but I could sense the tension in his muscles, the same way you can sense when someone beside you in bed is still awake.

Hawken had reached the end of her already-limited patience. "Don't be shy, boys. Someone's got to be first."

The pudgy man, Dudson, stood up. He articulated his words carefully, striking every syllable. "I'll go first. Worst thing that can happen is they send me back to Bucks. At least my cell there was warm and didn't smell like farts all night."

"Hail, Fartacus!" one of the men said.

Foss opened and closed his hands, as if to keep the blood circulating through those sausage-size fingers. "Enough!"

It might have ended there if not for Hawken. "What's the matter, Dudson? You have a better job offer than cutting trees?"

Dudson flushed a shade brighter. "You think it's funny, but you're not working outside all day in the freezing cold, waiting for a tree to fall on you like it did on Lovejoy."

Who was Lovejoy?

"That's enough, Dudson," said Foss.

"Yessuh, massa!" said the sex offender.

"I said that's enough!" The floor shook as Foss stepped down off the dais and crossed the room to Dudson's table. He seized the soft-looking man by the arm and pulled him away from the table.

"Ouch! Ouch!"

Each of the other sex offenders in the room had frozen in place, as if playing a game of statues.

Foss looked like he could have flung Dudson into the next room if he had chosen to. The man was seriously angry. "The rest of you, remain here," he boomed. "You'll be called when it's your turn to be interviewed. You have my permission to step outside briefly if you need to smoke. But don't force me to go chasing you."

There could be no doubt: The men who worked for Foss were terrified of him.

Foss dragged Dudson into an adjoining room. Clegg and Hawken followed close behind. The door swung shut.

I could hear the sound of breath being exhaled.

"What are we supposed to do?" I whispered to Pulsifer. "I thought we were going to be part of the interviews."

"Hang out for a minute while I go see what's up."

Pulsifer disappeared through the far door. The men began to whisper among themselves and cast furtive glances in my direction. I had dealt with enough felons to know that most of them had no fear of law-enforcement officers, but these ex-cons were as timid as jackals. That Dudson character might be defiant, but the rest were frightened of doing anything that might result in their probation being revoked.

And why shouldn't they be frightened? As long as he had Shaylene Hawken backing him up, Foss could work these men into the ground and risk no fines from the government, because who among them was going to report that their work conditions were unsafe or they weren't being paid a minimum wage? As long as POs like Hawken kept sending him warm bodies, Foss would turn a profit.

If Adam had been even half as rebellious as I was, he wouldn't have stood for it.

While I waited for Pulsifer to return, I took the opportunity to poke around. A fetid odor hung in the air: a combination of grease, wood ashes, burned coffee, and Murphy oil soap. The room had all the charm of a cash-strapped summer camp for troubled boys.

I made eye contact with an old man sitting by himself at a corner table. He had crazy hair that stood up in every direction like a cartoon character who'd just been struck by lightning. It took me a few seconds to realize that I recognized him.

"Wallace Bickford?" I said.

"Yeah?" He was missing assorted teeth.

"It's Mike Bowditch."

Not a flicker of recognition showed in his eyes. He just kept smiling his jack-o'-lantern smile.

"Jack's son," I said.

He seemed to suck in his stomach. "Jack's dead."

"Don't you remember?" I said. "I was with the police that night they raided your cabin looking for him."

Wally Bickford had been one of my father's several sidekicks, a former logger who had received a traumatic head injury in the woods and had made his living thereafter as a trapper and collector of roadside cans and bottles. The last time I'd seen him had been during the manhunt. Search dogs had tracked my dad to the squalid shack where Bickford was then squatting. The brain-damaged man had been wounded during the ensuing police assault on his cabin, but my father had already managed to slip through the closing net.

I remembered hearing that the district attorney had drawn up accessory charges against Bickford for aiding my dad in his escape but that a judge had ruled Wallace wasn't mentally capable of understanding his crime. So how had he ended up in Pariahville?

"What are you doing here, Wally?"

"I work for Don."

"Did you come here from jail?"

"I got probated out of Windham last year." He twisted his little finger inside his ear to remove some wax.

"Why were you incarcerated?"

"For looking at pictures."

"Pictures of kids?"

"They looked old enough. Those photos don't come with ages on them." He began to rise from his chair. "I need to take a piss."

The judge who had sent him to jail on a child pornography rap must not have had the same qualms about his limited mental capacity. I pressed my hand on his bony shoulder and pushed him back onto the bench. For years, I had felt sorry for Bickford, but I was having trouble summoning sympathy for a collector of child porn, brain-damaged or not.

"Tell me about Adam Langstrom," I said.

"He ran away."

"What else?"

"He called Don names. They fought."

"You mean physically? With fists?"

He ran his fuzzy tongue over his lips.

"Foss gave Adam a black eye," I said, assuming he'd correct me if I was wrong. "Did Adam have any other enemies here? People he was afraid of?"

"I mind my own business." He began to push against my hand. "Don said I didn't have to answer questions."

I tried smiling. "You and my dad were friends."

He had rheumy eyes. They blinked very slowly. "Used to be. He took my ATV and never gave it back."

"Foss is lucky to have someone with your logging experience working for him."

His broken smile made a reappearance. "Some of these guys— they don't know—they don't know shit about what they're doing."

"There must be accidents all the time."

"Some."

"Like what happened to Lovejoy." Dudson had referred to a man by that name having been crushed by a falling tree. "Was Adam Langstrom here when Lovejoy was killed?"

Bickford closed one eye but kept the other open. The nature of his mental disability made it hard to figure him out. He usually seemed slow-witted, but I felt I might be seeing a glimmer of some residual intelligence.

"I need to take a piss," he said again.

After I released my hand from his shoulder, he just about ran to the bathroom.

Year after year, logging appeared on the list of most dangerous professions in the nation, second only to commercial fishing—and far ahead of law enforcement. By all rights, the Occupational Safety and Health Administration should have done an investigation of any deaths that occurred at this company. But Pulsifer had suggested that Foss ran his operation off the books with the complicity of POs like Shaylene Hawken and other government employees whose hands he might have greased.

I had no proof that the dead man was connected in any way to Adam or his decision to run off. Had he and Foss fought over the safety conditions of the workers in the woods? Had he threatened to go public? It would explain why Adam went looking for his Glock at his mother's house.

I found myself yearning to imagine my brother in something other than an ignoble light.

When Pulsifer finally returned, I could see that he was steamed. He motioned me toward a quiet corner.

"Foss won't let us talk to any of his guys," he said.

"Won't Clegg go to bat for us?"

"He tried," Pulsifer said. "But this is Foss's property. He doesn't have to allow any of us here without a warrant."

"But I need to tell Clegg about the gun Adam got from his mom's place," I said.

"Call him later. If you went marching in there now, Foss would terminate the interviews in a heartbeat."

"Even Foss can't stop Hawken from talking to her clients."

"What does she care? There are ten more Adam Langstroms who need jobs and housing. Foss makes her job a hundred times easier. Why would she want to mess up a good situation?"

"I've been asking myself the same thing," I muttered.

"I should have known coming here was a stupid idea."

"It was Clegg's idea, not mine."

Pulsifer's ill temper seemed to be rising from its cobra basket again. "What is it about you that causes serious lapses in judgment? Is it some sort of contagious condition you carry around, infecting everyone you meet?"

"What's that supposed to mean?" I said.

"It means I'm ready to get out of here." Pulsifer faced the room with his lip twisted in disgust. "I can't even stand breathing the same air as these scumbags. It makes my skin crawl, thinking about the shit they did to end up here. I wish someone would take a match to this place and burn it to the ground."

Where had I heard that sentiment before?

"What a colossal waste of time this was," said Pulsifer.

Speak for yourself, I thought.

24

Snow was falling from the high boughs of the evergreens as Pulsifer and I walked back down the road toward his truck. I could hear the clumps dropping in the woods around us. The crossbills were still up there in the treetops, chittering at one another and feeding on cones, although I could no longer see the birds.

Glancing through the barred shadows of the trunks, I saw the Ford Explorer Interceptor parked beside Pulsifer's Sierra. Officer Russo was down on one knee in the snow, examining something amid the litter of fallen needles. Instead of the uniform he had worn at Widowmaker, he was wearing a midnight-blue snowmobile suit, but he had pinned his badge to the front and had his gun belt strapped around his waist. The snowsuit made him look inflated, and he was already a large man.

He straightened up when he heard the crunching of our boots and wiped the snow from his gloves.

"Russo," said Pulsifer.

"Hey, Gary." The man's smile, like all of his other features, was so mild as to be unmemorable.

"What are you doing up here?"

"Saw you guys pass by before and thought I'd come up and see if you all needed help."

In addition to being a security guard at the resort, Russo was a sheriff's deputy, so it was possible he had heard about Langstrom's truck and knew that Clegg was planning to pay Foss a visit this morning. The detective wouldn't necessarily have kept the plans secret. Still, I found his presence on the scene to be suspiciously coincidental.

"Do you remember Warden Bowditch?" Pulsifer asked.

"I am afraid Mike and I got off on the wrong foot. My apologies." He said this without a hint of contrition in his voice.

"What were you looking at?" I asked.

"Just some animal tracks, trying to figure out what they are."

Pulsifer stepped over and gave the ground a quick glance. "Those are from a mink."

In fact, the prints had been left by an ermine—a long-tailed weasel—but I decided not to correct Pulsifer, knowing the foul mood he was in.

"So we saw you parked outside Logan Dyer's house before," I said.

"I wanted to see how he was doing."

The thing about Russo's face, I realized, was that it had the artificial softness of a sculpture, as if Madame Tussaud had tried and failed to fashion his likeness from wax.

"Is Dyer sick?" I asked.

"That's what I wanted to know. He's missed a lot of work lately, called in sick, but Elderoy doesn't want to terminate him without cause."

"So you came out here to see if he was faking?" I said.

"You know how the job is," he said, meaning police work. "You never know what the day will bring."

My work had never involved checking up on employees who had claimed to be ill.

"So is he faking?"

"He says he's been getting migraines. That's hard to double-check. He told me he thinks he might have a brain tumor. He is certain he is dying." The security guard shook his head in a robotic gesture that was supposed to suggest sadness. "I told him to see a doctor if he was so concerned. I tried to talk some sense into him, but there is a limit to Logan's ability to understand things."

I remembered Pulsifer asserting that Dyer wasn't dumb but that his speech impediment made people assume he lacked intelligence. I thought he might jump in to defend Logan. Instead, Pulsifer changed the subject. "How did you do in Florida? I never heard."

"Fifth place," said Russo. "I had an off day. I should have finished in the top three."

"World Speed Shooting Championships," explained Pulsifer. He waggled his thumb at me in typical mocking fashion. "Bowditch is always the slowest draw on the course."

Russo turned his doll-like eyes on me. "You need to stop thinking before you shoot."

I had heard that advice before—in many contexts.

"Your brain is your enemy in competition," Russo continued. "You need to make every move automatic."

"Thanks for the tips."

The security guard pointed into the woods, in the direction of the dining hall. "How's it going up there? Clegg getting anything useful?"

"Foss kicked us out," said Pulsifer. "He's only allowing Clegg and Hawken to interview his workers. You'd better not let Foss see your vehicle, or he'll go full volcano."

"Too bad," said Russo. "I'd love to poke around this place. I've never been past the gate."

"No?" said Pulsifer with a perplexed expression. "What about when that Lovejoy guy got crushed?"

"That's right," said Russo, "but that was in the woods. I never got a tour of the compound."

"Maybe someday," I said.

"How long are you sticking around?" Russo asked me.

"Undecided."

"Enjoy your stay."

No one could be this banal unintentionally, I thought.

Pulsifer waited for Russo to leave first; he didn't explain why. Then we started back down the slippery slope.

Logan Dyer was in his open garage, tinkering with his snowmobile as we drove by. I was surprised to see him outside, since Russo had claimed he'd called in sick.

Pulsifer slowed to a stop and rolled down his window.

Dyer dropped whatever tool he'd been using and ambled out to meet us. His sleek Plotts, which must have been sleeping inside the garage, ventured out into the plowed drive, baying like hellhounds before their master silenced them with a command.

Dyer hadn't changed out of the clothes he had been wearing the day before, I noticed. His unshaven cheeks looked even scruffier and his eyes seemed even more deeply set into his skull.

"Morning, Logan," Pulsifer said.

"Hey, Warden." Dyer leaned on the side mirror. The gesture struck me as presumptuous and disrespectful. If it had been me, I would have told him to get his grimy hands off my truck.

"I understand you've met Warden Bowditch."

"Came by with Mink last night," he said thickly. "Never met a hero before."

From anyone else, I might have interpreted his constant references to me as a hero as a sarcastic insult. But Dyer was hard to figure.

"Hello again," I said.

"So what's with the cop convention this morning?" Dyer tilted his chin toward the hilltop. "Did one of those perverts ass-fuck another without permission?"

Pulsifer barked out a laugh. "A cop convention! See, Mike, I told you Logan was a clever guy."

"Sounds like my ears should've been burning," said Dyer. "But I guess it's too cold for that."

"We ran into Russo just now and he said he came out to check up on you. He said you've been having migraines."

"Feels like there's a golf ball between my eyes."

I leaned forward. "Maybe that's why you didn't recognize that picture I showed you of Adam Langstrom."

A muscle twitched in Dyer's hairy neck. "I remembered who he was later. Used to see him around the mountain before he went to prison. My memory needs to be jogged sometimes."

Pulsifer tugged on one of his earlobes; it was red from the cold. "Have you gotten any coyotes yet this season?"

"Some," he said. "I got one last week. A thirty-pounder."

Evidently, his migraines hadn't slowed down his hunting. I looked past him at the two Plott hounds lying in the driveway, focused entirely on their owner. They were big, streamlined animals with fierce eyes and muscles that rippled beneath their brindle coats.

"With the dogs or over bait?" Pulsifer asked.

"With the dogs."

"What did you use to get him?"

"Smith & Wesson M&P 15 Whisper." Dyer turned his attention from Pulsifer to me. He ran a dirty hand through his filthy hair. "Russo said they found that missing guy's truck. Said there was blood all over it."

"That's right," I said. "Don't be surprised if a detective named Clegg knocks on your door later."

"Me? What for?"

"He's handling the criminal investigation into Langstrom's disappearance and will want to get a statement from you."

"Me? I didn't see nothing." His speech became harder to understand the more agitated he became.

"You might have," I said. "You might not have realized it at the time. Everyone going in and out of Foss's drives by your front windows. And you said your memory needs to be jogged from time to time."

Dyer took a step back from the window, his shoulders tightening. "Those perverts shouldn't even be running around loose. Who cares if they kill each other?"

"Not me," said Pulsifer, reaching for the shift. "You take it easy, Logan."

We drove in silence for fifty yards, until Dyer's house had disappeared behind the trees. Then Pulsifer swung his head around to look at me through his mirrored glasses.

"What the hell was that about?" he said.

"What?"

"Don't give me that bullshit. You were trying to rattle Logan. What was up with that?"

"There's just something about him that seems off to me."

"Because he hates child molesters? So what does that make me? Jesus, Bowditch. All those years of standing up for you in front of disciplinary committees, hearing about you sticking your nose where it doesn't belong—I never thought I'd get to see it up close and personal. But you really are a piece of work."

Pulsifer had been in a rotten mood all morning, and I knew anything I might say in defense of my actions would only irritate him more. When we arrived at Route 16, he turned in the direction of Bigelow and Flagstaff and hit the gas hard. He wasn't making any pretense of wanting to get me back to my Scout and out of his district as soon as possible.

The day was shaping up to be a beauty. The snow was sparkling, brighter than crushed diamonds, where the sun hit it. We passed the dead tree where the owl had been roosting, but it had flown away along with the birders.

Visiting the logging camp with Pulsifer had brought back a memory I had done my best to repress. It was the memory of a drive I had taken with Warden Tommy Volk a year and a half earlier, when I was new in the Sebago region. Volk had wanted me to know where the worst dirtbags lived because I would be policing his district on his days off.

Pulsifer might have dismissed southern Maine as a suburban la-la land. But on that day, Volk and I had visited fenced compounds where barking pit bulls announced our approach, trailer parks where men pimped out their teenage girlfriends for heroin, and former farmsteads where the only crops still being grown were sold in Baggies for three hundred dollars an ounce.

But the memory that had lingered longest was our last stop of the day.

Toward dark, we had pulled up in his patrol truck to an anonymous split-level house: the kind of exurban home I wouldn't have looked at twice under normal circumstances. A single light shined from a second-story window, but all of the others were dark.

"I've saved the worst for last," Volk had said. "The guy who lives here is pure evil. Do you want to meet him?"

"Who is he?"

"No one you'd ever notice."

Volk chewed tobacco constantly, not even removing it while he ate. He spat a stream of brown saliva into a stained coffee cup. We sat outside the nondescript house, staring up at the lighted window and listening to the engine idle.

"What did he do?" I asked finally.

Instead of answering, Volk did something that made my heart seize up. He hit his pursuit lights and sirens, bathing the dead-end street in blue hellfire.

The outside light came on, the door opened, and a man appeared on the front step. I couldn't see him well from that distance, but he seemed to be middle-aged, with a fat face and square glasses. His dress shirt was untucked on one side, as if he'd come directly from the bathroom, and his athletic socks were so phosphorescent white, they seemed to glow in the dark.

Volk switched off his blues, but the siren echoed in my head.

"Hope I didn't wake you, Pete," Volk whispered, more to himself than to me.

The man stared sleepily at our truck while he tucked his shirt into his pants. Then, without turning his back to our vehicle, he stepped back inside the house and closed the door.

"Who was that?" I asked.

"Peter Hamlin."

"Who?"

"You never heard of the Pied Piper?" Volk stuffed a fresh wad of tobacco between his cheek and gums. "He used to be the music teacher at Pondicherry High School—married, kids, the whole nine yards. Then a girl in the school band slit her wrists. In the hospital she told a nurse that Hamlin had been having sex with her—all three holes. When the state cops raided his house, they found pictures of him with three other girls. One of them was a niece of my first wife."

"Jesus," I said.

"Hamlin 'tried' to kill himself when he was out on bail, hanged himself in a motel room, but I guess he wasn't able to go through with it, the fucking coward. I don't know who his lawyer was, but he must have been the best that ever was. The asshole did only ten years in the Maine State Prison. Can you believe that? Ten years? His wife divorced him, changed her name, moved out of state with the kids, but somehow that dirtbag kept the house. I think it's technically his mother's, and she lets him live there."

The state of Maine doesn't have laws dictating how close a sex offender can live to a school, day-care center, or playground, but I knew that some towns had passed their own ordinances. Whatever statutes Pondicherry might have put into place wouldn't have applied here anyway. Hamlin had no proximate neighbors.

"How long has he been out?" I asked.

"Five months," Volk said, growing redder. "I have made him my personal project. I come over at all hours. Blast my siren. I want him to know he's being watched. I want him to think I'm a crazy motherfucker who doesn't give a fuck about the law. I want him to have a heart attack from fear."

The inside of the truck smelled of Volk's sickly wintergreen dip.

"So he's called the Pied Piper because he was a music teacher?" I asked. "Or because of the Hamlin/Hamelin thing."

Volk seemed confused; I don't think he was familiar with the locale of the German folktale.

"Hamlin wanted those girls to play his skin flute," he said simply. "That's how the fucker got his name."

In my career as a law-enforcement officer, I had accompanied regular police on bail-compliance checks, and I'd seen firsthand the damage child molesters can inflict on the most helpless of victims. I had seen horrible things that had torched whatever faith I'd once had in the essential goodness of human beings. So, however much I disliked being made his unwitting accomplice, I wasn't about to rat out Tommy Volk.

Then, three months later, I had heard the news that Peter Hamlin had burned his mother's house down with himself inside. His charred skeleton had been found inside a bedroom closet, of all places. There were no signs that his death had been anything but suicide, and as vicious as Volk could be, I couldn't imagine him plotting such an elaborate and brutal death for the Pied Piper. On the other hand, I had little doubt that the pedophile had felt driven to take his own life.

What I had tried so hard to repress was my emotional response to the fire. Some of it was guilt. I'd wondered if I should have told someone in command about Volk's campaign of harassment. There had also been a sense of relief. I was glad that one evil man, at least, was no longer at large upon the earth. But there was something else, too: a buoyant feeling in my chest. It was satisfaction, I realized.

I had never felt that emotion before at the death of another human being.

25

Do you ever look at the registry?" I asked Pulsifer as we neared the Bigelow crossroads.

He flicked the wipers to clear the windshield of the salt and dirt being splattered on us by every passing vehicle. "The sex offender registry?" he said. "No, but I know where the local predators live, if that's what you're asking. If one of them moves into the area, I hear about it around town. People spend hours on that site, looking to see if they know anyone. It qualifies as a recreational activity up here."

That hardly surprised me. In my experience, rural people, having few distractions, especially enjoyed prying into one another's business. Without gossips and grudge holders, Maine game wardens would be out of business.

"I've been wondering about Nathan Minkowski," I said.

For the first time all morning, Pulsifer burst out laughing. "Mink! That's right. You were supposed to tell me about your close encounter."

"I gave him a ride home yesterday from town."

"What was he wearing?

I closed my eyes and summoned his image. "Fur hat, lumberman's coat, jeans, pack boots."

"That makes sense," Pulsifer said. "Yesterday was an even day."

An even day? I didn't understand what that meant. "There was something off about him," I said. "I wondered if he was on the registry or something."

"Not yet." Pulsifer turned the steering wheel suddenly in the direction of the village. "Let's see if he's out on display this morning."

Up ahead was a gas station. It had old-style signs that needed to be changed manually when the price of gasoline rose or fell, and vintage pumps that wouldn't take credit cards. Because it was such a beautiful morning, there were lines of vehicles in both directions. Not many places to fill up in Bigelow, evidently.

"There he is," said Pulsifer with a broad grin.

I saw a few men pumping gas, and a short blond woman in a fur coat using a squeegee and paper towels to clean a windshield. But no Mink.

Then the realization dropped on me with the force of a Texas hailstone.

"Oh my God," I said.

Pulsifer swung into the lot and hit the brakes. "I honestly don't know why Erskine puts up with Mink, looking like that. You'd think it would hurt sales to have a cross-dresser standing at your gas pumps all day, offering to clean your windshield for a buck. It's not the kind of thing your average tourist expects to see in Bigelow, Maine. Erskine told me about one old lady who stopped in and asked about the nice blond woman who used to wash windshields. The funniest part was that Mink was standing there the whole time in his men's clothes."

The gas station owner might have had a tolerant heart, but I was beginning to understand why Mink might have been banned from the general store.

I popped open the door. "I want to say hello."

Mink had quite the winter wardrobe going: waist-length fur coat, black ski tights, fur-lined boots. His wig was long, blond, parted in the center, and feathered at the ends.

"Mink!" said Pulsifer. "You're looking lovely today."

"Up yours," Mink said in his normal deep voice. His cosmetics were, if anything, even more elaborate than his clothes: fake eyelashes, mascara, rouge, scarlet lipstick, layered over a foundation thicker than pancake.

"How's it going, Mink?" I asked.

"Fine until you ass clowns got here."

The car Mink had been cleaning took the opportunity to drive off. He swung the squeegee back and forth in the same irritated manner a cat flicks its tail.

"How did you get into town this morning?" I asked.

"Walked, same as usual." I didn't know if he changed his voice with strangers, raised it a couple of registers, but he didn't seem to be actively trying to fool anyone into thinking he was a woman. "I don't get many rides when I dress this way."

"I thought this was a brave new world," said Pulsifer. "Isn't transgendered supposed to be the hot new thing?"

"I ain't transgendered."

"I don't know the politically correct term."

"I don't give a shit about politics. I wear women's clothes sometimes because I like it. Did you guys just come here to give me the prod? Because I got work to do." He pointed with the squeegee at the line of cars.

Pulsifer reached into his pocket and pulled out a crumpled dollar. "This is for the last car."

Gary could be a true dick when he wanted.

"Go jump in the lake," Mink said. But he still took the dollar.

I followed Pulsifer into the station, where a graying, bespectacled man stood behind the register.

"Morning, Erskine."

"It was until five seconds ago," the owner said.

"Erskine, I want to introduce you to Mike Bowditch. He's a warden down in north Massachusetts."

"He means southern Maine," I said. "Pleased to meet you."

The old man scowled. "I know who you are."

He must have been another person my father had made an enemy out of. I could imagine my dad on a bender, driving off from one of those old gas pumps without paying, daring the old man to give chase or call the cops on him.

Pulsifer and I filled Styrofoam cups with coffee and returned to the counter.

"This used to be A. J. Langstrom's station," Pulsifer said, "before A.J. got sick of his wife's escapades and moved out of state. You ever hear from A.J., Erskine?"

"Why the hell would I?"

"I thought you two might be Facebook friends."

"Isn't it a little early in the morning to be a pain in the ass, Gary?" Erskine said.

"I was trying to explain to Mike here why you let Mink hang out at your pumps," said Pulsifer. "Don't you get complaints?"

"Sure I do. But so what? It's my store. I can do what I want."

"You're a better man than me," said Pulsifer.

"That goes without saying." The old guy kept a deadpan expression, but I was beginning to sense that maybe they really didn't dislike each other, but that this was a skit they performed regularly. "I heard Jim Clegg was up at Don Foss's place this morning."

"Where did you hear that?" Pulsifer asked.

"One of John Cabot's drivers saw his cruiser turn up that road."

I hadn't considered the idea that Cabot and Foss might have been business rivals, but it made perfect sense; they were both loggers.

Pulsifer took a sip of coffee. "Erskine, you're better than Google when it comes to information around here."

"I suppose it has something to do with Amber's son?"

"Don't you mean A.J.'s son?"

"I mean exactly what I mean."

Another belated revelation: Adam's questionable parentage was a topic of conversation. I wondered if anyone had ever fixated on the strong resemblance he bore to Jack Bowditch.

The old man scratched one of his hairy ears. "I don't know who they thought they were fooling, passing that boy off as A.J.'s son all those years. He looks no more like A. J. Langstrom than I look like George Clooney."

"When was the last time you saw Adam Langstrom around, Erskine?" I asked.

"Last time I saw him was before he went to prison. That prick knows he's not welcome here. I caught him stealing gas once. Can you believe that? Stealing gas from the same store his own 'father' used to own?"

A woman, dressed from head to toe in expensive Moncler ski apparel and carrying a five-dollar bottle of water, cleared her throat behind us. We paid for our coffee and stepped aside so Erskine could ring up the sale.

"Have a good day, Erskine," said Pulsifer.

"Yeah, yeah," said the old man.

We found Mink enjoying a cigarette outside the door. The filter was red with lipstick. He made no secret of having been waiting for us.

"And another thing," he said.

Pulsifer said, "Mink, have I ever told you how hard it is for us to have a conversation when you're dressed like that?"

"That's your issue," he said. "So what's this I hear about Langstrom's truck?"

"What did you hear, exactly?" asked Pulsifer.

"I heard someone found it over near the SERE school. The window was busted and there was blood inside."

"I can neither confirm nor deny that report."

Mink sniffed up a line of clear snot that had begun to run from his nose. "So did he kill someone or did someone kill him?"

"Maybe he just hit a deer," said Pulsifer, winking at me.

"And it landed in the seat beside him? You dopes don't really believe that."

"Stranger things have happened. Besides, didn't I hear once you had psychic powers? Maybe you can help Detective Clegg with his investigation."

"Laugh if you want, but I got a sixth sense about things. My mom is half Roma. That's what Gypsies call other Gypsies."

"Maybe you should dress as a fortune-teller sometime," said Pulsifer. "You know, with the red kerchief and the bangles."

"Go jump in a lake."

Mink dropped the butt on the wet ground. He smacked his bright lips and readjusted his wig. When the woman in the Moncler ski suit stepped out the door, he wasn't shy about checking out her rear end.

Lauren Pulsifer's Ford Explorer was gone when we arrived back at their farm. She must have let the goats out of the barn, since several of them were making trails through the snowy pasture. They had heavy, hairy coats.

I shaded my eyes with my hand against the sun. "Are those Angoras?"

"Cashmeres. You wouldn't believe what we get for their wool. You sure you don't want a tour of the farm?"

"I should head home."

Seeing Mink in women's clothes seemed to have lifted his spirits. Either that or his hangover had worn off. He helped me dig out my Scout at least.

"You should call DeFord this morning and tell him you've been up here," he said, "Didn't he tell you to keep a low profile to help the AAG make a stronger case against that Michaud bitch?"

"Too late for that."

"You are exceptionally bad at following helpful advice, Bowditch. It's almost a gift."

"So you've told me."

As I backed out of the dooryard, he waved like a beauty queen riding by on her float: limp-wristed, with a pasted-on smile. Always the comedian, Pulsifer.

Heading back into town, I turned left at the blinking light and took my second tour of the day through beautiful downtown Bigelow. Mink was back at the gas pumps, but he was too engrossed in his work as a freelance service station attendant to notice me.

Wait until I told Stacey that my hitchhiker had turned out to be the town drag queen. She would insist on us driving up here again to see Mink in the flesh. Stacey was, if anything, a more curious person than I was.

First, she needed to accept my apology, of course. She had given me no guarantees that she would.

I knew that at this very moment she must be up in the Forest Service helicopter. The stubborn woman couldn't take a single day off from work to rest in bed and recover. It took me a few seconds to realize who she reminded me of in that regard.

I passed the apartment complex where Amber lived but didn't see her Jeep. Had she recovered enough from her grief to return to the Sluiceway and beg for her job back? Her manager didn't seem to be a sympathetic sort.

I decided to take the long way home. I followed Route 27 southeast through Stratton and Wyman Township, skirting the edge of the Bigelow Range. As I approached the Sugarloaf ski resort, I saw the first trails, across the valley, white against the dark green of the mountain. From a distance, I picked out the skiers and boarders, small as specks, and I thought of lines of ants exploring a bowl of sugar. I crossed the bridge over the Carrabassett River and came to the village at the base of the mountain. It reminded me somewhat of the string of businesses outside Widowmaker, the difference being that these seemed to be thriving.

It was a picture-perfect day to be out on the slopes. When all of this was over, I promised myself that I would head up this way again. It had been too long since I had gotten out my old skis.

An hour later, I arrived back in civilization in Farmington. I stopped for lunch at the McDonald's at the edge of town. In my head, I heard Stacey's scolding words about my miserable diet, the toll that cholesterol and sodium were taking on my arteries. I thought briefly of ordering a salad but broke down and got a Big Mac. And extra-large fries, of course.

Someone had left a newspaper in the booth. I paged through it while I picked at my fries, until I came to the editorial page and saw a column written by Johnny Partridge titled "A Soft Landing for Sexual Predators." It was an "exposé" of Don Foss Logging that portrayed the bare-bones compound as a woodland paradise where child molesters and serial rapists enjoyed luxurious accommodations and gourmet meals on the Maine taxpayer's dime. I couldn't find one true sentence in the piece, but that hardly mattered. All Partridge cared about was causing an uproar.

Maybe Foss's gravy train was about to go off the tracks.

My phone buzzed. Half of my fellow diners were gabbing away on their own cells, so I felt free to take the call.

"This is Bowditch," I said.

"Warden, this is Joanie Swette from Pondicherry. We met at the house with the wolf dog."

Preoccupied as I'd been with Adam's disappearance, I had almost forgotten about Shadow.

"Hi, Joanie. Thanks for calling me back."

"I tried you a couple of times yesterday, but the call kept dropping."

"I've been up in the mountains."

"Oh, it must be beautiful." She waited to see if I would say something out of politeness, then plowed right ahead. "You asked me to call you when the DNA tests came back. It usually takes weeks, you know, but it turns out that Shadow has a tattoo."

"A tattoo?"

"On his stomach. No one saw it at first. Shadow began showing signs of stress at the shelter, not aggression, but you could tell that he had some pretty bad associations with cages. He was fine in the carrier, but he really freaked out at the shelter. Eventually, Dr. Carbone decided to sedate him, because it was the only way he was going to be able to draw blood. He was afraid of being bitten."

That poor animal, I thought. I'd seen canids in zoos and wildlife parks, and almost without exception they'd worn grooves along the inside borders of their pens from nonstop pacing.

"So that's when he discovered the tattoo," I said. "What did it tell you?"

"It's a registration number. It seems that Shadow's from Montana."

"Montana?"

"The number was assigned by the Montana Fish, Wildlife, and Parks Enforcement Division. Shadow is a high-content wolf dog. Almost pure wolf, basically."

The smell of the fried burger had begun to nauseate me. "How did he end up with a drug dealer in Maine?"

"No one knows, but it seems his original owner died recently. The wardens in Montana contacted the relatives for us, and they didn't even know their uncle owned a wolf dog. They're ranchers, and they hate wolves. They said we should just put him down."

I pushed the tray away with such force, it nearly slid off the table. "Jesus."

"I know," she said.

"So what happens now?"

"Normally, we'd try to find someone to take him, someone with a license to possess wildlife. There used to be a wolf dog sanctuary just across the border in New Hampshire, but it went out of business."

"You said 'normally.' What does that mean?"

She took a breath. "Under the law, the vet is supposed to euthanize a wolf dog if there's a potential danger to the public."

I was having a hard time hearing above the clamor of the restaurant and felt compelled to raise my own voice. "But you said Shadow wasn't aggressive."

"He killed a deer."

"What's the name of the vet?"

"Dr. Carbone."

"Can I talk to him?"

"I'm not at the shelter. And Dr. Carbone is up at Sugarloaf for the weekend. He has a condo there."

The thought of swinging around and driving back into the mountains occurred to me before I realized how mad I would seem, showing up unannounced on the doorstep of the man's second home. "Can you get a message to him? Tell him I'll find someone to take Shadow. There's no need to put him down."

"Dr. Carbone is a good vet."

"I'm sure he is."

"He doesn't make decisions like these lightly."

"Joanie—"

"I hate it, too, but—"

"Joanie, I understand. But you have to promise me that nothing will happen to Shadow before I have a chance to talk to Dr. Carbone. Will you do that? Will you promise me?"

"Yes."

"Thank you. He can call me anytime, day or night."

"I will let him know that."

It was only after I'd signed off that I realized that everyone at the surrounding tables was staring at me.

26

Two hours later I arrived home and discovered that the plow had erected a wall of ice and snow as high as my chest between the road and my driveway. Having no other choice, I ended up parking exactly where Amber had parked—in the middle of a dangerous curve—while I chipped away at the frozen barrier with a shovel and an ice chopper.

I had spent two tiring days on the road, and for what? I had been too late to save Adam Langstrom, if he had even been worth saving. By all accounts, my half brother had been an arrogant asshole who had brought his problems on himself. And now he was probably dead. Did it even matter who had killed him or why? As a law-enforcement officer, I was supposed to think it did. But I was having a hard time caring about closure.

Then I thought of Amber. She might have been a shallow and self-centered person, but I still felt heartsick when I envisioned her alone in her dark, smoky apartment, having lost the only thing outside of herself she had ever loved.

Meanwhile, the wolf dog that I had ostensibly rescued was facing lethal injection, all because of me. I hated to imagine the existence Shadow might have had if he'd lived out the rest of his days with Carrie and Spike, but at least he wouldn't be headed to the death chamber.

How could I be so indifferent to the fate of my own half brother and so distraught about a dog I'd met for a matter of minutes?

I was as lathered as a racehorse by the time I'd finally cleared a drivable path from the road to the garage. I parked the Scout inside and let the descending door plunge me into darkness.

I carried an armload of hardwood into the living room and dropped the logs beside the stove. I thought of the Pulsifers' house, full of loud children and scampering dogs, and realized how tired I was of living alone. Stacey and I had avoided discussing the idea of moving in together because most of her work as a wildlife biologist needed to be done up north. But that was just a bullshit excuse. The truth was, we were both afraid of commitment.

After I had made a fire, I peeled off my dirty clothes and stood under the showerhead until the water began going cold. The stitched wound on my arm reminded me of a black centipede. I applied a clean bandage.

I was shaving at the sink, with a towel around my waist, when I heard my cell buzz in the hall. The phone was still in the pocket of my pants, which I'd tossed on the floor.

Even before I answered, I knew from the number on the screen who was calling me.

"Hi, Charley," I said, glad to hear from my old friend.

From the background noise, I could tell that Stacey's father was in an echoey space, surrounded by jabbering people.

"Mike." His voice sounded strange—flat.

"I've been meaning to thank you and Ora for Christmas. You really didn't have to go to all that trouble. And it was so nice of you to invite Aimee Cronk and her kids."

"Mike," he said again.

"What's wrong?" I felt pressure beginning to build behind my eardrums.

"There's been an accident."

"What kind of accident?"

"A Forest Service chopper went down an hour ago near Clayton Lake. Some ice fishermen out on Lake Umsakis said they saw it crash." He paused and I heard my pulse pounding in my head. "There are rescue teams heading to the scene. A buddy of mine out of Ashland just got through to me."

I could only manage one raspy word. "Stacey?"

"The fishermen said it went down hard and fast in a pretty dense woods. There was no distress call."

I rushed to my closet. "I can be on the road in five minutes."

"It'll take you seven hours to drive that far, Mike."

"Then fly down here and pick me up!"

"I'm in Bangor, at the hospital with Ora. I brought her here for a colonoscopy. I can't leave before she wakes up. I couldn't do that to her. My Cessna's back in Grand Lake Stream. But I'll probably bum a ride with someone over at BIA. I'm sorry, but there's nothing you can do right now, young feller."

"There's got to be something."

"Say a prayer for my little girl, and don't give up hope. Stacey's a tough one. Toughest there is."

And then he was gone.

Not again. Not again.

Eighteen months earlier, one of the scariest men I'd ever met had held a gun to Stacey's head, and I'd discovered, for the first time in my life, what it was like to feel helpless when someone you love is in mortal danger.

Not again. Not again.

I didn't care if Clayton Lake was half a day's drive from my house. I would race up there with lights blazing and siren screaming.

I grabbed my field uniform from the closet and my combat vest and my gun belt. I would call the Division G headquarters in Ashland once I was on the road. The IF&W office up there would have more information.

It felt as if the volume had been cranked up in my head. My thoughts were louder than normal. The last time we'd spoken together, we had argued over my having lied about my injuries: "You should have called me from the hospital. If you don't understand how much that breaks my heart, there's nothing more to say. I'm not interested in being with someone who'd rather be lonely than be loved."

And then her final text message to me: "I am having trouble forgiving you."

If that was it—if those were her last words to me—I couldn't imagine what the rest of my life would be like.

I started up my patrol truck and I backed out so fast onto the road that the driver of an oncoming car had to slam on her brakes. I pulled forward to let her pass.

She gave me an annoyed toot on her horn.

I needed to calm down before I killed someone or myself. Slowly, I backed out onto the road and turned in the direction of Windham, where I could pick up the Maine Turnpike and begin my journey north.

Amber had said she'd felt the moment of Adam's death as a physical blow. But she had been his mother.

Mink claimed to have psychic powers that forewarned him of bad things to come.

But I felt nothing except a buzzing in my nerves, as if they might short-circuit at any second.

I reached for my cell to push the autodial for Division G. Just as I did, the phone vibrated in my hand. The screen showed the number of the Ashland office.

"Yes?" It was more of a rattle than a word.

"Mike?"

I braked so hard against a snowbank, I heard ice scrape paint from the side of the truck. "Stacey?"

"It's me," she said. "I'm all right."

My mind wouldn't believe the evidence of my ears. "What happened? Where are you?"

"There was a crash," she said, her throat thick with mucus. "The helicopter."

"I know." The words were coming out as gasps. "Your dad just called me."

"He did? How did he—"

"It doesn't matter. Where are you, Stacey?"

"Ashland. Graham wouldn't let me go up with them. We argued about it. He wouldn't back down. Told me to go back to bed. Everyone in the office thought I was on board the chopper. They didn't know I'd gone back to my place."

I covered my eyes with my cupped hand, as if in shame, and my palm came away wet. I had never felt so happy, so relieved, so overcome with disbelief. And then I realized how selfish these emotions were.

"They're all dead, Mike," she said, sobbing. "Graham, Marti, Steve. We just got word."

"Oh God."

"It could have been me, should have been me."

"Don't say that."

"Graham was always so funny." She sounded horrible. "I can't believe he's dead. And poor Marti—she just graduated. And Steve was such a big soul, so full of life. I'm having chills, Mike. I can't stop shivering."

Suddenly, I, too, was shaking. "I know, I know."

"I need to sit down."

"Do they know what happened?"

"The chopper just went down. Steve never even radioed that there was a problem. It's a beautiful day up here, too. Light winds, clear skies. It doesn't make any fucking sense."

"Maybe there was a mechanical malfunction."

"It's a fucking brand-new Bell." She coughed away from the phone. "Steve was always going on and on about what a dream it was to fly."

"Could something have happened to him in the air?"

"Like a heart attack? Maybe. I can't believe they're dead. I keep expecting to hear them coming back from the helipad."

"How come no one knew where you were?"

"I stormed out of the office when Graham said he didn't want me coughing and sneezing on everyone again. I was so pissed." She took a sharp breath. "Oh God! That was our last conversation. I can never take back the things I said."

It was the same harrowing realization I'd had a few minutes earlier, when I'd thought about the last time she and I had spoken.

Stacey began to sob harder. "So I went back to my room. I tried to sleep, but the medicine made me jittery. When I walked through the door, people looked at me like I was a ghost. Everyone thought I had been on the chopper. I feel so horrible now. I should have been with them. It doesn't feel right that I'm alive and they're dead."

I rubbed my forehead with my hand. "But you're not! You're alive, Stacey. I wish I could be there with you."

"Why?" She sounded genuinely surprised.

"To comfort you."

"I'm not the one who needs comforting. I shouldn't be sitting here sobbing. My friends' dead bodies are still out there in the wreckage, and their families are sick with grieving. I need to do something."

"You should think about your own family. When your dad finds out you weren't on the chopper—you need to call him. You need to call him right this second."

"Right. Of course. Shit."

"Call me later."

"I'll call you when I have some news. I can't promise when that will be. Good-bye, Mike. I love you."

"I love you, too."

A big eighteen-wheeler went barreling past and caught me up in its wake. For an instant, my truck rocked from side to side in the slipstream. I finally remembered to hit my hazard lights, but it seemed a little late at that point.

27

When I returned home, the house seemed altogether different. No one else had been there while I had been away. The temperature was more or less the same as when I'd taken off down the road.

And yet I found myself overcome with that paranoid feeling you sometimes get when you step into a favorite room and you perceive that some small item has been moved. You can't put your finger on what it is, but your subconscious can sense that something is different. The more you try to identify what has been changed, the more agitated you become. It is how some people end up pulling out their own hair.

I found myself wandering from room to room, unable to sit still. I removed my combat vest and gun belt again, changed out of my uniform and back into jeans and a T-shirt, then decided I should run a few miles on the treadmill in the basement to burn off some steam, which meant putting on my shorts and sneakers. But I had barely started running when my legs started cramping and I was overcome with exhaustion, and I found myself sitting down on the weight bench with a towel over my head.

It wasn't until I lifted the towel that I felt the fabric was wet. My hands slid down my cheeks when I touched them. I had been crying without even realizing it.

I made my way upstairs and removed the bottle of bourbon from the cupboard. I held the label up to my eyes for a long time, examining the elegant signature of James B. Beam, then dumped every last drop down the sink.

Eventually, I wandered into the living room and threw my sore body across the sofa. I closed my eyes, but the bulb overhead was so strong, it made the inside of my lids turn bloodred. I thought about getting up to turn it off, but I didn't really want to go to sleep, either. My nerves were still too raw.

I reached for the television remote and was surprised to find that the New England Patriots were playing a night game. It must have been the play-offs. I started to watch, but the loud voices of the announcers sounded like air horns in my oversensitive ears, so I hit the mute button.

I needed to talk to someone.

I tried Kathy first, but I got a voice-mail message. She had become an early riser in her late middle age.

I wanted to give Charley and Ora space.

Call Pulsifer? No way.

I scrolled through the list of recent calls and touched the name of Captain DeFord. It was as if my finger acted of its own accord. The phone began to ring.

"Mike?" he said. "What's going on?"

"There was a helicopter crash up near the Allagash. Did you hear about it?"

Why had I called DeFord, of all people? This man I was talking to was the captain of the Warden Service, not a chaplain or a grief counselor. He was my superior officer, and I barely even knew him.

"I was just on the phone with St. Pierre. He's coordinating the recovery operation. What a tragedy."

I tried to keep emotion out of my voice. "The initial reports were that Stacey Stevens was on that helicopter. But it turns out she wasn't."

DeFord knew Stacey was my girlfriend. He was also well acquainted with her parents. "Have you had a chance to talk with her?"

"A while ago."

"How is she doing?"

"About as well as you'd expect."

He paused. "How are you doing?"

The reason I had called DeFord, I now realized, was in the hope that he would ask me that question.

"Not great."

"You've had a hell of week, haven't you?" he said quietly. "Are you sure you don't want to talk with Deb Davies?"

"Maybe, I don't know. Stacey was supposed to be on that chopper, but she was too sick to fly. It was dumb luck that saved her."

The same way dumb luck had saved me from Carrie Michaud's knife, I thought.

"I am not so sure," DeFord said. "I am one of those people who believe things happen for a reason. We just don't know what it is until later. Sometimes we never know. But we have to believe there was one. Otherwise, how do we keep going?"

I found myself chuckling.

"What did I say?" DeFord asked, sounding a little irked.

"No offense, but the Reverend Davies is in no danger of losing her job to you."

"Well, I'm glad to hear you laugh," DeFord said, and I could detect a smile in his voice. "How are your shoulder and arm?"

"Healing."

"Even with all the running around you've been doing up around Rangeley?"

The television flickered from a beer ad back to the game. "You heard about that?"

"Pulsifer told me."

I should have figured he would rat me out. Damn him.

DeFord went on: "Gary said you've been assisting Jim Clegg with information about that missing sex offender."

"His name is Adam Langstrom."

"How do you know him?"

I took a moment to consider my words. "I don't, really."

DeFord had to mull over my unexpected answer. "So what made you take an interest in him?"

"Langstrom comes from a town where I lived when I was a kid. His background seemed so familiar to me. And I hadn't been back in those mountains since my dad died." None of these statements was an actual lie, strictly speaking. "I wanted something to keep my mind occupied, and crossword puzzles aren't my thing. So I decided to drive up there."

"Nearly dying is a traumatic experience. Everyone reacts differently to it. When I saw you in the hospital, I was worried about you."

"Because of my history? I can't say I blame you."

The captain paused. "Am I going to receive a complaint about you? Is that why you're calling?"

"What did Pulsifer say?"

"He said you're a pain in the ass but a hell of a good investigator."

"Really?"

"He said you're wasting your talents, and I should assign you to the Wildlife Crimes Investigative Division."

I was dumbfounded. Not in my wildest imaginings would I have expected Gary Pulsifer, of all people, to have vouched for me, especially after the way our day had started.

"I told him I agreed," continued DeFord. "But if we're going to get the colonel on board, you're going to need to promise me something first."

"Anything."

"Stay out of trouble for a while."

"I can't do that, Captain. It doesn't seem to be in my nature. But I won't knowingly violate any rules or regulations."

"Or laws? It would be helpful if you didn't break any of those." I sensed a smile in his voice again.

"Or laws," I said.

He sighed. "I guess that will have to do."

On the television, the New England Patriots had marched down the field to score a touchdown.

"There's one more thing," I added quickly.

He laughed. "There's always one more thing with you."

"I want to go back to work. It's only ten stitches, and they're healing fast. Can you clear me to return to duty?"

"You'll need to see a doctor first."

"But I really do feel fine."

"And if the doctor agrees, you can discuss the matter with your sergeant. Good night, Mike. Don't take this the wrong way, but this has been one of the more unusual conversations I have had in my career."

When I hung up the phone, I realized the agitation I had felt before was gone. I no longer wanted to pull out my hair or scratch off my skin.

Using a package of frozen moose meat from the freezer, I made chili while I listened to the television in the next room. Even the obnoxious announcers no longer bothered me. The Patriots were moving on to the next round of the championships. It felt good to hear other people celebrating.

Stacey never called back that night, and I couldn't say it surprised me. She had never been forced by her superiors to see a counselor in the aftermath of a fatality or a traumatic event. No one had ever encouraged her to give voice to her grief and guilt. As a result, she maintained her heart as a sort of Pandora's box. Keep everything locked inside, and it will all be fine. The problem was that sooner or later, that box was going to open, and that was when her demons would come flying out.

All I knew for certain was that talking with Captain DeFord had helped me. I felt better for having asked for help.

Even so, the thought of having almost lost Stacey kept me awake late. My mind churned around and around, reliving those terrible minutes between my conversation with Charley, when I had feared she was dead, and the near coronary experience of having the phone ring and hearing her voice on the other end.

After a while, I gave up trying to sleep and got up before sunrise to make coffee.

The kitchen windows were so dark, I could see my reflected self moving from sink to fridge to table. Until the doctor cleared me to return to duty, I was still in limbo. I couldn't engage in any work-related activities.

I sat down at my laptop while I ate my cereal and checked my e-mail. Nothing from Stacey, but there was a message from Pulsifer, dated the previous afternoon, that I had missed seeing:

Heads-up. DeFord might be giving you a call. I didn't tattle, so you shouldn't have any problems unless you go out of your way to piss him off. Wait, that means you're definitely going to have problems.

Talked to Jim Clegg, too. He had been expecting you to call him. What happened there? Anyway, he spoke with Amber himself and she told him about the gun.

Another piece of news. Clegg said someone in the crime lab owed him a favor and expedited the test on the blood recovered from the Ranger. The type was AB positive, same as Langstrom's. That's a rare blood type, too.

Jim is headed back to Pariahville tomorrow. He has a couple more questions for Foss.

I scrolled down the list of other e-mails, most of which were department-related, until I came to a second message from Pulsifer posted later in the evening:

Just heard about the crash at Clayton Lake! How is it possible Stacey wasn't on that chopper? Has she ever taken a sick day before?

I owe you an apology, too. Sorry I was so dickish this morning. I was mad at myself for slipping. It wasn't you. I'd been building up to it for a while (ask Lauren). But I went to a meeting this evening and got my one day chip, which is the only one that ever matters.

I wasn't ready yet to use the word *friend* to describe Gary Pulsifer. There was a dark side to the man that made me want to keep some distance between us. But he had made an effort at making amends, and I was grateful.

I checked out the Web sites of the Maine newspapers. The helicopter crash was the lead story on all of them, but there were no details in the reporting that I hadn't already heard. The flying conditions had been close to ideal, so weather was unlikely to have been a factor. The pilot, Steve Cobb, was only fifty-six and had been flying since the Gulf War. His widow was quoted as saying he'd recently had a physical that showed his cholesterol was on the high side, but otherwise he was as physically fit as a middle-aged man could be.

At seven o'clock sharp, I called Stacey's cell. There was no answer.

On a hunch, I tried the IF&W field office in Ashland, assuming that the crash investigation and recovery operations would mean someone was already in the office.

A woman with an unfamiliar voice answered. "Department of Inland Fisheries and Wildlife."

"This is Warden Mike Bowditch. Can I speak with Stacey Stevens, please?"

"Oh, hello, Warden. Stacey isn't here."

"Can you leave a message for me?"

"She might not get it for a while. She took a snowmobile out to the crash scene last night."

"What?"

It was sixty-some miles from Ashland to Clayton Lake along the infamous American Realty Road, a gravel thoroughfare maintained by loggers and nicknamed the "Reality Road" by locals because it leads through the wildest stretch of Maine.

"We tried to talk her out of it, but you know Stacey."

"She's going to catch pneumonia!"

"All I can tell you is that she radioed in when she arrived at Clayton Lake. So you don't need to worry about that at least. If she radios us again, I'll let her know you called."

I thanked the unnamed woman and restrained myself from punching the nearest wall. Did Stacey honestly believe the recovery team and crash investigators needed her help? She could be so selfish in her recklessness.

As I put my cereal bowl in the sink, I caught sight of myself in the kitchen window again.

"Don't even say it," I told my glowering reflection.

28

As I thought about the day ahead, I realized there was something productive I could do that wouldn't violate my agreement with DeFord to refrain from rule-bending activities. I would make it my personal mission to find someone willing to adopt Shadow.

I started researching what Maine state law had to say on the subject of wolf hybrids. Like most legal language, it resisted clear interpretation. Title 7, Section 3911 gave game wardens six days to dispose of a wolf hybrid at large before ownership of the animal was transferred to a shelter for it to be put down. Did that mean I was still the legal custodian of Shadow as the warden who had confiscated him? After five minutes of scratching my head, I pulled up Kathy's number and hit the call button.

My former sergeant picked up on the second ring.

"Mike! I heard about that crash up in the Allagash. Did you know Stacey was not on board?"

"Not until she called. I thought I was talking to her ghost."

"Jesus! Is she all right?"

"Not remotely. I just called the field office in Ashland and a woman there told me Stacey took a sled out to Clayton Lake because she wanted to 'help.' She practically has walking pneumonia as it is."

"And what's this I heard about you being on the sharp end of a knife?"

"That's another long story, but the short version is that I am fine. I'll tell you all the gory details later, but right now I have a question. Do you know anyone who would adopt a wolf dog?"

"So that animal you called me about really was a hybrid?"

"Afraid so. I've been looking at the law book, and I think I have six days to find a home for him before he's euthanized. Am I reading that right?"

"I never had to deal with that situation, but I'm guessing the language is vague enough that, unless the department formally transferred ownership to the shelter, you can take him around to people who might consider adopting him. It won't be easy. Most of the wolf dogs I've met have been holy terrors, especially those with the higher wolf content. What's your guess about this one?"

"I don't have to guess. He came from Montana, and the state had him listed in its registry. He's ninety percent wolf."

"Ninety percent!" Kathy said. "That's a wild animal, Mike. That's not a pet."

"I was hoping you might consider taking him."

"No."

"Please, Kathy. You have a permit, and you're so good with dogs. Pluto has been gone nearly two years and—"

"Mike, you need to stop right there."

"I'm sorry."

"You should be."

It had been rude of me to try to foist Shadow onto my friend. When Kathy was ready to adopt another dog, she would no doubt want an animal bred for search-and-rescue operations, one she could train. Wolf hybrids were probably the worst-possible animals for the work she did.

"What about some sort of sanctuary?" I asked.

She gave the question some thought. "Well, there's nothing in Maine."

"There used to be one in New Hampshire, but I heard it closed."

"Fenris Unchained didn't close," she said. "That was just a rumor because the guy who runs the place had a heart attack, and they thought he was going to die. Somehow, he recovered and is back to taking wolf dogs. I don't know if he's accepting new animals, though. More and more states are banning wolf hybrids. "

"Where's it located?"

"Just across the border in the White Mountains. I've never been there, but I heard it's a funky place. Do you want me to make a call for you?"

"Yes! Thank you, Kathy."

"What is it about this particular animal that's gotten to you?"

"I feel responsible for him."

"There's got to be more to it than that."

"I can't explain it. If you saw him, you would understand, I think."

After we'd signed off, I pondered the matter some more.

Being a game warden means dealing daily with dying and dead animals. In the course of a shift, you might be called upon to shoot a rabid fox or kill a moose whose brain has been turned into Swiss cheese by parasitic worms. The thrash-metal band Megadeth once put out an album titled *Killing Is My Business . . . and Business Is Good*. I hated the music but thought often of the title. In the course of your career, you see hundreds of dead deer, bears, moose, geese, ducks, turkeys, coyotes. The list goes on.

Game wardens couldn't afford to be sentimental about wild animals. Those feelings were a luxury that belonged to first-world people who no longer had to think about the cycle of predator and prey—people who could afford to remain ignorant of how life actually played out on planet Earth.

One of the perks of being a warden is that the department allows you to use your patrol truck on your days off, provided you reimburse the state for your mileage.

I put on civilian clothes over my long underwear—L. L. Bean boots, jeans, wool shirt, and Carhartt coat—and went out into the freezing garage.

Most days, I lived out of my patrol truck. A warden's pickup is the closest thing he or she has to an office and supply shed. Most of the gear I carried was standard from season to season: binoculars, an old-fashioned pager to receive messages when I was miles from the nearest cell tower, a camouflage jacket and pants, a spotting scope, a first-aid kit, a Mossberg 510A1 tactical shotgun, a Windham Weaponry AR-15 rifle, boxes of all kinds of ammo, evidence bags and body bags, a come-along, multiple thicknesses of rope, a sleeping bag, a GPS, a camera, crime-scene tape, flares, safety cones, et cetera.

I didn't normally travel with an animal carrier or catch pole, but I knew I would need the carrier at least on this trip. The department had just given us new talonproof gloves that extended up the arm to the elbow. They were comparable to the bite sleeves worn by dog-catchers. I threw my new gloves onto the passenger seat.

As I got behind the wheel, I saw my father's dog tags dangling from the rearview mirror. I'd forgotten that I had hung them there. I could hear Amber's last words in my head as clearly as if I were back in that smoky room again. *I thought you were a good person. I thought you were loyal. But you're just as much of a heartless bastard as Jack was. What kind of asshole son doesn't even claim his dead father's ashes?*

A son who had been utterly betrayed by his father?

I had no idea what had become of my father's ashes. I assumed that the state of Maine had some protocol for dealing with the un-wanted remains of the indigent and outcast. I figured there must be a twenty-first-century equivalent to the old potter's field. But I wasn't entirely sure where to begin looking for it.

I flicked the dog tags so that they jingled, then backed out of the garage.

The Lakes Region Animal Shelter was located in a nondescript build-ing along busy Route 302, which is the main road from Portland into the White Mountains of New Hampshire. It was one of those long, low rural structures that had probably been half a dozen things over the years—day-care center, dentist's office, travel agency, beauty salon—but which was now the temporary home for wayward cats and dogs waiting to be returned to their owners or in need of new ones.

From the icy parking lot, I couldn't see the pens at the back of the building, but I could hear the barking of dogs, large and small, let outside into the open air. At least the people who ran the shelter had had the courtesy to choose a headquarters far from the nearest residences. There was an auto-body shop across the highway, but otherwise nothing but white pines in either direction.

A buzzer sounded as I stepped through the door. I breathed in the earthy scent of cat litter and dog hair gone airborne. Muffled barks made their way through the walls. The entry was decorated with pictures of animals up for adoption and posters that offered veterinary tips for pet owners.

A thin, freckle-faced young woman appeared from another room. She was cradling a tabby under her arm. It had a bandage on its foot, a plastic cone around its neck, and a displeased expression on its small face.

"Hello?" she said in a stuttering voice.

"Good morning," I said. "I'm Mike Bowditch, the game warden who rescued the wolf dog that you're sheltering."

Rescued seemed a cruel word under the circumstances, given Shadow's likely death sentence.

Her eyes widened. "Really? That's so awesome. Oh my God, he's such a beautiful animal."

"How is he doing?"

"Dr. Carbone said he's actually very healthy." She stroked the cat's back, but to no good effect. The tabby continued to glower. "Those awful people didn't abuse him at least."

"That's good to hear." When I reached out to touch the cat's fur, it gave a hiss. "What's this guy's name?"

"Gremlin."

"What happened to him?"

"He got caught in a trap. Those things should be outlawed! Talk about animal cruelty!"

I doubted she would have liked me if I'd told her I'd gotten a junior trapping license the month I'd turned ten. I reached into my wallet and found a business card. "If you ever have problems with dogs or cats getting caught in traps, give me a call, and I'll go have a talk with the trapper."

"You'd do that? That's so sweet of you."

We smiled at each other while she stroked the cat.

"My name's Kendall," she said out of the blue.

"Can I speak with the director, please, Kendall? It's about Shadow."

"Let me put Gremlin back in his cage, and I'll go get Phyllis."

"Phyllis is the director?"

"Uh-huh. I'm just a volunteer here. I just started three weeks ago."

After Kendall disappeared into the next room, I checked my phone. There were no messages or texts from Kathy yet. I hoped she was having luck persuading the founder of Fenris Unchained to accept Shadow. If he didn't, I had no idea what I would do next.

Kendall returned after a few minutes, accompanied by a stocky middle-aged woman wearing granny glasses, a hand-knit sweater, felt pants, and sensible shoes. Her clothes were absolutely covered in dog and cat fur.

"Phyllis Murray," she said, shaking my hand solidly. "I'm the director here."

"Mike Bowditch."

"You're the warden who saved Shadow, Kendall tells me."

I removed my knit cap out of old-fashioned politeness. The way Phyllis was dressed, she struck me as the old-fashioned type. "That's right," I said. "I appreciate your taking care of him for us."

"Are you here to see him one last time?"

The implication being that his appointment with death was imminent. "No, ma'am. I'm taking him to be adopted."

She didn't stand more than five feet tall, but when she straightened her back, she seemed to grow in size. "I am confused. Shadow chased and killed a deer. Dr. Carbone has already declared him to be a danger to the public."

"I've found a sanctuary in New Hampshire willing to take him," I said, hoping it wasn't so much a lie as a prematurely told truth.

"That Fenris place?" Her eyes went to heaven. "Have you ever seen that so-called sanctuary?"

"No, ma'am. Have you?"

"No, but I've heard stories." Phyllis Murray was not a woman who was easily swayed. "We're not allowed to release a wolf dog that poses a danger to the public, even to a person licensed to possess wildlife. I'm sorry, but those aren't just shelter rules. Our hands are tied by certain laws."

"That's not entirely true, legally speaking," I said. "Title 7, Section 3911 gives my department six days to dispose of a wolf hybrid at large, before the shelter can claim ownership. That means I'm the one who is still responsible for him for the time being."

"Are you certain of that?" she asked.

"Yes, ma'am. The Warden Service is committed to doing everything we can to keep these animals from being put down. I saw on your Web site that this is a no-kill shelter."

"Normally."

"So we have the same goal here. Fortunately, Shadow has gotten a reprieve. Now if you'll excuse me, I've got a long drive ahead of me today. I'm going to go get a carrier out of the back of my truck, and I'll be right back."

I stepped outside before she could respond. Outside, traffic was moving at a steady clip in both directions. The cold air smelled heavily of auto fumes. I lifted the dog carrier from the bed of my truck and returned as quickly as I could to the shelter.

Phyllis Murray hadn't been idle. While I'd been outside, she had gone to retrieve Shadow's folder and was examining every document with great care. "My understanding was that everything had already been decided."

"Is there anything in there granting the shelter ownership of him?" I asked, hoping that no one at IF&W had signed any papers yet. I hadn't considered the possibility that somebody in the department might have unwittingly sabotaged my plan.

"No, but—" she said.

"Then let's go get him."

Phyllis Murray raised her eyes from the folder. Then, to my surprise, she laughed out loud. She had been torn between two aspects of her personality, I realized: the side that believed in strict adherence to rules and regulations, and the side devoted to saving animals at all costs. In the end, the better angels prevailed.

Still smiling, she handed the folder to Kendall. "Let's go get him."

The three of us passed through a series of rooms before arriving, finally, at the kennels. The floors were concrete, with inset drains, and there were overhead fans mounted in the ceiling that recirculated the air. The odor of urine and feces was overpowering, and the barking was so loud, it hurt my ears.

Dogs of all sorts—purebreds and mutts—surged forward, pressing their wet noses against the cages to meet us. One elderly beagle licked the steel links, unable to reach my hand.

Phyllis Murray had to shout to be heard above the animals. "We had to separate him from the other dogs. They're terrified of him."

There was a vacant kennel between Shadow and his nearest neighbor, a shivering gray mutt who looked like he was still too close to the wild animal down the lane. The black wolf dog stood in the back of his cage. He didn't approach, make a sound, wag his tail, or signal in any way that he acknowledged us. At a glance, you might have mistaken him for a stuffed animal in a museum diorama—until you stared into those eerie gold eyes.

"Isn't he, like, the most awesome thing you ever seen?" said Kendall.

"He's magnificent," said Phyllis Murray.

"How often do you let him outside?" I asked.

"We don't."

"Why not?"

"He found a spot along the bottom where the cage had broken loose of the concrete and started to attack it," Phyllis Murray said. "I didn't even know there was a hole there. He almost got out."

I crossed my arms and stared deeper into the wolf dog's uncanny eyes. To make eye contact with a predator is usually a prelude to a fight, but Shadow and I were still sizing each other up.

"Do you have some protective gloves you can put on?" Kendall asked. "We have some you can use."

"I won't need them," I said.

The schoolmarmish Phyllis Murray replied, "Yes, you do."

"He knows I'm his friend."

"Friendly dogs can tear your arm off under certain circumstances. You need to put on the gloves."

She disappeared into the adjoining room and returned with heavily armored gloves that extended past the elbow. I put them on.

I squatted down beside the carrier. "Hey, Shadow."

His eyes bored into mine. If this was going to be a challenge, would it be better for me to assert myself as an alpha? Or should I accept the role of a harmless beta to lure him close? With domestic dogs, you always want to show them who is boss. With wolf hybrids, I had absolutely no clue.

"OK, Kendall," I said. "You can open the door."

For protection, the two women kept the chain-link door between the wolf dog and themselves.

I held my breath.

None of us moved for the longest time.

And then, without further enticement, Shadow trotted forward. He ducked his head and stepped into the plastic carrier as if he'd been trained to do it. He was such a big animal, he barely fit when I closed the gate behind his tail. In the cramped box, he was going to have trouble turning around on our long journey up into the mountains.

"He really does know you're his friend," said Kendall, amazed.

"Here," said Phyllis Murray, taking a handle. "Let me help you with that."

The woman was remarkably strong. The two of us lugged the heavy crate through the series of rooms and outdoors without having to pause to rest.

"I'll take it from here," I said.

"You'll throw out your back," said Phyllis Murray.

I squatted down so that I would be using my leg muscles, and then I grabbed the two handles and pushed hard against the ground. It was like deadlifting a hundred-pound barbell. Getting the carrier onto the truck gate took everything I had, and I knew I was going to be stiff for days afterward. The wolf dog growled and flicked his tail. I crawled into the bed of the pickup and pushed the box until it was right behind the cab, out of the wind. Then I tied the kennel tight with bungees to the frame of the truck.

"Call us, please, when you get there," said Phyllis.

"I will."

"It means everything to us to know they're safe."

I hadn't driven three miles when the phone buzzed. It was Kathy.

"You're in luck," she said. "The sanctuary is going to take your wolf dog. The guy I spoke with sounds like a character. He made me promise to make a donation to his cause in exchange for taking the animal on short notice. I hope you brought cash, because I don't think he takes credit cards."

"That is awesome," I said, chuckling. "But I wish you'd called me half an hour ago."

"What did you just do, Grasshopper?"

"My good deed for the day."

29

After I had crossed into New Hampshire, I stopped at a rest area to get my bearings.

The Fenris Unchained Wolf Refuge had a Web page that looked as if it had been built in 1990 and not updated since. I recognized the name Fenris as belonging to a monstrous wolf out of Norse mythology. The site consisted mainly of pixelated photos of wolf dogs inside a border of Nordic runes with a flashing button to click if you wished to make a donation. No driving directions were given—the refuge didn't welcome drop-in visitors—but Kathy had gotten route information from the guy who ran the place. His name, she'd told me, was Dale Probert.

By my rough calculation, I guessed it would take an hour to get there, allowing for traffic. I checked on Shadow, who had somehow found a way to lie down in the tight carrier. He sniffed my hand, then went back to sleep.

I decided I had better get moving if I wanted to be home before nightfall.

The summit of Mount Washington was hidden in clouds of its own making. It was the tallest mountain in New England. Even more noteworthy, the highest winds ever measured on the planet, 231 miles per hour, had been recorded at the weather station at the top.

Mount Washington was a killer and not to be underestimated. I remembered the time when my college friends and I had gone back-country skiing down the face of Tuckerman's Ravine. All of the sensations I had felt that glorious April day came back in a rush: the burning in my quads as I trudged up the ridge, carrying my skis over my shoulder; the surprising warmth of the spring sun on my face; the moment of stomach-dropping fear at the top; and then the burst of adrenaline as I pushed off into space. Skiing had always made me feel so alive, even more so because it had never come easily to me.

Maybe when Stacey visited again we could try it, but when would that be? Not until after the funerals. I'd had more brushes with death than any man my age should have, but I had never lost three close friends in a single day.

I stopped at a market in the failing mill town of Berlin and got an Italian sandwich, a bag of salt and vinegar chips, and a jug of water. At the meat counter in back, I bought a package of stew beef for Shadow. I had a feeling that the stomachs of near wolves were not well adapted to digesting kibble made from soybeans and corn.

I pressed the chunks of beef one by one through the metal gate. He took them gently, as if not wanting to nip my fingers with his fangs. He even held his mouth open while I poured water from the jug into his throat. This was, indeed, one of the smartest animals I had ever seen.

Kathy had told me to turn east off Route 16, cross the Androscoggin River, and then head up the backside of the Mahoosuc Range. As I climbed out of the valley floodplain, I found that the roads grew worse and worse with every passing mile. Eventually, I couldn't see the paving beneath the compacted layer of snow. Kathy had told me to watch for a signpost. When I passed a weathered rail carved with Viking runes sticking up out of a snowbank, I felt confident I was on the right path.

The woods around me were mostly young evergreens with an understory of poplars and willows. The trees had been cut hard a couple of decades earlier, which might have explained how Dale Probert had gotten the acreage cheap. Few buyers viewed clear-cut hillsides as investment opportunities. I checked my cell phone and saw a NO SERVICE message. I had entered the geographical middle of nowhere.

I reached for my pager and clipped it to my belt.

The road evened out along a ridgetop, but I found my eyes rising above the ragged skyline. Up high, in the distance, circled dozens and dozens of black birds. They were not crows. They were ravens, recognizable by their shaggy throats and wedge-shaped tails. Their calls carried across the winter landscape: a chorus of croaks, rasps, chortles, and knocks.

I rolled down my window to listen, and that was when I heard the wolves.

In my life, I had heard hundreds of coyotes and even more dogs, but never anything like this except in television shows. Wolves had been extirpated from the Northeast more than a century ago. Never in my life had I expected to hear them howling in the wild mountains of New England.

I wished Stacey could have been here to share the moment with me.

Suddenly, Shadow started howling as well. Which only excited the others even more. A few ravens peeled off from the others to have a look at us.

I spun my tires, I was in such a hurry to see what was ahead.

When I finally crested the last hill, the scene that greeted me could not have been further from my romantic imaginings. The refuge was located at the bottom of a basin between clear-cut hillsides. It seemed to consist of a rusting mobile home, a handful of weathered sheds, and a checkerboard of wire-fenced pens. Each scrubby enclosure housed a handful of wolflike dogs of various shapes, sizes, and colors.

As I rode the brake down the hill, a skinny old man emerged from inside the trailer.

I climbed out of the truck and raised my arm. "You must be Mr. Probert."

"And you must be the warden with the wolf." His voice was harsh as a raven's, little more than a rasp.

He was wearing a leather hat, glasses that darkened in the sun, and a sweatshirt with a wolf airbrushed on the front. His slim-cut jeans only made his long legs look thinner. Cigarette smoke trailed from the butt clutched between his fingers.

I introduced myself and we shook hands. Probert's face appeared even more gaunt, with just the thinnest layer of skin covering the bones. If I were to come upon his skeleton sometime in the future, I felt that I would be able to recognize him from his skull alone.

"Well, let's have a look at him," he said.

I moved around to the back of the truck and leaped into the bed.

Probert peered over the side. "High-content animal," he said, expelling smoke with every word. "Ninety percent or so, I would estimate. What's this handsome fellow's name?"

"The people who had him last called him Shadow."

"That won't do," said Probert. "An alpha like this deserves a kingly name."

"How do you know he's an alpha male?"

"You see the fierceness in those eyes?" When he spoke, the skeletal man used his cigarette as a prop, waving it in the air for emphasis, pointing the orange tip to draw attention. "I'll tell you right now, if I were to let him loose in one of my pens with another alpha, there'd be a dead wolf in five minutes. What is his history? How did he come to be in your possession?"

"A couple of drug dealers got him from another drug dealer, who got him from who knows where," I said. "But there's a tattoo on his belly saying he came from Montana originally. No one knows how he got to Maine."

"I am sure it was an odyssey," he said. "But he looks healthy enough, and your lady friend said he's been neutered and vaccinated. She is quite the pistol, your lady friend. I'd hoped she might be coming with you."

"This is quite an operation you've got," I said, surveying the acres of fenced pens.

I still couldn't get over the howls I was hearing, or the aerial show overhead. To think that the ancient partnership between wolves and ravens, long gone from this part of the world, had re-formed here was nothing short of awe-inspiring.

Probert led the way. "Come on, I'll show you around."

We followed a dirty, trampled path to the first chain-link enclosure, where a couple of animals that looked more like German shepherds than wolves rushed forward, wagging their tails. The snow inside was grooved from the trails the animals had made, littered with chewed bones, and stained with urine. The fence looked to be about twelve feet high, but the unshoveled snowbank on the opposite side provided a natural ramp. It wouldn't be hard at all for one of them to escape, I thought worriedly.

"Good day, ladies." Probert extended his long fingers to be licked.

I judged the pen to be about an acre in size, maybe an acre and a half, with an island of short firs in the center. From the depths of the evergreens, a third wolf dog peered at us. It had the recognizable long legs and snout of the wilder mixes.

"That's Macduff," said my guide. "He's a little shy. Bad story there. Terrible abuse and neglect. The people who had him in Pennsylvania never changed his collar, and so as he grew, it began to strangulate him. Amazing that he even made it here. Macduff has the distinction of being the only one of my brothers and sisters to bite me. It happened as I removed him from his crate, and no, I haven't yet become a werewolf."

Brothers and sisters? I wasn't so sure Probert didn't howl at the moon occasionally.

The wolves had grown louder since I had arrived. The arrival of the newcomer, Shadow, was causing a commotion.

"How many animals do you have here?" I asked above the howls.

"Thirty-seven at the moment. Housed in six pens. Each is a perfect pack structure, with an alpha and beta pair running the show. The way of the wolf."

"And you run this entire refuge yourself?"

"My apprentice, Kara, is off on a 'meat run,' as we call it. A slaughterhouse generously gives us its scraps. Wolves prefer the company of females to males. They associate our sex with death and danger, I have come to believe. And with good cause."

"They seem to like you."

"That's because I have taken the time to learn their language. Wolves communicate in all manner of ways, from their posture to their facial expressions. Their vocalizations are more nuanced than they might seem to the untrained ear, more complex than that of dogs. What you hear as yips and yaps, I hear as full sentences. But if you really want to see into the soul of a wolf, you need to look into its eyes."

Dale Probert and Don Foss couldn't have been any more different physically, and yet they both shared an inflated sense of self-importance and a mannered way of speaking, as if they had attended the same preschool eons ago. But whereas I had doubts about Foss's motives, it was clear Probert sincerely cared for his wolves. As run-down as this refuge might appear, he seemed to be doing his best to create a true sanctuary. Unlike Pariahville, this was a place of protection and caring, not exile and exploitation.

It's the word *sanctuary* that's tripping me up, I told myself. I was drawing a false equivalency between the two operations. What mattered was finding the best home for Shadow, and if this was it, then so be it.

Meanwhile, overhead, the ravens wheeled.

30

Probert continued his lecture as we tramped from pen to pen. He told me horror stories of animals that had lived their lives in dark cellars before coming to him or had arrived with gruesome wounds he had been forced to stitch himself. ("I am an autodidact and a veterinarian self-taught," he declared.) The wolf dogs looked healthy enough, and clearly the old man had devoted his life to this makeshift shelter.

"This is our transitional pen," Probert said as we finished our circle. "This is where I'll introduce our newcomer to his new pack members."

A longhaired dog rushed up to the fence as we drew near, and if I hadn't known better, I would have sworn it was a purebred collie. Its tail was swaying and its mouth was open, but there was a desperate look in its eyes, as if it had been falsely imprisoned. Couldn't I see that it was here by mistake?

"Luna is low content, but we love her just the same," Probert said.

Suddenly, the pager on my belt began to flash and beep. There was a reason the Warden Service still used those antiquated messaging devices: They worked even when you were well out of range of a cell tower. I recognized the number as Gary Pulsifer's.

"Can I use your telephone?" I asked.

"As long as you're not planning on calling Timbuktu."

"No, just Maine."

"We're practically standing on the Maine border here," Probert said. "The state line isn't even a mile to the east."

243

Probert lit another cigarette, using the smoldering butt of one to ignite the next.

I made my way into the nearby trailer. The smell of smoke had penetrated every swatch of fabric: curtains, carpets, and furniture. The walls were paneled with fake wood and decorated with snapshots of assorted wolf dogs, along with a disorienting number of pages torn from past *Sports Illustrated* swimsuit issues. An old rotary telephone sat on a desk beside an overflowing ashtray.

"Gary, it's Mike."

"Where are you?"

"New Hampshire."

"Where?"

"I'm over in the Mahoosucs. There's this sanctuary for wolf dogs."

"I'm not even going to ask," he said. "You need to get over here. Something's happened at Foss's place."

"What do you mean?"

"Clegg was heading up to the compound again, but no one answered at the gate, so he decided to walk in. A hundred yards up the road, he found one of the sex offenders shot dead. Clegg hightailed it back to his car and called for backup. I'm heading out there."

"Wow."

"I know. You need to get over here."

I calculated the distance in my head. "Gary, I'm more than an hour away."

"You spent the past few days poking around Pariahville, trying to find out what happened to Adam Langstrom, and now there's been at least one murder there. Do you have other plans or something?"

"By the time I get there—"

"Who knows what will be happening. But we might just need you."

This was Pulsifer at his most devilish. The man knew exactly how to tempt me.

"It's your choice," he said, and hung up.

Ever since I'd learned the blood in Adam's truck matched his rare blood type, I had been positive he'd been murdered. I'd let my suspicions harden into certainties. But what if he had survived whatever had happened inside his pickup? I could easily picture him returning to Foss's place to exact some kind of vengeance.

My father's face appeared when I shut my eyes. His face, my face, Adam's face.

Not again, I thought. It can't be possible.

I stepped out into the cold air to the excited howls of wolves. While I had been on the phone, a pickup had descended into the refuge and parked beside me. The driver was a woman, early thirties, on the heavy side, and even from a distance I could tell she was no beauty. But Probert was beaming at her as if she had stepped straight from one of his bikini posters. They were both leaning over the bed of my truck, cooing to Shadow.

The old man straightened up. "Warden, this is my apprentice, Kara. Kara, this is Warden Bowdoin."

"Bowditch. Nice to meet you." The blood was rushing so quickly to my head, it was making my brain ache.

"Your wolf is gorgeous!" She was wearing heavy rubber gloves that I associated with dirty jobs done in dirty places.

"He's not mine," I said. "Listen, I'm afraid I have to go. Something important has come up."

"And miss feeding time?" said Probert.

He stepped to the other pickup and, with all the theatricality of a birthday party magician, pulled loose a blue tarp that had been covering the contents of the bed. Kara's truck was filled with severed pig heads.

"Disgusting, I know," he said, "but the wolves consider them to be delicacies."

"I had pig cheeks once," said Kara. "Kind of rubbery, but not bad."

"I really have to get going," I said again.

"Then we should introduce your passenger to his new family," said Probert. "Did your lady friend mention how reliant we are here on donations?"

Without thinking, I reached for my wallet and removed three twenties, leaving myself with a few ones.

"Thank you." The old man crushed the bills in his tight fist. "Kara, can you help the warden get that kennel out of his truck?"

"I can do it," I said.

I jumped up into the bed and unlashed the cords that held the plastic box in place. Shadow had begun to grow restless. He was twitching his tail and making a strange noise that reverberated from deep inside his powerful chest.

"He doesn't sound happy," I said.

"He's just excited," said Probert. "He knows this is the first day of the rest of his life."

I squatted on my haunches and stared through the grate at the wild animal inside. Ever since I had arrived here, I had begun to think of him that way: not as a wolf dog or a wolf hybrid. Shadow was a wolf.

I rubbed my chin and then my eyes. I shook my head as if in disagreement with someone I alone could hear.

Probert was the self-professed wolf whisperer. What did I know about these animals? Once again, Shadow and I locked eyes. His irises were streaked with dark flecks I hadn't noticed before. His pupils were as black as Pleistocene tar pits.

I climbed to my feet. "You know, I think I am going to take him with me."

"Huh?" said Probert.

"I don't mean any offense, but this isn't the best place for him."

"I can't imagine where you think he might be better off," said the old man. "This refuge is the best of its kind in the world."

I certainly hoped that wasn't true.

"He'll be happy here, you'll see," said Kara. "Come visit him in a few weeks."

"He belongs among his own kind, Warden," said Probert. "Your lady friend told me he would be euthanized unless we gave him asylum. Perhaps you've grown too attached to him and are not thinking through the consequences of your actions."

I laughed out loud.

"Excuse me?" he said indignantly.

"It's nothing," I said. "It's the story of my life."

Driving down out of the mountains, I was overwhelmed by the foolishness of what I had just done. I had lied and connived to rescue Shadow, and then, when I had finally found a sanctuary for the wolf,

I had upended my plans, and for what? Because he had communicated telepathically that he didn't want to be imprisoned in one of those sad pens with a wrongfully accused collie?

The idea of becoming one of those people who projects their personal emotions on animals depressed me. Even more so when I reflected on the death sentence the wolf still faced if I didn't succeed in finding an angel willing to care for him. It seemed like every possibility had already been exhausted.

I'd even paid Probert sixty dollars for the privilege of changing my mind. The old man would undoubtedly put the money to good use. Buy some more pig heads or renew his subscription to *Sports Illustrated*.

For the moment, I had more pressing concerns.

If Clegg had gotten no response when he phoned Foss's office, it suggested multiple casualties might be waiting for the first responders. The cops arriving on the scene would have to assume the presence of an active shooter. It was every police officer's worst nightmare.

Before the Columbine shootings in 1999, police had been taught to respond to active shooters by securing a perimeter around the scene and waiting for a tactical team to arrive. The folly of that approach only grew more and more apparent as massacres began to multiply at high schools, on college campuses, in churches, and outside women's health clinics.

At the Academy, I had been taught the new standard: immediate action rapid deployment. The term was fancy jargon for swarming the shooter. Don't sit around waiting for a negotiator. Mass murderers don't negotiate. Sure, SWAT teams are highly skilled, but how many more innocents might die while the first officers on the scene sit on their hands? Pulsifer and the others would have no alternative but to rush into gun sights, while all I could do was say a silent prayer and do my best not to collide with a deer.

Light snow had begun to fall. It sparkled like broken windshield glass from the patches of bare pavement. I drove fast along Route 16, well over the posted speed, until a light came on my dashboard telling me I was close to running on fumes. I stopped for gas in Errol, New Hampshire, the last town of any size between Berlin and Rangeley.

I leaned over the side of the truck bed to have a look at Shadow. He was adapted to live in subzero temperatures, but I hated the thought of keeping him cooped up in that cramped box. Every time he opened his mouth, steam escaped from between his fangs.

"Are you going to run off if I let you out?" I asked him.

That old geezer in the Green Beret shirt had told me he'd seen Shadow riding in Carrie Michaud's truck. I decided to risk it.

I found a bag of beef jerky in my rucksack and waved it outside the kennel gate so he could get a whiff of the dried meat. Shadow began to whine and saliva dripped from his ragged black lips. As I opened the gate, I wondered if he would snatch the bag from my hand—or my hand from my wrist—and sprint away into the nearby woods. But I managed to lure him out with scraps of jerky. I led him from the bed, around the side, and into the passenger seat.

"Good boy," I said, as he hopped up into the Sierra.

He stared hard at me until I dumped the rest of the jerky at his feet.

A man I hadn't noticed before came over from the next gas pump, holding a quart cup of fountain soda. "What kind of dog is that?"

"Have you ever read Jack London's *White Fang*?" I asked.

"My wife reads. I don't have time for it." He sipped loudly through the straw from the ice at the bottom of his cup.

"It's a good book."

"Look, mister," he said, "if you don't want to tell me what your dog is, that's your business. But you don't have to be a dink about it." Then he wandered off.

I got back behind the wheel and looked over at the hundred-pound wolf sitting beside me, steaming up the windshield.

31

Dusk was creeping up fast as I crossed the state line into Maine. I turned up the police radio. Multiple officers, identifiable by their call numbers, were arriving on the scene in Kennebago. An ambulance from the Northstar base in Rangeley was en route. Two other wardens I knew in Division B—Bill Gordon and Jeff White—radioed in. And I had miles yet to go.

My father's dog tags swung back and forth before my eyes like a hypnotist's watch. Shadow seemed mesmerized by them, as well.

"What do you think?" I asked the wolf.

He paid me no attention.

"Is Adam still alive? He can't be, right? With all that blood in the truck?"

Shadow sighed through his nose and then began licking one of his sooty paws.

"You're not going to help me, are you?"

The wolf raised its eyes back to the white road.

Even with lights and sirens clearing the way through downtown Rangeley, it took me another hour to arrive in Kennebago.

The side road up to Foss's compound was blockaded by two police cruisers. Their drivers—sheriff's deputies in brown parkas and reflective safety vests—stood on Moose Alley, directing traffic past the scene. Despite the best efforts of the dispatchers, the radio chatter had brought out the inevitable rubberneckers.

As I came up on the first shivering deputy, I rolled down my window. He had red cheeks from the cold, which made me think of a father who had let his little daughter put makeup on his face.

"What's the situation?" I asked.

"They're still counting bodies up there."

I had feared as much. "Any of our guys?"

"No."

That was a relief. "And the shooter?"

"Gone with the wind."

"Any idea who we're looking for?"

"Man, I'm just directing traffic. What kind of dog is that?"

"Belgian Malinois," I said, not wanting to start a conversation.

"Big fellow! Hang on a second and I'll let you through. A bunch of wardens are already up there."

I had beat the television news vans at least. But the media would soon be descending on this spot like ravens on a dead moose. The mass murder of sex offenders at a remote camp in the Maine woods was a national story—an international story, in fact. The information officer for the Department of Public Safety was soon going to be the most sought-after interview in the state.

The deputy backed his car up to let me through. Within a hundred yards, I began encountering emergency vehicles of all sorts parked along the road. I passed Logan Dyer's house and noticed that the windows were dark and the garage door was closed. Dyer was the nearest thing Don Foss had to a neighbor, which made him both a potential witness and a suspect, since there had been no love lost between them.

Suddenly, Shadow let out a howl, and I nearly hit my head on the ceiling. This was the first time I'd heard the wolf in full throat, and I began to understand why medieval villagers had cowered inside their huts after dark.

In response, Dyer's hounds began baying loudly from inside the house. Logan had mentioned using his Plott hounds to hunt coyotes. Shadow snarled—an even more ferocious sound. He had good reason to be on edge. Those big dogs were his natural enemies. Where was Dyer? He didn't seem the sort to leave his prize hunting dogs home alone.

An ambulance approached slowly from the opposite direction. Its emergency lights were off, which could mean only one thing: There was no one left to be saved in Pariahville.

I pulled against the right snowbank to make room.

The emergency medical technician at the wheel rolled down his window so we could have a chat. He was a big woodsy guy with flushed cheeks and a white beard. His partner, beside him, looked ashen.

"Have you been up there yet?" the driver asked in a deep baritone.

"No, I just arrived."

"Imagine the worst death scene you've ever worked and then multiply it by ten. Most of them were killed in their bunks or trying to get out of them."

"What about Foss?"

"The shooter gave him special attention." The EMT's tired eyes grew wide as he spotted Shadow beside me. "Holy hell! What in the world is that beast with you? Is that a wolf dog?"

"I had to confiscate him from some drug addicts," I said. "He's a sweetheart, though."

"I'll take your word for it!"

I was eager to return to the subject at hand. "So the state police think it was just one guy?"

"One guy with an AR-15 and a whole bunch of clips."

That wasn't much help. Black guns, as some people called them, were as common up here now as M1 rifles used to be in the Maine woods after World War II. Their omnipresence was why the service had equipped us with Windham Weaponry MPCs; we had been in serious danger of being outgunned at every firefight.

"He was a regular Audie Murphy, too," the EMT said. "That's what I'm hearing. The CSI guys are still mapping the scene up there. Maybe they'll find it was two shooters. They're leaving all the bodies where they fell until they can finish photographing everything. They said they'd call us again when they're ready for us to cart them away. They're going to need a caravan of ambulances for that job, let me tell you." He scratched his woolly beard. "I didn't think I could ever feel sorry for those men, after the things they did. I used to say that prison was too good for them, but now—"

He didn't finish the sentence. He just rolled up his window and drove away.

Adam had been a good shot. I'd seen the evidence in the deer mounts on his bedroom walls. But he had taken a Glock handgun from his mother's apartment, not a semiautomatic rifle. Unless he had used the money he'd taken off Josh Davidson to buy a carbine.

Dyer had mentioned owning a black gun, too. A Smith & Wesson. I forgot which model.

But, really, the list of potential suspects was close to endless. All it would have taken was for one crackpot to have read Johnny Partridge's inflammatory column about the pampered pedophiles of Kennebago. The worst-case scenario was some unaffiliated vigilante—just a random kook with a gun—who had traveled in to do the job and had now disappeared back wherever the hell he'd come from.

As I neared Foss's gate, I came up on a cluster of wardens gathered around an unmarked patrol truck. They were all wearing headlamps and looking at a topographical map spread across the hood. Sooner or later, I would have to show Shadow to them, and I would need to explain what he was doing in my pickup, but I had sped all the way up here to find out what had happened. Show-and-tell could wait a few minutes.

I left the wolf in the truck and buttoned up my coat to join the others.

"Hey!" I said.

Pulsifer glanced up. With his headlamp, he looked like a coal miner. "What did I tell you guys? Bowditch can't help himself."

"You make me sound like a compulsive gambler."

"Your words, not mine."

"Good to see you, Mike," said Bill Gordon. He was Pulsifer's sergeant, despite being nearly a decade younger. Gordon was new to the division—he had worked up in Aroostook County for years—and had never met my father. Many of the other area wardens shared Pulsifer's hatred for the late Jack Bowditch and still treated me as the son of a cop killer. Jeff White, the other warden present, fell into that category.

"You want to bring me up to speed?" I said.

"CID is controlling the death scene," said Gordon. "They want as few people as possible disturbing it, which is why we're down here. Word is it was a regular bloodbath."

"More like a turkey shoot," said White.

"And none alive to tell the tale," added Pulsifer, as if quoting some famous novel I didn't recognize.

"So most of them were shot in their bunks?" I asked.

"All of them except Wallace Bickford," said Pulsifer. "He must have been out taking a leak, because when Clegg found his body, the old dude's wang was hanging out of his union suit."

Poor Wally, I thought. A pathetic ending to a pathetic life.

"What about Foss?" I asked.

"Clegg found him outside his trailer," said Pulsifer. "Don must have heard the shots and screams, because he came out with a big old Ruger 500. Got a couple of pops off, too, before the shooter made Swiss cheese out of his face."

"Any sign that the shooter was wounded in the exchange?" I asked.

"No," said Gordon. "This guy knew what he was doing. He made sure to walk on the road and keep to the heavily traveled paths. It's going to be wicked tough picking out his boot prints from all the others."

"What about tire tracks?"

Pulsifer removed his glove and used his index finger to trace a wavy line on the snow-dotted map. "My guess is he took a snowmobile up here. There's a spur trail a quarter mile away that goes across a bridge over the Dead River and up past Kennebago Settlement. It connects with Route Eighty-nine of the ITS on one end and the Black Fly Loop on the other. I can ride from my house here and cross only two paved roads."

"Which means he could have gone anywhere," said Gordon. "And he has a full day's start on us, too."

"What did he use for rounds, .223's?" I asked.

"No, .300 Blackouts," said Jeff White.

Now that was interesting. I hadn't come across many hunters who used that particular cartridge. "Aren't .300 Blackouts supposed to be a good fit for a gun with a suppressor?"

"Quieter than a vulture's sneeze," said Pulsifer.

"His choice of cartridges is distinctive," I said. "Maybe the detectives can use that."

Jeff White turned his head toward me, blinding me with his head-lamp. He was a veteran officer who worked out of Kingfield and was one of the wardens my father had bested time and time again. "Maybe you should go up there and help them out."

I tried to pretend I hadn't heard the insult. "Has anyone spoken with Logan Dyer yet?"

"Can't find him," said Gordon.

"I heard his dogs baying inside his house." I turned toward Pul-sifer. "Doesn't that seem strange to you? That he would leave them alone?"

Pulsifer adjusted the strap of his headlight. "Yeah, I'm sure we're going to get word that he's a person of interest. Adam Langstrom, too."

"Langstrom?" asked Jeff White. "Isn't he dead?"

"Someone with his blood type bled a lot in his truck," I said.

"I heard he and Foss had a fight," said Pulsifer. "Maybe he came back looking to even the score."

"By massacring everyone?" The disbelief in my voice seemed stri-dent in my own ears.

And where had Pulsifer heard that Adam had tussled with Foss? Gary hadn't been in the room for my conversation with Wallace Bickford. And I had never mentioned the black eye to him.

"For all we know," I said, "what happened to Langstrom could have been a dry run for what happened here last night."

"You mean someone's on a rampage, executing sex offenders?" said Pulsifer. He sounded more excited than horrified.

"Just once I wish things would happen like they do on TV," said Jeff White. "You know, the killer leaves a partial thumbprint on the dead man's eyeball."

"Except Foss doesn't have eyeballs anymore," said Pulsifer.

"There is that," said Gordon.

32

What was so surreal was that it had become a beautiful night: the snow drifting through the beams of the headlamps, the frosted boughs of the evergreens, the pools of violet shadows at the edge of the light. The dreamlike scene reminded me of a Japanese woodblock print I had seen at the Colby Museum when I was a student there. Those college days seemed so long ago now. I had traveled so far since then.

I had to remind myself of the horrible event that had brought us all here. Up the hill, out of sight, evidence technicians were snapping photographs. A K-9 and its handler were running tracks between the buildings, searching for something, anything. Some unlucky cops had been given the task of bagging the dead bodies. The senior officers were on their phones with state police headquarters and the FBI, planning next steps. Because of the darkness and the absence of leads, the manhunt hadn't yet begun.

But down at the gate, the woods seemed eerily serene. There was not a hint of wind. Fat flakes of snow floated nearly straight down. We were all waiting for orders, and there was nothing to do until the instructions came down from on high.

Not everyone was as spellbound as I was.

Jeff White stamped his booted feet to drive blood into them. "This waiting around is bullshit. What if this maniac is on a killing spree? He could be headed to Sugarloaf or Widowmaker next."

"This wasn't random," said Gordon. "Our guy has a hatred of sex offenders."

"Who doesn't?" said White. "You might as well add half the people in the county to the suspect list, including me."

255

"Are you confessing, Jeff?" asked Pulsifer, giving White one of his grins.

"I won't be crying in my pillow tonight," White said. "I'll admit that much."

Jeff White reminded me of Tommy Volk and some of the other wardens I knew who believed in a code of rough justice they'd picked up from watching Westerns. I had been a history major, and I had read once that the Old West depicted on-screen bore no resemblance to the reality of that era, when men voluntarily surrendered their six-shooters before going into saloons and when bank heists were rare enough to count on two hands. Men like White and Volk preferred the myths, since they validated their own violent preconceptions.

"They didn't deserve to be gunned down in their sleep, Jeff," I said.

"Fuck you, Bowditch," he said by way of a counterargument.

To clear my head, I decided to check on Shadow.

The wolf whined when he caught my scent in the air. I shined my flashlight inside the truck and saw a pool of urine on my passenger seat. I knew I should have let him out sooner.

"Is that him? Is that your wolf dog?" Pulsifer appeared at my shoulder as if from a puff of smoke.

"He's not mine."

"Then why are you driving around with him?"

"Because I am trying to find him a home," I said. "I was in New Hampshire visiting a refuge for wolf hybrids. The people there would have taken him, and they seemed nice enough. I just didn't like the vibe of the place."

"You're too softhearted for this job," said Pulsifer.

"I'm getting kind of sick of hearing that."

"I hate to tell you, but Jeff is right," he said. "Lots of people are going to cheer when they hear a bunch of sexual predators got put down. Whoever did this will end up being a folk hero."

What if it really had been Adam? Might he have seen executing the other sex offenders as some sort of act of redemption? Hadn't he told his mother that Pariahville deserved to be burned to the ground?

Pulsifer seemed intrigued by Shadow. "What do you think would happen if you let him out?"

"I'm afraid he'd run off."

"Or eat some little girl in a red cape," he said.

"Doesn't the wolf eat the grandmother?"

We heard a sharp whistle. I turned and saw Sergeant Gordon waving us back up the hill. I would have to mop up the piss later.

"Listen to this," Gordon said. "Someone shot up a house over in Eustis this afternoon. An old guy was inside watching television. Suddenly, glass started exploding everywhere and he hit the deck. Bullets were tearing up the walls, but he managed to crawl into the bathroom and hide inside the tub. The only thing that saved him was that his son and a bunch of his drinking buddies came riding up on their snowmobiles. By the time they could get the old guy to explain what had happened, the shooter was gone."

"Who is the guy?" Pulsifer asked. "What's his name?"

"Ducharme."

White and Pulsifer grunted simultaneously.

"Let me guess," I said. "He's listed on the public registry."

"Ducharme fondled his seven-year-old niece," said Pulsifer. "He inserted various objects into her, if I remember correctly. When he got out of prison a few years back, Joe at the Bigelow General Store got a bunch of business owners together, and they banned him from entering their establishments. The only reason Ducharme probably didn't end up here with Foss is that his born-again son took him in."

"It looks like our vigilante is just getting started," Pulsifer said.

"He probably figured what the hell," said White. "'I already mowed down ten of them. Why stop now?'"

"So here's what's happening," said Gordon. "We're all getting our own personal predator to protect."

"You are shitting me," said Jeff White.

The sergeant rubbed his bare hands together and blew on them. "If this guy is going from house to house, using the registry to pick his targets, then we have a general idea where he might be headed next."

"There are dozens of names on that list, just in this area," I said.

"Shouldn't we be out on our sleds?" asked White. "If this guy is riding a snowmobile, then we should be out looking for him on the trails, not parked in front of some pedophile's driveway."

"Major Carter says it's all hands on deck tonight, until he can get more of his own men up here. But I expect tomorrow you're going to get your wish. They'll have planes in the air first thing in the morning and we'll be setting up checkpoints all over Franklin and Somerset counties."

"Crazy night," said Pulsifer. "The safest people in these mountains are going to be convicted sex offenders."

Gordon got on the phone again to confer with the state police. Then he huddled with Pulsifer and White to give them their assignments. Pulsifer was given a pedophile nearby in Coplin Plantation. White got a statutory rapist in Rangeley. Neither warden seemed delighted with his chosen blind date.

"What about me?" I asked the sergeant.

"You haven't even been cleared for duty, Bowditch. Isn't that what I heard?"

"Yeah, but I can help."

He removed a key fob from his pocket. "Actually, Jim Clegg said he wanted to talk to you. He should be down in a few minutes."

"Did he say what it's about?"

"Not to me," he said.

I returned to my truck and used a towel to wipe up the urine. I tried letting Shadow out to see if he needed to shit, and sure enough, he did. It was the biggest pile I had ever seen come out of a canine.

How to get him back inside the truck now? I found a box of protein bars I kept in the glove compartment, ate one, and fed the rest to Shadow, who chomped them to pieces, Cookie Monster–style. In my Internet research, I had read something about wild wolves eating twenty pounds of meat a day.

I had no clue how to care for this animal. Maybe I should find a motel room for the night, then swing back to Fenris Unchained in the morning. Hopefully, Dale Probert would forgive my change of heart.

Every time headlights appeared, cutting a hazy arc through the darkness, I figured it must be Clegg, but I was always disappointed. I watched the first ambulance return to begin transporting the bodies to the medical examiner's office in Augusta. It was followed by a second and a third.

Another vehicle approached from the direction of Route 16, a Ford Explorer Interceptor. I recognized it at once by its midnight blue paint job. I scrambled out of my pickup and stepped into the road.

Russo rolled down his window. I got a whiff of the peppermint gum he had been chewing. "I didn't expect to see you here," he said.

"I could say the same thing."

"Thought I'd come over after my shift was done and see how I could help." Russo's bland face reminded me of someone who'd been injected with Botox, so that every muscle was paralyzed.

"I don't suppose you've seen Logan Dyer today," I said.

"No, I haven't. In fact, that's one of the reasons I'm here. Logan's been calling in sick a lot. He's been convinced he has a brain tumor."

"Yeah, you told me."

"This morning, he didn't even bother to call."

"Really?"

"I'm worried about him. There was no answer at his door just now when I knocked."

"Did Dyer's dogs start baying when you knocked at his door?"

Russo turned his head away from me to face the hill. "You know, they did, and I thought it was strange. Logan never goes anywhere without his Plotts."

His face began to glow, and I realized it was from the lights of another vehicle coming down the hill, its beams shining inside his SUV. I turned to see who it was, and it was Clegg. Instead of moving his Explorer aside, Russo unbuckled his lap belt and stepped down into the snow beside me.

Detective Clegg kept his engine running as he emerged from his cruiser. He walked toward us with his hands deep in the pockets of his brown uniform parka. His nose and cheeks were rosy from a long day spent outdoors. His chalk white hair was standing up, as if he'd just removed a hat.

"Lieutenant," said Russo, greeting Clegg by his official rank.

"Russo. Who's that with you?"

"Mike Bowditch," I said.

"Just the man I was looking for."

"Why is that?" asked Russo, as if it was any of his business.

"I spoke with Amber Langstrom yesterday and she mentioned that you came to her apartment."

"I apologize. I'd been meaning to talk with you about it."

Clegg shrugged. "Doesn't matter now. But she told me you found a box of her son's guns there."

"That's right," I said. "He took a Glock with him. His mom sensed he was afraid of someone in particular and wanted it for self-defense. Did you find any nine-millimeter shells up there?"

"Not yet." He removed his bare hands from his pockets and rubbed them together for warmth. "Is it possible Langstrom also had an AR-15 rifle?"

"Possible, I guess. I found a Ruger American in a .30-06 and a Winchester 76 in .30-30. Both with boxes of ammo. I didn't see signs of an AR-15, and Amber didn't mention his having any other rifles."

Clegg raised his face to the falling snow. I could tell he was trying to work through a puzzle in his head.

"I heard that you found .300 Blackout rounds up there," I said.

Clegg lowered his eyes. "That's right."

"Nothing else?"

"Nothing except some casings from Foss's revolver."

I got a look at Russo in my peripheral vision. He was standing stock-still. "Detective, I'd like to talk with you about Logan Dyer," I said.

"We don't know where he is," said Clegg.

"Dyer didn't show up at work today," interjected Russo. "Usually he calls if he's sick, but he didn't this morning. I just knocked at his door, and his dogs are inside. That's very unusual for Logan, to leave his dogs alone."

My jaw nearly dropped. Russo had just laid out all of my suspicions as if they were his own.

"We did a check on his house," said Clegg. "Made a sweep around the exterior, looked in the windows, but we didn't have cause or authorization to go inside. We saw the dogs. They look mean as hell. What breed are they?"

"Plott hounds," I said before Russo could jump in. "Detective, when Gary Pulsifer and I last talked with Dyer, he mentioned going coyote hunting with a Smith & Wesson AR-15."

"What caliber?" asked Clegg.

"He didn't say."

"Do you remember the model?"

I tried to transport myself back to that conversation. Tried to visualize Dyer standing outside the window of Pulsifer's idling truck.

"Smith & Wesson M&P 15 Whisper," I said.

For the first time since we'd met, Russo showed a real expression. He was astonished, whether at the specificity of my memory or about the implications of what I had just said, I couldn't be certain. But his mask had finally fallen.

"I know that gun," he said. "Dyer showed it to me. It's chambered in only one caliber: .300 AAC Blackout."

Clegg removed his phone from his pocket and began tapping in numbers. I didn't have to guess who he was calling or why. The detective was going to ask a judge to sign off immediately on a no-knock warrant. Russo had just provided a cause for the police to break down Logan Dyer's door.

33

In real life, suspicious deaths are rarely mysteries. A wife dies in what looks like a botched robbery; her husband probably did it. A child falls down the stairs and breaks her spine; look first to the baby-sitter. Most criminals are morons. They don't have the mental capacity to plan elaborate schemes worthy of Professor Moriarty or Hannibal Lecter. With few exceptions, the simplest explanation for a crime is the correct explanation. The butler almost always did it.

Police officers are human. Sometimes, because we want our work to be more exciting, or because we have a need to demonstrate our brilliance to the public and colleagues (and especially our superiors), we reach too far in our theories. Catching the guy who robbed the bank without a mask probably won't get you promoted. Catching the Night Stalker or the Green River Killer will turn you into a living legend.

Dyer was a loner who loved guns. He had recently been showing signs of instability, according to Russo. He had a legitimate grievance against his neighbor, Foss, for making it impossible to sell his family house and begin life anew somewhere else, where people didn't associate his name with a fatal chairlift accident. Motive, means, and opportunity—what more did you need? Nothing, in the eyes of the law.

To me, this realization carried extra sadness. It meant that Adam Langstrom was almost certainly dead—likely the first of Dyer's victims. The caginess with which Logan had evaded my questions about my missing brother suggested as much. Would we find Adam's dead body inside the darkened farmhouse?

* * *

I returned to my truck to put on my ballistic vest and get a gun. I didn't care that I hadn't been cleared to return for duty. With officers spread across two counties, protecting sex offenders, Clegg needed every available man now.

For the sake of my truck, I moved Shadow back into his carrier. He whined and bristled his fur. He wasn't some mythological creature, I had to remind myself. He was a living animal, and he was unhappy.

Then I called the IF&W office in Ashland again.

"Is Stacey back?" I asked the same woman I'd spoken with before.

"She stayed overnight in Clayton Lake. Do you want the number for McNally's?"

It was a sporting camp outside the flyspeck village, not far from where the helicopter had gone down. Presumably, the owner was providing lodging to the investigation and recovery team.

I dialed the camp. A woman with a creaky old-sounding voice answered. "McNally's."

"I'm trying to reach someone who is staying with you. She's a wildlife biologist with the Department of Inland Fisheries and Wildlife. Her name is Stacey Stevens."

"Is she the pretty one?"

"Yes."

"She's not here, dear. She left to go back to Ashland a couple of hours ago."

I thanked her and tried to decide what to do. Stacey was speeding along on a snowmobile in the dark on the Reality Road, as out of touch as a person could be. I dialed her cell phone and waited to leave a message.

"It's me," I said. "I am in Kennebago again and about to go on a raid into the house of a man named Logan Dyer. You're going to hear about him soon. He murdered eleven people up at Don Foss Logging. I think he killed Adam, too. He's on a vigilante crusade to kill sex offenders. Anyway, he's dangerous. Stacey, I am so sorry for having lied to you before. And I know you must be grieving for your friends in ways I can't even imagine. But I just wanted you to know, in case something happens to me tonight, that I love you."

I felt sick to my stomach when I hung up. But there was nothing more to do now except to get ready. I attached my service weapon, a SIG Sauer P226, to my belt. I unlocked my Mossberg 590A1 from its case and hung it from its sling over my shoulder. I took up my catch pole with the noose on one end. Then I removed my brand-new talonproof glove from behind the seat. I had thought I might need the bite sleeve for Shadow.

Strange the way things work out.

I found Clegg putting on his ballistic vest at his vehicle. He seemed to have gained weight since he had last adjusted the Velcro straps holding it in place. He was having trouble getting the fit right.

"Did you get the warrant?" I asked him.

"Got the warrant. Also put out a BOLO." The acronym had replaced APB in police jargon. It stood for "Be on the lookout."

"Can I help you with that?" I asked, meaning his vest.

"No, I've got it."

"How well do you know Dyer?" I asked.

"Logan? I've know him his whole life. I started my career in law enforcement just like Russo, doing security up at Widowmaker. I knew Logan's dad. Scott was a good man right up until the crash that killed his wife and daughter. Afterward, he was broken. He did his best, but you could see it in his eyes, hopelessness. The chairlift accident was what pushed him over the edge. He'd tried to get the owners to shut that lift down, but they'd refused. It didn't matter. Everyone blamed him, and he blamed himself."

Having finally secured his vest, the detective pulled his parka back on over it. His face had turned a shade of purple from the exertion.

"Logan wasn't more than eighteen when Scott shot himself," Clegg continued. "Eighteen or nineteen. And then suddenly his father was dead, and he was living alone in that big house. I hadn't seen him in a while before the other day. But I noticed he'd let himself go. He used to be a handsome kid. Shy as hell, though. Scott told me once that if a girl ever winked at Logan, he'd probably faint dead away."

"Detective!" someone called from the darkness.

But Clegg wasn't finished saying what he needed to say. "I

knocked on his door first thing this morning, before I found the carnage up at Foss's, but there was no answer. I heard the dogs barking, though, and thought that seemed strange. Later, when we were searching outside his house, I didn't want to admit to myself what I already knew. Sometimes I think the best part of this job is getting to know the people in your community. It's also the worst thing."

I knew what he meant.

"Let's go get this over with," the detective said, moving past me down the hill.

If Dyer was at large, hunting sex offenders, then it was unlikely we were going to be charging into a firefight. Some criminals had been known to booby-trap their properties—I knew so firsthand—but I suspected the biggest danger we would face, breaching the building, would be Dyer's two hounds.

The dogs were baying even more loudly and aggressively. Their supersensory hearing had picked up the sound of approaching vehicles and voices. Back up the hill, in the bed of my truck, Shadow responded with occasional howls, which had officers looking at one another with startled expressions.

A fresh-faced deputy, whom I'd never met, took a look at my gloves and catch pole and said, "You on dog duty?"

"I will be if needed."

The young guy had his shotgun already in his hands and wasn't practicing particularly good muzzle control. His name tag said Cauoette. "Man, I am pumped. It's like an adrenaline high."

I had a hunch about him. "When did you graduate from the Academy?"

"I'm scheduled to go this spring. Is it as tough as they say? I'm hoping it is. What's that term? *Crucible of fire?*"

If Cauoette didn't wash out after the first week, I would be surprised. I stepped clear of the rookie and made a vow to myself that as we entered the building I would stay behind him, where he couldn't mistakenly blow a hole in my back.

Clegg turned to face the assembled officers. I counted seven besides myself: two state troopers, four officers from the sheriff's department, and a state police forensics technician who would not be part of the assault.

Then it hit me: Russo was missing. Where had he gone? I hadn't noticed his SUV leaving, but I had been distracted with Shadow and thinking about Stacey. I would have thought a competitive shooter, currently employed as a glorified security guard, would have been eager to get in on a no-knock raid.

"Gather round, people!" said Clegg. "So here's how we're going to do this. We're going in two teams."

"Aren't there three doors?" asked a trooper behind me.

"We'll have a team posted outside the third one. But we have dogs to deal with inside and only two officers with bite sleeves."

"Why can't we just shoot them?" someone behind me whispered to himself.

Clegg must have had good hearing. "Those dogs are not to be killed unless an officer is at risk of dire injury. We've got television reporters lined up along Moose Alley in both directions. I don't want to be the one who goes in front of the cameras and explains why we had to shoot two of this guy's pets."

The detective spent five minutes laying out his plan. One officer would breach the door with a sledgehammer and then step back, allowing two others to enter: one armed with an AR-15 carbine and one assigned to subdue the canines. I had never wrestled a dangerous dog before, but I had seen it done on occasion, in person and in videos, and hoped I could manage the jujitsu involved. We would move quickly to clear the house. Once it was secured, the forensics guy would assume responsibility for searching the premises.

"Everybody good?" Clegg asked after he had finished separating us into teams. "You understand your assignments?"

"Hoo ya," said the overeager rookie, Caouette.

I followed a deputy holding a sledgehammer to the front door and took my place beside a trooper armed with a carbine. Given the tight quarters, I decided to leave my catch pole propped against the house.

I didn't expect Clegg to give the signal as fast as he did, but the next thing I knew, the deputy was swinging the hammer and the door went flying inward off its hinges. A trooper with an AR-15 stepped quickly into the breach, and I followed just in time to see both hounds lunging for him. I threw myself between the man and the attacking dogs. I shoved my padded glove into the open mouth of one of the animals and kicked at the other, catching it in the haunch.

The dog began shaking its head viciously, and I felt tendons and ligaments straining to move in ways they were not supposed to move. The other hound went for my calf, but the trooper beside me knocked it on the head with the butt of his gun. It howled in pain and retreated out of my line of sight.

I was totally focused on my own attacker.

The Plott was incredibly strong for its size and weight. I tried manhandling it away from the door to give myself more room to maneuver, and nearly tripped over a coffee table. Flashlight beams crisscrossed the room in a geometrical pattern as I wrestled with the hound. I heard shouts and then an explosion.

Someone had fired a gun.

I lurched upright, pulling the dog free of the floor, and then thrust my arm forward, twisting my wrist. It landed on its back, its ribs and soft belly exposed, its four legs clawing at the air. I dropped my knee on its stomach and felt its fangs loosen as its lungs emptied of air. Immediately, I spun the hound back over and grabbed its collar, pulling and twisting. I straddled its back and pressed my knees tightly against its haunches. The dog shook its head and snapped, but I didn't stop squeezing.

The overhead lights came on. I glanced around and saw a bathroom to my right. Using all my strength, I hurled the gasping dog through the open door and pulled it shut before it could catch its breath.

"Where's the other one?" I shouted.

"It got out!" a female voice cried from the kitchen.

Another gunshot sounded. This one came from the backyard.

All around me cops were darting into rooms. I heard heavy footsteps racing upstairs, boards creaking on the second floor, then voices shouting.

"Clear!"

"Clear!"

"Clear!"

I turned to Clegg and pointed at the bathroom. "Don't let anyone through that door!"

The snarls coming from inside as the angry animal tried to break free made the point for me.

I made my way through the living room, noticing heavy blankets covering the windows and the pervasive smell of mildew. I passed through a formal dining room that hadn't been used in decades and entered the kitchen, where I found a female deputy sitting on the linoleum with her hands clutched to her thigh and blood oozing between her fingers. She had cast aside the bite sleeve she had been wearing to put pressure on the wound.

"Are you all right?" I asked, crouching beside her.

"I don't know."

The back door was open to the night. I heard yet another gunshot in the clearing behind the house.

"I'll be right back," I said.

I smelled gunpowder the second I stepped onto the back porch. An officer stood in the falling snow. It was Caouette, of course. He was staring down the barrel of his shotgun at the second-growth timber behind the farmhouse.

"Son of a bitch!" I heard him say.

The hound had vanished.

"Didn't you hear the sergeant?" I said. "No shooting."

"That fucker bit Carly."

"Route Sixteen is only a quarter mile from here," I said. "The reporters are going to have heard those shots. Will you stop pointing that gun at me and start practicing some goddamned muzzle control?"

Caouette dropped the barrel toward the snow. "Where's the other one?"

"Safe and secure," I said.

The dog's prints led in a straight line from the back door toward the trees. I followed them through the calf-deep snow. The light was lousy, but I found the splatter of dark spots melting the snow. The impact had knocked the dog off its feet, but it had regained its footing and loped down the private snowmobile trail Logan Dyer had cleared from his property to the network of interconnecting paths that Pulsifer had showed us on his map.

I knew from hard experience that nothing is more dangerous than a wounded animal. I also knew what I had to do.

I removed the talonproof glove and crossed the yard to the porch, where the hotheaded deputy stood watching me.

"Did you find it?" Caouette asked.

"No, but I will."

"Why? What for?"

"Because you don't leave a wounded animal to die in the woods!"

Inside the kitchen, a trooper was applying a pressure bandage to the leg of the injured deputy. Her face had good color, which was a positive sign. I continued through the house and out the front door. I was going to need my snowshoes if I was going to track down that poor dog and put it out of its misery.

34

I returned to the house with my snowshoes under my arm, bracing
the single-point shotgun sling against my other side. Cops who
had been part of the raid were trickling out through the busted door.
The evidence tech didn't want any inexperienced patrol officers mess-
ing up potential evidence.

I found Clegg inside the living room, conferring with a state
trooper with corporal chevrons on his sleeve. Both of them had put
on latex gloves. The detective waved me over when I stepped across
the threshold.

"Any ideas how we're going to get that dog out of the bathroom?" he asked me.

"Call a real animal control agent. I can recommend a good one in
Pondicherry if you're willing to pay her mileage." I kept my hands in
my pockets to avoid touching anything. "If you don't need me, I've
got to go track down a wounded dog."

Clegg looked none too pleased. "I heard the shots."

I moved my gaze around the ratty room. It was less of a man cave
than a man cesspool. "Find anything interesting?"

"Logan sure likes video games," said Clegg, pointing to the big-
screen television. "First-person shooters primarily. He's got one hell
of a collection. And he drinks a lot of Mountain Dews."

The trooper chimed in: "Also, his snowmobile is gone."

"What about Adam Langstrom?" I asked.

"What about him?" said Clegg.

"Is there any sign he was here?"

"It's a big house, and we've just started to search."

In the winter, before they begin to hibernate, certain snakes will gather together and roll themselves into a writhing ball. That was how my stomach felt.

"I need to go find that dog before the snow covers its tracks," I said.

A phone rang in Clegg's pocket. He glanced at the number on the screen and winced but answered anyway. "Yes, this is Clegg." He made various affirmative noises to signal he was listening and then he covered the receiver with his hand. "A bloody dog just ran out onto Route Sixteen from the woods. Some of the reporters tried to approach it, but it ran off toward Redington."

I turned toward the broken-down door. "I'm going to get my truck. Maybe I can catch up with it before it gets hit by a plow."

From another room came a voice: "Lieutenant!"

A deputy beckoned through the doorway. He pointed a gloved finger at the table.

A stack of white computer paper lay in a perfectly neat pile. In a house littered with filthy socks, dirty dishes, and dog-chewed hambones, the pages were noteworthy for having been so carefully arranged.

Standing behind the white-haired detective, looking down over his shoulder, I could read only the first paragraph:

From: Logan Scott Dyer
To: America
Subject: Last resort

As I do not expect to survive the coming days or have my appointed hour in court, I hereby leave this statement of purpose to explain why I have had no choice but to take drastic and shocking actions to protect the children of this community. I know I will be villified by the media as my father was, a great man dragged down by lesser beings. When the evil are allowed to prosper and go free while the pure of spirit are condemned to suffering and death, we must admit that this once-great country is sick with a moral cancer that must be cut out tumor by tumor.

"Christ," said the trooper. "It's a goddamned manifesto."

"That's why he left his dogs here," I said. "He doesn't plan on being taken alive."

Clegg covered his face with one of his big hands. When he let go, there were red marks in the skin from the pressure of his fingers. "This day just gets worse and worse. I've got to call Major Carter."

The detective stepped aside to place his call. The trooper and the deputy both remained fixated on the manifesto. I could tell they were itching to turn the page and read more but were reluctant to touch it, even wearing gloves.

"It doesn't sound like him," I said.

Both men looked at me.

"Dyer has a speech impediment, which makes people think he's dumb. I don't think he is, exactly. But these words don't sound anything like him. The man shovels snow for a living."

"Maybe he took courses online," said the deputy. He hadn't meant the comment to sound as stupid as it did.

It wasn't my job to deconstruct Dyer's prose style, in any case. I needed to find his wounded dog and either save its life or end its suffering. I repositioned the snowshoes under my arm and stepped back outside into the picture-perfect winter evening.

The two frostbitten deputies were still standing at the intersection, directing traffic, but they had been joined by half a dozen vans and SUVs painted with the logos of television stations from across Maine.

I didn't want to roll down my window to ask which way the dog had gone. I knew one of the reporters would use the opportunity to stick a camera and microphone in my face. Fortunately, one of the deputies guessed what I was doing and pointed me in the right direction after he moved his cruiser aside for me to get out.

As soon as I was past the last parked vehicle, I hit the gas until I began to fishtail. In the bed of the truck, the dog carrier shifted and Shadow yelped; I hadn't secured it as well as I should have. I let up on the pedal. That would be the last straw: careening off the road on live television and sending a caged wolf tumbling into space.

I shouldn't drive too fast anyway, I thought. I didn't want to miss a sign. The cold was probably crusting the blood on the dog's pelt. But every once in a while, I caught sight of a print in my high beams. The wounded animal seemed not to want to leave the flat openness of the road for the deep snow. Only if it felt cornered would it seek cover in the trees. Or so I hoped.

After a mile, I happened to glance in my rearview and saw head-lights approaching quickly from behind. They seemed low to the ground. The car behind me accelerated when it was twenty feet from my rear bumper. I tapped the brakes to put a scare into the driver. But he just swung out into the passing lane and gunned his engine.

It was a Mercedes coupe with a Thule ski box, a New York plate, and a Sugarloaf sticker. The idiot at the wheel probably hadn't even realized I was a law-enforcement officer. The anger that had been simmering inside me for hours seemed to reach a sudden boil. I was just about to hit my blue lights and push the gas pedal to the floor when a voice in my head—Stacey's voice—told me to take a breath.

Of all the things that had happened throughout the day, *this* was what had finally set me off? An entitled asshole from out of state driving too fast on a snowy road?

Rage could make a man so stupid.

I thought of Logan Dyer, sitting in his dark, damp living room, pointing a pretend gun at a flickering television screen, imagining that the creatures he was blasting into oblivion weren't aliens or monsters, but, instead, the real men living a mile up the road. At a certain point, he had stopped seeing his neighbors as human beings at all. In his twisted imagination, they had become tumors to be cut from the flesh before the corruption festered.

If he was using the registry of sex offenders as his guide, then at least we might have a chance. We could be relatively certain the name of his next victim was on a list we already possessed. "Pick a pervert," as Jeff White had said.

But who said Dyer was using the registry?

That had been the assumption we'd made after we'd gotten word about the other man, Ducharme. Because his name was on the list, we had leaped to the conclusion that the next person Dyer targeted would also be found online. It was the rationale Major Carter had used to deploy law-enforcement officers to the residences of every registered sex offender within a hundred-mile radius.

But what if it wasn't so? What if Dyer was merely working off his own local knowledge of who was and wasn't a "pervert"?

Pulsifer had said that Ducharme had been banned from busi-nesses in the area as part of a coordinated campaign.

Nathan Minkowski had also been banned—at least while in drag—from the Bigelow General Store.

Except Mink wasn't a sex offender. He was, to the best of my knowledge, a law-abiding person. He just happened to like dressing up in women's clothes and parading around in public. In the eyes of a man like Logan Dyer, though, that made him a carrier of moral disease, a vector of contagion, a cancer to be excised. I remember the contempt in Dyer's eyes when he saw Mink riding beside me in my Scout.

If Mink's name wasn't on the registry, it meant no one was protecting him.

The strange little man had no idea of the evil that might be headed his way.

The road up to Kennebago Settlement had a four-inch coating of snow unmarked by tire tracks. No one had been in or out for hours, at least by conventional motor vehicle. But a man on a snowmobile had other ways of gaining access to the isolated homesteads on the northern slopes of East Kennebago Mountain.

As I crossed the bridge over the frozen Dead River, I put in a call to Pulsifer. I wanted someone to know where I was going and why. The phone rang for half a minute before it kicked me to voice mail.

"Gary, it's Mike. I don't know if you've heard yet, but Logan Dyer is the shooter. He left a confession inside his house. The guy's a vigilante on a suicide mission to assassinate sex offenders. I'm heading up to Mink's house in Kennebago Settlement. No one was assigned—"

The call dropped.

I remembered how I hadn't been able to get a signal until I had reached Route 16. Would Pulsifer even receive my voice mail? I could turn back and try again from the highway or take my chances and keep going.

I kept going.

The forest fell away as I climbed above the river floodplain, and I found myself passing through a vast white pasture. The windows of a farmhouse glowed, soft and warm. Wood smoke corkscrewed from the chimney. I was turning my attention back to the road when

I caught sight of a light moving fast along the tree line. It was a snowmobile. I braked so hard that Shadow let out another yelp. The rider turned sharply in my direction. Then another bobbing light appeared: a second sled following in the tracks of the first.

I kept my foot on the brake as two kids on pint-size sleds went zipping across the road behind me, their engines roaring like chain saws. The snow machines left an echo in my head long after they had disappeared into the far woods.

I nearly missed the driveway up to Mink's house. The last plow to come by had piled a particularly steep bank at the entrance, nearly as high as the top of my truck. I shut off my headlights and idled a hundred feet up the road before I turned a corner. Then I pulled over and parked in the shadows of the pines. I wanted to hide my truck from sight in case Dyer came up the road behind me.

I lifted my shotgun from the backseat and stepped out into the cold, pulling the shotgun sling over my right shoulder. I tried to close the truck door as quietly as I could, but the night was so still, the sound of the latch catching was as loud as a rifle bolt being shoved forward.

I whispered to the caged wolf, "No howling. Agreed?"

I waited for my eyes to adjust to the low light. Then I began moving slowly forward, hugging the shadowy side of the road.

When I came to the snowbank heaped in front of Mink's drive, I had no choice but to scramble up it. The surface was hard with chunks of ice, but there were slick spots where my boots had trouble gaining traction. I dug my fingers into the frozen pile and pulled myself up and over the obstacle.

The snow was deep on the other side, nearly up to my crotch. Did Mink not own a shovel?

I labored forward up the steep drive, feeling sweat begin to soak my long underwear. I had no clue how far the cabin was from the road, but I could smell the tangy aroma of smoke from a woodstove. I found the odor reassuring. So far, I had seen no signs that Dyer—or anyone else on a snowmobile—had ridden this far up the mountainside. Maybe I had been mistaken about the next name on the vigilante's kill list.

The drive twisted and turned for another fifty yards before the cabin finally came into view through the trees. Mink had said something about it having been his father's old hunting camp, and that was exactly what it looked like: a small peak-roofed structure constructed of hemlock logs and mortar. I couldn't imagine that the inside was insulated, and I had no idea what Mink did for water. But there was a formidable pile of chopped wood not far from the porch, and a stump with an ax driven into the top.

The windows were aglow behind faded curtains that looked like repurposed bedsheets. I paused at the edge of the little clearing and listened. I heard music playing, a recorded voice and instruments performing an old song I didn't recognize. A man's deep voice belted out the same tune karaoke-style. Mink had a bona fide set of pipes.

I exhaled and watched the steam that had been building up inside me shimmer and dissipate into the air.

I doubted the little man received many friendly visitors, especially on midwinter evenings—or on any evenings, for that matter. I had to assume he owned a gun, since everyone in this part of Maine seemed to, including ex-cons like Adam Langstrom, who were forbidden to possess firearms.

"Mink!"

He continued to sing at the tops of his lungs.

"Mink!"

His voice ceased. But the radio continued to play.

"It's Mike Bowditch!"

One of the curtains was peeled back from the windowsill, and I saw half of his face peek out. Mink seemed to be wearing a white mask.

"I've got a gun!" he shouted in his deepest voice. "You'd better not come up here!"

"Mink, it's Mike Bowditch. The game warden!"

I stepped forward into the clearing with my arms raised over my head, my shotgun swaying by my side. There was no way Mink could see me clearly if he was looking out from a lighted room. But I hoped he could make out my silhouette and recognize the gesture as one of someone coming in peace.

He stepped away from the parted curtain. The radio went silent. A moment later, the front door cracked open. He had changed from a 1970s blonde to a Jazz Age redhead.

"What the freak are you doing here?" he demanded.

"Can I come in? It's going to take a while to explain."

"How do I know it's really you?"

"Go jump in a lake!" I said.

The door opened wide, and I saw him in his full glory. He was wearing a kimono and fuzzy slippers. His new wig was styled in a pageboy cut. I seemed to have caught him in the middle of a facial.

As I stepped forward into the light spilling through the door, the suspicion left his face. I plodded forward, kicking snow with my boots, until I reached a cleared path that ran around the woodpile. There was a big plastic sled tilted against the logs, presumably to be used to haul wood and other items up from the road.

"I get gawkers sometimes," he said as I climbed the stairs. "Kids mostly. They come up here on a dare to see the freak show."

"Kids can be cruel."

"Yeah, yeah. Tell me something I don't know." I hadn't noticed the derringer in his hand until he tucked it into his pocket. "So on what account do I have the pleasure?"

Crossing the threshold, I felt as if I had stepped into a sauna. The room was lit entirely by kerosene lanterns, which made an audible hiss as they burned. The decor wasn't feminine in the least. There were outdoorsy watercolors on the walls of men fishing and shotgunning ducks. A trout creel hung from a nail beside a bamboo fly rod. An ancient deer head—a ten-point buck—stared down from above the fireplace.

To my right was a kitchenette with a propane stove and a refrigerator. To my left was a big bed that had been expertly fashioned from shaved and shellacked logs. This was one of the coziest cabins I had ever seen.

I had so many questions about his unique living situation, but they would have to wait. "Mink, you need to get out of here."

"Huh? Why?" He grabbed a cloth from the sink and began rubbing off the moisturizer or whatever it was that made his face gleam.

"Logan Dyer murdered Don Foss and all his men last night. Then

he tried to kill a registered sex offender named Ducharme over in Stratton. Dyer left a note saying he was going to kill all the 'deviants' he could find before the police stopped him. We don't know where he is, but we think he's riding a snowmobile on the backcountry trails. He's definitely armed and dangerous. I'm here to get you to safety."

"So I'm a deviant, am I?" Finished with the facecloth, he tossed it into the sink.

"Those were his words, not mine."

"I always knew that guy was a creep. He had a look in his eye, gave me the chills."

"You need to get your stuff together."

"Screw him. I ain't going nowhere."

"Dyer is extremely dangerous. He's killed eleven men with an AR-15—that's the civilian version of a military rifle. You can't protect yourself here with just a derringer."

"You don't get it," he said, his mouth tightening. "It's the principle. I ain't a coward."

"Taking precautions doesn't make you one."

"Have you asked around about me?" He sneered. "Yeah, I bet you heard stuff. How I'm a freak for dressing the way I do. Probably a secret flamer, too. But I know one thing: No one ever called me a coward." He touched his bent nose. "You think I got this from being a coward?" He peeled up his lip to reveal a broken tooth. "Or this?"

Perspiration had begun to slide down the side of my face from the heat of the room. "Mink," I said.

"I live the way I want to live, and people can think whatever the freak they want, just so long as they don't treat me like someone to push around. I ain't afraid of no one, including that jerk straw Dyer."

I couldn't force the man from his home; this wasn't a mandated evacuation.

"What if I stay here with you, then?" I said. "Will you allow me to do that?"

"You mean like as my bodyguard? Who am I, Whitney Houston? No freaking way. Now, if you'll excuse me, I gotta go tinkle."

He opened a door at the rear of the room. I had a quick glimpse

of a self-composting toilet and a copper bathtub like the ones you see in cowboy movies. Then he shut the door.

What to do? I couldn't just sit in my truck at the end of his drive. There were too many ways Dyer could slip past me, and if he was using a noise suppressor on his AR-15, as I suspected, I might never even hear the shot that killed Mink. Plus, I had no idea what I was going to do with Shadow. I doubted the cold bothered him, under his heavy wolf's coat, but keeping him caged up in the tight confines of that carrier was cruel.

I checked to see if I had a cell signal. No such luck.

"Do you have a phone here?" I asked through the bathroom door.

"The company won't run the lines this far."

The door opened and Mink emerged. He had changed out of his kimono into a fuzzy pink sweater and blue jeans. He had straightened his wig and applied a thin layer of lipstick, red-orange to match his hair.

"I think I gave you the wrong impression about what's going on here," I said.

"I don't want to be impolite, but—"

"Just hear me out."

His sweater seemed to be made out of some kind of synthetic fiber. He must have gotten lipstick on the front. There was an incandescent red spot just below his throat. Then the strangest thing happened: The spot vibrated.

I threw myself forward and knocked him to the floor just as the window behind me shattered.

35

I never even heard the gunshot.

The impact of our collision knocked the wind from Mink and the back of his head hit the floorboards hard. I rolled off him and looked up to see the laser sight of a rifle moving like a jittery insect around the room. Dyer was trying to find one of us in his scope again.

"It's him," I said. "He's out there."

Mink moaned.

The shot had come from the front of the cabin. The bullet had shattered the same window Mink had peeked through. I propped myself up against a wall and pumped a shotshell into the chamber of my Mossberg.

Dyer had a high-powered rifle with a laser sight. He had the darkness to hide in and could circle the building, waiting for another shot. He had fired only once, which meant he was patient, not prone to getting overexcited. There was no way for us to contact the outside world for help. And for all I knew, Pulsifer had never even received my message telling him where I was headed.

To put it mildly, I was having trouble identifying a single advantage we might have.

"Is there a back door?"

"There's a window," Mink gasped, still out of breath.

I glanced at the cast-iron stove in the kitchen. Behind it was a large rectangular window. It had hinges on the top, so that it could be lifted inward. Lots of old logging cabins had these setups in their kitchens. A man could stand outside and pass logs for the stove through the open window to someone inside the kitchen.

Mink had rolled over onto his stomach. His big eyes were

following the laser sight around the room as if hypnotized by it, the way a cat might be.

"Here's what we're going to do," I said. "I'm going to provide some covering fire while you go out that back window. Here are the keys to my truck. It's a hundred yards up the road from the end of your drive. I want you to take it and get the hell to the nearest house with a phone. Dial 911 and tell them there's an officer who needs assistance at your address. Tell him Logan Dyer is shooting at me. That should get their attention."

His lipstick was smeared. His body was pressed so tightly against the floorboards, it looked like he had been squashed by a giant foot.

I kicked him in the arm. "You're not a coward."

He nodded.

I shimmied on my elbows and knees through the shattered glass toward one of the unbroken windows. Carefully, I raised the edge of the curtain. I brought my head up, hoping to obtain a target rather than just firing blindly, but as soon as I did, the glass above me exploded.

I rolled to the other window, raised myself onto my knees behind the cover of the wall, then swung out into the open and fired a shot at the trees. I pumped another shell into the chamber and fired again.

I ducked behind the wall just in time to see Mink's legs as he went tumbling through the kitchen window.

The little man could move pretty fast if he needed to.

The laser dot reappeared against the far wall of the cabin. I watched the quivering red light search the room. Now with two windows broken and two curtains torn, Dyer was going to have multiple angles, multiple lines of sight into the building.

The red dot winked off.

Maybe he was waiting for me to show myself again.

I tried to regain control of my breathing. My ears ached from firing the shotgun.

The laser appeared again, zipped back and forth against the opposite wall, and then vanished.

Dyer hadn't seen Mink go through the window or run off down the hill. This might just work, I thought.

I moved to the other window and fired a random shot into the trees. The percussive boom of the Mossberg left my ears ringing. It took a solid minute for them to return to normal.

In the distance, I heard an engine turn over. Mink had made it to my truck. Now he just needed to turn around and get the hell out of there.

But if I could hear the engine, so could Dyer. He would know that I had stayed in the house to provide cover for Mink's escape.

I took a chance, rose to my feet, and went running across the room and into the kitchen. I threw myself through the open window and landed face-first in a pile of snow. I blinked my eyes to clear them and then grabbed the side of the building to help regain my footing. I must have knocked my knee on the sill, because a shooting pain went through it as I straightened up.

I heard another engine off in the woods. The noise it made was almost a high-pitched whine: Dyer's snowmobile.

I hadn't considered the possibility that he might give chase.

I stumbled around the front of the cabin and looked down the steep hill. The holes my legs had left in the snow, climbing up from the road, made a zigzagging path. I took another step, felt my knee buckle, and grabbed at the woodpile for support. Birch logs rolled down, one after the other. Something else fell to the ground. It was the plastic sled Mink used to haul wood.

I glanced at it, glanced at the hill beneath me. I let my shotgun drop; the Mossberg swung on its sling against my side. I bent over, took hold of the sled by the edges, tried to get whatever momentum I could, and then belly flopped on top of it.

Headfirst, I went flying down the hill.

Then my shotgun slipped over the edge and began to drag against the surface. The sled turned sideways, and I flipped over. I had a glimpse of the sled continuing on without me. And then I began rolling over and over on my side, the way kids do when they're playing, only with less control. The sling came loose from my shoulder, and I continued down the slope, my shotgun now lost.

I came to rest fifteen yards from the snowbank at the end of the driveway. My parka and pants were as white as if I had rolled in powdered sugar. Snow was packed into one of my ears. I had lost my knit cap, too.

I crawled on hands and aching knees to the bottom and pulled myself over the frozen bank. I staggered out into the road, then turned in a circle. I looked up the road and down the road. I cupped my hands around my stunned ears and listened.

Two engines: a truck above me and a snowmobile below.

The truck was revving and revving. Mink must have gotten himself stuck while trying to turn around.

Meanwhile, Dyer was moving to cut us off.

I limped uphill on my gimpy knee. My right hand fell to my hip. At least I hadn't lost my SIG, too.

The sound of the snowmobile began to grow louder. Dyer was speeding straight up the road behind me.

I came around the corner and saw, through a sheer curtain of snow, my precious patrol truck wedged sideways in the road. The headlights showed how deeply the front was buried in a snowbank. The tires spun purposely, turning snow into ice. The Sierra wasn't going anywhere without being winched free.

Mink kept pumping the gas, revving the engine, spinning the wheels.

I staggered toward the driver's door, when suddenly I saw my shadow stretched out before me.

The snowmobile had turned the corner, too, and now its headlights were aimed directly at us, illuminating this tragicomic scene.

I glanced over my shoulder as the sled came to a stop. I couldn't see past the glare, but I knew what was about to happen.

"Get down!" I shouted as I grabbed the frame of the truck bed.

I pulled myself over the edge and tumbled onto the liner, my head knocking Shadow's carrier. I could have sworn I felt something brush my pants leg, but I didn't hear a shot. The wolf dog let out a growl.

The term most people use for suppressors is *silencers,* but that is a misnomer. A gun, fitted with a sound moderator, isn't silent, nor does it make that muffled *thwump* that you might have heard in movies. That noise is the invention of Hollywood sound engineers. An AR-15 rifle fitted with a suppressor makes a popping sound, less intense than the typical blast of an unmuzzled barrel, but loud enough to be heard from a distance of thirty yards, which was how far Logan Dyer was from my truck when he began unloading on us.

I heard the driver's window explode first and then a second round took out the spotlight. The third bullet pierced the door. The fourth and the fifth were directed at me. Both of them tore clean holes through the steel frame of my vehicle, mere inches from my boots.

The shooting stopped.

"Mink?"

To my right, I heard the sound of the passenger door opening and then the thud of a body falling to the ground. I heard movement, clawing in the snow. At least the truck was between Mink and the vigilante.

Inches from my face, Shadow had his fangs bared. For a moment, I wondered if the wolf had been hurt. The growl coming from deep within his chest made the hairs rise along my arms. I pulled my .357 loose from its holster and readied myself to sit up and begin squeezing off what were likely to be the last shots of my life.

Shadow growled again. The return fire was bound to strike the carrier. In my carelessness, I had doomed this hapless animal, as well. For the briefest instant, the sound transported me back into Dyer's house as I'd charged through the door with the bite sleeve on my arm. An idea came to me.

"I have your dog, Dyer!"

There was no response.

I tried again. "Your dog is in the back of this truck with me! I have it in a carrier! Listen!"

I knocked the side of the crate with the barrel of my pistol and Shadow let out another snarl.

"You're going to kill it if you keep firing," I said. "Or maybe I will."

I heard the crunch of boots on snow. Heard him advance a few more yards, then stop.

"Let her go," Logan Dyer said.

"No way! You'll just start shooting again."

"I won't! I swear."

I pretended to mull over his promise. "I have your word on that?"

"Yes!"

Now if only the angry wolf wouldn't bite my face off. I repositioned myself in the truck bed, made sure the grip on my weapon was secure. Then with my left hand, I reached up and squeezed the lock to open the carrier gate.

Shadow came charging out and leaped gracefully over the edge of the truck onto the road.

"What—" I heard Logan Dyer say.

As he recoiled from the shock of seeing a wolf coming toward him instead of his hound, I sat up, took aim, and fired a shot into his chest. He toppled straight back. The carbine went flying.

I pulled myself out of the truck bed and barely managed to maintain my footing. I kept my weapon leveled at the man on the ground. My knee twinged with every step. And I was pretty sure I'd popped my stitches.

Shadow had gone bounding past Dyer, seemingly intent on making his escape, but to my surprise, the wolf had stopped in the road and turned. He was now watching me as I advanced on the unmoving vigilante.

I heard footsteps behind me. "Holy moly! Did you get him?"

"I got him. Are you all right?"

"I'm all right. Is that a freaking wolf?"

"Yes, it is."

"Holy moly!"

I kicked the AR-15 away from Dyer's outstretched arm. I stood with my gun pointed at his heart. His foot twitched, and then his hand, and then he let out a moan. For an instant, it seemed he might be rising like a zombie from the dead.

I bent down and poked his chest. There was no blood. My finger touched some kind of hard plate.

Damn, if the son of a bitch wasn't wearing a bulletproof vest.

I dragged Dyer to a birch at the side of the road and handcuffed him with his arms wrapped around the trunk. Shadow had retreated farther down the hill, but he continued to watch. I had a brief thought that if I left the helpless vigilante alone, the wolf might devour him. It would have been a fitting punishment in my opinion, but I was already going to have a hard time explaining the events of the past few hours.

So it had been Dyer after all. All the signs had pointed to him.

He'd left a signed confession on his kitchen table. Who else had I been expecting?

I slapped his stubbled face to get his attention. "Dyer! Wake up!"

He groaned. When he opened his mouth, I saw his stunted tongue.

"Where's Adam?" I said.

"Fuck you."

"What did you do with Adam Langstrom?"

"Fuck you."

"Talk to me. Tell me where he is."

He started to giggle. I slapped him again—this time just for the hell of it.

Mink perched himself atop a snowbank and offered a running commentary that was heavy on constructive criticism on what I should be doing.

"You sure he can't slip out of those cuffs? I knew a guy who could dislocate himself. How come your truck doesn't have bulletproof glass? He shot it all to kingdom come. I'm lucky he didn't hit my liver or some other organ. This has been an unusual night!"

"You lost your wig," I said.

He clapped his hand atop his head and let out a curse. Then he slid down from his place of observation and began searching in and around the truck for his red-haired mop.

I told Mink to keep an eye on Dyer.

"Where are you going?" he asked, looking up from his hands and knees.

"I'm taking his snowmobile down the road until I can get a signal. I'll be back as soon as I can."

"What about that freaking wolf?"

Good question.

Dyer had a nice sled, a Yamaha Phazer—vintage, but he had maintained it well. When I opened the throttle, I needed to hang on for dear life.

I finally got a cell signal down past the farm where I had seen the kids chasing each other on their snow machines. I dialed the state police dispatcher and gave him the rundown. He told me there were units in the area.

The snow, which had been falling steadily all day, had finally begun to lighten up. There were a few intermittent flakes, but whereas the night sky had been a uniform gray dome before, now I could make out the backlit outlines of clouds moving southeast across the valley. A cold front was pushing down from Canada.

I removed my glove and ran my fingers up my sleeve and over the stitches on my arm. The threads had ripped, and there was some sort of fluid oozing from the wound. Yet another scar to remind me of yet another moment of carelessness.

Funny, though: That night outside Carrie Michaud's seemed an age ago now. For reasons I could not explain, the firefight with Dyer—an even closer brush with death—had unchained me from the mortal dread I had been dragging around for the past week. I felt fully alive again in body and soul.

36

My conservative estimate was that a dozen officers responded to my call. The road up to Mink's place looked like rush hour with all the emergency vehicles lined up one after the other. With so many people bustling around the scene, asking me questions, offering thanks, I found it hard to focus.

Dyer was unlocked from the birch and taken to the back of Clegg's cruiser and left there until the detective could finish his work.

I walked Clegg and a couple of state police detectives around the cabin, giving them the minute-by-minute replay. Another trooper escorted Mink inside to get an independent statement from him on what had happened. Even though I was receiving congratulations from deputies and EMTs whom I had never met—the hero of the hour—I knew that our accounts would be compared and contrasted, and that I might be called upon to explain any inconsistencies in our stories.

A deputy found my shotgun buried in the snow and returned it to me.

Shadow had disappeared into the woods. I kept looking for him at the edges of the trees, but he was gone.

Maybe, in the future, he would be glimpsed by backcountry skiers up on Widowmaker or caught in the headlights of sledders racing at night along one of the trails to Quebec. I could imagine the department getting occasional calls from people who were insistent that they had seen a wolf—not a coyote or a dog, but a wolf. Wardens and wildlife biologists would politely take the statements of these eyewitnesses, and then they would write off the reports as cases of mistaken identity. Wolves were not secretly returning to Maine to reclaim their ancient hunting grounds. That was just a myth.

With all the vehicles lined up along the road, I didn't notice the midnight-blue Ford Explorer Interceptor at first. I looked around for Russo but didn't see him in any of the clusters of cops. Eventually, my gaze drifted to Clegg's cruiser.

There was Russo, standing beside the open back door, talking privately with Dyer. No one else was within twenty feet of them. I glanced around, looking for Clegg, but the detective must have gone up to Mink's cabin.

I was seized by a sudden panic. I had the image in my head of Jack Ruby shooting Lee Harvey Oswald in the gut. As quickly as I could on my injured leg, I limped over to the cruiser.

"Russo!"

"Bowditch," he said, his face as blank as usual. "Congratulations."

"Get away from him."

"What? Why?"

"Did Clegg give you permission to talk to him alone? You shouldn't be talking to him before the detective does."

Russo nonchalantly closed the cruiser door. "I think you've jumped to the wrong conclusion, buddy."

"Where did you go before?"

"Where did I go when?"

"You dropped this bombshell about Dyer having a rifle that fired the same-caliber bullets as those found at Foss's, and then when the time comes to break down his door, you're nowhere to be found."

"I had a call back at the mountain," he said mildly.

"That can be checked, you know. Whether you actually received a call."

I stepped forward until we were nearly chest-to-chest. The man's body gave off no smell or heat.

"Are you all right, Warden?" he said. "You seem confused. You might want to have an EMT check you out for a concussion."

"So what were you saying to Dyer just now? What were you telling him?"

Russo paused. His expression was as unreadable as always, but I thought I saw a flicker of amusement behind his eyes.

"I told him that he was fired," he said. "What else would I be telling him?"

And then he stepped past me and returned to his vehicle. His headlights came on. I watched him do a perfect three-point turn and then drive away.

When I looked in on Dyer myself, he gave me a smile that showed off his discolored teeth.

"What did Russo say to you just now?" I asked. "Tell me what he said."

"He said I'm going to be famous." I found myself wanting to slap him again across his smug, triumphant face. Whatever else Logan Dyer was, he was no patsy. He had killed twelve men that I knew of, starting with Adam, and nearly including Mink and me. But I still couldn't believe he had written that so-called manifesto, couldn't believe he had planned and executed his vigilante campaign alone. I had to sit down on a snowbank to cool off.

Pulsifer was the last warden to arrive, and he pretended to give me holy hell for my ruined truck. "I am no insurance adjuster, but I would file this one under 'totaled.' Don't be surprised if your rates go through the roof, Bowditch."

Gary helped me transfer my gear from my truck to his—the stuff that hadn't been shot full of holes, that is.

"What about these?" he said when we were almost done. He held out my father's dog tags. In the artificial light of the emergency vehicles I read the stamped words again, as if for the first time:

```
BOWDITCH
JOHN, M.
004-00-8120
O NEG
NO PREF.
```

I sucked in my breath.

"What?" asked Pulsifer, narrowing his eyes and sticking out his chin in that foxlike way of his.

"Have you ever heard the expression 'Blood doesn't lie'?"

"Yeah. Why?"

I put the dog tags around my neck and tucked them under my T-shirt. I didn't pause to think about what I was doing or why. The metal felt cold against my chest.

"Maybe I'll tell you someday."

I stayed with Lauren and Gary Pulsifer again that night. I'd asked Clegg to call me if he got any information out of Dyer, thinking I'd hear from him in the morning. But the detective called even before we'd finished the hot chocolates Lauren had made to warm us both up.

I took the phone into the Pulsifer's guest room, which was as drafty as ever.

"He confessed to everything," Clegg said. "As soon as I started back to Farmington, he started talking. He said, 'Yeah, I killed them all. Langstrom, too. I'm guilty, and that's all I'm going to say. If you want to know why I did it, read my letter.'"

"His letter?" I said.

"That word struck me as odd, too. I said, 'Are you referring to your manifesto?' And he said, 'Yeah, my manifesto. That letter I wrote. All my reasons for doing it are in there. Read it and you'll understand why. I'm guilty, and that's all I'm going to say.'"

"So what were the reasons he supposedly gave in his 'letter'?"

Clegg answered as if he might have had the document in front of him. "It starts with him having a revelation that he has only a short time to live, and that he decided the best way for him to spend his final days was in dramatic action, taking extreme measures to protect the children of Maine, since the criminal justice system has failed so mightily. He claims this country was founded on vigilantism and the only way 'to take it back' is by adopting the methods of our Founding Fathers. It's quite a lengthy document."

"That sounds a lot more like Johnny Partridge than it does Logan Dyer. Don't you think?"

"Speaking for myself, I would say yes. Speaking for the state of Maine, I am not sure it matters."

"How can it not matter?"

"Because you caught him in the act of trying to kill Nathan Minkowski and yourself. Because every bit of physical evidence we have found so far connects him to the massacre of those men. Because he had means, motive, and opportunity. And because his 'letter' tells us exactly why he chose to leave Langstrom's truck near the SERE school."

"What reason did he give?"

"So that its discovery would gain international attention for his crusade. The navy base is already the preoccupation of conspiracy theorists. He sees himself as the inspirational leader of a vigilante insurrection that will sweep the nation."

"There's more to this, Clegg. There has to be."

"What do you mean?"

"I mean, what if Dyer was put up to this? What if he was goaded along by someone else? He's already unstable, and he thinks he's dying of a brain tumor, and so he's going to be easy to manipulate. Someone tells him he'll be a world-famous hero if he wipes out all those sex offenders."

"Who do you think is manipulating him?"

"Russo."

Clegg's tone turned sour. "What reason would Russo have had to mastermind something like this?"

"He wouldn't, which is why he would make such a good middle-man. People think those Night Watchmen are just a bunch of tough-talking old drunks. I did, too. But they hated what Foss was doing—bringing 'human garbage' to their mountain resort—and his business was in direct competition with Cabot Lumber. When I met Russo at the Sluiceway, he didn't act like the head of security at Widowmaker. He acted like he worked for Cabot."

"Mike—"

"I know it sounds crazy, but at every stage of this thing, there's been one of those Night Watchmen involved. First it was Torgerson showing up outside the SERE school. Then it was Partridge publishing an incendiary column the day before the massacre. I don't know how Adam Langstrom fits into it all. Maybe Russo told Dyer to kill him as a dry run, to see if he could go through with killing the others. But I think Foss was the real target all along."

There was silence on the other end of the phone.

"I think you should get some sleep, Mike," Clegg said at last in a patient, fatherly voice. "Those aren't accusations you should be making in public without any proof. You're starting to sound like those conspiracy theorists we were just talking about."

"If I was one of the Night Watchmen, that's exactly what I'd hope you'd say."

"Or it could be that it's all coincidence, and Dyer is a better letter writer than you think he is."

"Yeah, I guess."

"Well, we'll know more in the morning."

"Why's that?"

"Because Dyer's manifesto also spells out exactly how he disposed of Langstrom's body. He says he lashed it to a tire wheel and then pushed it off a bridge over the Dead River. In the morning, the state police are sending a dive team to check out the water under that bridge. You're welcome to watch them if you'd like."

"I wouldn't miss it," I said.

I had barely hung up the phone when the door opened and Flotsam and Jetsam rushed into the guest room and began sniffing around my legs. As I scratched their heads, I found myself thinking of Shadow again. Would he be able to survive alone in the wild, after having spent so much time with humans? Yes, he would, I thought. There was something about that animal that made me regret all the times I had scoffed at New Agers for worshiping wolves as magical creatures possessed of special powers. Shadow might not be a deity, but that big brute was a survivor.

The phone buzzed again. This time it was Stacey. I stretched out atop the still-made bed. The dogs jumped up to join me.

"I got your message," she said. "Are you all right?"

"I am now."

"What happened tonight?"

"I promise to tell you the whole story," I said, "but first I need to hear how you're doing."

"Shitty. You were right. I shouldn't have gone out there. I saw things—I wish I could unsee them."

"You need to come home."

"I'm worried it won't help."

"I'm not."

"You promised to tell me the whole story of what happened to you. Begin at the beginning."

And that was what I did.

The next morning, I awoke early to go watch the state police divers begin their search for Adam's corpse. Pulsifer was waiting in the kitchen with two cups of coffee. "You're not going to get far without a vehicle."

"I figured I'd steal one of yours."

"Another charge for the disciplinary committee."

As I had expected, the temperature had plummeted after the snow moved out, and it took us so long to scrape the frost from the windows of Gary's patrol truck that I needed to pry my fingers loose from the scraper. I never knew the living could also suffer from rigor mortis.

"Do you know what the state does with unclaimed bodies?" I asked Pulsifer.

"I've always assumed the ashes end up in the back room of some funeral home. Why do you ask?"

"It's just something that's been on my mind."

We drove in silence back toward Kennebago Settlement, both of us agreeing without saying so that it was too cold for further conversation.

A deputy had blocked the road to the bridge with his car to prevent nosy people from approaching the scene. It was my friend from the other night, the one who had pointed me in the direction of the wounded dog.

"I heard it was hit by a car," he told me.

I had hoped the injured animal might still survive. I certainly didn't blame it for the actions of its vile owner.

Pulsifer and I walked to the bridge.

On too many occasions I had watched the Warden Service dive team retrieve bodies from the water: swimmers who underestimated the currents in a river, snowmobilers who overestimated the thickness of lake ice. Most of the corpses I had seen brought up from the

295

depths had belonged to young people. Younger than thirty. Younger than me. The young and the reckless.

Adam had been only twenty-one.

The river wasn't particularly deep, and the dark water, when the divers opened a hole, didn't seem to be moving particularly fast, but I knew that diving is always dangerous, especially under ice.

Mist rose from the moving water—it was so much warmer than the air. It almost seemed as if we were staring into hot springs.

I had expected a long wait, but the divers found Adam on their first descent. He was exactly where Logan Dyer's manifesto had said he would be. Everything Dyer had told the detectives turned out to be true.

And for reasons I couldn't explain, it made me all the more certain that he hadn't acted alone. But what could I do about it? I hadn't even been able to convince Clegg. I would have to be content in knowing that the man who had pulled the trigger twelve times would spend the rest of his life—however long it was—behind bars. Not all of the wicked are punished in this life; many bad men die peacefully in their sleep. The injustices of this world are why we so desperately dream of a better one yet to come.

The divers laid the corpse on a black tarp that they could zip up to form a bag. Then they began changing hurriedly out of their wet suits. The hole they had made in the ice was already refreezing.

The lifeless thing that they brought up resembled none of the pictures of Adam I had seen. Not the cocksure kid in the photo Amber had left me; not the angry defendant scowling at the camera at his trial; not the damaged ex-con from the sex offender registry. His skin was white, with some blue-and-purple mottling. His hair looked like black kelp except where the bullet had torn away part of his skull. If I hadn't been told who this sodden, crooked-limbed creature was, I never would have recognized him.

"I believe my testicles have fully retracted," said Puslifer through chattering teeth. "How about we get going?"

I was about to reply, when I heard shouting start up in the road behind us. The deputy was trying to block a woman from getting past him and rushing to the bridge. I recognized the lipstick red Jeep parked beyond the police cruiser.

Had her friend in the Rangeley police department told her where to go? The woman had a special gift for getting secrets out of men. Without a word to Pulsifer, I started back along the ice-hard road. My bruised knee was as stiff as if it were encased in a metal brace.

"Let me through!" Amber screamed. "He's my son! He's my son!"

"You can't, Amber," said the deputy.

He was strong, but she drove her boot, hard, into the top of his foot. The man went down, cursing, as if hit by a maul.

I moved to intercept Amber as she surged forward.

She tried to dodge me, but I had played cornerback in high school and knew how to guess which way a running person will turn by watching their hips. I got my arms around her before she could take another step. She tried the same stomp move on me, but I was ready for it.

"Stop, Amber," I said in her ear. Her hair smelled of marijuana.

"I want to see him."

"You will."

From a distance, it must have looked like we were dancing.

"I know you lied to me," I said. "I know Adam isn't my brother."

She ceased to struggle. She turned her anguished face to mine. She hadn't removed her makeup in a long time, and it was streaked and smeared from her tears. "What?"

"Adam couldn't have been my dad's son."

"But he is."

I could feel the cold metal of my father's dog tags against my chest. "My dad had O-negative blood. That's the same blood type I have. But Adam's records say he was AB-positive."

"But I'm AB-positive."

"A man with an O-negative blood type can't have a child who is AB. It doesn't matter what the mother's blood type is."

She stared up at me with eyes redder than any I had ever seen. "It's not true. Adam was Jack's boy. He was."

"I don't know how long you've known the truth," I said. "But you knew you were lying the night you came to me for help. You were desperate and out of options, so you tried the same lie on me that you used on my dad a long time ago. Did he ever believe you?"

Her body grew heavy in my arms. "No. He knew Adam wasn't his."

"Then how did you get his dog tags?"

"He left them in my house. They fell between the wall and the bed. We heard A.J. drive up and—"

"Whose son is Adam?" I asked.

She shook her head so that her dirty hair hid her face.

"No one's," she said. "Not anymore." And she began to sob.

37

Two weeks later, on my twenty-ninth birthday, Stacey and I fastened our skis on top of my Scout and we started off into the mountains.

It had been a bad time. Stacey was suffering, afflicted with grief, guilt, and anger, and there was nothing I could do but be present for her. I insisted that she stay with me until the services were over, since I lived so much closer to Augusta. Together, we attended the state-sponsored memorial for her dead colleagues, as well as two of the three private funerals. The body of the young intern who had been killed in the crash, Marti Menendez, had been flown back home to California for burial there.

Stacey didn't leave the house much otherwise, except to split wood. We had more than we would need for the winter, but I left her to her labors. She would open the garage door to let in the cold air and then she would go to work with an ax and a wedge, breaking logs down into smaller and smaller pieces. If she doesn't work through her anguish soon, I thought, I will have nothing to burn but toothpicks.

On the day before my birthday I left her alone to run an errand in Augusta. It took me most of the day, but when I arrived home, I found that she had cleaned the house from top to bottom. She had wrapped her thick brown hair in a kerchief, almost in imitation of a 1950s housewife.

"Consider it your birthday present," she said. "I forgot to get you one. I'm sorry I've been so preoccupied."

"I understand, and I have something to take your mind off things. We're going skiing for the weekend."

"Mike, I don't know if I'm up to it."

"You split two cords of wood yourself. I'd say you don't have to worry about your physical fitness."

"That's not what I meant."

"Do it for me."

She agreed, but she couldn't manage to show excitement at the idea of going away together. The thought of having fun seemed an offense to her dead friends. I had known the feeling, and I could tell what was going on behind those sad green eyes of hers.

We hadn't made love since the accident. She hadn't been ready. In bed, we lay on our sides, me behind her, hugging her tightly, as I had done every night since she had returned home, sometimes whispering reassurances when she cried, sometimes remaining totally silent until she had fallen asleep.

That night, however, she put my hand on her breast. I appreciated the gesture but felt she was doing it out of guilt, because it was my birthday the next day.

"We don't have to," I said.

"Just keep it there." She leaned her head forward and pulled her hair up and away from her neck.

I understood the invitation and began kissing her behind her ears.

She let out a soft moan, and I felt her nipple grow hard in my hand. I began to massage her breast while I nuzzled her neck. She rolled over on her back, and I held myself propped on my arms above her. She traced with her finger the bright new scar on my forearm.

"We don't have to," I said again.

"I'm tired of feeling nothing."

I moved her hand down my body. "Is this something?"

It was the first time she'd laughed in weeks. "It's something, all right."

The next day, we arrived at Widowmaker just before noon. Another front was moving in after the prolonged cold snap. Dark clouds were bunched up in the west, and the wind was blowing a mare's tail of snow off the summit.

"I still don't understand why you wanted to come here, of all places," Stacey said. "Why not Sugarloaf?"

"I have my reasons."

"You always do," she said with a smile.

We took the shuttle from the day-use lot to the base lodge, since it was too early to get into our hotel room. I saw Russo's midnight-blue SUV parked outside the resort's security office. Not all the wicked are punished. If I was fortunate, I would enjoy my weekend without having another encounter with that soulless man. Stacey was waiting for me when I came out of the locker room. Her green eyes were bright and clear, and she looked sexy as hell in her tight outfit. Holding our skis over our shoulders, we tromped toward the nearest lift. There was a line to get on, and we found ourselves behind two teenage boys with snowboards.

"Did you hear they're tearing down the Ghost Lift?" one of them asked the other.

"No way!"

"I know. I always wanted to go inside there. It was supposed to be haunted."

"Yeah, right."

"No, I'm serious, dude. My bro went in with his friends, and he said they saw something—like a ball of light."

"Was your brother high?"

"Dude, my bro is always high."

The line crept forward, and finally it was our turn to get on the lift. We shuffled up to the blue line and waited for the chair to hit the backs of our thighs. We sat down fast and felt the rushing sensation of being whisked up into the air. I pulled the safety bar down across our chests.

I couldn't remember the names of the trails that Elderoy had pointed out. They all ran together in my head.

"When was the last time you went downhill skiing?" Stacey asked me as we passed over a bunny slope packed with children and newbie adults. "You sure you don't want to try something easy first?"

"It's a little late for that. Besides, you only live once."

"You only die once, too."

A snow squall began to rock us back and forth. We were about sixty feet above the mountainside—no surviving a fall of that height—and I imagined what it must have been like that horrible day that lift had broken and people went tumbling to the ground.

Stacey interrupted my morbid thoughts. "I saw on Facebook that Cabot Lumber is expanding," she said.

"Makes sense. Cabot just lost a major competitor. I can introduce you to the Night Watchmen après ski if you want."

"I don't want to meet any of the people you told me about. Let's have all our meals in our room."

"Fine by me." The cold stung my teeth when I smiled.

"I also saw on Facebook that Dyer was getting fan mail."

"That's no surprise, either. He did what a lot of people dream of doing. Logan Dyer acted out a bunch of collective fantasies."

"You said he wanted to be a hero."

As we neared the top of the lift, I spotted the ski patrol shack where I had met Josh Davidson, Adam Langstrom's only friend in the world, according to his mom. I hadn't heard whether Amber had held a funeral for her son. If so, it must have been a lonely affair.

"Do you believe in conspiracies, Stace?"

"What, like Area 51?"

"I'm talking about in real life."

"I think there's a lot about what goes on in the world I'm glad I don't know."

"I wish I felt the same."

We pushed the safety bar up. As we slid clear, Stacey turned in the direction of the nearest trail.

"Wait," I said.

I reached down and unfastened my boots from my skis.

"I've got to go do something first," I said.

"You should have taken a leak at the bottom."

I propped my skis over my shoulder. "I'll be back in fifteen minutes."

"Fifteen minutes! How much coffee did you drink this morning?"

I smiled and waved and began to hike up above the chairlift, heading in the direction of the old Ghost Lift. My father's dog tags bounced against my sternum. I had decided to keep them as my own amulet of protection. They had been with me the day Carrie Michaud's knife went astray, and I had no better explanation for my deliverance.

This close to the summit, the trees were all stunted or disfigured from the high winds and cold. It was a deceiving landscape. A white spruce might be eighty years old yet no taller than a Christmas tree.

I kept climbing until I saw the cairn of stones poking up from the snowdrifts, the spot that marked the summit. I paused in the lee of the wind and looked out at the white landscape at my feet. Over the past two weeks, when I had thought ahead to this moment of farewell, I had imagined having a clear view of the mountains—a panorama from Bigelow to Saddleback—but it was not to be.

The wind rose to a full-throated howl as I reached into my jacket for the tin I had brought with me from the funeral home in Augusta. It was hard to imagine that an entire human life could be contained in something so small. Without ceremony, I unscrewed the top and tossed my father's earthly remains into the air. The wind caught the sooty ashes and bits of bone and blew them out among the snowflakes, over the wild land he had once called home.

Author's Note

There is no Widowmaker Ski Resort, but East Kennebago mountain, where I have set so much of the action in this novel, is very real and remains largely forested and undeveloped (long may it remain so). Nor does a Fenris Unchained Wolf Refuge exist, although I drew inspiration from the former Loki Clan Rescue, which I had the good fortune to visit before its demise. That sanctuary, I should add, has been reborn as part of the New England Wolf Advocacy Rescue Center, whose work I support. As I noted in my first book in the Mike Bowditch saga, *The Poacher's Son,* the villages of Flagstaff and Dead River were razed in 1949 to make way for a reservoir (i.e., Flagstaff Lake) for the Central Maine Power Company; I have resurrected these ghost towns again, in memoriam. In fact, many of the locations in this novel are fictional and should not be confused with actual places. That goes for the characters as well.

I owe a debt of thanks to the following people who each helped, in his or her way, to bring this book to life:

My agent, Ann Rittenberg.

Everyone at Minotaur Books, in particular Charlie Spicer, Andrew Martin, Sarah Melnyk, Paul Hochman, April Osborn, David Rotstein (for another rocking cover), and my copy editor, Carol Edwards.

The Maine Warden Service, especially Cpl. John MacDonald, Wdn. Troy Thibodeau, and Wdn. Scott Stevens.

Detective Sgt. Bruce Coffin (Ret.), of the Portland Police Department.

Nancy Marshall, Maine's best publicist.

Steve Smith, Esq., for information about the laws and policies pertaining to the prosecution and punishment of sexual offenders in the state of Maine.

Dave Perry, for giving me a night tour of the Sugarloaf ski slopes via snow cat.

Lee Kantar, of the Maine Department of Inland Fisheries and Wildlife, for taking me along on a helicopter ride as part of the department's 2012 aerial survey of moose in the North Woods.

Ron Joseph.

Dr. James Marshall.

Greg Drummond, Master Maine Guide and proprietor of Claybrook Mountain Lodge.

Allister Timms for proofing.

Derek and Jeanette Lovitch, of Freeport Wild Bird Supply, for expert bird guiding.

The gang at *Down East*.

Bob and Danny Lee, my lifelong friends.

My parents, for their steadfast support.

All the Doirons, increasingly too numerous to name.

And, as always, for everything, Kristen.